HERITAGE

BOOK I OF **ZERUA UNCHAINED**

BRADY E. MOXLEY

Disclaimer
This is a work of fiction. Names, characters, places, and incidents are either the product of the author's imagination or are used fictitiously. Any resemblance to actual events, locales, or persons, living or dead, is coincidental.

ISBN 979-8-9924545-0-5 (Paperback)
ISBN 979-8-9924545-1-2 (Hardcover)
ISBN 979-8-9924545-2-9 (eBook)

Edited by: Linnea Schroeder
Cover art by: Chris Taylor
Map art by: Manolis Karavidas
Beta Readers: Erizza Moxley, Mckenzie and Colby Holt, Papa Rotschy, Sammi Ekmark

For my wife, Erizza.
Thank you for always believing in me, throughout it all.

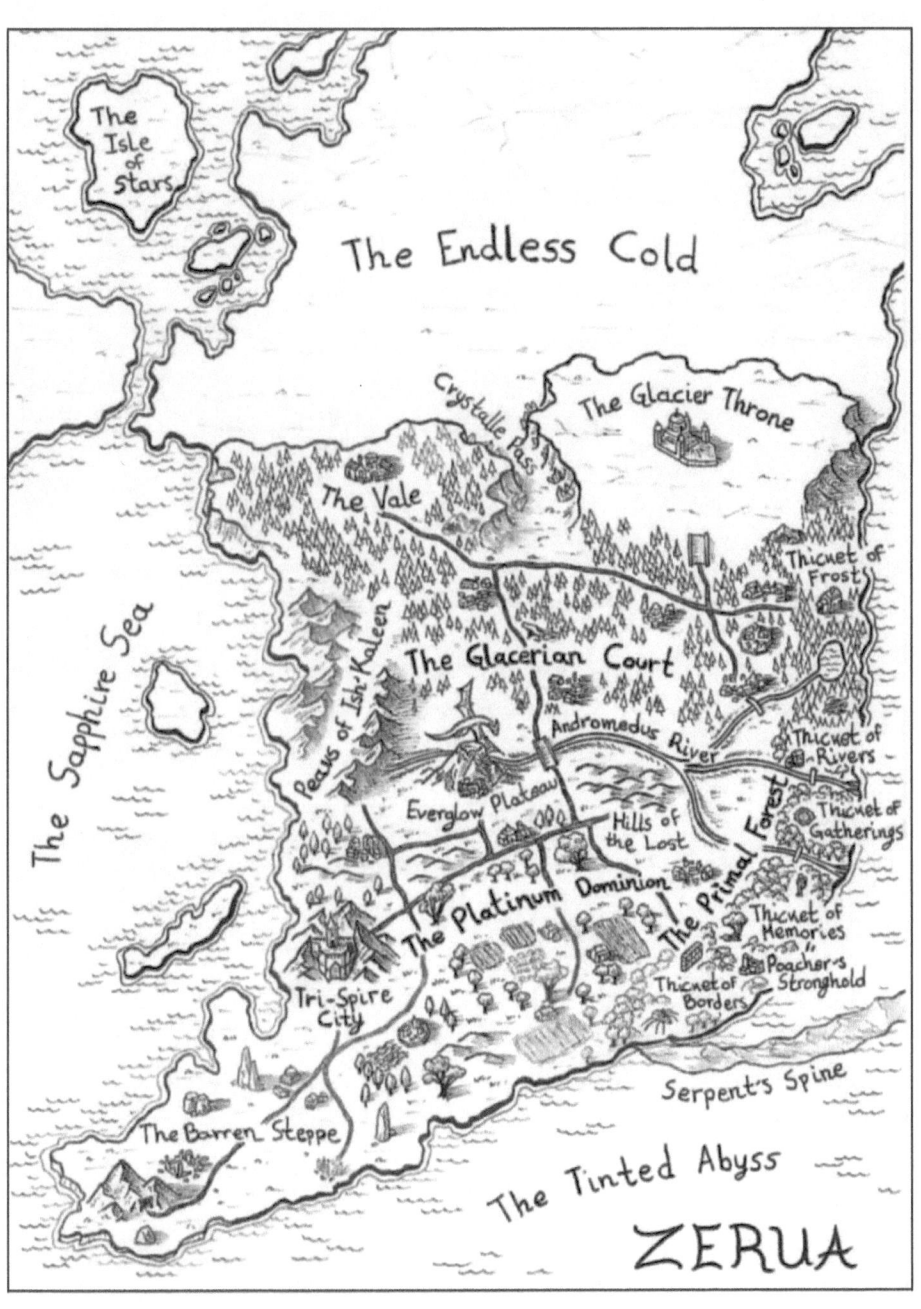

The Isle of Stars

The Endless Cold

Crystalle Pass

The Glacier Throne

The Vale

Thicket of Frost

The Glacerian Court

Peaks of Ish-Kaleen

Andromedus River

Thicket of Rivers

The Sapphire Sea

Everglow Plateau

Hills of the Lost

Thicket of Gatherings

The Platinum Dominion

The Primal Forest

Thicket of Memories

Poacher's Stronghold

Tri-Spire City

Thicket of Borders

The Barren Steppe

Serpent's Spine

The Tinted Abyss

ZERUA

Prologue: Deals and Consequences

T he darkness of the cramped tunnel encroached on the woman, her ragged breathing the only sound echoing off the rocky walls around her. Sweat coated her exposed skin as she pulled her way through the heated corridor. At last, as the tunnel bent, a small glistening firelight could be seen some distance ahead. A grunt of effort escaped her, as she forced her tired limbs to continue working.

Right hand, left hand, almost there...

Finally, with a last exertion, she pulled herself free of the compact tunnel, landing on her hands and knees. The space smelled of sulfur and ash as she gasped to catch her breath in the stifling heat. Getting to her feet, she took in her surroundings and a nagging thought returned to her mind: *was this a terrible mistake?*

With her worn leather boots lightly thumping on the obsidian floor beneath her, she approached the edge of a bubbling pool of lava. Before she could change her mind, she unslung her satchel and rummaged for the item that brought her here. Her fingers grasped a leathery tome and pulled it free. She still felt uncomfortable holding this accursed book. The cover appeared to be crafted from some tough leather, and the interior pages seemed to be made of tanned skin from a more...humanoid source. As if that weren't enough to ward the sane from ever touching the creepy grimoire, the binding was constructed from what could only be the tendons of the victims that were used to craft the pages.

With a shiver, she opened the book. She had come too far to turn back now. A light hiss escaped the tome as if it were breathing in the air around it. The woman stared as a flaming script began to crawl its way across the pages, leaving behind the now-familiar instructions.

Find your way to the burning core.
Walk until you reach the shore.
Bare your wish for the fire to hear.
Offer your blood, for we are near.

The woman set the book onto the rough stone floor and unsheathed the dagger at her hip.

Speaking loudly, she said, "Give me an army to defeat the dragon that terrorizes my village." Then, with a quick motion, she slashed her hand.

Blood dribbled into the lava as it sizzled away. Then, she felt a force grip her hand in place. The woman struggled to pull her hand back, but suddenly she felt her blood being pulled from the cut in her hand in extreme amounts. The liquid poured forth and began forming an orb that floated above the burning lava. Panic rose in her chest as she began to feel weak from the excessive blood loss. Falling to her knees, her hand remained in place held by some unseen force. She watched as the blood flow staunched and her hand fell limply to her side. Kneeling there, she weakly raised her head to look up at the swirling crimson orb as it took shape into a small floating figure with two wicked horns and a jagged tail drifting behind it.

The creature chortled and looked down at the woman. "Terribly sorry, I haven't had a bite to eat in centuries. I always forget how fragile you mortals are. I suppose we will have to do something about that if you truly want what you asked for, but enough blabbing. Let's get down to business."

Chapter One: Nearly There

T he evening breeze swept across the deck of *The Silver Gale* as it
crested the gentle waves. Ahead, the barest hint of shoreline could
be made out with a sharp eye. The smell of salt in the air, a constant
companion over the long months of travel, made its presence known once
more as a strong gust blew the leather jacket of a man standing at the bow
of the ship to one side. He leaned into the assaulting wind subconsciously
with his calf-high boots planted firmly on the rocking deck. As he gazed
out at the horizon with his piercing ocean blue eyes, he lifted a hand to
scratch the scruff on his chin, then slightly tilted his wide-brimmed
leather hat back to wipe the sweat from his brow.

"Colton," came a familiar voice from behind him. "I was
beginning to think you'd fallen overboard. Been looking everywhere for
you."

Colton turned to see his longtime friend strutting toward him in
his long fur cloak and leather attire. "Ah, Imbrose, I see you're feeling
quippy," He remarked in his deep twangy voice. "Would you have saved
me if I had?"

Imbrose shrugged, his eyebrows raising in mirth. "Maybe, maybe
not? Who can say?"

Colton snickered. "I was just taking in the first glimpses of land in months. Still can't believe we're about to be there. Feels like just yesterday I promised Gramps I would make the journey for him."

Imbrose reached his friend and laid his blue-tinted forearms on the railing and turned to look at Colton. "I'm still trying to believe there's land out there. Kinda thought you were sailing Ember and I to our doom if I'm being honest." Imbrose said with a chuckle. "Though, it would take a lot more than salty winds to ruin these luscious locks." He ran his hand through his black hair, revealing the ram-like horns that stuck straight back to encircle his head and marked him as one of the hellborn race he was.

Colton elbowed him. "Don't get too excited. I'm still not sure I didn't lead you and your 'luscious locks' to their doom as well." Colton gestured to the landmass on the horizon, which had already gotten noticeably bigger and longer since he had been standing there. "As far as we know, those are untamed wilds, my friend. I haven't the foggiest idea what could be awaiting us there."

Imbrose sighed dramatically. "You really know how to make discovering a new continent sound like a pain. Look, I've said it before, and I suspect I'll need to say it again: we chose to be here and we have been on countless adventures together before this one. If there is something big and scary in this new land, then we will fight and beat it. Most importantly, we will do it together, as we always have."

Colton turned and looked directly into Imbrose's icy-blue eyes. "This one is different. We are months away from home." He looked back along the deck of the ship then lowered his voice to say, "And the only person who has ever been confirmed to have set foot on that continent came back crazy."

Imbrose leaned close and whispered in Colton's ear. "Good news then. I'm already crazy." Colton scoffed and Imbrose pushed him roughly. "Colton...stop it! Enjoy the journey and know that Ember and I will be by your side, always."

4

Colton smiled at that and gave a weary nod. "Speaking of Ember, where is our fiery red head at?" Colton asked whilst turning to survey the busy deck.

Crew members scurried around going about their daily duties. What was more interesting though, were the massive crates of supplies being stacked near the port side of the ship where half a dozen rowboats were currently moored. They had come prepared, and were careful to keep the necessary provisions locked away even after rations were cut in half.

Imbrose placed a hand on Colton's back and began beckoning him away from the railing and toward the stairs leading below deck. "Who do you think sent me? She's been waiting to eat dinner for thirty minutes now, and you know how she gets when she's hungry."

Colton smirked as the pair stooped into the mess hall below decks, the bombastic chatter and the aroma of barely-washed bodies assailed them harshly as they entered. All along the center of the room rested a long plank table with a bench set to either side, all of it bolted to the ships deck to avoid any sliding during storms. Currently, the benches were stuffed full with the off duty crew, all eagerly piling mouthfuls of stale bread and dried meat into their faces while chasing it with flat ale. Despite the depressing rations, moods were high as the first sight of land had been called out around midday. Already people were discussing what treasures they may find and how they planned to claim them for themselves.

Barely noticed, Imbrose and Colton moved along the table trying to find their companion through the barely-lit interior. A resounding thud cut through the noise as Colton and Imbrose reached the halfway point of the table.

A sultry exotic-sounding voice reached their ears and they knew immediately who was responsible for the ruckus. "How many times do I need to dislocate your shoulder, Terran, before you finally get it into your skull that you…may…not…touch…me?" Those last four words

5

emphasized with a grunt of exertion and a pained groan from a male voice.

The boys pulled apart a small crowd gathering around the incident to see Ember, her long red hair cascading over her sun-kissed face, a look of disgust marring her otherwise beautiful features. She had her knee planted firmly between the shoulder blades of a man while her hands gripped his burly arm at an awkward angle. Her victim's face pushed aggressively into a loaf of bread on the table as he grumbled unheard insults.

Colton could easily see the man as Terran, one of the large group of mercenaries he had no hand in bringing on this trip. Smiling at the man's misfortune, he stepped around the gawking crowd in an attempt to reach Ember.

"I think you might break it if you go any further," Colton drawled.

"Good, then maybe he will think twice before he puts those grubby sausages he calls fingers anywhere near my butt again." With one last jerk and a shove, she sent the man sprawling onto the floor in a heap.

A chorus of laughter rose up as the man tried to right himself and then move to engage Ember again, a snarl on his face. "I'll gut you, you little–"

Colton's eyes drifted to Imbrose who was already pulling a jagged red dagger from its sheath.

"Take it easy," Colton cautioned. "We aren't trying to kill any–" Imbrose threw the dagger across the room. "one." Colton finished lamely as his friend vanished in a puff of red smoke.

A burst of reddish energy bloomed between Terran and Ember as Imbrose appeared out of thin air. "Ah ah ah, let's watch our mouths when speaking to ladies, shall we?" As the flash cleared Imbrose could be seen holding a glinting dagger none too gently between the man's thighs as he pulled the red dagger from the post just next to him.

Terran froze and looked at Imbrose with fury in his eyes. Imbrose in turn simply smiled and said, "Now turn around and trot off like a good boy, and maybe I'll allow you to keep your precious lads."

As the air became so thick it felt like soup, Terran finally grunted and turned to walk away mumbling something under his breath.

Colton stepped up behind Imbrose. "A little heavy, don't ya think?"

Imbrose shrugged and turned to meet his friend's gaze, a jovial smile plastered on his face. "Oh I don't know. I kinda hoped he would make his move. All the time I've spent on this tub has left my daggers feeling itchy. At this point, I'm praying there is some nasty beasty waiting for us when we make land."

Colton scoffed and gestured to the surrounding crowd. "Get going, you lot. We have a busy day tomorrow and you should be well fed." The crowd began to shuffle away, many still snickering as the atmosphere began to calm. With that, Colton moved to the other side of the table and sat down across from his two friends.

The two of them sat close to one another, even as Ember berated the blue man for being too impulsive and for nearly getting himself hurt. As Imbrose defended his actions, Colton's mind drifted as he began to play out what the next few days would look like. *How is a single ship filled with less than forty people meant to take a foothold in an unknown land with unknown dangers? Is this a mistake? Have I truly condemned my friends to some horrible fate?*

"Colton!"

Colton's mind focused as Imbrose shouted his name. "Huh? What did you say?"

"I said, he's got another thing coming if he thinks he can even touch me on his finest day," Imbrose repeated slowly, his eyes narrowing.

"Oh, uh yeah, Terran's just blowing hot air," Colton mumbled as Ember looked at him with concern.

Ember looked at him for a long moment, her too-sharp eyes seeming to read his thoughts. "Anyway, let's move on shall we? I want to hear about what Colton thinks we might be looking for once we get where we are going."

7

Colton looked up at Ember and nodded relief plain on his face. "Right, well we know very little aside from what Curtis tells us his Dad saw when he came over, and he wasn't exactly speaking sense when he came home. So, really it could be anything. I would just expect some crazy world ending threat or something to set the bar. That way we can only be pleasantly surprised if it is anything else."

"Has our fearless leader given any further insights on what is in his crazy Dad's journal?" Imbrose asked.

Colton drummed his fingers on the table as he responded. "Not really, mostly just if we get the sudden urge to start writing the word 'defiler' all over the ship in our own blood then that is probably the same thing that got his Dad."

"Lovely," Ember whispered. "But what I meant was, what are *you* hoping to find when we get there, Colton?"

Colton sighed and looked down at the table in front of him. "Well, as I've told you both, my family is from a ruthless tribe that used to live in the forests of Kelyfos. However, my grandfather escaped when he met my grandmother. The tribe wasn't too happy about this and tried to hunt down my grandfather and kill him for straying from their ways. Unfortunately for them, Grandmother Aileah had a small army at her disposal and essentially decimated the rest of my tribe."

Ember reached across the table and laid a hand on Colton's arm. In response, Colton placed a hand on top of hers and smiled gratefully at her show of empathy. "Oh I'm fine with it, they were a terrible bunch. I mean, what kind of religion believes that to become closer to their God, they have to blind themselves? It's just a shame my grandfather didn't get out before they did the same to him."

Colton paused, adjusting himself in his seat. "Anyway, as the tribe was dismantled, my grandfather was able to coerce some information from the leadership. The way he says it is that the tribal elder accused him of being 'just like those we fled from across the ocean.' Of course, no one has been foolish enough to attempt the trip over here until now, and

Gramps has gotten too old to make it himself. So, in an effort to honor him, I promised I would find these people who sent my tribe packing."

"Are we sure we want to find them?" Ember asked gently. "I mean, they scared away a tribe that blinds themselves. Are we sure they aren't worse?"

Colton shrugged. "The way he said it, it was almost as if they were sent away, not frightened into leaving."

"Well, do you know what exactly we may be looking for?" Imbrose chimed in.

"Not entirely, but after Gramps scoured our old tribe's records, he found mention of a blade that was given to them as a gift in hopes it would one day reunite them. Since the only blade of any real reverence was wielded by the elder, we assumed it had to be that one." Colton paused and patted the pommel of the blade strapped across his back. "*This* blade."

The sword was long, with its sapphire studded pommel sticking more than a foot above Colton's right shoulder, and the scabbard stretching well past his left hip. The hilt was wrapped in a fine leather, with a thick band of metal filigree in the center of the handle for the greatsword, segmenting it into two evenly spaced handholds. The crossguard extended eight inches to either side and ended in a cloverlike pattern.

"Still don't understand why you didn't try to learn to use the dang thing. You are strong enough to heft it," Imbrose teased with a chuckle.

Colton laughed lightly. "Be grateful I never tried! I'm terrible with a blade, and this one has plenty of blade to work with. I'd have lost an arm by now."

"That still doesn't really answer my question," Ember observed. "What do you want to find?"

"Well, I guess I want to find whoever sent us away with this sword, and I guess I just hope they're like me," Colton hedged. "Oh, and I hope they're all very friendly and very averse to self mutilation," he added quickly.

Ember smiled. "That would certainly be preferable." With a glance over at Imbrose she added, "If they are still around, we will find them! Can't be letting Grandpa Xander down now, can we?"

"Definitely not! He may be blind but he's still the only one able to find me while I'm sneaking around," Imbrose said.

The three of them laughed. Imbrose reached over and grabbed three mugs filled with frothing ale from near the center of the table, passing one to each of his compatriots and kept the last for himself. "A toast to the old man himself and to our foolish endeavor! May we be successful and return with stories to tell!"

They clinked mugs in a sloshing, disjointed cheer before drinking deeply. The moment of camaraderie offering a small respite from the fears of the future.

—

In the sparsely lit Captain's Quarters, a man sat at a desk covered in rolled parchments and journals. A flickering candle was the only thing illuminating the scrawling text on the worn journal he now flipped through. As he ran his fingers across the words written in his father's hand, he paused at a frantically written phrase: "Forest of Monsters."

"I suppose we will see, won't we, Father?" a cracked and broken voice said. Then, with a jerking motion, he slammed the journal shut and blew out the candle descending the room into darkness.

Chapter Two: The Landing

A soft *clang* of metal against metal jarred Colton from a drunk-addled sleep. Jerking upright, he turned to see the apologetic face of one of the ship's cooks as he went about clearing the table from the night before. Mouthing an apology, the cook moved to the nearest wash basin with an armful of dirty platters and mugs. A grunt escaped Colton's lips as he moved to cover his face from the perfectly placed ray of morning sunlight shining through the porthole across the room. As he blinked his eyes to clear the sleep and rubbed his aching head, he remembered he wasn't young enough to be drinking like this anymore.

A soft thud caused him to look down at the table and see another mug of frothing liquid being placed there by the same cook from earlier. "Hair of the dog, they say," he rumbled in a thick, lowborn accent.

With an assenting raise of the mug, Colton downed a swig of the same offending ale from the night before. As he winced through the unpleasant taste, he looked through the porthole once more, expecting to see the same endless expanse of ocean he had grown accustomed to these last few months. Instead, he saw trees. Massive trees, like the ones people wrote tales about seeing without ever actually having seen them.

He rose from the bench abruptly and jostled the table just enough to get Imbrose to start from his own sleep. Colton quickly hurtled the table, all sense of drunkenness having left him as he moved to the porthole to look at the new landscape. There he saw a long beach that stretched as far as the eye could see in either direction, and a treeline that did the same. The foliage was that of an exotic alien world, leaving Colton speechless. His eyes glanced down and saw rowboats had already gone ashore and many people were setting up an impromptu campsite. He could easily see one group was already gearing up for some sort of hunting party, no doubt in search of something other than bread and molding cheese.

As if remembering he had legs, Colton quickly swung around and went back to his slowly awaking friend. "Get up lazybones, we are missing the party. We've finally made it!" Seeing his friend was under the same influence of the night before, only much worse, Colton grabbed a half-drunk mug of water and dumped it over his friend's head.

Imbrose threw his hands up as if it had been boiling, and the inertia of the movement sent him toppling off the back of the bench. "Is that any way to wake a man who nearly died of alcohol poisoning last night?" Imbrose rolled to his hands and knees and promptly vomited all over the already stained planks.

"Yes, well, you did that to yourself, and besides, you absolutely need to see this," Colton chuckled apologetically, patting his friend's back.

Imbrose groaned and wiped his face before holding up a hand. They clasped hands and Colton heaved him to his feet, then steadied him as he looked ready to fall over again.

Imbrose looked around the table, obviously searching for someone. "Where did Ember get off to?"

"Probably found her bed like an intelligent person. Come on, look at this." Colton pulled Imbrose to the porthole and held him there as he tried to shade his eyes from the sunlight.

Imbrose let out a huff of air and his hand fell to his side. "Wow, I never thought I would be so happy to see trees." Then his eyes glanced downward and he pushed past Colton heading for the stairs. "Looks like someone is trying to steal first glances at the new continent. Come on slowpoke, we have history to make!"

12

Colton rolled his eyes and jogged for the stairs. As he crested the top and turned around to look at the coastline, he was blown away once again by the sheer scale of this new land. Everything seemed to be supersized in comparison to back home. The trees were massive sure, but monstrous fruit could be seen dangling temptingly just out of reach. He shook himself from his awe to see Imbrose on the far side of the deck arguing with a small group of men. Colton rushed over, already planning to break up whatever nonsense he was getting into.

"Oh, don't be like that Baldo! You know I beat you fair and square," Imbrose began as Colton reached them. "Tell you what, if you let Colton and I take this next one, I promise that you get first dibs on whatever fresh fruit I find!"

Baldo, a halfling in stature but a giant in personality, looked up at Imbrose unimpressed. "Or, I could simply go over now and get my own dang fruit, you little blue cheater!" Baldo shrieked with a high pitched but mature sounding voice.

"Alright, alright. You drive a hard bargain. How about I give you thirty gold coins and you let us take yours and Janshi's spot on the next row boat over." Seeing Baldo was not terribly impressed, Imbrose added, "And I promise to put in a good word with Ember on your behalf."

Baldo perked up at this and said, "Fine, but it better be a pretty good word. I still want the money and the fruit too. Oh, and tell the captain you are the reason we are late."

Imbrose stooped low, quickly dishing out the gold pieces and grabbing Baldo's hand at the same time. "You won't regret it! I always knew you as an honorable gnome!"

"I am a halfling you dimwit, now get going before I change my mind," Baldo half shouted.

Imbrose grabbed Colton and pulled him to the side of the ship near the rope ladder. "Yes of course! Thank you again!" Imbrose called over his shoulder as he lowered himself toward the now arrived rowboat.

As the two of them took their place on the rowing benches and began pulling away from the ship, Colton looked at Imbrose and smirked.

"What?" Imbrose asked innocently.

"Put in a good word with Ember, eh? Haven't you been trying to put in a good word for yourself all these years? Seems counterintuitive to talk up some other guy to the girl you fancy," Colton said through a chuckle.

Imbrose fake yawned. "Oh please, give me some credit. If I can't beat out Baldo for the affections of a woman, what use am I?" Imbrose paused and tossed a small coin purse at Colton. "Hold onto this for me, can't have him searching me and finding it when he finds out he's misplaced his coins."

Colton pocketed the pouch with a hearty laugh. "Never change, Imbrose Vanderbaan, never change."

They both laughed and the small rowboat pushed further from the ship and closer to the unknown.

After ten minutes of hard rowing, the two of them found themselves scraping onto the rough sand beach. Without hesitation, both men hopped over the side and began rushing up to the small group gathered near the treeline.

"I won't stop anyone who wants to from going into the forest. My father's journal made no mention of this place, so if anyone finds anything, make sure you report it back at once!" The authoritative–albeit scratchy–voice of their leader, Curtis Nezva, reached them as they approached.

"Hiya boss," Imbrose said as he slowed to a walk.

Without looking over his shoulder Curtis said, "Ah, so you two have finally decided to join us? Wonderful, please do me the honor of putting Genevieve and her men at ease by taking them into the woods. They haven't stopped complaining about the lack of security since we got here."

"Sure thing," Colton said as a flare of annoyance rose in his chest at the dismissive reception.

Without skipping a beat, Curtis returned to a small group of his mercenaries and ignored them as the two of them walked away, heading towards a broad-shouldered woman some distance off.

"Man, I hate that guy," Imbrose grumbled as they walked out of earshot. "Total jerk. No wonder he covers his whole body in rags, he's probably just a scrawny, sad, little man underneath all that."

Colton grunted his assent but didn't say anything more. He knew a little about why Curtis covered himself in rags, and it was the only reason Colton was able to convince him to fund this expedition.

The sand sank below their boots as they strode toward Genevieve and her two flanking guards. Sounds of wildlife could be heard coming from the jungle to their left. Colton's gaze drifted to the treeline as he listened to the abnormal calls the animals made. Something about them gave him chills. It was as if the beasts inside were conversing about them. Despite the loudness, Colton couldn't see a single living thing from the beach. That alone would have given him pause, but there was an energy that leaked from the forest. Something quiet, something hidden.

"Finally, someone with some sense," came the irritated voice of Genevieve.

Stirring Colton from his musings, he turned to look at the tall, strong woman before him. She wore a fitted set of plate armor and a large two-bladed ax clung to her back. With her plate helm clasped under one arm, she waved in Colton and Imbrose's direction. Her shoulder-length blonde hair caught in the breeze, as her hazel eyes shone in the sunlight. She stood tall, scanning the treeline, constantly alert for any danger.

"Do me a favor and tell me you have a plan to set this place up to be defended in case things go sideways," Genevieve said while she clasped arms with Colton and then Imbrose.

"Just getting situated myself," Colton said simply. "Wish I had better news. Though I can say that we should probably be getting to work on clearing some of this underbrush from near the campsite." Colton gestured to a few thick brambles.

"That is what I was thinking also. A beach isn't exactly the most defensible position given our backs are to the water, but Mister Mysterious over there wants to let his people pillage the forest blindly," Genevieve grumbled with a dismissive gesture aimed at Curtis.

"Well, how about you and your people start by clearing around the campsite while Imbrose, Ember and I head in and look for some food. With everyone fed, I'm sure we can come up with something concrete." Colton paused and placed a hand on the big woman's shoulder. "Not to worry, once we've gotten some fresh supplies, I'm sure we will sail further in whatever direction that journal of his says to."

Genevieve nodded and looked to her two compatriots. "Quinn, Gavin, get started on the western front, and find me Baldo, and Janshi." She turned to Colton. "Always happy to see you, Colton. I think I spotted Ember scouting further down the beach."

"Likewise." With a nod, Colton and Imbrose strode past, letting them get to work. "Weren't you supposed to tell her about Baldo?" Colton asked.

"Oh, I suppose I was. Ah well, I'm sure he'll be fine!" Imbrose said with a scoff. Then in a lower tone added, "He'll be fine right?"

Colton snorted. "Well, if he still has all his essential body parts when we come back, I suppose we'll know."

The two carried on in relative silence, save for the constant din of creature calls coming from the jungle. As they came around a low hanging branch that blocked any visual further down the beach, they spotted Ember poking at an oversized mango that was barely within the reach of her eight foot naginata. With a jump, she pierced the fruit and yanked it from the tree, catching both halves as they fell to the ground. Just then, she turned to notice Colton and Imbrose closing the distance.

"About time you two made it over here. I was beginning to think I should have slapped you both awake before I left. Here." She handed them both a half of the fruit and smiled cheerfully. "This place is really something, huh? Almost makes you forget how much you miss home."

"Almost," Colton said dimly.

Ember turned to look at him. "I cannot imagine being anywhere else, Colton Cobb. You two make it feel like home travels with me." Then, she looked down at the dripping fruit in their hands. "Go on, try it! It has to be the most delicious fruit I have ever eaten."

Both men brought the fruit to their lips and took a huge bite.

Imbrose moaned. "Oh by Meraway's long grass skirt, this is delicious."

Colton grunted his agreement as he took another big mouthful of the tender and juicy fruit. He finished it with two more big bites, and began walking toward the surf to wash his hands. As he squatted down, he heard Ember gasp behind him.

"Did you see that?" she asked as Colton wheeled around to face the duo. "I think I saw something watching us through the leaves."

Colton rushed back to their side and peered into the thick jungle. Nothing caught his eye as he scanned back and forth. His hand reached down and caressed his whip at his side as the lack of movement put him on edge.

"Maybe it was a deer or something," Imbrose offered hopefully.

"I don't know, but it looked pretty big," Ember whispered.

With one last look, Colton turned to his companions. "Let's head back toward the camp, then we can go in and look for food. Being this far from the rest has me feeling nervous."

The other two nodded emphatically and the three of them walked quickly back into view of the small campsite being erected some two hundred feet down the beach.

Chapter Three: Traps and Betrayals

With the eerie feeling behind them, they began to discuss how they planned to make their first expedition into the forest.

"The way I see it is we are probably going to be blind on all sides as we make our way in," Imbrose theorized while tracing a finger along their chosen entrance into the all-encompassing jungle foliage. "Though, if we carve our way through, it will definitely make it easier to get out when we turn around."

"How do you feel, Ember? Do you think you can cut through it?" Colton asked as he turned to meet her fiery gaze.

Ember scoffed and stepped forward as she swung her weapon in a long flowing arc. Without resistance, the vines and brambles in her path were cut clean and she stepped forward to press further into the opening she had created.

"Guess that's a yes?" Imbrose said with a shrug. "After you, your majesty," he added with a dramatic bow and a flourish.

"You are too kind…" Colton said, groaning, and made to follow Ember as she hacked her way through the thick foliage.

"Mister Cobb!" Colton turned to find the source of the female voice calling his name. Running up the beach was a woman in all black form-fitting armor. She wore daggers all along her doublet and greaves, and the lower half of her face was covered with a thin silk bandana. Her long brown hair was pulled back into a high ponytail and moved gently as she jogged to a stop in front of him. "I'd like to come with you, if you don't mind."

Colton smiled and shrugged. "Who am I to deny the Nightingale of New Eradin? Besides, I think we have a better chance of making it back based on how deadly I've heard you are with those daggers of yours."

"I'm grateful, and please call me Delphine," she said with a smooth voice and a slight bow of her head.

"Very well, but only if you call me Colton," he offered with a smile as he turned his back to follow Ember.

"Wait a minute, was that comment about being good with daggers meant to be a jab at me?" Imbrose whined.

"Whatever do you mean?" Colton asked innocently. "It's just nice to have someone with us who knows how to use them, is all."

"I know how to use them!" Imbrose snarled. "Keep it up and I'll show you, pal."

Colton turned to look at him and chuckled. "See, if you were Delphine, that might've scared me a little."

Delphine watched the exchange between them and Colton could've sworn he saw her face turn up in a smile underneath her silk cover. "Aren't we supposed to be following her?" Delphine asked, pointing past Imbrose's head.

Ahead, Ember had already nearly passed out of sight through the shredded foliage.

"This isn't over, bub," Imbrose threatened as he passed Colton to catch up to Ember.

With a shake of his head, Colton chuckled once more and jogged to follow.

After forty minutes of slashing from Ember's Naginata, the undergrowth cleared away and the party found themselves standing in a more standard-looking forest than what the shoreline would suggest. This far in, the thick brambles were nowhere to be seen, and instead, a person could easily traverse the floor of the terrain. What they assumed was a jungle had revealed itself to be a crowded forest. The canopy still blotted out the sun, but one could see hundreds of feet in any direction.

Colton marveled at the beauty of such a place, and wondered, just for a moment, if he should abandon the whole notion of blindly traveling around looking for someone he wouldn't know if he met them, and instead live here in this gorgeous place. A branch broke to the group's right and they turned to see a deer of some sort bounding away through the forest. Colton felt his hand relax as it moved from his hip and was grateful to see everyone was slowly placing their weapons back in their scabbards. Delphine had two daggers already in her hands and at the ready, but Colton hadn't even seen her move. *Deadly with daggers indeed,* he thought to himself.

"Well, aside from the massive difference in how it looks from the beach, it doesn't seem very lived in, does it?" Ember observed as she firmly sheathed her naginata.

Colton turned in a circle and saw the barrier of thick vines, thorns, and trees extended in a sort of wall in either direction. To him it was like crossing through a thick hedge only to arrive in a wooded glen.

"It's almost like the forest is trying to keep something out…" Colton thought aloud. "Or something in…"

Just then, an ear-piercing roar shattered the silence that had gathered among them. The whole group drew their weapons in unison and turned toward the sound. A loud *crack* and *boom* sounded in the distance as a large, scaled white body crashed through the trees, sending massive oaks sprawling in its wake.

"Down, now," urged Delphine, pulling Colton to the ground with her.

The massive creature stormed through the forest, causing the ground to shake beneath their prone bodies. At first, it sounded as though it were getting closer, but slowly the booms and creaking trees receded into the distance.

After what felt like an hour, Colton rolled to his side to look at the rest of the party and made a circle with his finger in the air while standing up. "Well, that was a lovely surprise," Colton said shakily. "We should probably head back to camp. People will be asking what that was, and I'll be anxious to see the hunting parties come back. Here's hoping there's only one of those."

The group all nodded in unison and all at once began moving to the small opening back toward the camp.

As they walked, Delphine moved to stand next to Colton. "Apologies if this is none of my business, but what are you hoping to find out here?"

Colton stepped over a large fallen log. "Well, Curtis hopes to learn what happened to his dad, I think. Though, I have my own motives for making the journey."

"Ah, I see. It just seems like we don't have much of a direction is all. It sort of feels like no one really knows what we're doing except Curtis. Something about the way he confidently chose to be the first on land makes me feel like he has a plan of some kind," Delphine confided as she turned to watch Colton's reaction.

"I suppose so. He does have his father's old journal, but from what he has told me, it's mostly just the ravings of a mad man," Colton said with a shrug. Stopping in his tracks, he turned to look at Delphine, his suspicions rising. "Why are you here, Nightingale? Aren't you supposed to be some royal assassin back home?" Colton's hand instinctively moved toward his hip.

Delphine stopped a few steps ahead of him and turned around. She cast her eyes down at Colton's hand and tilted her head. "Oh please, Colton, if I was sent to kill you, I could've done it a hundred times as we walked through the forest and you had your back to me," she scoffed with a dismissive wave of her hand. "No, but I am here for personal reasons. You see, Curtis–"

She was cut off as up ahead Imbrose shouted, "What is that thing?"

21

Colton looked to see Imbrose squatting down and poking a stick into a weave of roots and vines at the base of a tree. With one last look at Delphine, he pushed past her and walked to where the other two stood. As he approached, a small *ting* came from the spot Imbrose was poking at.

"I think it's made of metal or something," Imbrose said as he poked at it again.

Colton knelt and looked in where Imbrose was prodding. Inside, Colton could just make out a shining glint from some type of metal. What's more, he could swear that it looked a bit like a breastplate Genevieve would wear. Colton leaned forward and pulled a handful of vines away to reveal a plate helmet.

"Is that a person under there?" Ember exclaimed as she stepped in to pull away more vines.

The group worked quickly to uncover the figure that seemed to be leaning against the tree. Upon removing the last of the vines and moss, they pulled the figure out into the path they had cleared. The person before them was covered from head to toe in full plate armor with no visible skin. The armor itself looked slightly worn, but all together in pretty good condition. As Colton leaned in to look into the visor, his eyes caught on a small scratch on the side of the helm. With a closer look, the scratch revealed itself to be six letters that had been etched into the metal: F.R.I.E.N.D.

"Think he's dead or just passed out from the heat?" Imbrose asked from over his shoulder.

"I don't know, could have come out looking for us and couldn't make it out wearing all this armor," Colton said as he reached for the visor.

Raising the visor on the armored figure, a pinkish vapor escaped from within. Colton backed away and swatted at the air in front of his face. However, the vapors, when inhaled, made him feel slightly drowsy as he caught himself by placing a hand behind him. Colton's vision swam as he struggled to keep his eyes open. Suddenly, the figure lying on the ground in front of him sat up and turned to look at the rest of the party.

22

Colton's hearing blurred together as he watched people reach for him and call his name before he fell back onto the soft forest floor, unconscious.

—

Colton blinked his eyes to see himself lying on a cot next to a crackling campfire. The stars twinkled high in the night sky. *It's night time? Just a moment ago it was midday,* he thought to himself. He turned to see Delphine sitting on a stool next to his head as she leaned forward onto her knees.

"Nice of you to finally wake up. Whatever that poison was that came out of Friend's helmet, I had never seen anything like it before. Wasn't sure how to help you after the first hour, but then you went and slept like the dead for eleven more." She looked up and checked the sky. "Almost to the exact minute I'd say. Curious."

"What happened?" Colton groaned; his throat parched from hours of breathing hot air.

"Well, after you sniffed the pink smoke, you passed out. Then we had a pretty intense conversation with the guy in the armor, who we have taken to calling Friend due to the carving on his helmet. He claimed to have no knowledge of the vapor or how to counteract it. After a bit more grilling we decided to get you back to camp so I could see if it poisoned you. Friend was even nice enough to carry you. When none of my antidotes worked and your condition didn't worsen, I volunteered to sit here as your vigil until you woke up. The others took Friend to meet with Curtis, and they have been at it ever since," Delphine explained as she helped him sit up on the edge of the cot.

Colton rubbed the heels of his hands into his eyes as he tried to clear his foggy head. "What do you mean 'Friend?' Doesn't he have a name?"

Delphine clicked her tongue. "Well that's the most interesting bit. He's not one of ours, and he doesn't remember a thing about himself. The only thing he could say is that he's been 'looking for a group of people who live in the forest' and 'the knowledge he has must be shared.' Funnily enough, he couldn't remember any of the knowledge he was supposed to be sharing, but he seemed happy enough to be up and about. His eyes were captivating though. They seemed to burn like embers briefly before dowsing themselves. I could've sworn I saw an actual fire in his eyes when he first sat up."

Colton's mind spun, though he couldn't tell if it was from the bizarre information or the after effects of the poison. The sense of foreboding that had been following him since he stepped off the ship once again descended. Determined not to get swept away, Colton did his best to put on an almost casual, dismissive air. "Hmm, that's odd." He reached out toward her. "Help me up. I need to figure out what's going on." Colton said as he held out a hand.

As Delphine helped him up, she gestured to a tent that had light peeking through the flap. "They're over there. Good luck! If you plan to go back out tomorrow, I would love to tag along so we can finish our conversation from earlier."

With a nod, Colton disengaged from Delphine and moved to the dimly lit tent as the voices from inside became easier to hear. Colton stepped in to see Ember questioning the metal man as both Imbrose and Curtis flanked her on either side.

"–you can certainly understand why your story simply doesn't add up– Colton! How are you feeling?" Ember cut herself off as she stood from a stool across from the armored man who sat on a stool of his own with his back to him.

"I'm fine, just anxious to meet my 'Friend' here," Colton replied easily as he stepped around to get a better look at the man. "So, I'm Colton Cobb, nice to meet you."

The visored face looked up to meet his gaze and then stood to his full height of almost seven feet tall. Colton tilted his head back to look up at the figure.

"I have been told it is customary to shake hands when meeting someone new." The voice that came from the man was robotic in nature with a seemingly very measured speech pattern. "A pleasure to meet you, Colton Cobb. I am Friend." Then, the figure raised both of his hands and waved them back and forth on either side of his head, and then promptly sat down and looked back at Ember.

Colton stared dumbstruck at Friend. "Well, I think I will just take a seat over here," Colton said as he gestured to the last remaining stool next to Curtis.

"There have been a lot of interesting interactions like that," Ember noted dryly. "So, Friend, where do you come from?"

"I cannot recall, but I do remember it being fairly warm, I believe," Friend intoned with his monotone voice.

Colton turned to see Curtis digging through his father's journal. Then, he placed his finger on the page and looked up at Friend. "Do you know where the cloudstone is?" Curtis blurted.

Friend turned to look at Curtis. "Cloudstone? What is this thing you speak of?"

Curtis closed the leather-bound tome and set it on the table behind him. "Cloudstone, the rock with bluish veins that run through it. It floats when it is properly smithed."

Friend pulled his finger up to his head, which was the first human-like gesture the man had made since Colton walked in. "I am sorry, what you describe sounds familiar, but I cannot remember."

"Do you think if I showed you some it would help you remember?" Curtis asked as he rose to his feet.

"Perhaps…I would have to see it to know for sure," Friend intoned as he watched Curtis cross the room and lift the tent flap.

"Follow me! I think I have some I brought from the ship." Friend stood and began following Curtis from the tent. The others looked at each other and shrugged, then got up to follow his lead. Once outside Curtis placed a hand on Colton's chest. "Get some rest, you three. I'll find a place for Friend to sleep tonight, and you all can take another crack at him tomorrow morning."

Colton hesitated for a moment. "Are you sure you're safe with him by yourself?"

Curtis nodded emphatically. "Oh yes! If anything happens, we will be next to the campsite. I had your tents set up that way." Curtis pointed toward a second campfire some thirty feet along the beach.

"Well, alright then…If you need anything, just yell for us," Colton said as he looked curiously at Curtis.

"Certainly, off you go." Curtis turned and ushered Friend toward a stack of crates near the shoreline.

"I'm not the only person who thinks that was weird right?" asked Imbrose as he adjusted his cloak over his shoulders.

"Definitely not…" Colton said while stifling a yawn. "Truthfully, I'm still exhausted though. I could definitely use some normal, non-magically induced sleep."

Imbrose's eyes lingered on the two figures walking away from them, suspicion plain in his expression. "Well, let's get some sleep and see what Friend remembers in the morning. If Curtis hasn't chased him away from excessive questioning before then," Imbrose muttered.

"Meet back here at dawn?" Ember asked.

"Sounds like a plan to me," Imbrose said as he pulled his cloak tighter around himself.

Colton nodded and began walking toward his tent. On his way there, he noticed Genevieve and her people off to one side drinking merrily. She waved him over, and he shook his head while waving his hand. Then, with a playful dismissive gesture, she returned to her revelries.

Once inside, Colton reached down for his whip at his side only to find his weapons belt was missing. Deciding someone must have taken it off him to help him stay comfortable while he rested, he reached over his shoulder and grasped the hilt of the long greatsword. With a sigh of relief, he resolved to find his whip in the morning. With a practiced ease, he unbuckled the weapon from his back and laid it on the small desk that had been erected for him. With a stretch, he kicked off his boots and plopped himself into bed, closing his eyes.

26

His mindeye immediately bombarded him with the images he had seen that day. From the massive trees and fruit to the monstrous white reptile he saw tearing those same trees down just by moving through them, and lastly to Friend, his first confirmed piece of evidence that something else lived in the forest. The idea that he was among the first people from another land to sleep on stranger shores sent a shudder through him. Just then, a moment of unease passed over him, and as quickly as he felt it, it vanished. There would be guards posted all night, and he needed some sleep. Forcing himself to relax, he rolled over and sleep finally came over him.

—

Screams, running, sounds of battle.

Colton bolted upright as he glanced about trying to get his bearings. The screams from outside intensified as a figure passed in front of his tent at a run, only to be flattened as a giant form pounced on him out of nowhere. His screams cut off in a gurgle as whatever had just landed on him finished him off by tearing out his throat. Colton rolled out of bed and grabbed the hilt of the greatsword. With a grunt of nervousness, he pulled the blade from its scabbard and marched out to meet the chaos ensuing outside.

All around, people were dead and dying. Bodies half eaten, or just eviscerated beyond recognition, littered the beach. However, people were fighting, but it was *what* they were fighting that caused Colton to freeze in place. Monsters of massive proportions flooded out onto the beach. No two were the same. A small group had the bodies of monkeys but the mouths of chittering insects. Another looked like a bear with six legs as it pinned someone helplessly to the ground with four paws so the other two could disembowel the victim. Colton turned just in time to see the creature who had killed the man that woke him up stalking in his direction. The creature was long and lithe, like a panther, but its size was all wrong. With a body that easily stretched up to fifteen feet long and a height that was close to five feet, Colton felt terribly ill-suited for this

27

fight. However, he raised his blade all the same, the weapon feeling unfamiliar in his grasp.

With a snarl, the creature bared its six-inch-long fangs and leapt at him, attempting to end the fight the same way a second time. Colton reacted quickly, sidestepping the attack and bringing the blade down toward the creature's neck. Unfortunately, he misjudged the weight of the weapon and the swing was sluggish, giving the creature time to nimbly dance away from the worst of the blow, resulting in only a small cut on its front right foreleg. This time, the creature charged directly at him and lashed out with a mighty swipe of its razor-sharp claws. Colton barely had time to get the blade up in time to intercept the massive paw, the force of the blow sending him stumbling through the loosely-packed sand landing on his back. He tilted his chin to his chest to see the creature already bounding toward him preparing for another pounce.

Colton grasped for the hilt of the sword realizing he must have dropped it while he stumbled. In a moment of divine grace, Colton found and levered the sword upright with its sapphire jeweled pommel buried in the sand next to his left hip.

The beast roared as it descended, excited by the kill it was about to make, only to be impaled through its throat all the way to the hilt. Warm blood spewed onto Colton's chest and face and he coughed, trying to keep himself from swallowing it. The blade dug even deeper as his hand lost its grip and the hilt was pushed into the sand by the sheer weight of the mighty beast.

Though even in its death throes, the creature's mouth snapped open and shut as it neared his face. With nothing left to do, Colton punched the creature in the snout, attempting to keep its teeth from getting any closer. The force of the impact was just enough to cause the massive panther to slouch off of him and fall to his left, which could have very easily saved his life, for the creature itself had still fallen on his legs and the weight was immense. He felt like his knees were locked in a painful vice and he began to fear the worst. Quickly, he rose to a sitting position and began digging into the sand to give his legs a place to weasel out from under the freshly-killed corpse. He felt the weight ease off and then he pulled his legs free in a puff of sand.

Standing up, Colton wiped the blood from his eyes and tested his weight on both legs. Nothing appeared to be broken, but he felt bruised all over. The blow from the creature's paw had forced the crossguard of the greatsword to hit him in the chest. Rubbing the spot it had hit, he looked down at the titanic beast he had felled by dumb luck.

"I thought you were a goner!" exclaimed a gruff female voice to his right. Colton turned to see Genevieve and her four guards come running down the beach toward him. Baldo had taken a nasty gash on his shield arm, but he still wielded his short sword with determination. Otherwise, the others had various forms of superficial wounds and were all covered in gore; no doubt they had been busy at work themselves this bloody evening.

Colton looked down at himself as he panted. "To be honest, I kinda thought so too. That sword isn't really a weapon I've practiced with," he admitted, pointing at the now-exposed hilt buried in the creature's throat.

"Well, you can't go into battle without your shoes on," she said while gesturing to his bare feet. "Go get them and we'll wait for you here. Be quick about it, I have a feeling we have lost quite a few tonight and the survivors are going to need our help."

With a curt nod, Colton splashed some water on himself to remove some of the grim and raced back up the beach and into his tent. Breathing frantically, he cursed as he pulled his boots over his sand-covered feet knowing it was going to be a pain to wash them out later. Then, he latched the scabbard for the greatsword across his back and threw open a small strongbox he had wedged under his bed. Inside was a whip he had been working on. Only this one had a long blade weaved into the end. Thinking there was no time like the present to give his new prototype a try, he strapped the belt holding it around his waist and moved toward the open tent flap. As a last thought, he leaned back and

29

snatched his wide-brimmed hat off the desk and strode out onto the beach once more.

This time, he felt far more comfortable and began analyzing the situation with a trained and calculating eye. He could see people having more luck than he initially thought fighting off the beasts of the forest. Aside from a small group of insect-mouth monkeys strewn about where Colton had seen Genevieve and her people drinking the night before, he also saw a blue-cloaked figure and a redhead with a long polearm carving their way through the animals with wicked efficiency. As he scanned the carnage, he could see a small group of wounded trying to escape to the row boats only to be overtaken by some horrid moose-like creature. He turned and gestured to Genevieve as she wrenched the long blade from the panther's throat and began moving to meet up with him.

"So, what's the play, boss?" Genevieve asked as she handed the blade over to Colton.

With an effort, Colton shoved the still blood-soaked blade into its scabbard with a cringe. *Another mess to clean up,* he thought to himself. "We need to support the defenders over by the other campfire. It looks like they're holding their own and pushing the creatures back, but I bet there are still some who are in need of help. You guys push down to the shoreline and keep the beasties off our row boats. I am going to push on with those two," he said pointing at Ember and Imbrose, "and I will meet you all at the campfire when these things have been dealt with."

With a nod, they set off toward the giant moose that was currently charging the wounded indiscriminately. Confident they could handle it, Colton moved to meet up with his compatriots.

Imbrose threw his jagged red dagger at another giant wolf that attacked Ember's blindspot. With a thought, he teleported to where it drove home into the wolf's flank. Grunting, he ripped the dagger along the canine's side, spilling its innards onto the sand. The creature yowled and crumpled to the ground, dead. Ember spun and brought her naginata down onto the back of a giant multi-colored frog, carving clean through its spine. Extracting her blade, she turned to face Imbrose.

"Thanks for that. Didn't want to give up the chance to end this thing. Its poison must've been pretty potent to do that," she said while pointing to the half-melted face of a fallen mercenary.

Imbrose stood up breathing heavily. "Of course! Who else would I pester if you got yourself eaten by a giant wolf?"

Ember chuckled and was about to respond when a roar broke up their conversation. To their right, the six-legged bear that had been tearing through the defenders had finally set its sights on the two of them.

"Now that's an angry teddy bear," Imbrose quipped. Wasting no time, he burst into action, moving with incredible speed to slash three times at the bear's exposed side. The bear's extra leg swatted quickly at his feet, knocking them out from under him and sent him sprawling. Groaning, Imbrose just barely rolled away to avoid the bear's massive front paw from coming down on his right leg. Scurrying backwards, he tried to find his feet as the bear advanced on him. Just then, a loud *crack* split the air as a long blade appeared in the beast's eye attached to a braided whip leading to Colton some fifteen feet away.

The creature roared in pain and wheeled back onto its hind legs as Colton ripped the blade from the creature's eye socket. Seizing the moment, Ember quickly drew her weapon across the bear's neck and then in a smooth motion, slashed across the base of the creature's skull as it toppled. The two attacks served to sever the beast's head and it crashed down into the sand without another sound.

"About time you joined us, and I thought *I* was a heavy sleeper," Imbrose teased as he accepted a hand from his best friend.

"Sorry, I had to avoid being eaten by a giant cat," Colton fired back as he smiled at the two of them. "Besides, it looked like the two of you were doing just fine without me."

"Maybe, but we aren't done yet," Ember said while pointing to a waving Delphine near the jungle's edge.

The trio advanced across the battlefield to meet up with Delphine. As they reached her, she started talking quickly. "During the melee, Friend ran off into the forest the way we had gone earlier. All I could hear

31

him say was that he 'needed to get away' and 'couldn't afford to take any detours,' then he disappeared into the woods. I was going to go after him, but then I saw you three and figured I should at least wait until you got here."

Colton sighed, and scanned the campsite. People were fighting off their last opponents as he made eye contact with Curtis across the din of battle. With a nod, Curtis gestured to the forest and Colton turned, a resigned look on his face, to the rest of the group. "Boss wants him back. I'd better go get him. Besides, he won't last a night out there by himself with the whole forest riled up like this."

"Well not by yourself, you idiot," Ember chastised. "We are coming with you obviously."

"Huh? Oh yeah! Let's go into the death forest and save a perfect stranger while not getting eaten!" Imbrose cheered sarcastically.

"I mean, I already planned on going in, so what are we waiting for?" Delphine asked.

Sighing, but not saying anything else, Colton strode into the darkened interior of the forest of monsters.

—

Navigating through the dense vines and undergrowth proved to be more of a challenge than Colton had originally anticipated, and more than once he found himself drifting off the cut path from earlier. When Colton finally burst free of the bramble into the more open forest beyond, he took a big breath of relief. Following quickly behind, the other three found themselves at his side. They surveyed the area, trying to ascertain where Friend may have gone as a crack of a twig in the distance caught their attention. Colton crouched and started moving toward the ruckus, carefully placing his feet to avoid making too much noise. Finally, as he crested a mound of dirt, he saw Friend kneeling on the ground looking at something.

"Friend!" Colton called quietly.

Friend looked over his shoulder and stood up. "I cannot go with you and Mister Curtis. I need to find the people who live in these woods."

Friend spoke in a normal volume voice, which to Colton sounded like screaming in their current circumstances.

"I don't know where you think we're forcing you to go, but you should come back to the safety of the campsite at least until morning." Colton looked around, ready for something to jump out at any second.

"You people are here for greed, and I won't be a part of that. Besides," Friend continued as he pointed at the ground, "I am nearly certain that the people who reside here have already been watching us."

Colton leaned back at the accusation. "Greed? What do you mean? We set out on this adventure to establish communication with other societies. We seek to only trade and share, not steal."

Friend tilted his head as he looked up at Colton, measuring his words. "You speak true, and therefore I must wonder. Are you a very good liar, or have you been deceived?"

Colton let the words hang in the air. "What do yo–"

"Well, well, well. I have to say I was a little nervous we wouldn't find you lot in this darkness, but all that racket made it easy indeed."

Colton turned to see several darkly clad figures had completely surrounded their group, and at the front of the strangers was the speaker: Terran.

Colton uncoiled his whip in an instant as his companions did the same with their own weapons. "Terran, what are you doing out here?" Colton asked as he bided his time to analyze the situation unfolding before him.

Terran's lips curled up into a cruel-looking smile. "It's not obvious? I've come to show my appreciation for being interrupted earlier," he sneered as he pointed to Imbrose.

"Very brave of you to bring your goons." Imbrose taunted. "Though I suppose it makes my life easier. This way I don't have to hunt them all down after I'm done with you."

"Curtis won't be pleased to hear you're out here trying to hurt his own people. Even if you do manage to kill us, he will have your head,"

Colton warned as he counted twelve assailants. *Bad odds,* he thought to himself.

"Who do you think sent us? Your usefulness is at an end, Mister Cobb," Terran said as the group of mercenaries began to close around them.

With a massive effort of concentration, Colton silenced his mind and reached out to connect his thoughts to Imbrose. He hadn't tried to use his ancestral abilities for so long now, and the connection caused him to develop an immediate headache.

Go for the four on your right. Ember should follow. I'll take out the two on my left and we'll have to see where it goes from there, Colton thought toward his friend.

Leave the idiot for me, Imbrose replied simply, then with a flick of his wrist he threw his dagger at the first man to his right, kicking off the engagement.

Chapter Four: The People of the Forest

E veryone burst into motion at once. The would-be assassins tried to overwhelm with raw force as they charged the group, banking on their superior numbers. Colton turned his back on the fight to his right, knowing Imbrose and Ember would make them pay dearly, and instead focused on the two rushing up the dirt mound with their swords brandished. Flicking his wrist, he sent the blade on the end of his whip flying for the chest of the man on the right. With impressive speed, the man ducked to avoid the instant kill shot and instead took the blade in his arm. Adapting quickly, Colton yanked on the handle of his whip and pulled the man off balance sending him stumbling into the pit where Friend was conjuring flames from thin air.

Before Colton could observe any more, the other man was upon him swinging a downward cut for his neck. Deftly, Colton dodged to one side while holding the whip handle in his right hand and punched the man in the face, breaking his nose. With his left hand, Colton pulled the bowie knife from his belt and jammed it into the man's jugular. A choking sputter escaped the mercenary as he fell off the knife and onto the ground grasping at his throat. The sound of a bow string pulled Colton's attention to the other side of the pit, just in time to see the crossbow bolt slam into his left thigh.

"Son of a…!" he exclaimed as he scanned to find the shooter. His face dropped as he saw the other three across from the melee all had crossbows and another one was pointed right at Ember's back.

Time slowed as the bolt left its crossbow, arching directly for Ember who had no idea she was about to be shot in the back. Colton coiled his whip and lashed out toward the crossbow bolt. In his mindseye, he could see the exact trajectory of the bolt and where it would strike her, so he aimed just in front of her back trying to catch the bolt at the last second. He watched in horror as the bolt inched closer to her and his whip seemed to be moving too slow, then with a blink of surprise he watched as the blade lashed upwards and cut the bolt in two causing it to fall limply to the ground behind her. With a swing above his head, he brought the whip into a circle above him and then flicked it at the offending crossbowman. The man was so stunned by what he had just witnessed that he was dead before he registered the knife embedded in the side of his head. Colton ripped the blade free and spared a glance down at Friend in the pit.

To his delight, Friend had turned his flames on the man he had sent down there a few moments ago. Friend looked up as the man at his feet screamed and nodded, then he climbed up the embankment to engage the other two crossbowmen.

As Colton turned, he could see the other side of the battle was going poorly. Imbrose had received many wounds and was retreating away from Terran, who looked fresh. Ember was engaged in a two-on-one and Delphine was struggling to get some distance between herself and a brute of a man with a large maul. By his count, five of Terran's men were dead and that meant it was seven versus five, but he could only see six. Then, he saw a glint of steel as the last mercenary slashed Imbrose across the back. Imbrose cried out and fell to his knees as the man brought the blade up to thrust through Imbrose's heart. Horrified and knowing he couldn't make it in time, Colton could only watch as Imbrose glanced his way.

A blast of bluish energy erupted from a nearby treetop, blowing a hole through the man and sending him sprawling to Imbrose's right. Terran's eyes glanced up to see another bluish beam strike out and hit one of Ember's enemies, allowing her to dispatch the second. Surprised by the display, Colton searched the intervening party, but couldn't see anyone.

Seizing the initiative, Imbrose sprung to his feet and closed the distance with Terran. Who recovered slowly and tried to stab lazily toward Imbrose as he charged. With a flourish, Imbrose wrenched the blade from his hands and spun around behind him, embedding Terran's own blade through his back and out through his stomach.

"Lucky sho–"

Terran was cut off as Imbrose dragged a blade across his throat and threw him to the ground. "Sorry, didn't catch that, mate," Imbrose said as he stepped away from Terran's body and fell to one knee.

Two more shots at quick succession from the treetop sent both the maul wielder and the last crossbowman into the afterlife.

Colton took a deep breath and then let it out in a hiss as he felt a searing pain in his leg. Glancing down, he remembered for the first time the crossbow bolt sticking out of his thigh. With a groan, he dropped onto his butt, letting his wounded leg stretch out in front of him.

"Who are you people?" a soft, twangy female voice called from the darkness of the tree.

Ember was the first to recover. "We come from a place far from here and I assure you we mean no harm."

"Your friends there would tell a different story," came the cool reply.

"As you can see, they were no friends of ours. Who do we owe our thanks to?" Colton asked while still sitting on the soft dirt floor.

A beat of silence followed, then a rope flowed down the side of the tree, and a darkly clad figure shimmied down the rough cord with grace only years of practice could accomplish. As she landed and turned, the firelight from Friend's still-burning hands illuminated her features.

Her emerald, green eyes glanced over the group with a guarded expression as she brushed one of her long locks of dark curly hair from her face. Her skin was darkened by the sun and she wore minimal green leather armor and thigh-high leather boots. As she took another step forward, Colton could make out a pistol of some sort grasped in her right hand as she placed it in the holster on her upper thigh. Most notable though, she carried a long rifle strapped across her back and the barrel was still giving off small vapors of energy having been discharged very recently.

"You can call me Orielle, and I live here in this forest."

Colton's eyes lingered on this woman's striking figure as she introduced herself. A sharp cuff on the back of his head from Delphine allowed him to find his words. "Ow…Ah, well, thank you very much, Orielle. My name is Colton Cobb, and this is Delphine, that's Ember, and the lucky blue guy you saved is Imbrose." Then Colton turned and looked at Friend. "Oh, and that's Friend, but as far as we can tell he seems to be from here."

Orielle shifted her weight to one hip, taking a more relaxed posture. "A pleasure to meet you all. I'm glad I was able to help."

Colton froze as he heard her speak this time. Her accent sounded very similar to his own. He hadn't realized it right away since he'd only ever heard his family speak with such an accent. "Well, I would like to stand and shake your hand, but I'm afraid my leg won't let me," Colton continued with a smile.

"Oh, well do you mind if I have a look at it? I have some experience with crossbow wounds," Orielle asked as she stepped closer.

Colton slightly flushed involuntarily. "Yes please!" he said a little too loudly. Then he added, "I would greatly appreciate it."

With a nod, Orielle approached Colton and kneeled next to his wounded leg. "It looks like it missed the bone and it's in the fatty bit of your thigh. So, it should be safe to remove."

"No, please don't worry about me. I'm sure I won't bleed out from the gash on my back!" Imbrose whined from across the clearing.

38

"Oh shut up you big baby, and let me see," Ember said as she walked over to inspect his injuries. "How are you Delphine? Friend? Anything serious?"

"I am fine. They could not pierce my armor," Friend reported from across the pit.

Delphine held a hand over her left forearm. "It will probably scar, but I'll live. Thank you for your concern."

Orielle reached down and picked up a stick. "Here, you're going to want to bite down on this."

Colton looked down and took the stick with a nod. Then, he placed it in his mouth and nodded once more. With a swift tug, Orielle yanked the bolt from his thigh and placed a thick piece of fabric from her satchel over it. Colton let out a sharp grunt and bit down on the stick in his mouth, bearing the pain in relative silence.

"The poultice on that cloth should stop the bleeding and speed your recovery. Though in a few minutes, it should dull the pain to a manageable level," Orielle explained as she stood and looked around at the carnage left from the battle. "This much blood is going to attract some big predators. We can't stay here, and it sounds like you folks need a safe place to bed down for the evening. Good news on that front, as I have a small outpost not too far from here." She turned and looked down at Colton. "Can I trust you, Mister Cobb?"

Colton met her intense, but startling beautiful gaze. "Absolutely, ma'am," Colton said earnestly.

Orielle held his eyes for a moment longer then smirked and looked away. "Never been called a ma'am before." Gesturing toward the wounded, she stood and moved to tend to their wounds "We'd better patch you up quickly, and get moving."

Ten minutes later, the group was bandaged as best as they could in the middle of the jungle and were slowly making their way through the dark with Orielle as their guide. There were multiple times where she held up a hand and some terrifying roar could be heard in the distance and the party would go still. Only after Orielle gestured for them to keep moving, did they dare move from their position.

Time stretched on and the shadows of the night grew longer. Colton had no idea how long they were able to sleep before the attack, but now that the adrenaline of the fight was beginning to fade, he felt himself growing tired again. Eventually, the numbing effect on his leg wore off and every step sent a fresh wave of pain through his body. Then, just as he was about to ask for a break to catch his breath, Orielle walked up to the side of a tree and knocked on the trunk in an intricate pattern that Colton couldn't keep track of in his pain-addled state. Colton leaned against a nearby tree panting hard as sweat dripped down his face from the stress of the trip on his injured leg. Tentatively sparing a glance to his right, he saw Imbrose slumped against Ember with his left arm draped across her shoulders. He seemed to be barely conscious and lifted his chin slightly to look at Colton and managed a weak smile.

"Don't worry about me, pal. I'm tougher than I look," he wheezed in raspy breaths.

"Hush now," Ember whispered while staring at the tree impatiently. "Any idea how long this is going to take? He needs to find a bed and medicine. I may be able to find some nearby, but I need to get him comfortable first." Her words coming out clipped, and laced with worry.

Orielle turned and looked at Imbrose, sympathy plain on her face. "Don't worry, Ember. Joel will have what he needs." Then a hollow thunk sounded from inside the tree and the hidden door pulled inwards and raised up out of sight.

A man stood in the doorway looking out at their wounded and disheveled group, and turned to look at Orielle. "I see you found some strays." The man wore similar themed clothing as Orielle, only a bit more bulky. He also wore a dappled green cloak and sported the same accent as Orielle.

"Let's talk inside, Joel. He needs some rest and one of your tinctures," she implored, gesturing at Imbrose.

Joel looked at Imbrose and Colton then his face softened. "Very well, looks like the guy with the hat isn't doing well either." He stepped aside and gestured for everyone to enter. "Follow me."

The group gratefully moved to allow Imbrose and Ember in first as the rest followed close behind. Once inside, Orielle lowered the door back into place and threw a latch to drop a heavy piece of metal to block it from being forced inward. Colton turned and looked further into the hidden outpost. The entrance led to a small staircase downward into a well-lit subterranean living space. As Colton limped down the stairs and into the large room, he saw the man known as Joel gesture to a couch made of a tree log cut in half and moss packed on top to give it a plush seating surface. Quickly, Ember lowered Imbrose down onto the moss and then kneeled next to his head, whispering something no one else could hear. Joel walked to a nearby cabinet and opened it, circulating through the glass vials held within. Then he pulled one that had a green liquid swirling around inside it and rushed to Imbrose's side.

"Here, this will drop his fever and give his body the strength to recover. Though, it will put him in a deep healing sleep, and he likely won't be able to travel for multiple days, perhaps a week." Joel handed the vial over to Ember.

She nodded and leaned closer to Imbrose, and Colton thought he saw her eyes welling with tears. Then, after a few hushed words were exchanged between the two, she helped Imbrose drain the vial and he lay back with a contented sigh. Within moments, he fell unconscious and Ember rose and looked at Colton for the first time since they had arrived. Now he could easily see her usually indomitable demeanor was shattered as tears free fell down her muddied cheeks.

"Colton…" she said weakly.

Ignoring the pain in his leg, he moved to her and pulled her into a firm hug. Ember wept into his shoulder as he silently held her. Over her shoulder, Colton looked down at the pale face and slowly rising and falling chest of his brother in all but blood and closed his eyes tightly. Sleep deprivation and the pain threatened to overtake his emotions, and

41

the more he thought about what he had brought his friends into, he drifted ever closer to the brink. With a shuddering breath, he forced his own nerves down as he pulled Ember gently away from him. Her eyes were swollen as she tried and failed to control herself.

"He'll be just fine. Get some rest Ember. It's the best we can do for him right now. Something tells me this nightmare is just beginning," Colton murmured as he looked over at Joel. "Is there some place she can lie down and sleep?"

Joel nodded and pointed toward another door on the other side of the room. Ember wiped her eyes and walked back over to Imbrose, kissing him on the cheek before walking toward the door and opening it. Then she stopped and looked over her shoulder at Colton, the fire returning to her eyes once more.

"Don't you dare blame yourself for this, Colton Cobb. Do you hear me?" she said with the warning plain in her face.

Colton held her gaze and nodded. "We'll get to the bottom of this, I promise."

"I know, but Curtis better hope he isn't to blame for this betrayal or I'll…" She cut herself off with a frustrated growl. "Get your leg looked at and wake me up if something changes with him." Then she moved through the door and closed it behind her.

A heavy silence followed as Colton stared at the closed door, then he turned and looked at the rest of the group. Delphine stood just inside the entryway looking at Colton with alert but sad eyes. Friend walked up to Colton and rested a hand on his shoulder awkwardly, then walked past him to sit in a nearby chair. As Colton turned back toward the door, he could see Orielle entering and made eye contact with her, a soft smile caressing her lips. She stood there for a moment, her eyes locked on him until Joel moved to hug her tightly.

"I was starting to worry. Why were you gone so long?" Joel asked.

Colton averted his gaze, feeling awkward for witnessing such a moment for some reason. His eyes glanced around the interior once more.

The entire space was homey and held a certain inherent comfort. The rich aroma of pine lingered in the air, making him take a deep inhale of the relaxing scent.

Realizing his leg was throbbing, Colton slowly lowered himself into a chair across from Imbrose and watched him intently, adjusting the blade on his back as he did so. He could vaguely hear Orielle and Joel speaking as he thought to himself. *Don't you die on me. We still have so much to do, so much to see.* Colton's eyes drifted to the floor and he slowly removed his hat and set it on the small stump table to his right, a long breath escaping him.

"–truthfully I wasn't thinking! I just saw people in need and knew we could help!" Orielle's rising voice roused him from his musings. Colton turned to see Orielle disengaging from Joel's grasp as she walked over to the same cabinet with frustration in her posture. After a couple seconds of rummaging, she turned and looked at Joel from across the room with another vial in her hands, this one a pale white liquid. "Now, I'm going to help them, and you can either help me with that or you can sit quietly over there and brood." Turning her back on Joel, she walked over and knelt next to Colton, looking him in the eye. "I bet that leg is starting to really hurt again, isn't it?" she asked gently.

Colton couldn't pull his eyes from hers as she spoke but managed to respond. "I'd be lying if I told you it tickled," he remarked with a smile.

Orielle chuckled, causing Colton's chest to thump heavily. "Well, this stuff will numb it far more efficiently, and with another bandage soaked in healing herbs, you should be able to put weight on it again tomorrow." She began to remove his muddy old bandage and inspected the wound. "It looks like you avoided infection, so the healing will be quick." Then, she uncorked the pale liquid and looked at him again. "May I? It'll probably hurt a bit." Colton nodded and watched as she poured the liquid onto his leg. The pain was manageable, and he bit his lip as the pain faded to nothing in only a few moments.

Colton sighed as he slouched back in the chair in relief. "Wow, you weren't kidding. That stuff really works. What is it?"

"We call it Whiteshade. It's made from a type of poppy we cultivate back in our village. Living here, our people find a need for it rather frequently," she said as she bandaged up his leg once more and then sat in the chair next to his. "So, tell me about the group that attacked you."

Colton took a deep breath and watched as Joel moved to sit on the soft dirt floor near the couch Imbrose was on. "They wanted us to believe our leader had sent them to kill us off, and while I can't say for certain if that is or isn't true, I truly hope it isn't," he said as he looked over at Delphine.

Orielle leaned back and pursed her lips. "Ember mentioned you were from a place far from here. Where is that, and why did you come here?"

Colton turned to look at her. "I and everyone on this expedition hails from a collection of small continents to the east called The Archipelago of Ishnu. Specifically, we come from a continent named Chvost and a city named New Eradin. As to why we came...well, the initial purpose was to discover new land and civilization, and if possible establish communication and potentially alliances. The truth is more complicated, however, since everyone had their own reasons for coming, myself included." Colton finished by unbuckling the sword from his back and resting it against his uninjured leg.

Orielle leaned forward again as he spoke. "Why are you here, Mister Cobb?"

Colton chuckled slightly then looked between her and Joel. "Honestly, I think I'm here to meet the two of you." Seeing confusion cross their faces he continued. "Not just you, but your whole tribe." Colton then told them the story of his grandfather's tribe and their assumed splitting from a tribe across the ocean.

When he mentioned the sword and gestured to the weapon, Joel froze, finally seeing the weapon for the first time. "The sapphires on the hilt and pommel look just like the ones on Tyrrek's shield." He turned and looked at Orielle. "Do you think it could be…" Joel trailed off.

Orielle ran her finger down the side of her face as she nodded. "It must be…" With a turn of her head, she looked at Colton. "Have you ever felt a connection to the minds of others?"

"Yes, I've always been able to connect to the minds of those around me if they are willing, but it's easiest with my direct family members. Specifically, those who share blood with my grandfather." Colton looked back and forth at them hopefully. "Does that mean…?"

Orielle's voice echoed in his head. *It means we have far more in common than I initially believed. It means you and your family are Tyrkin.*

Chapter Five: The Maimed God

“A Tyrkin?” Colton echoed aloud.

Orielle broke the connection between them and nodded. “I suppose we should tell you the story of our people.” Orielle paused and gathered her thoughts. “During the Great Sundering two thousand years ago, our forefather, Tyrrek, was part of a group of adventurers. He was a renowned weapons master and could use any weapon ever made. Of course, back then, that trait was highly sought after because the titans that were placed here to protect our world began to war amongst themselves. Not a whole lot is known about who he served or fought for, but before the final confrontation he was badly injured. Ultimately, this kept him from joining the fight that ensued and he was stranded here on Zerua.”

Colton scooted to the edge of his chair. “So, that's what this place is called? Zerua?”

Orielle nodded and smiled, clearly enjoying his enthusiasm. “As you can imagine, he wasn't happy with being left behind and sought to find a way to heal himself so he could rejoin the others. See, his wife, Meraway, was one of the other adventurers and she decided she needed to go. Ultimately she, and the other adventurers, died during that fight, and Tyrrek never saw her again.” Orielle lowered her head at that. “Luckily, this was a time when the Gods roamed among us and to honor the sacrifice of their greatest champions they raised them all to Godhood themselves. This honor extended to Tyrrek as well, but he…well, he had made a deal with a coven of witches to heal him. This wouldn't have been a problem, except they did their job too well and made him immortal in the process, and the healing came conveniently too late to rejoin his friends. Thus, he was stranded in an immortal body, with the powers of a God, and no hope of ever seeing his beloved ever again."

"Geez, that's twisted," Delphine said from the dirt wall she was leaning on, speaking for the first time since they had arrived.

"Right?" Orielle continued. "It gets worse! After that war, the Gods decided that walking among mortals was too dangerous and so they sealed themselves away behind The Veil. Which basically means that Gods can't interact directly with those here in the living world ever again. So, Tyrrek was alone, and with no way to die to find his way beyond The Veil, he plummeted into a deep depression. We aren't certain how long it took, since we're basing this off memories from generations ago, but eventually Tyrrek decided to return to Meraway's home village, which was destroyed with the emergence of the forest we now reside in." Orielle stopped as she saw Colton waving a hand.

"Wait, wait. Did you say you are basing this off memories from centuries ago, and what's this about the forest being created?" Colton blurted in one breath, his voice reverberating off the low dirt ceiling.

Orielle nodded and held up a hand. "There's a lot you don't know, Mister Cobb, and there isn't enough time tonight for you to learn two thousand years of history. So, for now let me finish how our people came to be and during a future evening we can delve into more if you're interested."

Colton leaned back holding up his hands in surrender. He very much liked the idea of more evenings like this.

She paused for a moment, glancing at the cold firepit in the center of the room as if trying to regain her thoughts. "Ah yes!" she said while snapping her fingers. "When he got there, he managed to find her old home and a letter she had left for him. Within, he found a story she had written. The story was about a young man and woman who had fallen in love, but the woman was terribly sick and was expected to die very soon. So, in an effort to maintain their connection, they performed a magical ritual which would separate their spirits from their physical bodies. This allowed for them to escape together into the afterlife. Encouraged by the story, Tyrrek tried to perform such a ritual on himself, thinking that if his body couldn't die he could at least untether his spirit from it so he could move on. Unfortunately, the spell failed, but not entirely. See, Tyrrek accidentally created the two lovers from the story, only their spirits were…detached from their physical body. Initially, this proved to be very distressing for them, as they had no idea who they were, but over time, the two of them found a way to harness the energy their detached spirits gave them and they had children. That's us." Orielle pointed at herself, then Joel, and finally Colton.

Colton sat in silence for a moment considering what this meant, but it still didn't explain why he could speak to others in their minds. "So, how does that connect to the abilities I have? How does it work?"

Orielle shrugged. "Some of our greatest thinkers believe we transfer a piece of our spirit into the other person when we do it. To me, it's always felt like I'm sharing a hidden part of myself, so that could be it. Honestly though, I've always believed that something about the energy around us, connects us. It's as if we're more in tune with the essence of the world."

Colton watched Orielle as she talked. It was obvious she felt passion in what she was saying, and he couldn't help but smile. As he listened, he wondered if she felt awkward about sharing that "hidden part" of herself with him so soon after meeting him. To him, it felt as though he was stretching himself thinner when he did it, and it usually resulted in a pounding headache. He resolved to ask her why that was and if she could help him fix that later.

Delphine shifted from her place on the wall and walked closer to the rest of the group. "So, your whole race of people started from one couple?" she asked as she cocked her head.

48

Joel piped up at this. "Well no, because once Tyrrek finally accepted he couldn't escape, he decided to create more just like them. He decided that if he couldn't join her in the afterlife, he would honor her with the creation of new life."

"How is it that you know all of this?" Friend's deep voice cut through the air causing Imbrose to stir in his slumber on the couch.

Orielle lowered her voice to a whisper. "Let's save that for another time shall we?" She gestured down a hallway carved through the dirt. "There's a communal barracks down that hall on the right. You should all get some rest and heal. Tomorrow we can talk about what you all want to do, and how we can help."

Joel glanced her way with that last statement. It was clear he had some things on his mind that he wished to discuss with Orielle after the rest had gone to bed.

Colton stood and nodded at both of them. "From the bottom of my heart, thank you both. If it weren't for you, Imbrose would be…"

Orielle reached out and placed a hand on his arm. "But he's not, and he will recover. Something tells me you would do the same, Mister Cobb, for anyone you thought were in danger."

With a squeeze, she began to pull away, but Colton just reacted without thinking and grabbed her hand. Time stopped as they stared at one another for a long moment. There was something about the contact that left Colton feeling connected to her, as if their energy had, if but for a moment, become one. She didn't pull away, and he could tell she was trying to decide what to do, then he just blurted something out. "Please, call me Colton." Then he released her hand quickly.

Her hand lingered where he had left it for the faintest heartbeat then she smiled. "Very well, Colton. Sleep well." Then she stood and walked back toward the stairs leading toward the entrance. Joel stood, nodded, then followed in her footsteps.

Colton just watched her go, wondering if he had overstepped. He had forgotten Joel was sitting there, but he didn't seem angry. Perhaps he hadn't seen it. Delphine crossed in front of his vision and pulled up next to him. "Smooth, I couldn't tell you nearly crapped yourself at all. Let me know if you plan to do something like that again, I'd like to watch." Then she passed him, walking down the hallway laughing to herself.

Colton looked around the circular room until he finally met the eyes of Friend, who was staring directly at him. "Aren't you going to get some sleep?" Colton asked nervously.

"I don't seem to be tired," Friend replied.

Colton shuffled his feet awkwardly unsure what else to say. "Well, I should probably try and get some rest myself. I suspect tomorrow will be a long day."

"That does seem like a good idea," Friend said blandly. "May I ask you a clarifying question?"

"Uh, sure?" Colton, in fact, wasn't sure at all, but didn't have the heart to refuse the man.

"Was what you did with Miss Orielle considered a courting request?" Friend asked.

Colton stuttered. "Uhh…n-no? I don't think so."

Friend grunted. "How strange, I could have sworn that is what it felt like to me. Tomorrow, let us talk about Mister Curtis." Then he lowered his head to his chest and quit talking.

Colton stood there for a moment, his face burning as he considered the choice to grab her hand. He muttered to himself as he made his way down the hallway until he found a room with snores already coming from within. Colton rolled his eyes and walked into the darkened interior trying to find the bed furthest from the snoring woman. Realizing she had selected the middlemost bed, and it was likely on purpose, he sighed and laid down on the nearest one to him and pulled the pillow over his head.

—

Colton could not tell how long he slept, but when he awoke, he was refreshed. He rolled over to see Delphine had already gotten up and he could hear voices in the other room. With a grunt, he rolled off the bed and slipped on his clean boots, (*Did I clean these*) and made for the door.

It wasn't until he was halfway down the hallway that he realized he was walking normally on his wounded leg. *It can't possibly be healed. That is...* His thoughts trailed off as he unwound the bandage Orielle had placed on it last night. His eyes could not believe what he was seeing. The wound had completely healed over and was simply a red scar. *What was in that potion? If I'm feeling this good, I wonder how Imbrose is doing.* With renewed determination, he jogged into the main room to see everyone sitting and talking casually as they ate some fragrant smelling stew. The room went quiet as he froze when he entered, seeing Orielle before anyone else.

She stopped mid-chew and looked up at him from her seat on the floor and smiled. With a small wave, she finished chewing and started to open her mouth to say something, when a different, but a far more familiar voice broke the silence.

"I told you not to worry about me! I'm pretty hard to kill."

Colton turned to see Imbrose sitting upright on the moss couch with a similar bowl in his hands. He hadn't bothered trying to finish his bite before he spoke and received a disgusted look from Ember as he caught a stray piece of potato that flew out of his mouth, then popped it back in.

"I'm happy to see it, brother. You definitely had us worried to say the least; how are you feeling?" Colton asked as he accepted a bowl from Joel and sat down across from him, anxiously spooning some of the fragrant stew into his mouth. The meal tasted as good as it smelled and Colton let out a satisfied groan as he savored the flavor.

Imbrose swallowed. "I'm feeling pretty good! My back and pretty much everything else hurts like I was kicked by a mountain, but I'm finding Ember missed her calling."

Ember tilted her head and looked at him, the warning clear on her face. "What call exactly have I missed?"

Imbrose either missed the look or didn't care and winked at Colton. "With how well you have been nursing me back to health, you should have been a nurse."

Ember's eyes filled with fury and Colton braced for the clobbering Imbrose was about to receive, wounded or not. However, as fast as it appeared, the fury was replaced with mirth, and she laughed instead. "Well, maybe you should stop getting stabbed and I won't have to be."

"Perhaps, but you would make a very pretty one…" Imbrose added quietly and Ember looked away, her face darkening in shade. "So," Imbrose continued. "The group filled me and Ember in on the details surrounding your special powers and how that connects to them." Imbrose used his spoon to gesture to Orielle and Joel. "Does that mean it's a quest completed then?"

Colton sighed. "On the surface it seems that way, but if what Terran was saying proves true, we may have bigger problems." Colton looked over toward where Friend was sitting with his face plate down and a full bowl of stew in front of him. "What happened with Curtis last night, Friend?"

Friend turned to look at Colton upon being addressed. "After we left your company, Curtis took me to a crate full of some blue stones, which I now know as Cloudstone. When we got there, he started asking me more and more aggressively where the stones came from. At first I did not know, but the more he asked, the more a memory from my past began to surface. It came back choppy and incomplete and all I could remember was a sanctuary of sorts. A place people are not allowed to go unless invited. When Curtis pressed more, my mind began to spin and I started to feel faint, but then I remembered that the sanctuary is to the far north, beyond the Endless Cold. Afterwards, Curtis simply looked at me awestruck and then started telling everyone to get ready to leave. He said I was to come with him and show him where this place was. I resisted and his guards turned their weapons on me. For the first time since I had woken up, I genuinely felt…fear." Friend stopped talking and hung his head. "Then people started screaming and I took that opportunity to break away from them and run into the forest."

Everyone listened with rapt attention. The longer Friend spoke, the more informal and human-sounding he became. Colton was sure there was something more to him than what was obvious on the surface.

Orielle cleared her throat and spoke up first. "I'm so sorry, Friend…That sounds terrible."

Colton set his empty bowl aside. "Do you remember anything else from before we found you?"

Friend shook his head. "The only thing I remember is that I was supposed to find people who could save the knowledge I had. The only problem is, that I no longer remember what knowledge I needed to share."

Ember leaned over and placed a hand on Friend's armored shoulder. "I'm sure it will come back to you in time. I have learned that patience is the best remedy for these types of things." Then she turned to look at Colton. "What are we going to do about Curtis? Do you think he sent Terran after us?"

Colton rubbed his chin and considered the question. "I can't really say, but we need to go back and find out."

Ember nodded and stood up. "Orielle, how far are we from the beach?"

"About an hour's travel," Orielle replied. "I can take you back whenever you're ready." Joel grumbled a little bit, but didn't say anything in reply.

With a pained groan Imbrose began to try and get up.

"Not you," Ember said. "You are healing, and we plan to be right back."

"But–" Imbrose began.

"I am not asking." Ember insisted sternly.

Imbrose smirked and scooted back into his seated position and looked at Colton. "See? I told you she would make a great nurse."

Ember scoffed and turned to Friend. "What about you, Friend? Do you want to come back to the camp with us?"

Friend looked up and simply shook his head.

"Well, I'm coming," Delphine said.

Colton stood and crossed the room to where his sword and hat were lying. He could see the sword and scabbard had been cleaned thoroughly. "Well then. Let's get to the bottom of this," Picking up the sword he caught Orielle's eye and nodded toward the now sparkling scabbard as he began to strap it on. "By the way, did someone clean my stuff last night?"

"I did. Figured that putting your feet in sand-filled boots would be uncomfortable," Orielle said.

"Thank you. I was dreading having to do it myself." Colton chuckled.

Orielle nodded a smile on her face, pulled on her boots, and looked at Joel as he passed her rifle over.

"Be safe," he told her in a hushed tone. "Call if you need me."

"I will," Orielle promised as she hugged him and moved to the exit with Colton, Delphine, and Ember in tow.

Chapter Six: A Fallen Friend

T he sun was out in earnest as even the dense canopy only served to keep the stifling heat from escaping. As the hidden door closed behind them, Orielle waited for everyone to gather around.

"Right, so going back during the daylight will provide us with a bit more safety than before. Some of the most dangerous predators only hunt when it's darkest. Still, everyone should keep pace and not fall behind. Hopefully we won't run into anything, but I will stop if I see something coming." She paused, looking from each face, lingering on Colton. "Don't worry! Joel will take good care of him until we get back!" she encouraged cheerfully.

Delphine snorted. "Not if Imbrose annoys him to death with his obnoxious quips."

"Oh, I doubt Imbrose can irritate Joel. When Joel was a kid he was quite the little deviant. He's probably partly to blame for my adventurous spirit," Orielle said with a dismissive wave of her hand.

Colton chuckled. "Underestimate him at your peril! His dad was a pirate and his mother is likely the strongest mage on the face of Berrinos, so the guy had to stand out somehow. He just chose to use his wit to steal the stage." Colton paused. "Wait, what do people from this continent call the world?"

"We've always called it Berrinos too. Couldn't tell you who made that up," she said with a shrug. "We should get moving, it may be less dangerous, but it's far from safe to be out in the open." Waving for them to follow, Orielle started ahead of everyone.

As the group started walking, Ember scratched her head, pondering a question. "It seems someone, or something, had a hand in developing cultures all over the world." Ember rolled her hand in a continuing motion. "Hence the conversation we are having right now. I mean, how is it that we all know the same language?" she asked no one in particular.

"Well, based on the story Orielle was telling us last night, it sounds like the Titans made the effort to spread people around. I'm pretty sure I remember a story from one of my books as a child that said something like, 'The final battle between Titans occurred far to the east,'" Delphine chimed in while vaulting a fallen tree. "Now, that's assuming the story is true, and that they were referring to where the Archipelago is. Since we traveled to the west to get here and Tyrrek was left here during that final encounter, it stands to reason that populations probably moved more freely back then." Delphine snapped her fingers and pointed at Colton. "Not to mention this guy's family is originally from here."

Colton smacked his lips. "So much for being the first to find this place." Colton turned his head and noticed Orielle gaining even more distance from them. She had been quiet ever since they left.

"So, are you going to tell Ember what you did last night?" Delphine asked.

Colton turned to look at her, nearly tripping on an exposed root. "What do you mean?"

Delphine cocked her head with a sly smile. "You know, that awkward moment when you–"

Colton coughed loudly, causing Orielle to turn around with a questioning look in her eyes. With a sheepish smile, he gave a thumbs up and wheeled back on Delphine. "You know, for an assassin, you snore

56

like a bear with a cold." His voice was quiet but harsh, as he turned to catch up with Orielle.

"Ouch." Delphine placed her hands over her chest in mock hurt. Turning to look at Ember, she smiled and shrugged. "He's not wrong, when I go down, I sleep like the dead." She laughed as she started walking again and gestured at Colton catching up to Orielle. "Watch this, it should make for a good show. For such a handsome guy, he acts like he's never spoken to a woman before."

As Delphine's voice faded behind him, Colton pulled up next to Orielle. "Sorry about everything, Orielle. This is not how I imagined meeting the tribe," Colton apologized.

Orielle smiled slightly as she pulled some hanging creepers out of the way and passed beneath them. "To be fair, I never imagined meeting anyone like us from another continent."

Colton ducked to avoid the thick, almost fluorescent, green foliage."Well sure, but I know we put you out and I feel like we caused some problems between you and Joel."

Orielle paused and looked at him. "Caught onto that, did you?" Orielle shook her head slightly and kept moving. "For all the risky stuff he used to do when we were kids, he's extremely risk averse these days. I know in my gut that if he saw you guys get attacked like I did, he would've intervened even earlier. He's always been a man who thinks with his heart first."

"Sounds like you admire him," Colton said, feeling a lump form in his stomach.

Orielle chuckled. "I suppose I do! Even though he's my cousin, I've always felt like he was more of a brother to me."

Colton couldn't stop the smile from crossing his face. "Oh, well, do you have any siblings besides Joel?"

Orielle stopped walking again and screwed up her face. "Um…Yeah…"

Colton's eyes widened, unsure what he did to upset her. "I'm sorry! I shouldn't have been so nosy."

A sad smile crossed her face and she looked at him. "There's nothing to apologize for! I do have a younger brother named Jasper. He's...He's the most important person in my life." Orielle wiped a tear from her eye and gestured for them to keep walking. "It's just...he's really sick right now."

Colton cast his eyes down, trying to think of what to say, then decided to press forward. "Do you know what he has?"

Orielle tilted her head back and forth. "Sort of. You see, this forest can give and it can take." She swallowed hard. "Jasper was always a sweet boy. He actually helped me make this thing," she recalled while patting her pistol on her thigh. "But one day he just up and went missing without a trace. Everyone feared the worst, because there had been many kids going missing over the recent weeks." Orielle paused as she scaled a large broken tree stump. "After searching the whole village, we started sending out scouting parties. It took almost a month, but we found this cult who had a bunch of the kidnapped kids captured and held in cages. We rescued them, but the children had changed. They were nearly catatonic and wouldn't respond to anyone. We had to carry them all back to the village, and even then we couldn't figure out what happened to them. The place they were being held in didn't shed any light on what was causing them to act this way." Orielle paused, as if deciding whether or not to continue. "So I joined a group that was dedicated to finding a way to bring the kids back to their right minds. I was out on a patrol with Joel when we saw your party sailing toward the coast."

Colton cleared his throat as a large bird of prey squawked overhead. "Well, I wish I knew something about these cultists you're talking about." Throwing caution to the wind, he reached out for Orielle's shoulder, grasping it firmly. "I promise I'll help you with your hunt."

Orielle's head turned and looked at his hand, then she raised her hand and placed it on his own. "Thank you, but you barely know me. I couldn't ask you to risk yourself for me." Then she turned and started to pull from his grip.

Colton rushed to get in front of her and looked deep into her emerald green eyes. "You helped me when you didn't have to, and you say Joel would have intervened too. Would I really be one of you if I didn't do the same?"

A tear welled in Orielle's eye as she looked down and wiped it away. "You're a good man, Colton. If you truly mean what you say, then I'd be honored to have your help."

Colton placed his hands on both of her shoulders and lowered his face to look into her eyes again. "I mean it. I've never broken a promise."

He could see a smile on her face as she looked up at him. Then, a shadow fell across her face. "Colton, I–"

"This looks familiar," Delphine shouted from a nearby clearing.

Orielle moved past Colton without another word and moved to meet up with Ember and Delphine.

Colton stood there for a moment. Had he pushed too far? What was she about to say? Then, with a shake of his head, he turned to find the three of them standing in a familiar clearing. Only the last time he had been in this clearing, there had been bodies. Now, there were only dark stains in the dry dirt and drag marks heading off into various directions.

"Shouldn't be too much further," Orielle said. "If I remember correctly, the entrance you made to the beach is just around that tree over there." She gestured to a large tree that Colton did indeed recognize. "I'll stay here and wait for you. Given what I saw last night, I'd feel better not exposing myself on the beach."

Colton nodded. "Fair enough. How will we find you again?"

Orielle hesitated for a moment. "I can link my mind to yours, and we can talk from a distance. If something goes wrong, I'll do my best to help you."

Colton shifted slightly as he recalled the conversation from the night before. Merging minds was something special to her people, or was it *their* people? Regardless, he met her eyes. "As long as you're comfortable with that. I still don't really know how to do it without causing myself a massive headache."

59

"Not to worry. I can keep the link from my side," she replied.

Almost instantly, a surge of emotion flooded through Colton. Feelings like nervousness, fondness, guilt, and others that did not belong to him flowed through him. The emotions were suddenly cut off as Orielle's voice came through into his head clearly. *Remember to just think what you want to say to me and I'll be able to hear it.*

Colton smiled as her presence in his head settled the nerves he didn't know he was feeling. *Is this working?*

Orielle returned his smile and looked at him. *I can hear you.*

"If you two are finished, I would very much like to hear what Curtis has to say for himself." Ember's voice split the silence causing Orielle to drop her gaze abruptly.

"Right, let's get moving," Colton said. "We'll keep you updated, Orielle."

With a nod, the group split with Delphine, Ember, and Colton heading for the passage through the thick jungle back to the beach.

The trek back was made in eerie silence. The energy was one of nervousness. With everyone worried about what they would find when they got there. How many had survived the animal attack? Had anyone survived? Silently, he pushed his thoughts toward Orielle. *We are about to go onto the beach.*

A second later her voice came to him along with a feeling of worry. *Be careful…Please.*

Of course, Colton thought back.

As the final wall of vines blocking their visual of the beach was pulled aside, many things caught Colton's attention.

First and foremost was the fact that where there once sat a massive ship just offshore, there was now nothing but open ocean. Colton's eyes, barely believing what he was seeing, or rather what they weren't seeing, began to scan the destroyed campsite. The once corpse ridden beach was now cleaned. A single large funeral pyre had been built with the bodies lying side by side. The pyre had yet to be lit, but four figures could be seen on the far side looking up at them.

60

"What happened here?" Delphine asked quietly.

"Is that Genevieve?" Colton wondered as he saw a glint from her armor.

Ember's face contorted into a snarl and started toward the figures near the pyre. Delphine and Colton looked at one another, then followed in her footsteps. As the three of them approached, an armored figure, now clearly discernible as Genevieve, walked around the unlit pyre to meet them.

Genevieve clearly hadn't slept a wink with deep circles visible even through the grime on her face. She stepped within ten feet and held out a hand. "That's far enough, folks. Since you're stranded here just like us, I'd like to assume you weren't a part of this, but I need to hear you say it."

Colton held up his hands and stopped just in front of where Ember had frozen, staring daggers at the tall woman. "I have no idea what you're talking about Genevieve. We were attacked in the woods by Terran and his crooks. Imbrose is still hurt, but we needed to get back and make sure everyone was okay." Looking at the other three figures Colton recognized three of Genevieve's personal guard: Baldo, Gavin, and Quinn, but Quinn had a bandage wrapped around her midsection that was soaked in blood. There was one missing though. "Where is Janshi?" Colton asked.

Genevieve's eyes softened and she looked at a body lying on the pyre. Colton followed her gaze to see the tall man who had always been kind, lying there with his head in two pieces. "They attacked us without warning. Janshi didn't even know what happened before they split his skull from behind. Quinn took a spear in the side, but we were able to retreat up the beach as they boarded the rowboats and set sail," Genevieve grunted, obviously trying to keep her emotions under control. "Curtis gave the order. Anyone who wasn't one of his paid mercenaries was killed ruthlessly. I'm ashamed to say I saved myself as the massacre happened."

Ember spoke up. "It wasn't your fault, Genevieve. Janshi and the others knew that. Curtis is to blame, and his time will come."

61

"I'm sorry. Janshi was a good man. He was always kind and I don't think anyone had a bad thing to say about him. The fact that Curtis turned on you in that way only goes to show how far gone he really is," Colton offered in heartfelt sympathy.

Genevieve nodded without pulling her eyes from Janshi's body. Then she sniffed and straightened herself. "So, how did you guys make it through the night?"

Colton hesitated and reached out to Orielle. *Things are not looking good out here. We were betrayed by Curtis, and there are only four survivors. Would it be okay if we brought them with us? I trust each of them with my life.*

Orielle didn't respond immediately, causing Colton to look toward the forest for fear that the connection had failed, but then her voice entered his thoughts. *It sounds like we have a lot to talk about. If you trust them, then I do too.*

Colton smiled, honored to receive such trust. *Thank you, it means a lot that you feel that way.* Then, he turned to Genevieve and her team and told them the events of the previous evening from their perspective, leaving nothing out.

"With no means to follow Curtis wherever he has gone, our only hope is to trust Orielle and Joel," he finished.

Genevieve listened throughout. "Well, I'm glad Imbrose made it out. The man may act the fool, but he'd give you his last dollar if you needed it." She looked at the pyre once more. "We need to give them a proper send off. Then we can go."

The seven of them went about making small fires along the line of bodies. It didn't take long before the whole fifty foot pyre was caressed in bright flames. The group all bowed their heads and whispered prayers under their breath. Colton just closed his eyes. *Please give me the chance to avenge the warriors who fell here.* Realizing his thoughts probably passed through his and Orielle's link, he tensed, but relaxed as she responded.

You will, I know you will. Her voice washed over him like a soothing river during a hot day.

"Janshi, I'm sorry. You were a loyal friend, and I wish I could've given you a proper burial at home. You deserved that much. Know that I will carry your valor with me until my dying day," Genevieve swore in a proud voice. Then she turned to Colton. "Get us off this forsaken beach."

The group walked back to where they had left Orielle to find her sitting on a log cleaning the barrel of her pistol. As they approached, she looked up and scanned the new arrivals. "Hiya, I'm Orielle. It's nice to meet y'all."

Genevieve walked up to her and held out a hand. "It's nice to meet you too, Orielle. My name's Genevieve, that's Gavin, Baldo, and Quinn," she recited while pointing to them all in turn. "I appreciate you taking care of our people."

Orielle blushed slightly at the praise."Of course. Anyone would've done the same."

Genevieve shook her head. "Not everyone, and I'm not sure that if I saw people from another land fighting each other if I would even get involved. So, just know it means a lot and I'm grateful."

Orielle nodded and turned away clearly uncomfortable with the compliment. "You're welcome." She cleared her throat and looked back at the others. "We should probably get moving. This big of a group is going to attract some unwanted attention. Besides, once I told Joel about the betrayal, he said Imbrose had something he wanted to show you. It sounded important."

Colton stepped forward. "Lead the way."

The party picked their way through the lush forest. At one point, Orielle stopped to pluck some overly large berries from a purple-leafed bush, claiming these were rare to find this time of the year. The berries themselves smelled like a mixture between burning wood and a salty sea breeze. Their flavor was another matter entirely, with the outside tasting of unripe lemons, but the core of the berry tasting like a rich chocolate. At first, Colton found the berry difficult to stomach, but after a few bites he found it to be quite delicious if one could get the outside and inside in the same bite. After his third berry, he turned to see Ember still hadn't touched the one she was given.

"Everything alright, Ember?" Colton asked.

Ember sighed. "I suppose. Imbrose is okay, and we have a direction to go even though it feels like we are lost."

Colton arched an eyebrow. "But...?"

Ember glanced over at him with a conflicted look on her face. "I really wanted to confront Curtis. I feel like he has gotten away with something horrible, and I can't stop thinking about how bad Imbrose looked. I really thought I had–we had lost him."

Colton looked straight ahead spotting Orielle as she held some vines aside for everyone to pass under. "Curtis won't get away. When we get ourselves situated and we know where he is, we will go get him." Colton paused and smiled. "I've always known the two of you were...close. Even if you both have been dancing around it for our entire lives. He's too nervous and insecure to make a move, and you are too strong and stubborn to admit you feel the same." Ember wheeled on him, and he smiled placatingly. "I call it as I see it."

Ember's face cracked into a smile and she punched him on the shoulder. "Well, it seems you aren't as bad with women as Delphine would suggest." She walked a bit more in silence before piping up again. "I tried to ignore how I feel about him. He can be so enraging sometimes, but you know him like I do. He's gentle and loving. He could easily sit up in his ivory tower with his royal parents, but instead he journeys with us to try and save the world one silly joke at a time. He would do anything to save either of us, and that includes being reckless enough to start a fight in an enclosed ship with a guy who has fifteen goons at his back." She chuckled slightly. "Funnily enough, I really like that about him. Perhaps I am a bit reckless too."

Colton chuckled with her. "A bit? Why do you think I keep you two near me? If I'm not around, who's going to keep the both of you out of trouble?"

"Enough about Imbrose and I. We will figure it out. I am more curious who could have caught the eye of Colton Cobb," she teased as she shimmied her shoulders playfully. "What is it about her? I mean, you hardly know her."

Colton shrugged and pursed his lips. "I honestly couldn't tell you. There's something about the energy I feel around her that has me losing my ability to keep a clear head."

"Maybe she's a witch?" Ember asked jokingly.

Colton laughed loud enough for a few to turn their heads. "Maybe. Though I think there's more to her than I can see. Time will tell, I'm sure of that."

Ember nodded. "Don't wait too long, Colton. I know I sound hypocritical by saying that, but I have found that feelings are meant to be embraced."

Colton laid a hand on her shoulder. "Thank you, and you do sound like a hypocrite," he teased with a playful shove.

Ember smiled and fell into silence once again. Colton turned his thoughts inward as he considered her words. A panicked feeling washed over Colton as he worried Orielle had never cut the link between them, and she had heard everything. *Orielle? Are you still there?* When she didn't answer, he breathed a sigh of relief. This woman really had his mind tied in knots.

"Here we are," Orielle announced as they walked up to a familiar tree.

With the same knocking pattern as before, the door eventually pulled in and up to reveal the cozy interior once again, Joel standing faithfully at the entrance. To the right as he entered, Colton noticed a ladder climbing up the hollow tree into a darkened interior at the top. Assuming it must be some kind of lookout, he continued down the stairs to the circular common room where Imbrose was teaching Friend a game he used to hustle coins from drunk tavern goers.

65

"Keep your eye on the badger…" Imbrose intoned as he moved three cards in rapid succession. "Now, think carefully, which one is the badger?"

Friend thought for a moment while gripping his chin between his forefinger and thumb. "Hmm…Perhaps it was that one?" he guessed, pointing to the leftmost card.

Before even flipping the card over, Imbrose was already shaking his head. "Sorry, Friend. No dice I'm afraid." He flipped over a picture of a shark breaching the water. "That's how you play Badger Hole! That'll be fifteen silver pieces."

"I see you're feeling better," Colton drawled as he approached Imbrose and quickly seized his hand. "The problem here, Friend, is that you had no chance to win."

Imbrose looked at him with pleading eyes. "You wouldn't!"

Colton flashed a sinister smile. "Oh, but I would." Then he reached into Imbrose's sleeve and withdrew a card and flipped it over to reveal a badger. "The game is called Badger Hole because the dealer slides the badger up their sleeve right before they start moving the cards. Therefore, you were always going to lose."

Friend gawked at the badger and looked toward Imbrose. "Wow! Can I borrow the deck and try to be the dealer?"

Imbrose raised his nose at Colton. "You see? Some people recognize the beauty in the finer points of sleight of hand." He pouted, as he handed the deck over to Friend, a smirk playing at his lips. Friend seized the deck and quickly retreated to a corner to begin playing with the cards.

Colton rolled his eyes and sat down across from Imbrose. "So, you wanted to tell us something?"

The rest of the group had already made their way into the room and situated themselves preparing for what Imbrose had to say next.

He turned and looked at Genevieve. "I'm glad you guys made it out. I was sorry to hear about Janshi. I really liked the guy." Genevieve acknowledged the comment with a nod. "Anyway, I heard Curtis up and left. Figures, he was always a bit dodgy." Imbrose reached over and fumbled with his cloak. "Too bad he wasn't paranoid enough to guard this," he said, raising a weathered, leather-bound tome.

Ember gasped from across the room. "You stole his journal?"

Imbrose smiled proudly. "As I said. There is beauty in sleight of hand."

Chapter Seven: Monsters Within

"What's that?" Joel asked as he looked at the worn tome, clearly unimpressed.

"That," Colton began, "is the travel journal of Deegan Nezva. He's the first person from our homeland to have ever set foot on Zerua."

"He also returned so crazy that our own leaders refused to let him dock his ship and eventually ordered its destruction with him still on it," Imbrose elaborated as he flipped to the back of the book. "Which explains why the writing at the end is written in blood," he said as he turned the book so everyone else could see.

On the page was a winding scrawl of crimson writing with only one word repeated over and over again: *"Defiler, Defiler, Defiler."* The word became an unreadable smattering of far too much "ink" halfway through the last page.

"Why did Curtis have it?" Orielle asked as she recoiled from the disturbing nature of the writing.

"Deegan was his father." The cool voice of Delphine broke through the din as she approached Imbrose and held out her hand. "May I?" Imbrose shrugged and handed it to her, where she immediately started flipping through the early entries.

Colton eyed her suspiciously but decided to continue with the story. "When his ship was destroyed, it was believed that everything he owned sank with him to his watery grave. That is until Curtis approached the council of New Eradin with the journal, and begged for support to make a similar expedition here. They, of course, declined based on the state of his father upon his return." Colton scratched his head, nervous to share what happened next.

"What is it?" Joel asked as he leaned in.

Colton tilted his head with a guilty expression on his face. "Well, that's where I come in." He took a deep breath, and continued. "I've told you about my quest to come out here in search of our lost tribe at my grandfather's behest. So, when news about Curtis finding the journal and his subsequent request of the council reached my ears, I seized my chance." Colton paused once again recalling the memory. "I can still see his house. The front door had been broken off its hinges and I could hear the clatter of more things being broken from the inside. In hindsight, I probably should have recognized his instability at that moment but…I was desperate. I made a promise," Colton admitted as he bit his bottom lip.

Ember spoke up after a moment of silence. "His grandfather," she said, gesturing at Colton. "He's starting to get old, that's why he couldn't make the journey himself. So, all I have ever heard Colton talking about is 'fulfilling his promise to Grandpa Xander.'"

Colton nodded and sniffed, throwing on a stoic expression. "Curtis was easy to convince. He wanted to make the journey, even more so than I, but he was missing a ship that could make the trek. Lucky for him, I had spent the better part of a fortune to have a ship built for this specific purpose."

"She was a beauty," Imbrose recalled wistfully.

Colton smiled sadly. "That she was." Colton sighed. "After he agreed, I set about trying to recruit a crew who was crazy enough to do something that had already been expressly forbidden." He gestured around the room. "Then we set off before anyone could stop us."

Colton heard Delphine scoff and turned to see her toss the journal onto the couch next to where Imbrose sat. "Seems the apple doesn't fall far from the tree." She pointed an accusatory finger at the discarded book.

"Deegan landed on the coast of this forest with his three ships as well, and just like us, they were attacked the second the sun fell below the horizon."

"No wonder two of the vessels turned and set sail for home. Of course, it would've been nice to get a warning about the dangers they faced," griped Genevieve as she looked down at Quinn's bloody bandage.

Delphine nodded angrily as she pursed her lips. "He aptly names the place 'A Forest of Monsters,'" Delphine cursed under her breath and began pacing like a caged lion. "The monster planned to offload us here from the beginning."

Imbrose picked up the book and flipped open to a page he had marked. "Be that as it may, I found what happened next the most compelling." Imbrose ran his finger over the page until he found the spot he was looking for. "Ah yes, here it is. '*The cowards have abandoned me at the first sign of trouble. Today, I needed to squash a rebellion as my spineless first mate tried to mutiny and flee back home with our tails between our legs. I reminded him that if he didn't bring home some form of riches from this expedition, then he wouldn't have the funds to treat his wife. He fell in line, and we continued to the north, leaving the corpses behind for the beasts.*' Pretty ruthless if you ask me."

Delphine stopped pacing and visibly tried to hold back tears. "That 'spineless first mate,'" she spoke the words with a discernible note of venom, "was my father, and he left to try and save my mother from a long agonizing death. Ultimately, she did die, a shadow of her former self, believing he had sailed to his demise." Ember crossed the room and hugged Delphine tightly.

Imbrose continued hesitantly. "What this does tell us though, is which direction Curtis likely went."

Colton nodded remembering Curtis' interest in Friend. "That tracks. Friend, didn't you say the cloudstone he was asking for was to the nor–" Colton cut the word off as he turned to see Friend staring at the playing card in his hand, as the rest of his body trembled aggressively. "Friend? Are you okay?" Colton asked quietly as he and the rest of the room's attention focused on the metal man. Friend didn't answer and instead continued to shake, eyes fixed on the card. Colton moved tentatively to look over Friend's shoulder.

The card was that of a large dragon with red scales breathing a torrent of fire. Turning his attention back to Friend, Colton placed a hand on his shoulder. The metal was hot to the touch and the moment his hand rested on it, Friend's head jerked in his direction. Startled, Colton stepped back with hands raised and watched as Friend burned the card in his hand to ashes. In its place, a burning orb of fire appeared, swirling ominously.

Joel stepped forward first. "Woah, Friend. It's okay. No one is trying to hurt you." Joel's eyes glanced down at the roiling flame in his hand. "Why don't you get rid of that fire?" Joel implored. Colton risked a glance at where a pail of water sat a few feet away. Joel waved his hand to get Colton's attention and shook his head.

Friend stood there locked in place for a moment longer before he closed his fist around the flame, extinguishing it. A collective breath of relief echoed through the space. "I'm sorry. I appear to be recalling parts of my past. The memory I just experienced was quite…extreme," he said.

The group all exchanged looks with one another nervously. The wooden framing dangerously close to where Friend was sitting. "Not to pry, but it kind of looked like you were going to light this place on fire. Care to share what had you almost torching us?" Imbrose asked as he stared at Friend with wide eyes.

Friend nodded simply. "I was in a small town that was in the shadow of a slowly erupting volcano. I can't recall how I know, but that was normal and the volcano served as a source for our blacksmiths to forge the most impressive metal around." Friend paused and shuddered again, but continued speaking. "Then, a massive dragon attacked. My whole family was inside our small house when the dragon blew it to pieces. I remember feeling helpless as the dragon continued its carnage around the lower levels of the town. Only after reducing most of the population to ash did the beast land and declare herself master of us all."

Orielle placed a hand over her mouth. "That's awful."

"It most definitely was," Friend replied. Reaching up, he unclasped his helm and removed it for the first time. His charcoal-colored bald head was covered in intense burn scars. Friend turned and placed the helm on the ground while looking up at the rest of the room. For the briefest of moments, his eyes appeared to be on fire. Colton blinked, and when he opened his eyes again, Friend's had returned to normal. "Not to worry, I am myself again. You were asking about Curtis, correct?"

Colton opened his mouth to speak but closed it, then finding his voice he answered. "Y-yes, where did you say the cloudstone was?"

Friend tilted his head, recalling the conversation. "Ah yes, when he was questioning me, I recalled a story about cloudstone to the north. The memory was spotty, but the name 'Isle of Stars' came to mind." Friend snapped his gauntleted finger with a soft *clang*. "Also, 'the Endless Cold' was something I said, I believe. I do not know what that means." Friend stopped talking and scratched his head in what was the most organic motion Colton had seen from him.

Joel cleared his throat. "I think I can help with this. The Endless Cold is the expanse of ice that stretches off Zerua's Northern Coast. As for the Isle of Stars, it's a place of worship that some of our ancestors went to a long time ago."

Gavin, the youngest of Genevieve's guards, spoke up. "It sounds like we have a direction then."

Joel turned and looked at the man. "I wouldn't be so sure. The Isle of Stars is a closely guarded place and even its location is hidden. You may only go if you are expressly invited."

"That explains why the writing started getting a bit erratic," mused Imbrose as he looked at the journal. "Says here that they *'found a constellation on the surface of the ocean.'* Sounds like the place to me." Imbrose smacked his lips. "Unfortunately, they had already been sailing around lost for months by the time they found it. Then after that, it's just that word written over and over."

Colton screwed up his face in thought. This whole thing just felt like a mystery wrapped in a mystery, and it made his head hurt. "We can rightly assume he's going north, but he has a day of travel on us and we have no ship to follow him with."

"Well, he might use the Andromedus River to cross the continent," Orielle said, turning to Joel. "Don't you think?"

Joel tilted his head back and forth gauging his answer. "Maybe…if he does, then our people in the Thicket of Rivers will likely spot him." Joel looked at Orielle with an apologetic look on his face. "That would, of course, mean that we need to head back home to let everyone know what has happened here."

Orielle's eyes hardened as she looked at Joel. "You know I can't do that. We still haven't found anything."

Joel scanned the room uncomfortably. "Why don't we speak about this in the kitchen?" he said, motioning to a curtain blocking the visual into the next room. With a huff, Orielle stormed through the curtain into the room beyond. Joel looked at everyone else. "Apologies, give us a moment." Then he followed behind Orielle.

The room fell into silence until Imbrose spoke. "Well personally, I don't think of myself as nothing."

Ember rolled her eyes and looked at Imbrose. "It's not always about you. Besides, we are crashing whatever mission they were on before they found us."

Colton kept his mouth shut. He knew what they were looking for, and he also knew that leaving before they found it would be excruciating for Orielle.

A crash of shattering glass could be heard followed by Orielle yelling, "Why can't you take them? I won't abandon Jasper to his fate!"

Colton could hear Joel trying to reason with her, but he couldn't make out what was said.

Then, the curtain flew open and Orielle walked out and toward the entrance of the outpost. Joel followed after slowly and forced a smile on his face as he looked at the rest of the group. "We will leave in the morning. Get some rest." Then he moved to follow Orielle.

"So, anyone for a game of cards?" Imbrose said as the tension in the room grew thick.

A sharp crack rang out as Ember smacked the back of his head with lightning speed. "You're an idiot sometimes."

The evening went by slowly as everyone spent the rest of the day considering their own thoughts, with only a few words being exchanged here and there. When the time came for everyone to bed down, Colton laid down in his cot and tried desperately not to consider how dire their circumstances were. He may have come out here with the intent to stay, but he never meant for the others to be marooned so far from home. With so many questions circulating his head, coupled with the light weeping from Delphine's cot, he had a hard time finding sleep. Even when he did fall into unconsciousness, it was restless and nightmares invaded his mind.

———

Morning was a welcome respite. Colton awoke to find himself soaked through with sweat. Everyone else was asleep still except for Delphine, who sat on the end of her bed spinning one of her daggers between her fingers. She looked up as Colton rose to a sitting position himself. Delphine's tight ponytail looked disheveled and her eyes looked tired but determined.

"About time you stopped squirming," Delphine grumbled in a quiet voice.

Colton rubbed the back of his neck that had cramped uncomfortably. "Sorry about that. Did I keep you up?"

Delphine shook her head, sheathed her dagger, and moved to sit next to him on his bed. Colton slid over to give her some room. "I can't stop thinking about how my father must have felt being out here so far from home with a madman as a leader. Do you think at some point he just knew it was hopeless and that he wasn't making it home?"

"Never. He stayed for you and your family." Colton turned and looked at Delphine, and for the first time since he had met her, saw just another person. Until now, he had always unwittingly assigned her the

74

role of the fearsome Nightingale, a ruthless assassin who satiated her lust for blood through the legal murder of criminals. The woman before him was wounded, and all at once he realized why she had agreed to come on this mission. "You came to find him, didn't you?"

Delphine smirked. "Silly, isn't it? The expedition happened ten years ago. He is almost certainly dead."

Unable to kick her lower, Colton bumped her shoulder with his. "Or, he was left behind like us. He wasn't on the ship when Deegan got home. He could still be alive, Delphine," Colton said with confidence. "What were the odds that we would find Orielle and Joel, and yet we did! I've completed the life mission of my grandfather who had been holding onto the same dream since he was a boy. That's at least four times as long as your father has been missing. Besides, if we found friendly people, who's to say your father couldn't have as well?"

Delphine looked at the ceiling and sighed. "You're right. Thank you, Colton." She stood and brushed herself off, sniffing the air. "Smells like someone is making breakfast. Let's get it while it's fresh."

Colton watched her leave, then closed his eyes and steeled himself for the day to come. With a grunt, he stood and donned his hat and crossed to the door.

The rest of the group slowly trickled into the common area and eventually everyone was eating delicious food, even Friend, and was discussing happier times. All except Orielle who sat silently with minimal reaction when she was addressed directly. It was obvious something was on her mind and she wasn't pleased to be leaving empty handed. Eventually, Joel stood and told everyone it was time to leave. Within fifteen minutes, everyone was loaded up and standing outside of the outpost. Colton and the others were outfitted with some meager supplies, but to Colton's experienced eye, it looked like multiple days worth of rations. Joel explained the trip to the village would take at least three days, and along the way they would need to set up camp on the thick limbs of the massive trees in the forest.

The first day and night of travel was the hardest as both Quinn and Imbrose were both still injured, and the terrain was difficult to traverse without being hurt. As the sun rose on the second day, Quinn had almost made a full recovery with the help of Joel, and Imbrose was beginning to spar with Delphine during break times. Genevieve and her people were quiet with the exception of Baldo, who made a concerted effort to be near Ember as he regaled the troop with his heroic exploits during the beast attack. Orielle walked alongside Friend, who walked with his helmet under his arm more than not. This left Colton to marvel at the otherworldly beauty this forest displayed. Between the rays of sunlight permeating the canopy high above, and the vibrant alien colors all around, he found himself smiling at the wonder of it all. Even if some of the flora and definitely the fauna looked like they were waiting to take a bite out of him.

It wasn't until the middle of the second day, when the temperature was at its hottest, that Joel stopped and knelt looking at something on the ground. Colton moved to stand beside him and could see that he was looking at deep footprints leading perpendicular to their path. Colton's eyes followed the tracks until he saw a lone cloaked figure standing in the shadow of a large tree, their back to the party. Without taking his eyes off them, Colton fumbled to tap on Joel's shoulder.

With a jerk, Joel stood up and swept his arm through the air, cutting off Baldo's latest attempt to impress Ember. "Orielle, is that what I think it is?"

A screeching voice invaded Colton's mind, forcing him to his knees. *Your mind is weak, what a feast it will make for Him.* Colton clawed at his temples in pain, as his red-rimmed vision tunneled in on the creature as it turned around. *Have you heard His voice yet?* the voice screamed into his head. *You will,* It whispered. With that, the presence fled and the creature dropped onto the ground, seemingly unconscious.

Colton raised his hand and wiped away the tear forming in his eye from the pain only to see his hand streaked with red. In horror, he wiped furiously at his face to see that he had been crying blood. With shaking hands, he turned to see Imbrose crouching beside him, saying something he couldn't understand. The ringing in his ears caused him to wince as he rubbed them trying to gain his hearing back. Blinking his eyes, Colton took a deep breath trying to settle his thundering heart and looked over at Joel who had the same red tears running down his face. Colton heaved himself shakily to his feet and looked around him. Everyone was either looking at him, Joel, or Orielle who also held her hands over her face. As his senses returned to him, Colton turned and started stumbling toward the creature who had apparently done this to them. Almost immediately, his foot caught on something and he fell forward, his hearing returning to him.

"Woah, woah, what's going on Colton?" He could hear Imbrose's frantic voice beside him.

Colton rolled to a sitting position and placed a hand behind him to brace his weight. "That thing…" Colton coughed, his voice hoarse. "It spoke to me in my head. It told me my 'mind was weak' and that it would be a 'feast' for something."

Imbrose's eyes turned to look at the prone creature in the grass a few paces away. With a twist of his head, he yelled back at the group. "Genevieve, get that thing tied up. We need to find a place to let them recover."

The party set up a makeshift campsite as the three Tyrkin sipped some water and tried to compose themselves. Genevieve had tied the creature up, which was lying on the ground some feet away. Colton stared wide eyed at the cloaked figure's face. From the distance earlier and through the experience he hadn't been able to see it, but now he couldn't pull his gaze away. The creature's face looked like a mesh of mantis-like mandibles and crustacean exoskeleton. Its eyes were closed but they had an oddly human quality to the shape of them. The entirety of the monster, for Colton could think of it as nothing else, sent chills throughout his body.

"Are you okay?" said a quiet voice to his left as Orielle turned to talk with him.

Colton started as he heard her speak. "Y-yeah, how are you feeling?"

She rubbed her forehead. "Well, I feel like I was hit with a club over the head." Then when Colton didn't respond, she turned to look at the prone figure. "I wish this was the first time I'd seen one of those. However, I've never seen one offer themselves to captivity like that before. It was like it was waiting for us."

Colton grunted as pain lanced through his head again. "Do they always attack the mind?"

Orielle furrowed her eyebrows as she continued to look at the abomination. "Mostly, but none of them have been that strong before. In the past, we were usually able to resist them, but this one attacked as if our minds were his to play with." She paused and looked back at Colton. "Did it speak with you?"

Colton held her gaze and nodded slowly, his mind returning to the moment unbidden.

Orielle looked down, as a sense of discomfort flowed across her face. "He told me that my brother was lost, and that I would join him soon."

Colton considered how best to comfort her. "A creature like that feeds on despair. You mustn't allow its lies to take hold." Colton closed his mouth, unsure if it was appropriate to go on. Orielle still looked down at her feet, so Colton pressed forward. "Jasper needs you to be strong."

Orielle took a deep breath and let it out slowly, trying to compose herself. "You're right."

"That is the second time someone has told me that today. If people keep saying I'm right, I may get a superiority complex," Colton said with a chuckle.

Orielle smiled and waved her hand at him in a dismissive gesture.

"We need to keep moving." Joel's voice sounded out so everyone turned to look at him. "With this thing in our custody, we'll need to push through the night and get to the next outpost."

Ember rose from her seated position. "You hardly look like you're able to do something like that."

Joel stood and offered a hand to both Orielle and Colton. "It doesn't matter. Where there is one, there are countless more. We can't stay here." Joel crossed the campsite and grabbed his bag, pulling out a vial of viscous looking liquid and tossing it to Ember, who caught it deftly. "Rub that around your neck. It will keep the worst of the predators away while we make our way. Everyone needs to do it or we will be exposed." Joel then turned to Genevieve. "Do you think you can manage the prisoner? We'll need to move quickly." Genevieve nodded resolutely and called Gavin over to help hoist the body.

Colton strode over and nodded at Ember before picking up his own bag. "Are you okay?" she asked as she uncorked the bottle and recoiled from the smell.

"I'll manage," he said with an uncertain smile.

From that point forward, the group moved at a steady jog through the forest for hours. As darkness fell, Joel moved to the rear of the troop and Orielle led them toward some unknown destination. It wasn't long before roars and growling caused Colton to turn his attention to his left, almost losing his footing.

"Keep moving!" Joel shouted.

A feeling crossed over Colton as he felt as if he was being watched. Instinctively, he reached down and drew his long knife from his belt as he continued to run. Quickly, the whole forest came alive as the bushes all around them started shaking with the movement of massive creatures.

"There's no way we're going to make it, they're everywhere!" Quinn yelled from near the back.

Just then, Colton watched as Friend raised his arms to create a fireball in either hand and began to spray fire into the air in wide arcs on either side of the party while still running. Screeching pierced the night as everyone sped up their pace. Suddenly, the shape of a large primate lept from a nearby tree over the flames aiming for Friend, only to be impaled with a red dagger. Imbrose appeared at the hilt of the dagger a second later, still in midair, as he rode the corpse to the ground. Colton pulled him to his feet as he ran by and they continued on picking up the pace even further.

Behind him, he could hear a clash of steel and a grunt followed by Joel's determined voice. "I'm fine, we're almost there."

A cliffside fast approached through the darkness. As soon as Orielle reached it, she started frantically drawing an ornate pattern into the rock surface. Colton came to a stop and turned to watch everyone else catch up. Joel was cradling his left arm, and Colton pulled the man behind him as the forest smoldered at their backs. Friend, Colton, Imbrose, Ember, Delphine, Quinn, and Baldo all stood in a wide arc scanning the tree line. Colton unfurled his whip as he watched everyone ready their weapons.

"I need two minutes," said Orielle in a calm voice.

"You'll have it," Friend replied curtly. Then, he opened his faceplate and brought his hands, still burning, to either side of his face as he exhaled a breath. The torrent of flame that followed coated the entire treeline as Friend swept his head back and forth to cover the whole area in front of them. Colton recoiled slightly as he watched creatures that were once hidden in the darkness catch fire and run away whimpering.

As silence fell over the space, Colton's eyes glanced up to see large shadows moving through the treetops. The fires weren't going to be enough. The thought came over Colton like a bucket of ice water. Colton scanned the area and saw a small path off to one side. Maybe if he made enough noise, he could pull some of them away, and give everyone a chance to make it out.

With a resolved smile, he broke from the line, yelling over his shoulder. "Get out of here!" Then, he ran away from the screaming protests of his friends with renewed determination. The effect was immediate as he watched the figures turn and start tracking easier prey. "Come on beasties! Dinner's on me tonight!" Colton yelled as he ran. A pressure to his right caused him to instinctively throw his knife into the darkness as it caught a giant snake in its gaping mouth. The creature died instantly, and as it fell limply behind him, he kept running. The light of Friend's fires faded and darkness enclosed around him, and a shadow lunged for him. He rotated on one foot, dodging the attack while slashing up with his whip, catching the creature in the chest. Colton didn't even have time to check and see if it was dead before the next one was upon him. He ducked and dropped the whip handle and pulled his bowie knife in one motion. With all his strength, he jammed the knife deep into the furry sternum with both hands, but couldn't pull it free before the weight of the creature pulled it off to the side. Letting the handle slip from his grasp, he took stock of his surroundings.

All around him he could see the eyes of predators as they crept in on him. With a resigned sigh, he glanced over at his friends who were illuminated by the dying fire. He could see Imbrose fighting to pull himself from Genevieve's iron grip as she pulled him into the opening. He smiled again, realizing his idiotic ploy had worked. Returning his eyes to the creatures encroaching around him, he reached behind him and fluidly drew the greatsword from his back, and charged.

A sense of peace overcame him as he slashed through the first creature. He ducked another swipe to see the blade in his hand begin to glow. He could feel the blade grow lighter as if he, a man who had only wielded it a handful of times, could now call upon decades of bladecraft. A guttural yell escaped his lips as he felt something bite his shoulder, but somehow it didn't hurt. He made the wolf pay as he plunged the blade through its eye and shrugged off the now limp maw. Colton laughed as he watched the creatures back away from him. Without a moment of hesitation, he threw himself back into the fray. The next few moments consisted of the blazing blue light of the sword sweeping back and forth in the darkness while creatures fell before him. A thorny spike flew from the darkness and punched into Colton's abdomen, forcing him back against the rock surface of the cliff. Gasping for breath, Colton looked to see a field of corpses before him, but as he watched, more took their place and this time he knew he wouldn't be able to force them back.

Colton looked down to see a large porcupine quill protruding from his destroyed leather armor and coughed to see blood spill onto the forest floor. He closed his eyes and imagined the first time he met Imbrose. He was just visiting New Eradin for the first time. The massive spires of the city could be seen even from the deck of the ship he and his father sailed in on. As they docked, his father had kneeled down in front of him.

"Stay around the ship, Colton," he had said as he stood and moved toward the stairs that would take him to the city proper. "Don't get into any trouble!"

Colton had nodded and begun looking up and down the stalls. A wide-brimmed hat had caught his attention and he walked to speak to the merchant.

"Hey you!" a voice had called to him. As he turned his head, he saw a little blue boy with horns running toward him. "Wanna play hide and seek? I bet you won't be able to find me!" Then, the little boy ran away from him.

Colton blinked his eyes, returning to reality to see a large tiger stepping within inches of his face. The tiger sniffed him and snorted, the gust of wind causing him to turn his face. *This is it…* Colton felt consciousness slipping away as the creature pulled back its head and opened its mouth, a yawning portal to the afterlife.

The creature recoiled as a familiar red dagger appeared in its jugular. Then, that little blue boy appeared holding it, glaring down at him. "Sorry, mate. I'm not leaving this nightmare unless you're coming too."

Colton watched through blurred vision as a double bladed ax came down on another creature as Genevieve stepped through the swing and cleaved its head off. Then, they were all there, cutting through the beasts left and right.

Joel rushed to his side and pulled him onto his uninjured shoulder. "Hang in there, Colton! You're doing great," Joel urged as he looked over his shoulder. "Grab the sword, Imbrose, we're moving."

His last thought was: *How did I get so many loyal friends?* Then, his vision tunneled as he saw Orielle waving them toward an opening in the cliff.

Chapter Eight: Some Sage Advice

C olton gasped in pain as his eyes shot open to see Ember twirling her blood soaked naginata as the group retreated. Before his eyes closed again, he watched as Orielle shouted something his addled mind couldn't piece together and shot a blast of energy from her pistol past him. Colton felt himself slipping into darkness until someone pulled his wounded arm over their shoulders, and with the help of Joel, they pulled him into the darkened opening.

He could feel his eyes trying, no, *needing* to close. Someone slapped the side of his face, but he couldn't feel it. However, the impact forced his eyes open again to see Imbrose's face looking at him. His eyes were filled with frustration and worry as behind him, Joel ran down to a small hut that lightly illuminated. Colton's last energy reserves left him, and he let his head hang limp. It was just so dang heavy. The darkness closed in too quickly this time and he embraced it for the relief it promised.

———

Colton chased after the little blue boy as he ran through the market, leading him toward a large oak tree that leaned precariously over the surf, cascading into the supporting beams of the dock. A short, tan-skinned girl with long red hair stepped out from behind the tree and beckoned Imbrose toward her. Colton continued to give chase, determined to catch him.

As they came to a stop in front of the fire-haired girl, she put a hand on her hip and looked Colton up and down, unimpressed. "Are you sure he has what it takes?"

The horned boy turned and looked at him with a mischievous smile on his face. "Oh, I suppose we'll have to see won't we?" The blue boy pointed at him. "What do you think? Can you save us from *him*?" he asked as his finger moved to point out into the ocean.

Colton turned as a massive shadow emerged from the surf where the boy was pointing. What Colton saw made his blood run cold: a giant, coral-encrusted sea serpent with arms ending in three long, scissor-like fingers spaced every twenty feet down its endless body. The monster used its spindling fingers to pull its bulk further up the beach toward the three children.

"Don't worry, kid. I didn't actually expect you to save us. Stand back and watch the master work." The blue boy's voice had deepened significantly, and when Colton looked back at him, he now resembled Imbrose as he knew him. Behind him, the young girl had aged into Ember, holding her polearm with a determined look on her face as she stared at the nightmare from the depths.

Imbrose charged and Ember followed close behind. Colton tried to move his feet, but as he looked down, he saw he was buried in the sand up to his thighs. He looked up to see the creature impaled by Ember's naginata in its hand and shrieked. Ember held the powerful creature back for another moment before the force of the hand forced her naginata shaft to snap in half. Ember turned and looked at Colton with despair as the hand, with her naginata still lodged in it, slashed through her, sending her trisected body flying in various directions. Colton screamed as her head rolled up against his half-buried thigh, empty eyes gazing up at him. A second scream rang out as Colton looked up to see the creature open its gaping maw and bite Imbrose in half, leaving behind his legs to collapse with a wet sound. Colton dug at the sand furiously as he tried to free himself.

"We followed you to our deaths." Colton looked down to see the decapitated head of Ember speaking to him. "It's too bad Imbrose always looked up to you. I always knew you would get us killed."

Colton stared in horror as his friend spoke to him with such malice. "No! I will always protect you!"

"But you couldn't," the head taunted.

Colton yelled once again. "I'm sorry! I never should have asked you to come with me."

"Too little too late, I'm afraid. Both Imbrose and I are dead, and you are about to be *his* feast." The voice of Ember distorted as it spoke into the sinister scream from the creature in the forest.

Colton looked up to see the massive serpentine head open its mouth once again and descend towards him. "No!" Colton yelled as his world fell into darkness.

—

Colton awoke screaming.

All around him, he could see people moving about trying to restrain him while Orielle grasped the porcupine quill sticking out of his stomach. His armor had been stripped away and he was covered in blood and sweat as his mind raced to understand what was happening.

"Hold him down!" Orielle yelled as she looked down into his eyes. "Come on Colton, we're trying to help you!"

Colton felt his adrenaline spike as Genevieve and Delphine grasped his legs and pinned them to the table. Colton tried to raise his hand only to see Joel and Imbrose grab either arm and hold them down as well. Colton fought them, he had to get free to save them all!

Colton! His eyes locked onto Orielle as her voice echoed through his mind. He felt his muscles relax as she continued. *You are in shock, and I need to remove this quill before it pumps more poison into you.* Colton heaved for breath as his fight or flight instinct began to subside slightly. Orielle smiled at him warmly. *I'm sorry.* Then she grunted as she ripped the quill out of him and quickly placed a waiting bandage over the gushing wound.

Colton's eyes lolled as the pain proved to be too much and he fell into unconsciousness again.

———

Colton sat at a small dining table as he looked at the eloquent bouquet of flowers in the vase placed perfectly in the center. All around, he could see tasteful decorations, giving the space a distinctly lived in feeling. The smell of his grandmother's freshly baked apple pie filled the room, causing a smile to cross his face. His eyes locked on the centerpiece of the house. Down the hallway, he could see hanging above the fireplace a hand-painted portrait of his grandfather and grandmother hugging each other affectionately. Blinking, he glanced around the familiar dining room, and remembered he had come because his grandfather had summoned him. Turning his head to look toward the sink, he watched as his grandfather appeared, leaning against the counter. His simple clothes matched the unremarkable cloth wrapped around his eyes. Long white hair draped down his back as he scratched the scruff growing on his chin. Deep wrinkles etched into his face to show years of hearty laughter.

"Hi, Colton." His grandfather's voice, as deep as rumbling thunder, always gave him such comfort. "You look tired, boy. Have you been getting enough rest?" Colton stared at his grandfather wide-eyed, unable to formulate words. His grandfather sighed. "If I had known this journey would damage you this much, I'd have never asked you to go."

"Xander," came a gentle voice from the hallway, "he's a strong boy. He will find his way through this." Colton turned to see his grandmother as she crossed to embrace Xander. She moved with impeccable grace with a beautiful green dress flowing behind her. Luscious graying brown hair braided intricately cascaded behind her.

His grandfather in turn smiled lovingly as she wrapped her arms around him. "Yes, Aileah my dear, you are right."

"I'm always right," she said as she playfully tapped his nose with her finger, then turned and walked to Colton, offering her hand to him.

Colton reached out and took her hand as she pulled him to his feet, her startling hazel eyes gazing into him with deep concern. "Am I dreaming?" Colton asked.

"Of course you are, dear." Aileah smiled as she tilted her head slightly. "Is there something you wanted to talk to us about?"

Colton looked down, thinking. "I need some advice, I think."

Aileah raised his chin and kissed his forehead. "Let us speak in the other room." Then she grabbed his hand and led him down the hallway into a large space that housed the painting he was looking at earlier. Walking toward the plush couch that sat in the center of the room, she pulled him down onto the cushion next to her and looked over his shoulder as Xander took a seat in the large armchair diagonal from them. "Let's hear it then. What worries you so much?"

Colton closed his eyes. Why was he so worried? Then it came to him in a flood of anxiety as he opened his eyes to look at his grandmother. "How can I protect all of my friends? I feel like I've led them to their doom," Colton confessed as he felt a lump form in his throat.

Aileah nodded understandingly, never letting go of his hand. "You have a big heart, Colton. I know that it must feel as though you are responsible for everyone, but you aren't. Now I know that doesn't answer your question, and the truth is, there is no way to protect your friends. At least not in the way you are thinking."

"Your friends are their own people," Xander picked up. "You can protect them by guarding their backs and always stand up for them when others would diminish them." His grandfather paused. "But, as much as it may hurt, they will make their own choices and it could very easily take them out from under your protection." Xander tapped his chin. "There are also other forces that can pull them away from you. Such is life, son. Cruel at times, but that is why we live it while we can."

Colton bristled at this. "Are you trying to say that there's no way to save my friends?"

Aileah squeezed his hand and forced him to look at her. "Why do you think they came with you, Colton?"

Colton thought for a moment. "Because I asked them to and they wanted to go on an adventure. We always go on adventures together."

Aileah smiled warmly. "They came with you because they were trying to protect you."

Colton was at a loss for words at this revelation.

"Can't you see that while you are worrying for their safety, they are worrying for yours?" Aileah leaned closer. "Why do you think they pulled you away from that tiger's jaws?"

"The bond you have with those two is stronger than you give it credit for," Xander reminded. "Trust them to take care of themselves and protect them when they cannot. I know that the three of you will come home safe if you trust each other." Xander's face fell. "Just remember, no prison is inescapable."

Colton whipped his head toward his grandfather, but he was no longer sitting in the chair. "What does that mean?" He said as he turned to see his grandmother was also no longer sitting there. Colton turned in a circle as panic set in. "Hello? Where did you go?"

"Climb…" their voices said in unison.

"I don't know what that means!" Colton yelled as he stood from the couch. "Tell me what that means!"

The room folded in around him as a bright blue light forced him to shield his eyes.

Chapter Nine: The Cloudstone Railway

C olton dragged a heavy hand over his eyes as the same blue light flashed above him through the see-through ceiling of the room he was in. Streamers flashed by in a rapid symphony of color making him avert his eyes. He could hear a low humming coming from everywhere at once.

"I think he's waking up." A familiar voice could be heard near his feet.

Colton squinted his eyes as he took in the foreign surroundings. He was inside a small wood-paneled room that was just big enough to fit his prone form. Underneath him, he could feel pillows had been placed to cushion what would otherwise have been a long metal table. As he adjusted himself with a groan, he could make out two benches that ran lengthwise alongside the table he was laying on. Both benches attached to the wall at his head and extended almost all the way to the sliding door at his feet. Sitting on the bench to his right he could see Imbrose, whose voice he recognized from before, and Ember was sitting with a stern look on her face on the other bench.

"Well don't you look cheery," Colton said with a cough. "Anyone have some water?"

Imbrose stood and held out a waterskin for Colton to drink from. "Well, I'm conflicted," Ember said as she approached his left side. "On one hand," she began, holding up her right hand, "you aren't dead." She looked down and gave an exaggerated smile while nodding her head, then in a blink, her face returned to the serious one from before. "On the other hand," she raised her left hand, "you are an idiot, and if you weren't barely alive now, I would punch you in the face." Then she brought her fist down and stopped it just inches from his face, causing him to flinch, then playfully slapped it. "You boys are going to be the death of my sanity," she lamented as she sat down with a huff.

Colton looked at her in time to see her turn away from his gaze. Then he looked over at Imbrose who also bared a less than jovial demeanor. "It was stupid, but I understand why you did it." Imbrose leaned in close. "Do it again, and I'll kill you myself," he vowed as he leaned back with a sinister smile on his face.

Colton looked at his two best friends, and smiled. "It's good to see you guys again too." Then with a grunt of pain, began to try and sit up.

Imbrose moved to help him while looking at his bandage nervously. "If you start bleeding again, I'm not going to be the one to tell Orielle."

At the mention of her name, Colton remembered the foggy moment when he had awoken to see her preparing to remove the colossal quill from his abdomen and cringed. With a final burst of effort, he leaned against the wooden wall the table was built into and sighed as he tried to settle the pain running through his shoulder and midsection. Looking between the two of them, he asked, "Where are we?"

Imbrose tilted his head and sat back down on the bench. "We're on some kind of underground train. When we asked Orielle about it, she just said that it was a way for the people who live here to get from one point to another without too much trouble."

Colton pointed up at the glass like surface of the ceiling. "Is that why there's a blue light show?"

Ember turned to look back at him. "Not sure. She said it had something to do with cloudstone," she relayed with a shrug.

Colton nodded and lowered his head to look at himself for the first time. His right shoulder and abdomen were wrapped heavily in thick, green-tinted bandages, making him look more like a mummy than a person. With a wince, he reached down and pulled the bandage away from where the quill had stabbed into him. The wound was puffy and multiple sutures held the edges together. He could see it hadn't quite sealed together yet, and it would still be easy to pull a stitch.

"I suppose it was pretty bad, huh?" Colton said quietly.

Ember leaned forward and put a hand on his knee. "Yes, it was very bad. What got into you?"

Colton shrugged and regretted it immediately as his shoulder throbbed painfully. "I just couldn't imagine watching you guys be attacked by these...monsters after I was the reason you came here in the first place. If it hadn't been for me, you two wo–"

Ember held up a hand to silence him. "We would be sitting in some dusty nobles' house acting like we enjoyed the sixth course of a meal we wish had been over hours ago." Ember shook her head furiously. "No, sir. Not me, and could you even imagine Imbrose in civilized company?"

"Hey!" Imbrose protested in mock hurt.

Colton smiled slightly but was determined to carry on. "Sure, but you would both be safe."

Ember nodded, agreeing to the sentiment. "Oh yes, we would be safe, and bored as hell." Ember pointed back and forth between her and Imbrose. "We come from adventurers. Before they were nobles, they fought monsters and ventured into deep unknown caves. Now if you ask them, all they wish for is a chance to do it again." Ember smiled and bit her lip. "I miss them, but they knew we couldn't be ourselves at court. We need this," she said, gesturing to their surroundings. "Who knows? Maybe one day the three of us will settle down and become old and bored like our parents, but right now, we are right where we are supposed to be."

Imbrose leaned forward. "You can't protect us from everything. We made the choice to join you, and I for one, haven't regretted it for a moment!" Imbrose shoved Colton's leg roughly, and Colton chuckled through the pain of being jostled. "Come on! Where is your sense of adventure? We're in a new land, surrounded by amazing things and you're trying to kill yourself before we even get started."

Colton raised his hands in surrender. "Alright, alright. I hear you both, and I couldn't have asked for better company. I just worry about the two of you, is all."

Ember smiled. "And we worry about you. Why do you think we came back for you?"

Colton fell into silence, remembering the dream he had with his grandparents and how they told him cryptically, "Get them back."

Suddenly, his hat landed on his lap. "Now, enough of this melancholic talk. You have a woman to thank," Imbrose said as he held out his hand to help Colton off the makeshift bed.

Colton reached down to grab the hat and placed it on his head, then took Imbrose's hand. Nodding, Colton began the agonizing effort of getting to his feet.

Walking proved to be more of a challenge than he thought. At first, it was the nausea, then it was the weakness. His body seemed to be revolting at his movement, and it wasn't until he had Ember on one side and Imbrose on the other that he was able to walk at all. As the door slid open to reveal the corridor, Colton looked up once again to see the blue lights flashing rapidly. However, what he hadn't seen before was the earthen top of the tunnel they were traveling through, passing by at inhuman speeds. Realizing that looking up was not a good idea to keep his balance, he lowered his head to look forward and finally felt his feet get under him. Waving his friends away, he hobbled down the hallway under his own meager strength toward what sounded like scattered laughing and talking.

Upon reaching another sliding door, Colton pulled it open to see the rest of the group gathered around a small table against the window of a much larger rectangular common room. Everyone turned at once as Orielle stood and crossed the room to him.

"You're awake!" Orielle said, looking over his bandaged torso. "How are you feeling?"

Colton grimaced, but managed a smile. "I feel as good as one who has recently been impaled possibly can be," he said. "I hear I have you to thank for saving my life. So, thank you."

Orielle blushed and turned her head away. "Oh, well, you're very welcome. I'm glad we were able to bring you back." The room fell into an awkward silence. Finding her voice again, Orielle gestured to a nearby green cushioned couch. "Shall we sit? We've been waiting to discuss what happens next until after you woke up."

Colton nodded and moved to sit down on the couch with a pained grunt. "Hey, unless you want to keep walking around half naked for everyone to see, put this on," Imbrose said as he tossed a linen shirt his way.

"I wasn't complaining," Delphine pouted as she turned the chair Orielle had been sitting in around and plopped down.

Smirking, Colton pulled the shirt over his head and gingerly around his wounded shoulder. "So, tell me what's going on. As in, where are we now, and where are we going?"

Joel piped up at this. "We are currently traveling on what's called the Cloudstone Railway. It was found around three hundred years ago, and we have been using it to traverse the dangers of the forest ever since."

Colton looked up through the top of the clear ceiling where the flashes were continuing rhythmically, and pointed. "Is that the cloudstone there?"

Joel shook his head. "No, best we can tell it's some sort of barrier that forms around this train as we move along the rail. Otherwise, I suspect we wouldn't be doing so well moving at this speed. However, the cloudstone must play a role in its function."

Colton cradled his head between his forefinger and thumb. "Why is it always cloudstone?" he asked no one in particular. "I assume this is what you meant when you said your ancestors visited the Isle of Stars long ago?"

94

Joel nodded. "Honestly, aside from this railway, we have no clue what else cloudstone could be used for. We don't even know how it works for this train. The only thing we do know is that the Isle of Stars is a place of legend and people do not go there."

"Well that won't stop Curtis. He will go anyway, if he doesn't freeze to death first," Colton scoffed in a clipped tone.

"I'm hoping we can prevent that," Orielle said. As everyone turned to look at her she swallowed and continued. "Back at the outpost, we told you the story of the origin of our people. Now it's time we told you about who we are now." Orielle looked over at Joel, who nodded. "We, Tyrkin, live in these places called thickets, and there are eight in total around the Primal Forest."

Colton adjusted himself on the plush couch. "How do you survive out here though?"

"The thickets themselves are surrounded by a protective barrier that we presume Tyrrek himself put in place," Orielle explained. "The one we are from is called the Thicket of Memories." She gestured to Joel and herself. "It functions as a sort of cemetery and school for our people."

"Odd combination," Genevieve noted quietly.

Joel grinned. "In any other culture, I would have to agree with you, but for us, those who have passed are the greatest teachers a person could ask for."

"So, it's true then?" Friend asked. "Do you have a way to save knowledge?"

Orielle pursed her lips. "We do, but it's a fairly guarded secret. How did you find out about us, Friend?"

Friend furrowed his eyebrows. "I can't recall. Just that I needed to get to your tribe and give you the knowledge I possessed."

Orielle scratched her temple. "Well, even if you had found us, it wouldn't have been possible, unfortunately." Friend's face fell and he looked away. "Only because the magic we use is only compatible with our physiology. Trust me, we have friends who aren't Tyrkin, and if we could save their memories as well, we would!" Orielle added quickly.

Colton wrung his hands in front of him. "So, how do you do it?" he asked tentatively.

Orielle's eyes shifted from side to side nervously. "When one of our people reaches the age of ten anywhere in the Primal Forest, they are then escorted to our thicket where they begin their tutelage. Shortly after they arrive, we show them how to manifest their spiritual energy to create a flower which holds all of their memories," Orielle revealed. "Then, at the end of their life, their spirit seeks out that flower and resides within it, so they can teach the next generations."

"So…" Ember began, "Children from the current generation learn from the experiences of those who lived before them by communing with these flowers?"

"We call them Dream Bloom," Joel said quickly. "And yes, by touching the petals of an existing flower, a person can look back into their lives for guidance."

"That's actually kind of beautiful," Delphine said.

Orielle nodded. "It is. When you're going through something that you feel no one would understand, it brings a person peace to know that there's probably someone who *does* understand, and you can watch how they navigated the same situation."

"There must be millions of Dream Bloom by now though," Colton said. "How do you keep track of which one is which?"

"Oh, there are millions." Orielle confirmed. "That's why we usually put our flowers in familial groves, and we have multiple Grove Tenders whose sole job is to categorize who is who. Though, even that is tough because at this point, the Dream Bloom covers the entirety of our thicket. It's a gorgeous sight to behold in the evening."

Colton smiled, excitement welling in his chest. "I can't wait to see it."

Delphine cleared her throat. "You mentioned you would like to stop Curtis. How do you intend on doing that?"

Orielle looked over at her. "Well, one of our largest thickets sits right next to the Andromedus River. If I were sailing north with the intent of reaching the Northwestern Coast of this continent, I would need a place to cut across. Therefore, he should travel right past the Thicket of Rivers."

"Okay, but how do you plan to get word to them quickly enough?" Delphine pressed, her anxiety plain to see.

"We can communicate with one another over very long distances," Joel said as he held up a small metal locket. "Inside is a petal from Orielle's Dream Bloom. Whenever I touch it, I can link my mind to her, no matter where she is." Joel let the locket drop to his chest again. "The Keepers of each thicket can communicate with one another using the same method." Colton opened his mouth to speak. "And before you ask, the Keepers are the leaders of each thicket." Colton closed his mouth and gave a thumbs up toward Joel.

Delphine leaned back in her chair, apparently satisfied. "Do these rails go all the way to the Thicket of Rivers?"

Orielle nodded. "Yes, they reach each thicket and other outposts."

With that Delphine stood. "Well, that's settled then. We should just continue on to the Thicket of Rivers."

"Hang on a second there," Imbrose said. "This Thicket of Memories could be a place of invaluable information about the world we find ourselves in. We can't just bypass it on a wild goose chase."

"Speak for yourself," Delphine scoffed, her words carrying a sense of dismissal. "I came for Curtis, and I won't give up on a chance to give chase."

"If I may…" Joel began. "He may not take the river, and that would mean you would need to continue to our furthest settlement to the north, the Thicket of Frost. Even then, he may not stop, and beyond that you enter the Glacerian Court. We have no sway over the people who live there, and you could be just as easily mistaken as an enemy by them. Perhaps it's safer to reside with us here until we know for sure where Curtis is going."

Delphine kicked her chair over. "I'm going after him, dammit! Nothing you say will stop me! I have tracked prey far more dangerous than that coward, and not a single one of them could escape me," she seethed as a mad look came over her.

Colton tried to stand, but couldn't and let out a groan of pain. "Delphine," he cautioned while wincing through the pain. "No one is doubting your ability to kill him. We just don't know anything about where we are."

"Then give me a map!" Delphine shouted.

Colton frowned, worried he couldn't make her see reason. "If you die out there to some unknown threat, how will you kill him then?" Colton asked.

Delphine deflated slightly and looked at the floor. "Please, Colton. I need to do this. I'm not well suited to sitting around and waiting while the one I chase runs further away." She looked up at him with imploring eyes.

Colton opened his mouth to try one more time to bring her around when Genevieve spoke up. "She may have the right of it, Colton."

Colton turned and looked at the armored woman. "What do you mean?"

Genevieve glanced at her compatriots. "We came here to discover new civilizations before anything else. Seems to me that traveling north and speaking with this Glacerian Court is exactly why we came." Turning to Joel she added, "Are they openly hostile?"

Joel shook his head. "Well, no, and we trade with them often. Which is not something we can say about the Platinum Dominion."

"Who are they?" Ember asked.

"The continent is split into three…kingdoms, if you will." Joel said. "To the east you have the Primal Forest that spans from as far south as south goes to as far north as north goes. The Andromedus splits the continent perfectly in half horizontally, and it serves as a border between the other two nations, the Platinum Dominion to the south and the Glacerian Court to the north."

"Why don't you trade with the Platinum Dominion?" Colton asked.

"Mainly because they constantly attack the Primal Forest's borders with the intent of seizing more land. We lose people constantly to the waves of beasts they displace by doing it," Joel said somberly.

"So, it sounds like Delphine's plan to go north, whether it be for the right reason or not, is something we must do," Genevieve concluded.

"Genevieve...I need to speak to the people from the Thicket of Memories. It may tell me what happened to our tribes to cause their fracture," Colton implored quietly.

"Which is why," Genevieve began, "Delphine, Baldo, Gavin, Quinn, and myself will go north as envoys to the Glacerian Court, and if we find Curtis, we put him down for good measure."

Delphine, having been trying to calm herself throughout this conversation, looked back at Colton waiting to hear his next words.

Colton grumbled under his breath. These people were trying to break apart the last remnants of companions he could openly trust. If he didn't feel the need to follow through with his own mission, he would probably go with them, but he needed to stay. Looking at Ember and Imbrose, they both gave him grim nods.

Sighing in frustration, Colton scanned the rest of the room. "Very well, if Joel and Orielle agree to let you use the railway as means to get further north, you have my blessing." His gaze turned on Joel. "Is there a way we can communicate with them on their travels?"

Joel scratched his chin. "Well, we do breed falcons that carry our letters to other thickets if the news is less dire. I'm sure you can communicate that way. Otherwise, our town mage, Arcadia, may have a way I don't know of."

"Alright then. Gear up before you leave. I can't have you starving to death on the road," Colton muttered. "Joel, how much longer until we arrive at your thicket?"

"I suspect we'll arrive sometime tomorrow afternoon. Then, after we tell the Keeper what's going on, you can make your appeal," Joel said.

Colton nodded, then forced himself to his feet. "Think I'll try to get some rest. I'd like to be able to stand under my own power when I meet the Keeper."

Imbrose moved to help him, but Colton waved him off. Frustration over the willingness of the group to separate, even for a good reason, carried him through the pain as he worked his way down the corridor again.

Chapter Ten: Thicket of Memories

T he next day went by quietly as everyone came to terms with the plans for the future. Colton spent most of his time investigating the train and found a small parlor which had a sitting space looking at a wall made entirely of glass on the side of the locomotive. Sitting there, he was able to calm his frustrations from the day before and, more importantly, begin to understand why he was feeling so angry about it. Until now, the group had been on the same trajectory: a path which included everyone who was from the Archipelago staying together in this strange world. They had survived horrors together, and now more than half of them wanted to split up and go north.

Colton sighed and placed his head in his hand. Though if he was being honest, it wasn't because they wanted to leave. It was because he felt compelled to stay. In his heart, he knew he should feel an overwhelming urge to chase Curtis down and end the threat Colton himself had unleashed by convincing him to come in the first place. However, something about this place was becoming more comfortable the longer he stayed. He winced as a twinge of pain echoed from the wound in his stomach, reminding him of the dangers that existed on this beautiful continent. At the end of the day, Curtis was such a small concern for him. Nodding his head, Colton came to terms with the fact that Curtis would likely die out here all on his own with no support.

A fresh wave of annoyance at the party breaking apart to hunt him down caused Colton to screw up his face. Why couldn't they see the treasure trove of information that may be gathered? Afterall, this Thicket of Memories could be like a new home for them. A little voice sounded off from the back of his consciousness: *For them, or for you?*

He scoffed and stared through the window as blue light flashed rhythmically. The light was flashing slower now, and Colton had felt the whole train slowing marginally for the past hour. It was almost time, and he knew that Genevieve and the others would want to leave quickly.

The door behind him creaked as someone came through. Colton assumed it was Imbrose or Ember, since they hadn't checked in on him recently. However, he was surprised to see Delphine sit down in the chair next to him.

"I'm sorry for losing my cool yesterday," she apologized in a soft voice.

Colton turned away from her and looked out the window again. "It's fine. As an assassin, it makes sense that killing Curtis would be your top priority."

Delphine visibly winced at his words. "Is that all I am in your eyes? An assassin with a target?"

Colton bit his lower lip, feeling instant regret for his insensitive words. "No, of course not…"

"I won't deny that a certain need for revenge has consumed my thoughts recently," Delphine admitted, barely a whisper. "But I can't help feeling that he can lead me to my father."

Colton nodded as he cast his eyes downward. "I understand, and I'm sorry I can't come with you."

Delphine laughed lightly. "How could you? You've finally found what you and your grandfather had been looking for. It would be selfish of me to ask you to come on my journey." Colton nodded, but couldn't find any words to express what he was thinking. "Still, I'd hoped you would come."

Colton turned to her. Delphine was gazing at him in such a way that left him feeling like she had something to say, but was nervous. "What is it?" he asked quietly.

Delphine smiled and looked down. "I left New Eradin with the intent of finding my father and making Curtis pay." She paused gathering herself. "I never thought I would find myself developing feelings for someone."

Colton felt a lump forming in his gut as Delphine stood and walked over next to him. "Delphine…I'm flattered, but…" he began as she leaned closer to him.

"But I'm not the one," she finished sadly, then kissed his cheek lightly. "She's a lucky one, your woman of the forest."

Colton froze for a moment, shocked by the trajectory of this conversation. "I-I'm sorry…" he said lamely.

Delphine smiled and leaned back. "For what? We don't choose who we love. Besides, if I swung that way I'd be chasing her too." She placed a hand on his shoulder and walked back toward the door, letting her hand slip off of him. "No hard feelings from my end, Cobb. Follow your heart, and maybe when we meet again, you can tell me how you managed it."

Colton stood and looked toward the door to see Delphine turn her head. "Find your father, Delphine. He's out there, I can feel it."

Delphine nodded, and winked with a sly smile on her face. "No one can escape me."

Colton laughed and watched as she left, feeling a sense of both relief and sadness. He had grown fond of Delphine, even if it wasn't the same way she felt for him. Losing her would leave a distinct gap in their little troop, though he couldn't fault her for needing to leave. If the roles were reversed, he would have done the same. With a nod of finality, Colton exited the parlor, ready to embrace the next leg of this journey.

Two hours later, the train finally came to a stop and everyone disembarked into a damp underground system of caves. For the first time, Colton could see the rails they had been traveling on, and his breath caught in his chest. The rails themselves looked similar to those laid by miners back home, but what stood out to him was every six feet there were finely-worked, identical blue gems laid into the side of the tracks. Colton realized immediately that these gems were cloudstones. With the exception of the one Curtis kept on his person, he hadn't seen any others.

"Like I said, we have no clue how it works," Joel said as he pulled his bag over one shoulder and pulled up next to Colton. "As far as we know, it's been here since the beginning of civilization, but I suspect Tyrrek had something to do with it when he made the first of us."

"I've never seen anything like it. It makes you wonder what kind of power it takes to maintain," Colton pondered, a sense of wonder in his voice.

"The one thing we do know is that the cloudstone acts like its own powersource." Joel turned away as a man with a prominent belly approached. "Ulric! Always a pleasure to see you when we return!" he called, the jovial tone plain in his greeting.

"Joel! Orielle! What are you kids doing back so soon? I wasn't expecting you for a couple more months." The man's voice was gentle but hardy, like a man who spent equal time yelling instructions and sharing secrets.

"Well, we ran into some unexpected guests," Joel explained, gesturing to the group as they stepped off the train. Genevieve exited last, holding their gagged and bound prisoner. "Plus, we were successful. Found him waiting for us in the woods near the southern station."

Ulric's head tilted in confusion as he looked at the unconscious robed figure. "Waiting, eh? That don't bode well."

Joel nodded. "It certainly doesn't. Do you mind sending supplies down to the outpost we were at? We hit the healing herbs pretty hard."

"For sure, kid. You oughta get your hide up to your uncle. He's gonna want to see your little friend there," Ulric said, marking something in a ledger.

With that, Joel gestured for the party to follow them toward a circular tunnel leading upwards. Ten minutes later, a group of four Tyrkin were moving a large stone aside to let sunlight in as the group exited into the jungle once more. The biggest difference was the cliff they exited from was encased entirely in a thick impassible bramble filled with thorns as big as Colton was tall. The group followed the cliff face until they came to yet another circular stone, but there was no one to man this one. Orielle stepped forward and started to draw with her finger along the stone. Wherever her finger traced, a blue light stayed behind in a trail. After a few minutes, a beautiful glowing blue design covered the entire stone. Orielle stepped back to analyze her work then the entire sigil pulsed and the stone started to roll to one side.

"Alright folks, we're about to head in, so there are a few things you should know. When you step through that door, you're going to have a hard time remembering what happens for the next few minutes while we make our way through the bramble." Orielle paused and looked over at Colton. "Everyone except you, that is. Since we live in such a dangerous place, we have to use certain precautions to prevent those who aren't one of us from getting in."

"Will it hurt?" Imbrose asked.

Orielle chuckled lightly. "Uh, no. It should be similar to waking from a vivid dream. At least that's what I've been told."

"Don't worry, I'll hold your hand," Colton teased, reaching for Imbrose's hand.

"Keep your paws to yourself, mate," Imbrose barked, recoiling.

A nervous chuckle spread across the group as Joel and Orielle stepped through the opening. Colton held his arm forward to Imbrose to go first, then followed in behind. The moment Imbrose passed through the entrance, his shoulders slumped slightly and he shook his head.

"Woah, maybe I will take your hand," he slurred, swaying precariously to one side.

Colton reached out to steady him and watched as the stone opening behind them began to close. With an earthy thump, the passage was completely enclosed in suffocating darkness. Colton's breathing increased slightly as a brief moment of doubt creeped over him. After ten agonizingly long seconds, a small purple light pierced the darkness from the ceiling. Colton looked up to see a beautiful purple flower unfurl, extending its luminescent light down to illuminate the surrounding walls of the cave. Then, another appeared right next to it, and another. A wave of purple flowers rapidly blossomed across the ceiling, heading further into the tunnel of thorns. Suddenly, the blossoming flowers reached a split in the tunnel and instantly shifted down the right side, continuing into the distance.

"The flowers show us the way," Orielle's voice sounded through the echoing tunnel. "Stay close and don't go into the darker tunnels."

The party traveled on for a time until a bead of natural light could be seen around the corner. Picking up the pace, the light got brighter until eventually, Colton stepped out into a beautiful sight. Before him was a lush green valley a few miles long. The entire exterior was enclosed in the same bramble from outside, no doubt an effort to further protect its inhabitants. Winding paths snaked their way up and over small hills with circular houses dotting the landscape. Halfway through the valley was a large tree with what appeared to be purple veins running through its trunk. Even from this distance, Colton could see an opening at the base of the tree where people were entering and leaving. His eyes drifted upward to see rope bridges spanning the massive gap from one side of the thicket to the other. There were people who confidently strode across them as they swayed freely in the valley breeze. Hanging nest-like buildings could be seen all along the bramble.

"Aren't you a sorry-looking lot!" A deep voice from the left of the entrance pulled Colton from his sightseeing. Standing there was a scrawny man with a goofy smile on his face. "Heading up?" he asked as he gestured behind him.

Colton looked where he was pointing to see a flat platform that appeared to be attached to multiple pulleys.

"Not at the moment, Jerric," Orielle said, stepping forward. "Any idea where I might find my Pa?"

Jerric scrunched his eyebrows in thought. "Can't say I do! But I did see Luc–."

"Very well," Orielle interrupted, with an anxious tone in her voice. "We'll head down and look for him ourselves. In the meantime, we'll leave our prisoner here with you, if that's alright?"

"Certainly, miss," Jerric said, his smile dimming slightly.

Colton turned his head at the sudden sharpness of her tone. Until now, she had always seemed courteous, but something about what this man Jerric was saying had upset her. Colton caught Joel giving Orielle a side glance as the group moved past Jerric and down the switchbacks, leading to the rest of the valley.

The trip down was made in silence as everyone tried to take in the amazing sight they were beholding. Orielle led the lot of them, but kept a solid distance between her and everyone else. At one point, Joel even tried to catch up to her only to slink back, his face red with frustration as he fell back in line.

"What do you think that's about?" Imbrose asked, quietly sliding up next to Colton.

"No clue," Colton said, watching Orielle curiously.

As they rounded a final corner, the party found themselves being observed from all sides. People stepped off the path to let them pass, only to whisper amongst themselves as they did. The children were especially interested in Imbrose and his blue skin. A few of the smaller ones were rubbing their heads where Imbrose's horns grew from the crown of his head. After a moment, he turned dramatically and growled at them, only for them to growl back with giggles. Colton could see Ember smiling widely as Imbrose reached out to swipe at one of the children as they scampered away laughing louder. Eventually, one brave little girl walked up next to Imbrose and gestured for him to get closer. Leaning down, the girl whispered something in his ear, then ran off toward a group of her friends laughing all the way. Imbrose turned and looked at them with a shocked look on his face.

"What did she say?" Colton asked.

"She said she really likes my horns," Imbrose relayed in a matter of fact tone.

Colton stifled a laugh. "So, why do you look so shocked?"

Imbrose shrugged. "No one has ever complimented my horns before. It's nice to be noticed," he preened as he ran a hand through his hair.

"Oh, please," Ember groaned, still smiling. "You're insufferable."

As the three of them laughed and continued walking down the main thoroughfare, Colton's eyes flicked beyond Imbrose and Ember to a small cabin on the banks of a lake. There, sitting on the porch, was a hooded man who simply raised the clay mug he was holding in greeting. From this distance, Colton could not make out the features on the man and was swept along, quickly losing sight of the cabin behind a line of apple trees.

Colton dismissed the event as Orielle came to a stop in front of the door to a house. With a shaking hand, she knocked quietly on the door. As her hand pulled back for a third knock, the door swung open abruptly to reveal a mature, but still beautiful, woman. Colton recognized her as Orielle's mother instantly with the same curly dark hair and green eyes. In fact, the more he looked at her, the easier it was to see this woman as an older sister rather than a mother.

"Oh, Ori! I heard a rumor that you were coming home earlier than expected," the woman crooned, embracing Orielle tightly.

Orielle hugged the woman back, albeit a bit more tentatively. "Yes, Ma. We're back and I have something important to tell Pa."

"Your Pa will be home soon, dear. He's just finishing up at the grove." The woman, who Colton now knew as her mother, looked up to see Joel and moved to hug him as well. "Joel, sweetheart! Thank you for bringing my baby girl home safely!"

Joel hugged her warmly. "Of course, Aunt Lena! Though truth be told, she saved me more than I saved her."

"I don't doubt it," Lena said, chuckling. Her gaze flashed over the rest of the group for the first time. "Well now, it seems you brought home some guests. Mind introducing me?"

Orielle turned, her eyes darting around as if she was looking for someone. "Of course, Ma." Orielle introduced everyone in the group and Lena shook everyone's hand in turn. When she reached Colton, she stopped and held his gaze before reaching out and taking his hand.

"A pleasure ma'am. Your daughter is a wonderful woman, and she has saved my and my friend's lives at least twice in the two weeks I've known her," Colton praised, shaking her hand firmly.

Lena smiled sweetly. "The pleasure is all mine, Mister Cobb. You are most welcome here." Colton smiled back as Lena turned on her heels and walked back to the door. "Well, I must say, I hadn't expected so much company, but I'm sure I can throw together something. You all look positively famished." Colton felt his stomach clench at the idea of a proper meal, and saw a few others unconsciously place hands on stomachs. "Orielle, would you mind setting up the outside tables?"

"Sure, Ma. This way everyone," Orielle said as she gestured for everyone to follow her down a stone pathway leading around back.

A duo of circular tables sat in the center of a beautiful vegetable garden. The smell of fresh spices washed over the group as they made their way to the makeshift stone courtyard. Orielle made for a small wooden chest and set her traveling pack down next to it.

Flipping it open, Orielle jostled around inside before pulling out a stack of wooden plates and bowls. "Would you guys mind grabbing the other things inside?" Everyone moved quickly to try and assist with setting the table. As the group worked, the delicious smell of meat cooking began to waft through the garden. "Alright, go ahead and find a seat. I'll go check on Ma."

In a bit of a rush, the group moved to grab a spot, eager to sample whatever delectable meal Lena was preparing. A few moments later, Orielle came around the corner carrying a plate full of freshly cut fruits and vegetables and placed them on either table, then sat down between Colton and Joel.

"Not fair," Imbrose whined. "They got the fruit."

"Don't worry, she's just getting started," Orielle comforted with a smirk on her face.

Colton turned and snickered as he reached out and grabbed a bright orange tuber of some kind. The crunch that echoed from his bite left him feeling oddly satisfied, but it was the flavor that made him reach for another after downing the first.

Over the next twenty minutes, plates of meat, bowls of simmering stews, and sweet smelling beverages began to circulate out of the kitchen. "Is that woman a food wizard?" Imbrose asked as he stared longingly at the thinly sliced ham.

"Go on then! Eat up!" Lena's voice rang out from the open window in the back of the house.

"Ma!" Orielle called back. "Come out here and join us."

"A moment, sweetie. Just finishing up the pie," Lena hollered as she turned away from the window.

"Pie!" Imbrose half-shouted. "I think I'm in love."

"She's married, idiot," Ember scolded as she narrowed her eyes on him.

Needing no further encouragement, the group dug in. Colton filled his plate with both cooked and dried meats, a large slice of some kind of melon, as well as a healthy serving of mashed potatoes. He then reached over and topped both the meat and potatoes with a dark, lightly-spicy smelling gravy. Sounds of contentment began to rise around the garden as everyone ate their fill.

"Better put out another table setting, look who came to join us!" Lena said as she walked up the stone pathway with a handsome young man following behind her.

Orielle turned and immediately went pale. She stopped chewing and looked back at her plate. Closing her eyes, she swallowed her food hard, visibly trying to slow her breathing. After a moment, she opened her eyes and forced a smile on her face while standing up to meet the new arrival.

"Darling." The man embraced Orielle and leaned in for a kiss on the lips only for her to turn away ever so slightly at the last moment, kissing him on the cheek instead. "If I had known asking you to marry me would result in sleepless nights waiting for your return, I would have thought twice about it!" the man said with a joking tone.

"It's...good to see you, Lucas," Orielle stumbled tentatively. "Let me grab you a plate."

"Thank you, my love," Lucas replied warmly as he surveyed the group. "Hello everyone! You guys are the talk of the town."

"This is Orielle's betrothed, Lucas," Lena introduced as she placed an arm across his shoulders.

Colton's heart seized as the words left Lena's mouth. Lucas approached the tables and began to shake everyone's hand, but the ensuing introductions were drowned out by the ringing in his ears as he tried to come to terms with what he just heard.

Eventually, Lucas reached him and the world around Colton snapped back into focus. "Hi, there. Name's Colton," he muttered robotically.

"It's nice to meet you, Colton," Lucas said as Orielle handed him a plate and sat back down next to him. "Do you mind if I squeeze in there?" Lucas asked, gesturing between himself and Orielle.

Orielle looked over at Colton with an apologetic look on her face. "Uh, certainly," Colton said awkwardly as he scooched in closer to Imbrose.

Pulling his plate over, Colton watched as Lucas squeezed himself in between them and began filling his plate. Lena walked around the table and placed herself in the free spot that had been set for her.

Still filling his plate, Lucas glanced at Orielle. "So, tell me about your travels."

Orielle opened her mouth to speak, but no words came out. Joel rescued her. "Well, we set out to look for clues on what was going on with the kids…"

Joel's voice faded into the background as Colton's thoughts stole his focus. His stomach roiled and left him no longer wanting the delicious food still remaining on his plate. As Joel reached an exciting part of the story, Lucas exclaimed and bumped Colton's hand as he reached for his glass. The force of the motion caused some to spill out and onto Colton's trousers, leaving a reddish stain in the white fabric.

"Oh, so sorry, pal," Lucas muttered, glancing over his shoulder.

"Oh no!" Lena exclaimed. "Here, let me show you where the well is so we can wash it out."

"No, no, that's alright," Colton insisted, standing up. "You just sat down to eat. Point me in the direction and I'm sure I can find my way."

Lena, half-standing already, cocked her head then smiled brightly. "You're too sweet, Colton. Just around the corner there, you'll find it. You'll still need to give me those pants later. I have a special recipe that removes stains."

"Sure thing," he said and turned to walk away where Lena had indicated.

Once out of sight, he let out a breath he didn't know he had been holding. His heart pounded in his chest as he closed his eyes and put out a hand to steady himself on the house. He felt sick to his stomach as he tried to reconcile his emotions given this new development. He didn't really know how he felt about Orielle, but now that he knew she was betrothed, he couldn't help but feel…sad. Like the small flicker he felt when he was near her was snuffed out by a winter chill. The feeling sat heavy in his chest as he felt pain returning to the wound she had patched up days ago.

The sound of footsteps from behind caused Colton to stand upright and turn around. Imbrose peeked around the corner with a large red stain running down the front of his shirt. "I seem to have spilled something as well," he remarked with a sly smile.

Colton chuckled half-heartedly, still gripping his stomach. "It seems that way."

Imbrose approached and placed a hand on his shoulder. "How are you doing, mate?"

Colton slid down the wall onto his backside and sighed. "I'm fine. Just some pain from my injury."

Imbrose nodded slowly and pursed his lips, then moved to sit down next to Colton. "Ya know…Ember and I have been doing this little dance of ours for around twenty years," Imbrose said as he looked to the sky. "Can you imagine how it felt every time some sly little turd tried to hit on her?" Imbrose chuckled and dropped his head. "Felt like a ball of iron landed right in my gut, but I'd just smile."

"A bit different than her getting engaged, don't you think?" Colton asked.

"Engaged ain't married, mate. Life has a way of giving you just enough chances to get it right."

"I don't know. I just met her, so why does it bother me so much?"

Imbrose smacked his lips. "Feelings are weird, and for the life of me I still can't figure out why Ember won't get out of my head."

"It's because you love her, man. It's as obvious as that tree over there." Imbrose looked over at Colton pointedly. "What?" Colton asked.

"Nothing," he said simply.

"Sorry to bother you two," Ember said as she walked around the corner, "but it looks like Joel is going to show us where we can bed down while we are here."

Imbrose hopped to his feet quickly. "How much did you hear?" he asked with fear in his voice.

Ember smiled at him slyly. "Oh, hardly a thing." Then she walked back the way she'd come.

"Whoops. Guess the cat's out of the bag," Imbrose lamented, scratching his head.

Colton stood and clasped Imbrose on the shoulder. "It always was, pal." Then he moved to follow Ember.

Colton walked around the corner to see everyone was packing up to leave. Joel was shoveling the last remnants of pie into his mouth as he stood to grab his pack and waved over at Colton. Off to one side, Colton could see Orielle and Lucas talking.

"Come with me to get some cider," Lucas implored her softly.

"I-I can't," she declined timidly. "I mean, I want to, of course. I just haven't seen Jasper yet."

"Oh, I see," Lucas said dejectedly. "Well, if you find yourself with some extra time later, you know where I'll be." Sighing, he walked away from the gathering and Orielle's shoulders slumped in relief.

Colton averted his eyes as he made directly for Joel who had finally finished his last bite of pie.

"Sounds like Uncle George is going to be busy for a while. Why don't I get you guys settled and we can chat a little more along the way," Joel offered as he watched Lucas leave the garden.

"Lead the way," Colton said before stealing one more look at Orielle as she disappeared around the corner of the house.

Joel took the group out toward the barrier of the thicket. Along the way, he played tour guide as he pointed out a large circle that appeared to be a place for everyone in the valley to gather if needed. He also directed everyone's attention to various rope ladders leading to the nest-like buildings further up the massive bramble wall. The walk was short and eventually Joel pulled up to a small gathering of circular-shaped houses just like Orielle's.

"All of these are available for our guests. There are three beds per house and if you need anything else, Aunt Lena wants you to ask her. Once we get everyone rounded up, I'll come get you again so we can talk with the Keeper." The group looked around before moving to the different buildings in groups of three until only Ember, Imbrose, and Colton remained next to Joel. "Colton," Joel began, reaching out to grab his elbow, "if you're interested, I think I can show you a few things regarding your...powers. That is, if you aren't too tired," he added quickly.

"That sounds really good!" Colton said, his mood brightening significantly. "Let me just drop off my stuff, and I'll meet you right out here." Joel nodded and the three of them set off for one of the unclaimed buildings.

Once inside, Colton tossed his bag on the floor and spun around to head out again. "You two pick your rooms and I'll just have whichever is left."

"Be safe," Ember cautioned. "If you need anything, we will be here."

Colton smiled and walked out the door. Excitement bubbled up inside him as he considered the prospect of learning something about these powers that had always existed just beneath the surface. With a hop in his step, he rushed to meet Joel as he waved for him to follow.

Chapter Eleven: Unlocking One's Potential

C olton walked alongside Joel through the late afternoon sun in companionable silence, with a sense of safety for the first time in weeks. He still drew many eyes with his disheveled attire, but a sense of belonging fell over him that he hadn't experienced since before this expedition began. Presently, Colton had many things on his mind such as: what wonders he might learn from Joel, did finding this place mean his quest was complete, and what path would he follow after today? These questions plagued him as, for what felt like the only time in his adventurous life, he had nowhere else to be. Suddenly, a sense of sadness washed over him as a stagnant life wasn't one he imagined for himself, and if he were being honest, he silently hoped this particular adventure would be a long one. It was for that reason that he forced himself from his musings as he turned to Joel.

"Joel, can you tell me more about the thickets?"

Joel raised an eyebrow. "Sure, what do you want to know?"

Colton thought that over. What *did* he want to know? After all, this little preamble was simply meant as a distraction from his dark musings. "Uh, how many are there again?"

Joel considered the question. "Well, there is the Thicket of Frost to the far north, the Thicket of Harvests a bit further south than that. Then the Thicket of Rivers, which sits on the southern bank of the great Andromedus River." Joel held up a hand ticking them off as he went.

"The Thicket of Gatherings is right in the center of the Primal Forest, and it's where we go to meet as a people. Oh, and the Thicket of Hunters, they are the closest to us just to the northeast. There they pride themselves on their ability to acquire enough meat for all the other thickets." Joel paused and gestured around. "Then there's us, and one thing's for certain… Every single Tyrkin spends at least some time here, learning about our culture. However, our two southernmost thickets, the Thicket of Beasts and the Thicket of Borders, are the ones who defend us from the Platinum Dominion."

Colton looked at Joel's fingers. "So, eight then?"

Joel hesitated for the briefest moment before lowering his hand and nodding. "Eight in total, and they all serve a purpose to the greater whole. If the Thicket of Frost didn't trade with the Glacerian Court, we would lose out on some of the major crops the Thicket of Harvests provides. In turn, if we didn't tend the groves with our ancestor's memories, we would be a people without a history." The two of them rounded the side of a house and started walking into a field filled with sparring equipment and short to long range targets. "Not to mention, if the Platinum Dominion did manage to break through the Thicket of Borders, we would be exposed to their conquest. But worst of all, the beasts that exist in these woods would ravage the countryside. Countless lives would be lost."

Colton thought this over and another question came to mind. "So, how does the Thicket of Borders protect the entire western side of the forest? What keeps a creature from the north from leaving?"

Joel stopped near a drawn out circle on the ground, clearly meant for sparring. "Well, I've never been there, but from what I learned as a boy, there's a magical barrier that gives off an aura which…deters creatures from leaving." Joel set down his pack and started stretching. "Alright, so today I want to keep it focused on figuring out what power type you have."

Colton drew back slightly at the sudden change of topic. "Power type? Aren't we all using the same power?"

Joel bent over and touched the ground, while glancing back up at him. "Well sure, but we manifest it in different ways. Such as myself…" Joel stood up and shook himself loose before pointing out toward another circle in the dirt some distance away. "You see that ring over there?"

Colton squinted, the ring he was indicating must have been five hundred feet away. After spotting it, he nodded. In a quick motion, Joel took a wide stance and shoved his hand out in the direction of the indicated circle with his palm facing outward. Blue veins began to run down Joel's bicep and forearm, causing it to appear slightly transparent. As the energy reached his palm, a thin, oval-shaped swirl of energy began to form in his hand. Slowly, the blue energy began to grow vertically as if stretching to the ground, though it never grew in thickness. Colton turned to see a similar energy forming in the center of the far off sparring arena. Joel pushed into the energy, causing the veins in his arm to circulate the blue power even faster. Finally, Joel lowered his hand as a swirling portal solidified in space. Colton leaned forward to look through the shimmering glass-like surface to see himself and Joel from five hundred feet away, looking through the portal.

"I can create a portal to a location I can clearly visualize in my mindseye. It isn't a fast process, so it doesn't have many combat applications. I also have a limit on how far I can go. My current record is seven miles," Joel revealed with pride.

Colton gaped at the display. "It's incredible, man. How did you figure it out?"

Joel snapped his fingers and the portal popped like a bubble. "Well, as time has gone on, we Tyrkin have figured out that our powers come in three different types." Joel reached down and picked up a sparring sword. "One, which is what I just showed you, is movement or something to do with traveling. Best we can understand is we developed that to quickly traverse the jungle in relative safety. The second is what Orielle uses, and that's enhancement. The third, which is by far the most impressive and rarest, is healing. I think that's pretty self-explanatory." Joel swung the sword in a practiced flourish. "Let's start with healing, though I think you are more of an enhancement guy based on what I saw back in the woods." He pointed at Colton's stomach. "Have you tried healing it yet?"

Colton shook his head. "Didn't know I could."

"Well, give it a go! Close your eyes and focus your mind on your wound." Colton did as he was instructed. "Now, imagine the wound being stitched back together, with each piece of muscle and tissue returning to its original state."

Colton strained to find the power Joel described. "I can't feel the power inside me."

Joel grunted in acknowledgment. "Yeah, finding it for the first time is definitely the hardest. Try thinking about the first time you mindlinked with someone."

Colton thought hard and remembered the time his grandfather tried to instruct him in how to do it. "We have a connection, you and I," his grandfather had said. "Our minds are linked to the energy that flows throughout the world, and sometimes if we put our mind to it, we can send our thoughts to another." Colton remembered the sound of his grandfather's voice entering his mind. His presence had given off a sense of hurt that had been overcome by a life of joy. *You see?* His grandfather's voice had filled his mind in an unexpected swell of familiarity. *Most people's minds only extend to their own consciousness, but we are able to see and touch the strings that connect us all.*

Standing before Joel, Colton took a deep breath and allowed his senses to stretch beyond himself. He could feel the light breeze kissing his skin, the smell of pine and apples coming from somewhere in the valley, the sound of children laughing and the twang of a bow string.

There! A ripple of energy connected all of these things, even if they were all separated. They played into a greater whole, just like the thickets. Colton delved into himself, finding a blazing blue orb of light deep in his chest, pulsing gently. He could feel this center of him pulling on the strings of energy around him. With a concerted effort, he willed the orb of energy to heal the wound in his abdomen. The orb shifted but did not do as he asked. After a few more moments, he threw his eyes open with a gasp, sweat dripping down his face.

"And?" Joel asked expectantly. "Are you okay?"

Colton pulled the bandage away from his stomach even though he knew what he would see. The wound was still there, but the medicine he had been given seemed to have sealed the injury if not completely healed it. "No luck, I'm afraid," Colton announced, sounding dejected.

Joel clasped him on the back. "Not to worry, Colton. As I said, Healers are the rarest among us." Flipping the practice sword in his hand, Joel offered Colton the handle. "Here, let's see if you are a Spirit Smith."

Colton looked up and took the sword handle. "So, how does this one work?"

"I was hoping you would already know," Joel said. "After what I saw you do to those creatures in the forest, you are obviously extremely skilled with a sword. I also remember you calling blue energy to the blade in your time of need."

Colton gripped the sword in his hand and tried to remember what happened with the creatures in the forest. He recalled feeling alone, but content. However, he also remembered the sword giving him power and knowledge. Something about the feeling left him thinking that the sword had the power, not himself.

"I remember the sword gifted me with its power," Colton began, swinging the practice sword in a motion he recalled from that perilous fight. "I don't think it came from me."

"Hmm, well that would make sense that the weapon has its own power given it was Tyrrek's sword." Colton flipped the sword once more and handed it back to Joel. "So, it sounds like you are a Reach Roamer like myself," Joel said with a smile.

"What does that mean?" Colton asked.

"Essentially, we can walk across the Reach to move much quicker than others. At least that's what Tender Sully always said." Joel held up a hand to stop Colton's pending question. "Before you ask, the Reach is the energy which connects us all. It *reaches* from everything in existence to everything else in existence. Truthfully, I couldn't get my head around it either."

Colton scratched his head in confusion. "Do you think I could learn from…Tender Sully?" he asked curiously.

Joel suppressed a laugh. "Well, I'm sure you could, but Sully usually works with kids. You want Tender Terrance, he's the one who helps adults if they need help remembering something, or in some cases forgetting something."

"Who would want to forget something?" Colton asked incredulously.

Joel shrugged. "You might be surprised. Some people can't imagine living with the grief of losing someone close to them. It might seem cowardly, but I'm not sure how I'd feel if it were me."

Colton went silent as he processed that. He supposed that if something horrible happened to Imbrose, or Ember, or his grandparents, it might be hard to go on with that memory. Though without the memories, would he still be able to honor them?

"Enough dreary talk, let's get your powers out and about. I have a feeling we are running low on time," Joel said as he walked behind Colton. "Alright, this time I want you to focus on a distant point, say some fifty feet out." Joel pointed at a small sack lying on the ground. "Use that. Now this time, you need to imagine yourself standing where that bag is. It can also help if you picture what you might be seeing if you were standing there."

Colton screwed up his face in concentration and stared at the bag. Then, once he felt he had a good picture, he closed his eyes and felt for that orb of power deep inside him. This time it was easier to find and it seemed eager to oblige his request. Colton focused on that spot and imagined himself looking back at Joel's face and the field behind him. A blinding burst of light shot from the core of energy in his chest and pulled his consciousness with it on a ride through his veins. As he reached the end of his palm, daylight met his eyes and suddenly he was standing at the bag looking back at Joel, and his own astonished face. Colton looked

121

down and quickly patted himself and watched as the other version of himself next to Joel did the same thing.

"Don't panic!" Joel said quickly. "I've seen something like this before. This one is just an illusion, see?" Joel waved his hand through the still shocked version of himself leaving ripples of bluish energy as his hand swatted through him.

"Joel! The Keeper is asking for you." A child came running up to Joel as he yelled the news. The distraction caused Colton to lose his grip on the illusion and the power rebounded on him hard. Suddenly, he was looking through the other version of him's perspective then back again. He flipped back and forth multiple more times before the disjointed nature of it left him bent over hurling his lunch. From the corner of his eye, he could see the illusion version of him by the bag making the same motion for just a second before it popped out of existence.

After a moment, the nausea subsided and Colton felt a hand land on his back. "Should've warned you that if you let go too quickly, it will kick you in the guts." Joel patted his back sympathetically. "We had better get going then. The Keeper is a busy man, and he's probably already waiting for us." With that, he started walking back toward Orielle's house.

Colton wiped his mouth and stood up straight. "Can we come back and try again later?"

Joel smiled. "We might be talking with the Keeper pretty late, but definitely tomorrow if you're still interested."

Colton smiled back. He had actually done it! What would his grandfather say when he showed him his new trick? "Hey, why are we going back to Orielle's house?"

"Because the Keeper is her dad," Joel said over his shoulder.

Colton froze in his steps; it seemed there was even more he didn't know about this woman than he thought. With a shake of his head, he redoubled his pace to catch up to Joel.

Chapter Twelve: Enemies Revealed

Most of the populace had begun to turn in for the evening by the time Joel and Colton arrived back at Orielle's house. Lena, having apparently seen them from a window, appeared in the doorway to usher them both in. Entering the establishment caused a sense of nervousness to flow over Colton. Looking around the interior, he noticed the walls were covered in family paintings. He could see a timeline of their life in this home, and a small smile crested his face at the thought of his own childhood home. Colton stepped over a small pillow fort that had been made, with multiple hand-carved wooden animals littering the floor all around it. Each step further into the house impressed just how important family was in this abode. It was as if every little detail was placed specifically to remind any visitors that children lived here before anything else.

Looking into the dining room, Colton could see a group of adults sitting around a table discussing something in hushed tones. He couldn't help but feel like the display felt so out of place in an environment such as this. This was a place for children to play and be loved, and yet…times did not allow for that anymore.

Shaking from his thoughts, Colton started to make out some of the people sitting at the table as he approached. Delphine, Orielle, and Genevieve all looked up to see him and Joel come in. At the head of the table, a middle-aged man with a broad but approachable figure stood and held out a hand in greeting. Colton took the hand and was surprised by the roughness of his palm.

"George Dawson, it's a pleasure to meet you. I've heard quite a bit about you, Mister Cobb. Please, sit." The man gestured to an empty seat and sat back down.

He wore a green tunic and beige britches. Unruly brown curls with shocks of gray running through them covered his head, and a well-groomed goatee creased as he smiled broadly. His icy blue eyes, while friendly, seemed to observe the room completely no matter where he was looking.

"I hope you don't mind, I took the liberty of summoning your allies since I knew you were working with Joel," George said as he looked at Joel. "So, how did it go?"

"He's a Reach Roamer like myself," Joel announced with a pat on Colton's back. "With practice, I think he'll become one of the best of us."

"That's excellent news," George said cheerfully. Then a visible change washed over his face as he turned to look at Orielle. "I understand your hunt was successful?"

Orielle nodded. "Yes, Pa. We ran into a creature from that unknown cult we've been tracking, but it seemed to be waiting for us."

George rubbed his chin thoughtfully. "Most disturbing, and you say you left it at the gatehouse with Jerric and the others?"

Orielle nodded again, folding her hands on top of one another. "We did. I thought it was best to not drag something like that through the streets."

"That was very wise, Ori. I'm so proud of you," the Keeper praised as he placed a hand over Orielle's.

She looked up and beamed, and Colton felt himself smiling at the exchange. Her father's approval obviously meant a lot to her. "Thank you, Pa."

George squeezed her hands once and then pulled back to look at Colton. "Mister Cobb, I've heard Orielle's account of how she found you. However, I'd be very interested to hear things from your perspective."

This was it. If something went wrong now, everything Colton had strived for would be for nothing. While the Keeper seemed like a pleasant fellow, Colton had no doubt that he would kick his entire group out for the monsters if he thought they were a threat to the thicket.

George must have seen something on his face because his head tilted in confusion. "Is something the matter?"

Colton swallowed and steeled himself. "I want to start by thanking you for taking us all in, and showing such friendly hospitality," Colton began. "It would have been much easier to let us fend for ourselves out there, rather than save us."

George leaned back, his face dawning in understanding. "Saving you was the only thing to do," he dismissed, smiling. "You are one of us, and even if you weren't, we are guardians of this forest. Therefore, it's our job to protect those who are within it."

"So, you won't make us leave?" Colton asked.

George laughed gently. "By Tyrrek, no! You are all welcome to stay as long as you'd like." He paused looking at his wife. "In fact, we would love it if you made this your permanent home. It's time our two tribes were made whole again."

Colton smiled genuinely and looked toward Orielle. She smiled back and nodded as if urging him to accept. He wanted to accept of course, but he needed to go back home and get his grandfather for at least one more trip. Though, what about Imbrose and Ember? How would they feel if he made the permanent move to this new land?

"I'd love to accept your gracious offer, but before I do, I need to talk with my companions." George nodded his assent and Colton adjusted himself in his seat. "As to your original question, I'll tell you everything I know."

The Keeper listened intently without interrupting as Colton told him about the Archipelago, the months of seafaring across the Serpent's

Spine, Curtis' betrayal, and Deegan's journal. Even Lena found herself engrossed in the story, sitting down and remaining stationary for the longest period of time Colton had seen so far.

When he was finished, the Keeper sighed and scratched his nose. "Well, that is quite the tale."

"It is, and now we come to my only request," Colton continued, looking over at Delphine.

George raised an eyebrow. "Oh, and what might that be?"

"Some of my people feel the need to rid your world of Curtis, as we brought him to your shores. We would like the chance to remove him." Colton wrung his hands, trying to ignore old feelings. "We would ask that you allow some of us to travel north to the Thicket of Rivers in an effort to head him off."

George cast his eyes downward, considering. "I think it's noble that you would chase this man, and I shall help you in that endeavor as best as I can. Though, if I could say one thing on the matter…" Colton gestured for him to continue. "His choices aren't your responsibility, and what harm he causes will be his to reconcile with." With a nod, George looked to Joel. "See them provisioned and on their way when they are ready. I will admit, I had hoped you would stay a bit longer before leaving, Colton."

Colton looked up confused, then remembered he didn't specify who was going after Curtis. "Ah, well, I won't be going. Delphine and Genevieve, here, will be going with three more of us. Imbrose, Ember, and myself will be staying. Additionally, we would really be curious in trying to help Friend recover some of his lost memories."

"Friend?" George said questioningly, turning to look at Orielle.

Orielle smiled. "He's a gentle giant, but one that we couldn't do without. If it weren't for him, we probably wouldn't be having this conversation right now. He has some sort of fire magic which helped to keep the beasts of the forest at bay while we escaped."

"Intriguing, and you say he is originally from here?" George asked.

"As far as we know," Colton said. "He definitely didn't come with us from our homeland."

"Well, I'll make sure he meets with Terrance, and we shall see what we can do to help him." George placed his palms on the table. "If there is nothing else I can help our newcomers with...?"

Delphine, Genevieve, and Colton all stood up. "You've already done enough. Thank you once again," Colton said as he made for the door.

"Colton, if you don't mind, I'd like you to stick around for this next bit," George ventured.

Colton looked at Genevieve and Delphine. "It's alright, we need to get ready for tomorrow anyway," Genevieve dismissed. Colton gave them a solemn nod and placed a hand on both of their shoulders before turning to walk back to the table.

Once the door closed, Colton realized just alone he really was. Around the table sat Joel, Orielle, George, and Lena. He hadn't been separated from his own people like this since before they set sail all those months ago. Then again, weren't these supposed to be his people?

Colton folded his hands on the table, unsure what to do with them. "I realize this may be strange for you," Lena said gently. "Us asking you to stay behind alone, when only hours ago we were perfect strangers."

Colton shifted uncomfortably, but shook his head. "Not at all, I just wonder what it is I can do for you."

"I've been doing some thinking since I heard you were from our sister tribe," George said, his blue eyes locking onto Colton's. "I think it's fair you know what is happening around here if you are truly considering making our thicket your home. Meaning all of the good, and all of the bad. So, unless you object, I would welcome your counsel on the issues that have been plaguing us."

Colton straightened his posture. "I'd be honored, but I have no understanding as to how a thriving community should operate."

A knowing smile spread across the Keeper's lips. "Ah, but you do. You see, Joel and Orielle both told me how you stand up for your people, and how you put their needs above your own. You also don't strike me as a man who searches for power, and yet you are constantly burdened with it. That is what I see in you."

Colton rubbed his temple. "I will give what advice I can," he conceded finally.

"Very good!" George began. "Let us first discuss this captive you brought back with you. From what we understand, it must be from the same cult we suspect is responsible for some of our children's current state." He stopped talking to place a hand on Orielle's forearm. "Even our Jasper has been a victim of this strange affliction, and we have come no closer to figuring out what it is or how we can reverse it."

"Unfortunately, I'm not a doctor, so I really don't know what could be happening either," Colton retorted with an apologetic shrug.

"Be that as it may, collecting a prisoner has been a windfall we didn't expect. Most of the time, they kill themselves before they can be taken. Therefore, I can only assume this one wanted to be caught and that notion scares me more than anything," George continued.

"Hmm, so you mean to say that before now, you've never captured one alive?" Colton asked.

"Not a single one," Orielle affirmed. "That's why we were out there. We had been tracking a group of them moving south, and just before we found you guys, they vanished."

"That is odd..." Colton mused. "How do you plan to question it?"

Everyone turned to look at George. Apparently this hadn't been discussed yet. "Until we know that we can do it safely, we don't," George announced, eyes looking everywhere except at Orielle.

"What?" Orielle questioned, her voice rising slightly. "You don't plan to question him?"

George turned and looked at her. "We don't yet know what it wants, dearest. And until we do, we can't risk anyone getting hurt."

"What does it matter?" Orielle seethed standing from the table. "If we don't find a way to help Jasper soon, I'm concerned he won't get better."

128

"As am I, Ori," her mother whispered. "We just need to make sure everyone is safe."

"He isn't!" Orielle yelled as she pointed to the only closed door in the house. Then, when no one responded, she looked down at Joel with pleading eyes. "Joel?"

Joel smacked his lips. "He put three of us on the ground in no time flat. That has to be the strongest one we've run into yet." Joel stood as Orielle began to walk away with a scoff. "Ori, wait!" Joel called after her, but she was already opening and closing the door to what Colton assumed was Jasper's room.

"She's not wrong," Colton muttered just above a whisper. Everyone turned to look at him waiting for him to continue. Swallowing, he began, "This creature wanted to be caught, that's pretty clear. However, based on what you all have said to me, he's also your best lead into whatever's happening here. When the creature attacked me, it told me I would be a feast for *him*." Colton shuddered slightly at the memory. "It must be serving something else, and we have it, so shouldn't we press it for information?"

George scratched his chin. "Perhaps…let me think about it and we'll discuss our method for questioning tomorrow evening." Everyone around the table nodded. "I have one more thing to bring to everyone's attention, though I wish Orielle had been present to hear it… We found a man outside the thicket in the nearby woods." Lena gasped. "He appears to have been in some sort of fight and we were barely able to keep him alive long enough to bring him back."

"Did some beast get a hold of him?" Joel asked.

The Keeper shook his head. "No, he had three crossbow bolts sticking out of him by the time our scouts found him."

"Poachers, so close to our home?" Lena asked, raising a hand to cover her mouth.

"It seems that way," George confirmed looking over at Colton's confused face. "The poachers go by the name of Brotherhood of the Hunt, and they pride themselves on killing the biggest and meanest creatures this forest has to offer. Though we often find them prey to one animal or another."

"We are the guardians of this forest," Joel added proudly. "So, when they attack for no other reason than for sport, we have to get involved."

"They have also taken to harming some of our scouts as a warning. It appears they are getting bolder," George said pensively.

"What about this other fellow you found?" Colton asked.

A shadow crossed over the Keeper's face. "He's been very talkative. I get the feeling he's trying to hide his true intentions, but given the state we found him in, we couldn't simply leave him there."

"I see. What do you plan to do about these poachers?" Colton asked as the situation became clearer.

"We know they are held up inside some abandoned fortress directly east of us. I had considered sending a delegation there to treat with them in good faith, as we are not a warring people and want as little bloodshed as possible." George paused, folding his hands. "Though, I can't send people who aren't able to defend themselves if things go wrong. Which brings me to my request." Colton could see where this was going. "Given the news I received about your prowess in battle, I would ask that you and your people escort my delegation to and from this stronghold."

"I'm just as likely to get lost in the woods as I am to get eaten by some monster. I hardly think I'm qualified to escort your people from one end of this valley to the other, let alone out there," Colton countered, his memories of running through the forest flashing through his mind.

"I will be guiding them," Joel said. "We just need more people who can handle themselves in a fight if things go wrong. And don't worry, we have ways of safely traversing the forest. Last time, we were out of supplies and in a rush. We won't be this time."

Colton thought for a long moment then nodded to himself. "You've welcomed me into your home, so I'll go. I can't speak for my friends, but I'll ask, and knowing them, they'll probably jump at the opportunity."

"Very well, and thank you," George said as he stood from the table. "It has been a long day for you I'm sure, and I have kept you long enough. Please get some rest and we can discuss the details tomorrow evening over some dinner."

Colton stood and bowed his head slightly before making for the exit. "You know the way back?" Joel asked as he jogged to open the door for him.

"I think I can manage," Colton replied with a smirk as the two of them exited the house.

Joel laughed heartily. "Alright, well if you're feeling up to it, I'd love to show you the cider house tomorrow morning? Best breakfast in the valley."

Colton gave him a thumbs up. "You got it! Have a good night, Joel."

"You too," he called back.

The trip back to his guest house proved to be a bit more complicated than he thought, but after making a few wrong turns, he managed to stumble into the small courtyard of houses he and his friends were staying in. With a sigh of relief, Colton walked up and opened the door to his temporary dwelling. Putting his hat on the coat rack, Colton noticed something very interesting. Only the door to the leftmost room was closed, the other two were wide open.

"I suppose the cat is well and truly out of the bag," Colton murmured with a smile as he made his way to the rightmost room and closed the door behind him as softly as he could.

Chapter Thirteen: Impatience is Key

T he next morning, Colton woke to the sound of voices outside his door. Putting on his boots, he moved to the door and threw it open to see Imbrose and Ember abruptly stop talking to one another. Colton surveyed the two of them as Ember quickly went back to sharpening her naginata, and Imbrose started flipping through Deegan's journal far too quickly to actually be reading anything.

Colton smirked and let the silence hang as he walked to the nearby steaming pot of coffee. Glancing at the two of them, he used a nearby mug to scoop up some of the sweet-smelling liquid, then brought it to his mouth as he took a tentative sip. The flavor was rich but grainy.

Smacking his lips, Colton turned to see both of them had been looking at him but quickly returned to their tasks. A mischievous grin crossed his face. *Time to put them out of their misery.*

"So," Colton began, "when's the wedding?"

Ember huffed, discarding her whetstone and pointed accusingly at Imbrose. "I told you he would know; it doesn't take a genius to realize only one room was being used."

Imbrose closed the journal dramatically. "Well if you hadn't been so awkward when he walked out, that would have helped!"

Colton set his mug down and raised his hands. "Hey now! I've known for fifteen years. I was just waiting for the two of you to catch up." He smiled genuinely. "Truly, I am happy for the both of you. Now come here and give me a hug." Both of them rose hesitantly and moved to hug Colton. Once he had them both in a tight embrace, he chuckled. "Look at you two! All grown up!"

Imbrose shoved away from them in mock annoyance. "Oh, do shut up."

Colton laughed one last time then reached down for his mug once more. "Joel showed me how to do some pretty neat stuff yesterday! Wanna see?" Ember and Imbrose both looked at him with rapt attention and nodded.

Colton closed his eyes and imagined himself standing in the doorway to his room again. Tracing that same line of energy to the ball of power in his chest, he willed it to follow his instructions. Immediately, he felt himself pulled through space and opened his eyes to see his two friends staring at the illusionary projection he had left behind, cup still in hand. He brought the mug up to his real face to see the illusion copy make the same gesture.

"Cute light show, but what happened?" Imbrose asked as he leaned in to inspect his illusion closer.

"Here I thought you were observant," Colton drawled as the two of them whipped their heads rapidly in his direction.

"Holy shit!" Imbrose said. "That is wicked!"

"How did you do that?" Ember asked as she waved her hand through the rippling image.

"I honestly don't know," Colton admitted as he placed a hand on the doorframe to brace himself and the illusion popped away. "Still haven't gotten used to it."

"Still," Ember said, moving to help stabilize him, "pretty impressive!"

Colton chuckled ruefully as he waved her away. "I'm okay, just a bit nauseous is all." He straightened, rubbing his throbbing head. "Has Joel swung by yet?"

Imbrose sat down on a stool and crossed his legs. "Nope, and we didn't want to leave until you woke up."

Colton nodded and moved to sit down himself. "I got back pretty late last night. The Keeper has asked us to escort a delegation for him…" Colton relayed the information he received last night.

Ember tapped her chin as he finished his retelling. "So, they have been primarily a passive nation, and now they are being attacked by two separate entities. Sounds convenient at best and planned at worst."

"My thoughts exactly," Colton agreed, taking another sip of his coffee. "The question is, do we trust them or…?"

"Or what?" Imbrose asked. "Do we have any other choices? Seems to me that we are a bit stuck here."

"We could go with the others," Ember suggested quietly.

"I think we can trust them," Colton stated. "We owe them, that's for sure, but they aren't asking us for assistance with any expectations. They simply need help, and they don't know how to deal with these things." Looking at Ember, he added, "Besides, we have no idea what good we can do up north, but here we have a clear direction on how to help."

Ember wrinkled her face but nodded stiffly. "We are with you, Colton. Always have, always will be."

Colton stood and took in a big breath. "Joel asked if I wanted to have breakfast with him, are you two interested?"

The two of them looked at each other and Imbrose shrugged. "Sure, why not? If this is home for now, we should get to know the area."

The trio made their way outside into the morning sunlight to see a small pile of supplies that had been put in the center of the courtyard with Genevieve shouldering a pack.

"I was beginning to wonder if we would have to leave without saying goodbye," she shouted at them.

"Not goodbye, just see you later," Colton corrected as he clasped arms with her.

"As you say!" she conceded cheerfully. "We are about to head out, mind helping us to the gate?"

Colton reached down and grabbed a small crate of fruit. "Looks like you are armed for a settlement mission."

Genevieve chuckled. "When they said they would supply us for the trip up north, they weren't kidding."

The others slowly trickled out of their houses and began to pick up the supplies. Delphine made for Colton's side and looked pointedly down at the crate in his hands. "Planning to come with?" she asked.

Colton shook his head. "No, I just wanted to help you guys get everything loaded up." Delphine nodded slightly and moved to grab her own bag. "Has anyone seen Friend?"

"Yep, he left earlier with some guy who had a long beard," Gavin said.

Colton wondered if the big metal man was doing alright, and resolved himself to find him after breakfast with Joel. It had to be disorienting being by himself, and not knowing what his purpose was supposed to be.

Suddenly, a portal opened next to the pile and Joel stepped through, smiling. "Oh good, everyone is here. Let's get underway, shall we?"

The trip back up the gate included the same glancing looks they had been receiving on the way in. However, now the townsfolk seemed more at ease with their presence. Colton looked at the townsfolk and noticed that not a single one of them carried a weapon of any kind. This place had known peace for so long that it had no need for such tools of warfare. It put the request the Keeper had made of him into perspective, and only affirmed his choice to stay and help. In a place like his home, New Eradin, everyone walked around with their own sword or weapon of choice. These people wouldn't stand if there was any concentrated assault on the thicket.

Suddenly, their wary glances when they first showed up made so much more sense. Everyone in their troop was armed to the teeth, and unless there was some hidden weapon that could be used in case of attack, their small group could wreak havoc here. The bleak thought made him self-consciously wish he could cover the handle of the large greatsword hanging off his back.

Too quickly, they arrived at the gate and one of the guards came to relieve Colton of his crate. With a forced nod, he handed the crate over and turned to see his departing friends all looking at him.

"Take care of each other, and we will see you again soon." Colton felt a lump rising in the back of his throat, swallowing hard as he looked back up at them. "Please send word once you guys get to the Thicket of Rivers."

Hugs were exchanged and Colton watched the group begin to head through the entrance, when Delphine looked over her shoulder with a smile. "See you later, Cobb."

Colton nodded, unable to find any more words as they departed. The group disappeared around the corner and Colton felt a hand land on his shoulder. "We'll be seeing them again soon, mate," Imbrose said.

"Should we go with them, Imbrose?" Colton asked.

Imbrose smacked his lips and squeezed his shoulder. "No, I don't think so. We all have a reason to be in this new world, and yours is here."

"I'm still trying to figure out what my reason is," Colton mumbled, turning away from the tunnel.

"At first it was knowledge, but now I think it's more," Imbrose said.

Colton turned to look at him. "What do you mean?"

Imbrose smiled, and glanced down at the village in the valley below. "These are your people, right? Well, if I know you at all, you have an inherent obligation to help them." He paused and made a gun with his forefinger and thumb, a smirk tugging at his lips. "Besides, it's hard to turn your back on something that feels like it's meant to be."

Colton's eyes narrowed on his friend. "Right…Sounds like we should bring Ember over here to discuss what's meant to be."

Imbrose's eyes widened and his face flushed. "What's that?" he asked loudly, backpedaling away from Colton. "You're famished and can't wait to see what Joel has planned for breakfast? Oh yeah, me too."

"That's what I thought," Colton whispered, a grin pulling at the corner of his mouth.

Joel pointed down the hill toward the lake Colton had seen walking in the day before. "Down next to the lake, there is a delicious cider house that has the best apple turnover I've ever had. They also have eggs and bacon too."

"You had me at 'down next to the lake,'" Ember said as the group began their descent back into the valley.

The walk back down was fast, and with a much smaller group, the townsfolk seemed less anxious around them. As they reached the bottom of the switchbacks, Joel led them on a path toward a small patch of trees and a glistening blue lake. Colton glanced to his right as they passed the stilted cabin the man with the mug was on. This time though, he saw no man on the porch and instead saw only a dim light through a window. Before he could investigate any further, they turned left, putting his back to the lone cabin.

Passing between two trees, Colton could finally see a large, green-tinted house. It was unique in design compared to the other circular houses. This one had a multi-tiered, steepled roof with a wide front porch and stairs leading up to a door with a stained glass window. The party climbed the stairs and followed behind Joel as he confidently strode through the door which made a soft jingling sound as they entered.

"Take any seat you like!" A gentle, womanly voice echoed from the back room.

Surveying the interior, Colton saw upwards of twenty tables arranged around the space, with a set of spiral stairs leading to a second floor. Around half of the tables were taken by patrons and many of them were already feasting on a bounty of pastries and proteins alike. Colton's stomach grumbled as he continued to follow Joel to a nearby table with chairs arranged around it.

"This place is run by a lovely woman named Leilani. She's Lucas' ma," Joel shared as he sat down. "As far as I can tell, it has been in her family for generations."

"Well it smells delicious in here," Colton commented. The air had the sweet scent of cinnamon mixed with the savory smell of freshly cooked bacon.

"Just wait until you get to taste it!" Joel said happily. "So, have you had any time to talk about the Keeper's request?"

Ember reached for the full pitcher of water sitting in the center of the table and poured everyone a glass. "He told us, and I just have a couple of questions before we agree." She paused, sitting back down and taking a deep drink. "I couldn't help but notice there aren't many of you who are armed."

Joel nodded. "True enough, which is the main reason we need your help for this endeavor, but we have a few seasoned warriors."

"Aside from us, who else will be coming that has fighting capabilities?" Colton asked.

"Well, I spoke with Orielle this morning, and while she is frustrated with how things are being handled, she wants to come. Then there's Cartwright, he's the best swordsman we have. Lastly, our neighborhood tracker, Toku, will be coming as well." Joel said, putting a finger on the table for each one he listed off.

"How does a tracker count as a warrior?" Imbrose asked.

Joel snickered. "He's better at navigating these woods than anyone I know, and he can handle a sword good enough to survive in the forest for days on end, alone."

Imbrose raised his hand in surrender.

"That makes seven fighters then, right?" Ember asked. "How many are we escorting?"

"Two in total," Joel said as he cast around for a waiter. "The head delegate also has some baseline fighting experience, but it shouldn't be depended on."

"The way I see it," Ember began, "we owe you for saving our butts out there. So, Imbrose and I will join you guys. Afterwards though, we should discuss what our next steps should be given the fact our initial mission is mostly complete."

Joel regarded her seriously. "Absolutely, I think we can come to an understanding."

A young man walked up and greeted Joel warmly. After ordering for the table, Joel also asked the man to bring them some cider and sent him on his way.

"I hope you don't mind me ordering for y'all. I promise it will be a good surprise," Joel said as his eyes locked on an approaching figure.

Colton glanced over his shoulder to see Lucas walking up to their table and quickly turned back around to study his half-drank glass of water.

"Hi there everyone! Mind if I sit with ya?" Lucas' charming voice asked from behind him.

Joel hesitated ever so slightly, but then a smile crested his face. "Certainly! We would love to have you with us."

Lucas took a seat next to Joel and Ember as he reached for a glass of water. "So, how do you guys like it here so far?"

"It's very beautiful, and the people are very welcoming," Ember began, looking nervously at Colton.

Lucas nodded, taking a sip from his glass, and gesturing at Imbrose. "You are quite the topic of conversation among the kids. They seem to think you are the most interesting thing in this valley at present."

Imbrose chuckled. "I get that a lot, believe it or not."

Lucas laughed heartily. "Oh, I believe it. They're still trying to figure out if they should run and hide from you, or invite you to come play with them."

"What about you?" Colton asked abruptly. "What do you do around here?"

Lucas' eyes trained on Colton. "Well, I am the primary farmer for all of the food that people eat here. Everything except the apples, that's Ma's specialty."

Colton looked up and made eye contact with Lucas, a smile forcing its way onto his face. "Well then, thank you for all your hard work. I suspect I speak for everyone when I say it's well received."

139

Lucas held his gaze a second longer, then looked away with a pensive expression. The silence lingered a minute or so before Lucas looked over at Joel. "How is she?" he asked quietly.

"She's good," Joel answered. "Been spending all of her time with Jasper."

Colton thought he caught a slight look of disgust wash over Lucas' face, but it was gone instantly. "Well, I'm glad," Lucas said.

Mercifully, platters of eggs, bacon, and various pastries arrived alongside a pitcher of amber liquid with fresh cups. The waiter finished placing the food on the table, and with a nod from Lucas, left as quickly as he had come.

Not needing any further encouragement, the group began dishing out the banquet. As promised, the turnover was delicious, and left Colton once again reminiscing of home. In no time at all, the plates were cleared of food and everyone sat back luxuriantly in their chairs.

Feeling the need to walk off the meal and get some fresh air, Colton stood up. "I think I'm going to swing by the grove and talk with Tender Terrance."

Joel began to stand too. "Would you like me t–."

Colton held out a hand. "No, no. I'm assuming the grove is under the big purple tree?" Joel nodded. "If you wouldn't mind showing these two where they can train, I think they would appreciate that."

"Most definitely," Imbrose chimed in helpfully.

Colton grabbed the scabbard of the greatsword and shouldered it. "I'll meet you all there later." Joel nodded again, smiling. "Thanks again, Lucas," Colton said as he strode for the door, not waiting for a response.

Outside, the fresh air helped clear the shadow that had fallen over Colton's mood. Closing his eyes, he took in a deep breath and began to retrace his steps to the main road. Once again, his gaze was pulled to the shadowy cabin on the lake's edge. For a moment, Colton considered walking over and introducing himself, but then his sense reasserted its control and he pulled his attention away from it.

As his eyes caught sight of the main road, Colton watched Orielle walk by quickly, seemingly headed for the tunnel leading out of the thicket. He blinked several times, unsure if he believed what he was seeing, then realizing it really was her, he ran to catch her. She was already halfway up the first switchback by the time he reached her.

"Orielle!" he called out. "Where are you headed?"

Orielle looked over her shoulder at him and redoubled her walking speed. "Don't try and stop me, Colton."

"Try to stop you?" Colton asked in confusion. "From doing what?"

"From doing what I must. I will figure out what that creature knows, to hell with this caution. Kids are dying right in front of us and we just cower and wait," she snapped, the anger dripping from her voice.

Colton could tell she wouldn't see reason, and he wasn't about to get in her way. "Fine, but let me join you," he insisted quickly.

Orielle stopped and turned around, her face softening. "The Keeper will be upset. I can't ask you to come with me."

"You didn't ask," Colton pointed out, gaining confidence. "I promised I would help you with your brother, and I think this is a lead to helping him."

Orielle smiled, and embraced him. "Thank you," she breathed, her face pressed against his chest.

Colton swallowed, and slowly wrapped his arms around her. He could feel the heat rising to his cheeks as she squeezed him tightly. "Of course," he reassured quietly.

A long moment passed where neither of them moved, but then Orielle gently pulled herself free and wiped her eyes. "Let's get going then. People will figure out what I'm up to before too long."

Colton nodded and followed behind her up to the top of the hill for the second time today. This time, when they reached the top, Colton could feel his thighs burning from the exertion, and his breath came in rapid gasps.

141

Orielle turned and looked at him, her skin coated in a light layer of sweat, as she breathed heavily as well. "You alright?" she asked.

Colton nodded and held up a thumbs up as he belted over, catching his breath.

After a moment's respite, the two of them made their way to the gatehouse to see Jerric standing guard outside. "Miss Dawson!" he said, far more formally than the last time they had seen him.

Orielle approached him quickly. "Hello Jerric. I need to see the prisoner I brought in yesterday."

Jerric glanced at her nervously, then at Colton. "Uh, of course, Miss. He's through there," he stammered, gesturing through the door to his right.

Without another word, Orielle walked past him and disappeared inside. Colton stepped forward, but stopped at the entrance and leaned close to Jerric. "Get the Keeper," he urged quietly before following her in.

The interior of the prison was dimly lit and gave off a sense of foreboding. Colton quickly caught up to Orielle who had stopped halfway down the hallway. "Do you hear that?" she asked.

Colton listened and heard it. A quiet but determined chant of the same words echoed over and over again. The air chilled slightly as the chanting got louder. "Are you certain you want to do this, Orielle?"

She nodded, then stepped forward and threw the door open into the prison. Immediately, the smell of dirty bodies and stale air assaulted Colton's senses. Three prison cells lined the far wall, and each of them had comfortable furniture meaningfully placed inside. With the only way to leave the small jail being the doorway they had just entered through, the space felt cramped and uncomfortable. Colton's eyes drifted to the creature who was kneeling on the hay covered dirt floor in the center of his barred cell, completely ignoring the plush looking bed in the corner.

Suddenly, Colton could make out what was being said, but it still didn't make sense to him.

Va'Rul, Va'Rul, Va'Rul.

The words seemed to permeate the air around them and Colton felt himself straining to block the voice out.

Va'Rul, Va'Rul, Va'Rul!

The voice reached a crescendo and Colton watched Orielle walk forward and yell at the creature.

"What have you done to my brother!" she screamed, her voice cracking.

The creature's chanting cut off and the room fell into silence.

"Finally! I thought he would never shut up!" a youthful voice from the next cell over said. "Listen, I'm fine with being a prisoner, but at least put me in a different building. This guy is driving me crazy."

The creature's head rose and looked directly at Orielle through the bars. "Why don't you come on in and find out." The cultist tapped his temple as if goading Orielle into linking with him.

"Don't do it, Orielle," Colton warned. "He's baiting you."

"I need to know, and he has the information I need. I can feel it," she whispered back, her voice sounding reckless.

"We don't know what it can do!" Colton insisted, getting louder.

"Let's find out," she snarled before her body began seizing and fell to the floor.

The creature stayed upright, kneeling peacefully as if nothing had happened.

Frantically, Colton knelt next to Orielle and cradled her head as she shook violently. "What did you do to her?"

The monster's face twitched as if to smile. "Exactly what she wanted."

"Let her go right now!" he demanded, standing to take a threatening step toward the cage.

The creature shrugged. "I'm afraid it is not me you are contending with anymore."

Colton looked down at Orielle. Black foam gathered at her mouth and blood started to pour from her eyes and ears. With no other options, he closed his eyes and imagined himself inside the jail cell. A moment

143

later, he opened his eyes to see himself standing behind the cultist. With a fluid motion, he unsheathed his greatsword and beheaded the kneeling figure. A sick thump echoed as the head flopped onto the floor and its body collapsed.

Colton instinctively swapped back to where he was before and let his power fade, not even noticing how fluid it felt, and knelt next to the still shaking Orielle.

"Woah, how did you do that?" that same youthful voice called out.

"C'mon, Ori. What did you do?" Colton muttered as he carefully reached downward with his hand. Her body was cold to the touch and he could feel her breath becoming more and more shallow. "Oh Gods, you're freezing. What the hell do I do?" Colton questioned, his panicked voice surprising himself. He stood and paced back and forth, then an idea struck him. A stupid idea, but an idea. If he could mindlink with her, he might be able to pull her out of whatever she was dealing with. Looking toward the door to see if anyone was coming to help, he shook his head ruefully and knelt next to her again. He reached out and cradled her head as he pushed his consciousness into hers.

The world swam and Colton felt himself being pulled into a black abyss. He fell, listening to his own breathing as he grasped for anything to grab onto. Suddenly, a brilliant prismatic window opened below him, the only light in an otherwise black void, and he tried to aim for it. The air around him resisted his movements, but at the last second, he felt himself get pulled through the opening and thrown onto a hard surface.

Colton stood to take in his surroundings. All around him he could see little floating windows, but these didn't lead to darkness, they led to moments that were playing out from Orielle's perspective. Not just one, but many, over the course of decades of life. Each window, a memory. Colton looked down to see the floor below him was a reflective pool of ankle high water. The visual caused his head to spin as he took a step and the reflection ripped away from him.

A blast of light caught Colton's attention as he followed it back to its source. In the distance, he could see Orielle fighting off some creature made of shadow, only she was losing and the creature was moving in for the kill.

"Orielle!" Colton yelled as he started running toward the battle.

She turned in time to see him just before she was smacked by some shadowy hand. Orielle skipped across the surface of her mindscape and came to a stop twenty feet ahead of Colton. In the distance, the creature made for one of the windows of memories and opened its mouth to bite down on it, seemingly to devour it.

Sliding to a stop, he reached Orielle and could see that she had taken some hits. In the real world, he would be concerned for her life, and here he had no idea what kind of injuries may transition to her actual body.

"Stop him," she whispered weakly. "He's trying to eat my memories. If he does–" She cut off as she coughed a few times.

"It's alright," Colton soothed as he looked at the creature. "I've got him, you just stay here and recover."

Colton stood, and with a sense of ease, projected himself in front of the creature, drawing his blade in the same motion.

The creature came to a stop mere feet in front of him. In a blink, the creature's form shimmered and Colton could see its true self. This was the creature from his nightmare that killed Imbrose and Ember in front of him. Its coral-encrusted body with at least ten arms on either side stretched back at least thirty feet. Those same razor-like fingers clacked onto the ground as it stopped its massive bulk. Though something told him that this one was for real as it smiled a toothy grin at him.

"Colton Cobb, I had hoped to save you for another meal." The monster's gravely voice echoed throughout the space. "Though I suppose I am quite famished."

"Who are you?" Colton asked, glancing just behind the creature and placing an illusion there.

The beast let out a sinister chuckle. "I am the last great emperor, and I will devour your world to reclaim what we have lost." Then it lunged.

Colton sidestepped, but the creature telegraphed his maneuver and curved its long neck to catch him mid-air. With a thought, he swapped places with his image behind the creature and slashed down towards one of its back arms. The Blade of Tyrrek glowed in his hands as he cleaved through the arm causing the creature to roar and the arm disappeared in a burst of black smoke.

"You insolent whelp!" the creature screamed, turning on him. "I cannot be killed by the likes of you!"

Colton swapped back again and gashed the creature deeply along its turned neck. One of the many arms along its right side slashed with lightning speed, catching him before he could swap again. The force of the blow sent him cartwheeling across the space before landing hard in a splash. Dazed, Colton tried to get to his feet but the creature was upon him again biting down. This time Colton imagined himself in the air above the creature and closed his eyes. He hadn't tried to summon a copy mid-air before. He blinked and suddenly he was above the creature's striking head.

"Just die!" Colton yelled as he angled the blade downward for the base of the monster's skull. The sword began to glow so brightly, Colton had to squint his eyes as he plunged it hilt deep into the colossal snake-like titan.

The beast screeched as it thrashed, trying to throw Colton loose. He held on for dear life, but his hands slipped from around the grip of the blade, sending him flying through the air once more. With a grunt, Colton slammed into the ankle deep water again and felt bones snapping as he landed awkwardly. He hissed in pain as he watched the creature, sword still embedded in its head, limp toward him triumphantly.

"You see?" the creature cooed. "You cannot kill me, but I'll take your memories and life for believing you could."

Colton hissed in pain as he brought himself to a knee, unwilling to yield to this creature. Then, his eyes locked on the glowing blue blade still protruding up. It called out to him. This sword was bound to him, and it wanted to help him end this monstrosity. He willed the blade to return to him, and when he opened his eyes, the sword was in his right hand. Smiling, Colton raised the blade and prepared to take on the creature again.

A blast of energy flew from Colton's right to hit the creature in the face, then another. Colton turned to see Orielle on her feet, her pistols barking as she strutted toward the creature. Emboldened, Colton charged the serpent, slashing his sword in wide arcs as he cut through one arm after another. Eventually, the forest of writhing arms and fingers parted to reveal the long, coral-like body underneath. With a powerful swing of the sword, Colton bit into the beast's hide and drove the blade in deep. He pulled the blade back and brought it down again, intending to slice the monster in two. As the blade came down, the creature turned its head and lunged for him. He forced his head back to the task at hand, knowing he would be bit in half, but also knowing he needed to land this hit. Its strike went wide as another, much larger blast of energy erupted at its temple.

The sword hit true, and sliced through the monster like cutting through warm butter. He felt the reverberation from the sword clattering with the ground as the massive serpent writhed in pain. The bottom half of it immediately vanished into a thick cloud of black smoke as the head crumpled to the ground, it too slowly dissolving into smoke.

"Intriguing…" the creature managed before disappearing completely.

Colton turned to look at Orielle and felt himself get yanked away from behind, her mindspace disappearing into the distance.

With a start, Colton opened his eyes to see himself lying on the ground next to Orielle. She too was opening her eyes as she rubbed away the drying blood. He helped her sit up and she leaned into him for another hug, Colton embracing her back as she sobbed. His own head reeled from the casual use of his fledgling powers. Oddly enough, his sword lay next

147

to him, still glowing a furious blue as if it too were celebrating the victory.

The door flew open and Lucas stormed into the prison. He took stock of the situation, then moved to where the two of them were kneeling on the ground. Roughly, he inserted himself between them and pried Orielle from Colton.

"Ori! Are you okay?" he asked, nervously.

Orielle clambered to her feet, still crying, and pushed Lucas away. "Just stay away from me!" she cried out, running out of the prison and leaving Colton still kneeling on the cold floor.

Colton watched her go and then turned to look at Lucas, and glared into the back of his skull.

"I'll only say this once, Colton," Lucas began, his back still facing him. "Don't ever touch her again." Then Lucas walked down the hallway.

Colton felt his blood run cold. Not because of the threat, but because he could have sworn Lucas' voice sounded just like the creature he and Orielle had just killed.

Chapter Fourteen: Long Awaited Reunion

"Woof, tough break pal." a voice echoed from behind Colton's shoulder. "I really felt the energy between you two."

Pulled from his thoughts, Colton looked over his shoulder to locate the source of the voice. Standing with his arms looped through the bars was a young man who couldn't have been more than twenty years old. He wore ragged clothing and bandages all along his left arm, and smiled broadly as Colton finally made eye contact with him.

"Who are you?" Colton asked incredulously.

"Who, me?"

Colton nodded, gesturing around the rest of the empty prison. "I don't see anyone else here."

The man backed away from the bars and bowed deeply. "The name's Sero, at your service."

Colton turned away from him shaking his head. "Great, another showman," he muttered.

"What's that?" Sero asked.

"I said my name is Colton, nice to meet you," he lied, standing from his kneeling position. "But as you can see, I'm a bit preoccupied. Good luck to you." Then, he made for the door.

Sero rushed to the bars again. "Wait, wait!" Colton stopped and looked over his shoulder. "Can you get me out of here?"

"Afraid not, pal," Colton answered flatly, turning around and crossing his arms. "I have no clue what you did, and something tells me I'm already in trouble for doing what you just witnessed, so, sorry, but no." He moved to leave once again.

"Okay! But can you tell the leader guy something for me?" Sero asked.

Pulling on the handle, Colton paused. "What is it?" he asked finally.

"Tell him I know something about the Poachers or whatever. It's going to be important for them to know if they plan to take them out," Sero said quickly.

"Sure, I'll let him know. Anything else?"

"Um…Nope, I think that covers it," Sero said after thinking for a moment.

"Right. See you around," Colton dismissed with a wave as he exited the prison.

Once outside, he shook his head trying to make sense of the events that just occurred. It was obviously real, because Orielle had experienced it as well. Was that what happened to all of the children in the thicket?

Colton surveyed the valley as he stepped into the sunlight. Below him, he could see Orielle being cradled by her parents as they made their way to their home. However, he couldn't see Lucas anywhere. *Lucas…*Did he actually sound like that creature or was Colton imagining it? *He's obviously not the nicest person, but is it even possible that he's that…monster?*

He rubbed his temples, overwhelmed with the concepts he was considering. The idea that a creature like that could infiltrate a place like the thickets was absurd, and yet, the children were evidence enough. Taking a deep breath, Colton decided he needed to discuss this with the Keeper when things settled down.

His thoughts then turned to Orielle, as he considered the state she had been in when they were interrupted. Concern roiled inside him as he grimaced at what she must be enduring.

"To hell with your threats." Colton muttered, as he took a step to follow behind Orielle and her family.

As if she read his intent, Orielle glanced over her parents' shoulders and looked up at him, her mind reaching out to his.

I'll be alright. Just let me collect my thoughts.

Pausing mid-step, Colton responded. *Just…let me know if you need anything.*

I will. Her presence cut off abruptly, and she forced a slight smile before turning back around to be ushered away.

Battling with himself, he let out a deep sigh. He would give her the time she needed. In the meantime, he still wanted to meet with Terrance and get some answers. With a resolute nod, he looked at the purple tree in the distance and started off towards it.

—

The opening into the massive tree was crowded with people as they came and went. The low hanging boughs seemed otherworldly in size this close up, and the vibrant purple leaves swayed in the warm breeze. A familiar glimmer of metal caught Colton's attention as Friend stepped out and shook hands with a long bearded man. Bidding him farewell, Friend began walking down the path toward where he was standing.

Colton waved him down. "Hey, Friend! How are you doing? Didn't see you this morning."

Friend smiled genuinely as he approached. "Hello, Colton! I feel much better. Terrance was nice enough to help me remember some of my repressed memories. I think I have a better idea as to who I am, or rather, who I was." While he continued talking, Friend's face fell as if an unpleasant memory was invading his thoughts at that moment.

Colton waited for him to continue, but Friend's face grew more and more distant and he began to worry. "Friend? Are you okay?"

Friend's focus snapped back to him abruptly. "Yes. I think I need time to process what I have learned."

Colton nodded and reached up to pat his shoulder. "That sounds good. Let me know if you need anything."

"I will, do you know where I can find the nearest blacksmith?"

Colton flinched at the sudden change of topic. "I-I really couldn't say. Maybe down the road toward the market?"

Friend nodded, orienting his gaze that way. "Thank you, Colton." Then, he left without another word. Colton watched him leave and shook his head. The day just kept getting stranger.

Steeling himself, he moved up to the man who had walked out with Friend. He was a burly man with dark brown hair and a beard that stretched to the top of his abdomen. A big smile spread across his face as Colton approached him.

"Hail, friend," he greeted with a wave. "What brings you here?"

Colton swallowed. "I'm looking for a man named Tender Terrance?"

The man chuckled heartily. "Well, you've found him. What can I do for you?"

"Oh!" Colton exclaimed. "I'm not certain how to say this…" Colton let himself trail off as he tried to put together his request. "My name is Colton Cobb, and I'm from the tribe that broke off awhile ago. I'd like to know what happened."

Terrance's eyes widened as he listened to Colton. "You're what?"

"I'm–" Colton began again.

"I heard you, lad. Just trying to believe it too," Terrance said as he waved a hand at him. Controlling his shock, he turned to look at Colton once again. "It certainly was a while ago. Close to six hundred years ago." Now it was Colton's turn for his eyes to widen. The timeline he was speaking of didn't even seem conceivable. "Boy, this day has been an interesting one. First that tall metal man with amnesia, then you."

"You're telling me," Colton whispered.

"Very well, if you want to know what happened, I'll need to take you to the oldest part of the grove," Terrance mused as he started into the opening inside the tree.

Colton followed closely, worried he may get lost in the crowd of people. Though as badly as Colton tried to maintain eyesight of Terrance, he couldn't help but look around and take in the amazing interior. The further in they moved, the more luminescent purple light filled the space. Purple flowers coated the entirety of the space. The corridor was so packed with both people and flowers that the only light was coming from the flowers on the ceiling as bodies blocked the flowers along the walls. He could see the entire roof above them was made of thick interwoven roots as they seemed to knot themselves into a single mass.

Suddenly, Colton looked back down and could no longer find Terrance and began to panic. He gently moved a silver-haired elder out of the way, exchanging a polite smile and moved to where he had last seen Terrance. To his left, a tunnel broke off heading into a separate section of the tree. Standing just off the main path down the tunnel, Terrance waved at him to follow.

Breathing a sigh of relief, Colton followed him again, leaving the rushing crowd behind. This section was all but abandoned as the two of them pushed further into the Memory Grove.

"Down this way is where we take the students when they first start their education with us," Terrance informed. "Since this is the grove which houses the oldest living memories of our people, the kids need to experience it first before anything else."

"Are there any memories of Tyrrek down here?" Colton asked.

Terrance turned and looked at him, impressed, then continued down the hallway. "If only! I'm sure many would kill for the opportunity to see the world from a God's perspective." the Tender chuckled at the thought. "No, but we do have his shield down here. It felt like the best place to put such a relic."

153

Colton unconsciously reached over his shoulder to touch the hilt of his greatsword. "I have been told that this weapon once belonged to him as well."

Terrance rounded a corner into a large open area. "Then perhaps you truly are from the Tyrkin who left us so long ago. Here we are."

The whole circular open space was a field of purple flowers, some as tall as his knees. Colton's eyes were pulled to a movement on the far side as a small line of children emerged from the field and began to make their way to the entrance with an old man leading them.

Terrance bowed to the man as he passed. "Tender Sully," he said reverently.

The older man also bowed, but his age only allowed a small nod of his head as he continued walking with the children in tow. Colton watched the children, who all must have been around age ten, pass by in an orderly line heading back the way he had come. The last child in line stopped and stared up at him. Doing a double take, Colton was shocked to see the small boy's expression of blankness as he lazily blinked his green eyes. A sudden realization came over him as he studied the boy's appearance. Green eyes, curly dark hair, sunkissed skin, was this...

"Jasper," came the old man's voice from up ahead. "Keep up, boy."

Colton looked down at the boy, a sense of foreboding passing over him as the moment stretched. Then, a sinister smile spread over Jasper's face as he held Colton's gaze, the memory of when he appeared before the creature in Orielle's mind flashed through his head. The smile that invaded Jasper's face looked sickeningly like the beast from that nightmare.

Suddenly, a pair of frail hands closed around Jasper's shoulders and the smile dropped instantly. "Come on then, Jasper."

Colton watched as Jasper was led away and then turned back to meet Terrance's gaze. "That was odd. Haven't seen so much as a sigh from that boy for months now," the burly Tender wondered aloud.

"Yeah, odd," Colton echoed, still reeling from the incident.

"Well, we've made it." Terrance turned his attention back to the subterranean grove. "That there is the shield I was talking about," he said pointing to the far wall.

Colton followed his finger to see a large kite shield cradled in the roots. Alongside it, there was a distinct opening that fit the size and shape of the sword he now carried. Intricate markings flowed over the surface of the blue-tinted metal, and even from this distance, Colton could make out the same glyphs that ran along the blade. Feeling drawn to the shield, Colton walked toward it, careful to avoid stepping on the flowers that still glowed a constant purple.

The moment he stepped within ten feet of it, the glyphs on the shield began to glow a calming blue, just like the two times Colton used the blade in combat. As he took another step, the symbols pulsed and sent a wave of energy toward him. Stumbling from the force, Colton braced himself on the wall of the cavern to see every flower in the near vicinity to him fluctuate their color from the bright purple to the cooling blue of the shield. Colton could hear Terrance gasp behind him as the event subsided and the blue light faded from the kite shield.

"Wow!" Terrance exclaimed. "I've never seen it do that before. I wish Sully had been here! How do you feel?"

"I'm fine," Colton answered shakily as he caught his breath. "It felt like the shield was greeting a long lost friend."

Terrance grunted. "It has been said that the shield often seemed to be sentient in a way."

"This magic is beyond my understanding," Colton marveled, looking at the glyphs as they burned out with a sense of wonder.

"It's beyond all of us." He stopped talking and turned to look at Colton. "Come, let's commune with one of the flowers. This magic, I understand," Terrance said as he walked over to a particularly large one and sat down. He looked up at Colton expectantly and patted the ground next to him. "Come on now, I won't bite." Hesitating for a moment, he walked over and sat down as Terrance closed his eyes. "Good, now place your hands on the petals of the flower and let your mind wander."

Nervously, Colton reached out for the purple petals, his heart pounding in anticipation for what he was about to experience.

Chapter Fifteen: Delving Into the Past

T he velvety feeling of the petals caressing his fingers calmed Colton
from the stressful events of the day. With a deep sigh, he closed his
eyes and allowed his mind to wander as Terrance had instructed.

"Good." Terrance's voice sounded far and indistinct as Colton
could feel himself being pulled toward the flower. "Take a deep breath,
this next part can be disorienting."

A flash of light in Colton's mindseye caused him to flinch
backwards, but he felt himself being pulled forward at the same time. As
quickly as it had come, the light faded, leaving Colton standing in an
open glade next to Terrance. He could recognize the alien nature of the
Primal Forest all around him as he tried to gain his bearings.

"This memory is of the split between our two tribes, and it was
left by the leader of our tribe at the time," Terrance began. "In some
memories like this, you can actually feel the emotions of the person
who's memories we are seeing."

Colton watched as a man, in far more tribal wear than what Colton
had been seeing around the thicket, approached from behind a nearby
tree. Twigs snapped behind Colton and he turned to see another man
adorned in beads and purple flowers walk up to meet the first.

Instinctively, Colton stepped back to give the two individuals a
space to meet. Stopping twenty feet from one another, the man who wore

the beads spoke up first. "Tevin, it need not be like this. Please, reconsider."

Tevin, who Colton could now see was covered in scars, crept forward another step. "You do not follow the path of Tyrrek, Oren. The faithful strive to be as close to our creator as possible. You are misguided, and my people can no longer find peace among you."

Oren looked down in shame. "I fear I have failed you." Colton watched as another man stepped out of a swirling mist-like substance on the perimeter of the scene with a long scabbard laid across his forearms. Oren turned and accepted the blade with a nod before stepping closer to Tevin with the sheathed sword lying flat across his palms. "If you must go, please take his sword so that you may find your way home one day."

Tevin reached out reverently and accepted the blade. "I am grateful, though I fear we will not be coming back. We intend to sail to the east and see what Tyrrek has in store for us."

Oren nodded sadly, and Colton could feel the conflicted feelings of shame and loss passing through him. "Are you certain your mind cannot be changed, brother?"

Tevin smiled slightly as he handed the blade off to a man that Colton hadn't noticed before. "I'm afraid not. Do tell mother that I will miss her." Tevin paused, swallowing hard. "Farewell. May we meet again in the loving embrace of our father, Tyrrek."

Oren simply nodded as Tevin turned on his heel and strode away, the coast clearly visible through the trees as the memory faded to black.

Colton gasped as he pulled away from the flower and looked over at Terrance who was also catching his own breath. "That is not the same tribe my grandfather told me about," Colton breathed through heaving gulps of air.

"What do you mean?" Terrance asked gently.

"I mean, Tevin may have been misguided, but he does not represent the self-harming people I was told about," Colton elaborated, his breathing regulating.

Terrance hummed slightly, considering. "Shall we visit another memory? I think a bit more context would shed some light on your confusion."

Colton nodded and followed him to another prominent flower. This time when he entered the memories of the individual, it was easier and far less jarring.

The light fluttered away to display a much younger version of the Thicket of Memories. While the lake and trees were there, he saw far fewer homes, and the population appeared to be just on the cusp of a full civilization. The road was not nearly as crowded with people, however the most glaring difference was the lack of the massive purple tree toward the center of the valley.

Colton again took stock of his surroundings to see he was standing atop the large hill that led out of the thicket. He turned to see a group of men running up the tunnel toward where he was standing. Between them, Colton could see a man on a stretcher, his arm missing. The man appeared to be in intense pain, but was smiling proudly as the makeshift stretcher passed by at a sprint.

Colton's eyes were pulled upward as he saw a man slump into a chair. "Another one of the fanatics who think maiming themselves is the key to enlightenment went out to challenge the beasties."

A second man leaned against the doorway to what must have been the first version of the prison. "Well, one day they will all get themselves killed. I can be certain of one thing, Tyrrek would not want us hurting ourselves to be closer to him. He left for a reason. My opinion is that he left so that we could become our own people, and not base ourselves on some impossible to replicate hero."

The first man shrugged. "Maybe, I just can't stand seeing so many young ones being savaged in such a way. It fills me with a sense of dread." Colton felt the man's fear pass through him also. He found himself taking an involuntary step backward as he forced the feeling from his mind.

"You can't fix someone that is as misguided as him," the second man scoffed dismissively.

"No, you are probably right," the first one conceded, a forlorn look on his face.

The memory retreated from Colton as he found himself once again inside the grove sitting next to Terrance. "So, a group felt that they needed to replicate the injuries Tyrrek had to endure to become what he had envisioned for them?" Colton asked, his head spinning slightly from the transition.

Terrance nodded sadly. "Unfortunately, yes. From the memories I have witnessed from that section of time, they progressively escalated until it was untenable for them to stay."

"I see," Colton considered, laying his hand on the sheathed blade next to him. "Tevin and Oren were brothers, weren't they?"

"That they were!" Terrance confirmed, standing up. "Pretty close from what I have seen, but Tevin was always a misguided child and it transitioned to his adult life. Ultimately, he became the leader for what would later become known as the Tyrsworn."

"That name does sound familiar," Colton said, standing and picking up the sword. "Should I put the sword back?"

Terrance considered for a second. "I think not. That sword was given to your ancestors and unless the Keeper asks for it back, I think it should stay with you."

Colton pursed his lips recalling the stories his grandfather told him. "I'm not sure they deserved this."

"Why do you say that?"

"When they were here, they were maiming themselves in whatever way made sense at the time, but eventually they settled on ceremonially blinding their children." Colton shivered at the thought of being laid down on a stone slab as someone poured acid into his eyes. "The practice continued until my grandfather broke away and eventually destroyed them as they had become more like a cult than anything else."

"It saddens me to know our brothers and sisters from so long ago fell into such a terrifying place. Though it does seem Oren was right," Terrance said, his voice getting more upbeat.

"How's that?"

"The lost tribe found their way home," Terrance noted warmly, placing a hand on Colton's shoulder.

Colton smiled and nodded. "Thank you Terrance, you've given me much to think about. May I come visit you again if I have more questions?"

"Certainly, and please call me Terry."

"Terry it is! Now I should be going. I have someone I need to check in on," Colton said, his mind turning to the events of earlier once more.

"Right this way!" Terry walked out of the room and Colton followed, but just as he exited the room, he glanced back at the shield ceremonially caressed by the roots of the tree. Its brilliant runes pulsed once as if in farewell, then fell dark as Colton turned to leave.

The walk back was quicker than Colton remembered and before he knew it, he was shading his eyes as the afternoon sunlight made itself apparent. Bidding Terry farewell, Colton rejoined the crowded thoroughfare and made his way back to Orielle's house.

Upon reaching the humble home, Colton confidently strode up to the door, but held his hand an inch from knocking. What was he going to say? Shaking his head, Colton realized it didn't matter. He needed to face the Keeper sooner or later and explain his actions. Taking a deep breath, he rapped on the door three times.

A few moments passed, but then the door swung inward to reveal Lena standing there, her hands covered in fresh flour. "Mrs. Dawson," Colton began, "I wanted to check in on Orielle. Is she here by chance?"

Lena smiled and brushed her hands off on her apron. "Colton, dear. She's not here unfortunately, but do swing by later. I know George would still love to go over the details regarding the delegation to the Poachers."

Colton scrunched his eyebrows in surprise. "He's not angry with me?"

Lena tilted her head. "What for? You helped our little girl. How could we be upset with you in the slightest? If you're referring to her going to that prison in the first place, I'm afraid you couldn't have stopped her even if you tried."

Colton smiled slightly. "That's true enough."

Lena chuckled softly. "She got that stubbornness from me, sadly." Colton's smile widened at what an argument between these two probably looked like. "Thank you again, Colton. Though I must get back to my crust. We're having pot pies!"

Colton nodded and turned to leave. "I can't wait, see you then!"

The door closed behind him as he started to head back to the main road. A sudden crash of something breaking caught his attention as he turned his head to ascertain the source. The sound had come from around the side of the house. Unable to resist his curiosity, Colton walked around the building to see a small shack with a long sliding door that was connected to the side of the home. A yell rang out, followed by loud clatter as something shattered. Colton took a few more steps toward the shed as another, more pained scream echoed out, followed by a loud bang as the door shook from the impact. Colton took two quick steps to get to the door and heard the soft sobbing of someone inside. Immediately he could tell it was Orielle, and he reached for the handle.

A hand landed on his shoulder and he turned to see Lena smiling sweetly at him. "I've got this," she assured, gently moving herself between him and the door.

Colton nodded and took two steps back, then turned on his heels and quickly made his way in the direction of the training grounds.

Chapter Sixteen: A Mother's Love

Orielle slammed her hands down on the workbench in front of her, causing all of her tools to jump into the air a few inches. How had this become her life? She just wanted her brother to get better, and get back to what it was like before. Then Lucas had to ask for her hand...

Orielle stared at her hands as they trembled from the building rage inside her.

When she could hold it back no longer, her eyes caught on a glass vase. Impulsively, she reached out and grasped the vase in a tight grip. With a scream that sounded equally pained and angry, she threw the vase as hard as possible at the nearest surface, not caring for damage it may cause in that moment. The sound of shattering glass echoed back at her, but it wasn't enough to keep her own scream from reaching her ears. Heartbeat pounding in her chest, she reached for the nearest thing to her, and launched it with an even more guttural cry at the wall. The small object turned to powder as it connected, shattering in a shower of shrapnel. She squatted, screaming at the wooden floor, feeling her voice crack under the force.

Tears welled up in her eyes as the manic feeling built to a crescendo. Snarling, she lunged for her stool, grasping one of the legs and whipped it at the door to her workshop. With a final pain-laced bellow, she watched the stool ricochet off the wood-paneled doors and fall heavily to the ground. Her shuddering breath escaped her lips in ragged gasps as she slumped against the door. Drawing her knees up, Orielle buried her face and wept freely, as the rage left her in place of pain and deep sadness. She felt defeated and alone. Life had taken everything from her, and no matter how hard she fought to get it back, the Gods just kept moving it further away.

A small knock echoed off the door causing Orielle to cut off her tears immediately and glance wide-eyed up at the jiggling handle. "Just a moment," she managed as the panic began to set in. She couldn't be seen like this, and her workshop was a mess. Standing, she quickly moved to put the stool back as the door slid open despite her words.

Her mother poked her head into the small shed-like building and locked eyes with Orielle. "May I come in, sweetie?"

With a sniff, Orielle wiped her eyes and face, and gave a jerking nod.

Lena stepped through the door and closed it gently, taking stock of the destroyed room. "Oh, honey," she soothed as she quickly crossed to wrap Orielle in a tight embrace, her eyes welling once more. "I'm here."

Her emotions plummeted as quickly as they'd come, and Orielle slumped into her mother's arms, letting the feelings drain from her and onto Lena's shoulder. Her mind began digging through her painful memories, unbidden. From the moment she first noticed Jasper was gone, to the time she charged into that horrid cultist prison to find him curled up on the cold stone floor, unmoving. Then, a vision of Lucas approaching and getting down on one knee as he asked for her hand. A feeling of anxiety and discomfort as her traitorous mouth agreed to the engagement.

A tremor wracked her body as she heaved for breath between fits of sobbing. She no longer cared to put up an indomitable pretense. Instead, she felt like a little girl once more as her mother's embrace tightened even further. Squeezing her eyes shut, her mind pulled her to the latest in a field of failures as that creature baited her into mindlinking with it. The beast in her head had laughed as she fruitlessly tried to fend off its attacks. Then, *he* had arrived. Her scrunched up face relaxed slightly at the vision of Colton fighting off the nightmare for her sake. He too had been battered and yet he fought on, for her.

Lena pulled her back and looked her up and down. Orielle could feel herself slumping as all the fight left her. "Come, let's sit down." Orielle nodded numbly once more as she was guided to the same stool she had thrown earlier.

Her mother held her hands as Orielle began to control her breathing. "I can think of a few reasons you're feeling the way you are. Let's start with the obvious: Jasper's condition."

Orielle bristled, feeling the frustration rise immediately. "Ma, I don't want to talk about this."

Lena squeezed her hand tightly. "You may not want too, Ori, but you need to, sweetheart." Orielle opened her mouth to respond, but her mother held up a hand. "You have been trying to help for the better part of a year now, and he still remains the same. Trust me, it hurts me as deeply as it does you, and nothing would make me happier than to see both of my children whole once again." Lena paused, wiping a tear forming at the corner of her eye. "What's worse is that *both* of my children are broken. One is lost to us for reasons we don't know, but you are hurting because of the pressure you put on yourself."

"Who else, if not me? He's my brother, and I'm failing him!" Orielle yelled.

Lena leaned in and grasped either side of Orielle's head. "He's my son! Don't you think I feel your pain too?" Lowering her hands to her lap, Lena let her head droop. "I always hoped that one of these days you would come home with the answer and we could bring him back, but life is seldom that easy."

"I promise I'll find a way," Orielle vowed, taking her mother's hands into her own again.

"That's the problem, dear. You're going to kill yourself in the effort." Lena looked up and Orielle could see tears rolling gently down her face. "I can't lose both of you. I just can't."

"You won't lose me, Ma. I'm not going anywhere."

"I feel as though I've already lost you. There was a time when you wouldn't hesitate to share your pains with me, and now here you are hiding in this shed, alone."

Orielle slumped her head. She had felt alone, as if this were her burden and hers alone. She hadn't really considered how her mother felt about Jasper's condition. "I'm sorry. I just wanted to save him, for all of us," she whispered.

"We will save him together," Lena proposed, smiling through her tear-streaked face. "Please, let us be on this journey with you. We miss you, and Jasper wouldn't want you losing yourself along the way."

"How? How can we save him?"

Lena shook her head sadly. "I honestly don't know, but I believe we'll find a way to do it as long as we stay together, as a family."

Orielle couldn't think of any way to save Jasper, but she wouldn't stop trying. However, she had been feeling very alone, and that had caused her to hide where she used to be so open. Jasper's condition had changed them all, but Orielle had become an angry and depressive version of herself. She couldn't remember the last time she saw any of her friends and did something other than hunt down the cult that took her brother from her. When was the last time she had been home and had a family dinner? Orielle felt her eyes burn with fresh tears as she realized just how far she had pushed herself from her family. What was she doing everything for, if not for them?

"I'm sorry, Ma. I lost my way, but I want to come back home," she apologized, a barely audible whisper.

"Oh my baby girl," Lena sighed, pulling her into a hug. "We've always been right here."

The two of them held each other for a long moment before Lena pulled away once more, taking a deep breath and composing herself. "Now, let's talk about the reason you are so afraid to come home."

Orielle's heart picked up in rhythm as she considered not the reason, but the person who had her so stressed since returning. "I feel like I can't avoid him."

"Well, he is your fiancé. So, it would stand to reason that he would want to be near you," Lena reasoned, nodding her head.

"I know…"

"Why did you say yes if you didn't want to be with him?" Lena asked.

"I don't know. I guess I just figured you and Pa would consider it a good match, and I am getting old, so…"

"Oh, Ori! Your father and I had been sending that boy packing for years when he asked for your hand. We told him that it was completely up to you, and we stand by that now. You are only twenty-seven years old, and you have plenty of time to meet the right person," Lena counseled as she placed a hand on Orielle's knee.

"Then, you won't be disappointed if I…don't marry him?" Orielle asked hesitantly.

Lena pulled back in shock. "Me? Disappointed in you for not marrying a man you don't love? Honey, I would be more disappointed if you went knowingly into a loveless marriage." Her mother smiled, a bright warm feeling swelling in Orielle's chest as she did so. "As you know, I am originally from the Thicket of Rivers. I never once believed I would leave. In fact, I had quite a few young men who lived there that were determined to keep me there. However, none of them made me feel anything. When I saw your father at the Thicket of Gatherings, I fell for him immediately. He was never the strongest man, but he was gentle and kind. He left me wondering what it would be like to leave the place I had always known." Lena smiled at the memory. "He was very courageous, your Pa, and even stood up to a group of boys who were trying to win my affections. Though truthfully, what made me get on the next train here was the feeling of my heart skipping a beat when he first looked into my eyes."

Orielle smiled. "He was a charmer, huh?"

Lena laughed. "That he was, and still is!" Lena turned to look at Orielle again, her face more serious. "That is what I want for you, Orielle. You deserve the happiness of love, and to feel it from another person.

Whoever he is, I want him to make you feel safe and loved every single day of your life. Does Lucas do that for you?"

Orielle thought for a moment, but she already knew the answer. She paused now because she couldn't help but return to that last moment in the prison as she knelt on the cold floor while Colton held her.

"No," she affirmed with finality.

"Then you need to let the boy go, honey."

Orielle nodded, feeling lighter for the first time in months. "I will, Ma. Thank you for coming to check on me, and I'm sorry I've been so distant."

Lena stood and waved her hand dismissively. "You don't need to thank me, dear. Just come have dinner with us every now and again." Walking to the door, Lena stopped and turned around. "Oh, and I should tell you that we are having pot pies tonight."

"Sounds delicious," Orielle grinned, her stomach groaning as she thought of it.

"And..." Lena continued, dramatically, "Mister Cobb is going to be there. In fact, I had to stop him from coming in here himself. Told me he wanted to check in on you and make sure you were okay. Very sweet, wouldn't you say?" she teased with a wink.

Orielle chuckled, but couldn't stop her face from blushing. "Yeah, he is very sweet."

Lena placed a hand on the door and slid it open a crack, but paused. "Orielle?"

"Yes?"

"I am so proud of the woman you've become," Lena praised warmly as she walked out of the workshop.

Orielle smiled as the door slid closed. She wasn't alone, and it was time she stopped acting like it. She would help save Jasper, and she would do it with her family by her side. A feeling of contentment washed over her as she took a cleansing breath and looked around the room.

"What a mess..." she sighed.

Chapter Seventeen: Delegation's Deliberations

After leaving Orielle's house, Colton made his way to the training yard in an effort to meet back up with Imbrose and Ember. He arrived to see them in the midst of an intense sparring session where they seemed to be holding their own ground against one another. After a few more passes, Imbrose managed to gain the upper hand by simply waiting until Ember slipped slightly. Capitalizing on the accident, Imbrose swept her other foot and pinned her shoulders to the ground in the same motion. After exchanging a quick kiss, they both turned to see Colton observing the bout and quickly oriented themselves.

"Colton!" Ember squeaked, brushing off her robes. "I thought you were going to be at the grove?"

Colton smiled, the air growing heavy with embarrassment. "You guys are going to have to get comfortable around me with this new dynamic."

Imbrose threw an arm around Ember's shoulders. "You heard him, baby! Let's just do it right here and now!" he announced as he leaned in for another kiss.

Ember recoiled, a smirk crossing her face. "You wish, mister."

Colton laughed and crossed over to them. "That's perhaps one thing I don't need you getting comfortable doing in front of me."

"Suit yourself," Imbrose shrugged, holding up his hands. "So, what did you learn?"

Colton's smile faltered as over the next thirty minutes he retold the story of the tribes separating and the reasons for which it happened. Then, the mood took an even darker tone as he explained the event in the prison and the subsequent encounter with Lucas.

"Unnerving to say the least," Ember said, placing a hand on her hip.

"No kidding, but then I saw Jasper at the grove and he gave me some creepy smile that reminded me of the creature we had to fight," Colton shuddered, rubbing his forehead. "I'm beginning to think I'm losing my mind."

"No, I think that perhaps we are in the middle of something that is about to kick off. Can't say I'm enthused about that idea," Imbrose muttered, pursing his lips.

"I can't shake the feeling that we're supposed to be here," Colton worried.

"Maybe…" Ember contemplated. "If they need our help to guard their own people, they probably can't muster any sort of response to a full scale invasion."

Colton lowered his hand at the word. "Invasion? What do you mean?"

Ember shrugged. "What else would you call it when a nightmare monster attacks you in your head?"

"Fair enough," Colton muttered.

"Whatever it's called, we need to put it down in the real world," Imbrose said, drawing a line across his neck. "Something tells me it's not actually dead, no matter how many pieces you cut it into."

Colton hadn't had time to consider if the creature was well and truly gone. It would stand to reason that it was in fact still very much alive and well, given he only fought a version of it inside Orielle's mind. However, he genuinely felt that if he had died in that place, he himself would be dead, or at the very least, consumed. The thought sent chills up and down his body.

"I wouldn't even know where to start looking for such a monster," Colton lamented, shaking his head.

"Well, maybe Orielle learned something before you jumped in to help," Imbrose suggested. "Have you had a chance to ask her what happened?"

Colton looked down, remembering the weeping he heard on the other side of that door. "No, she was pretty shaken by the incident. Before I could talk to her, we were interrupted by Lucas and she left with her parents."

"Hmm…you said they want us to come back for dinner? Maybe we should ask her then?" Ember asked.

Colton bit his lip. "I don't know. She seemed pretty upset about it. I'm not very inclined to push her on it."

"Oh, come on! Orielle is made of tough stock," Ember scolded, smirking. "It'll take more than some creepy snake to send her running."

"I appreciate that, Ember!" Orielle's voice sounded from behind them as they turned to look at where Colton had come from. Approaching a jog, Orielle smiled as she stopped next to Colton. "It means a lot coming from you!"

Colton took a tentative step toward her, starting to raise his hand before thinking better of it. "How are you doing?"

Orielle met his eyes and nodded. "Like Ember said, it's going to take more than that to scare me off. If anything, it finally gave me something to chase after, so it wasn't a completely stupid thing to do. Most importantly, it gave me a name."

Colton raised an eyebrow. "Oh? You know what that thing is called?"

Orielle's eyes took on a glazed over look. "He called himself Va'Rul, and he plans to consume the memories of our people."

"Well, for a creature that eats memories, it sure chose the right group to go after," Imbrose commented passively.

"You're telling me," Orielle began, "but Ma sent me to let you guys know dinner was ready."

"We'd better be off then!" Colton said. "Wouldn't want to keep her waiting."

Orielle smiled and turned around to start walking back. "No wonder she likes you."

Colton kept a small distance behind Orielle, who was walking next to Ember, unsure what he should say to her despite having so many questions. He wondered whether or not he should mention Lucas' voice or his interaction with Jasper. Surely, she'd want to know, but would it do more harm than good? She had just come through something horrible, even if she was putting on a brave face.

Overwhelmed by conflicting emotions, Colton picked up his pace to catch up to them. "So, do you think you can show me a thing or two sometime?" Colton heard Orielle's voice as she turned to Ember.

"Sure! Though I will remind you that my techniques are pretty advanced. And while I can show you some basics so you can keep someone at bay as you gain your bearings, it is no substitute for real training," Ember said, noticing Colton's approach.

"Colton!" Orielle greeted, her voice a bit too high.

"I need to corral his highness back there." Ember gestured to Imbrose who had gotten distracted by a group of kids who began following him. "Imbrose, come on!" she called as she ran toward his now impromptu game of tag.

Orielle giggled as he fell on the ground dramatically, letting a child no older than five catch him. "He's quite the little ham, isn't he?"

Colton smirked as more kids piled onto him and Imbrose flailed, much to their delight. "Always has been..." He turned to look at Orielle, who seemed genuinely better than last he had seen her. "How are you doing, really?"

"Hmm, me? Oh, I'm much better now. Just needed to remember what really matters."

"I'm glad. I was worried about you."

"Were you now?" Orielle asked playfully. "Ma told me how she had to basically chase you away from my workshop."

"Wh-what? N-no! I was just trying to make sure you were okay!" Colton fumbled out the words as Orielle's face broke into a bright smile.

"I'm kidding," she teased, punching his shoulder lightly. Then she cupped her hands at her waist. "I appreciate you caring…It…well, it means a lot to me."

"Of course…" Colton answered awkwardly.

"I wanted to thank you properly for your help at the prison–"

"It was nothing," Colton interrupted.

Orielle smiled sweetly. "It was everything. If you hadn't put yourself on the line to help me, I don't think I would be here right now."

"Anyone would have done it," Colton countered quietly.

"But you did," Orielle insisted, placing a hand on his arm. "So, I wanted to do something for you, since I know you wouldn't ask for yourself." Colton swallowed, his mind trying to imagine what she could be talking about. "Do you remember how I told you about the mage that lives in our village?"

"Oh, yeah. Her name is Arcadia, right?" Colton asked.

"Yep, that's her! Well anyway, she thinks she can get your family over here if someone on their end can draw the sigils she used for her transportation circle."

Colton's eyes widened as her words set in. "You mean…"

"I mean, I think we can help skip the months of boat travel, and bring our tribes together properly," Orielle offered.

Colton paused for a moment, the mere possibility of seeing his family again filled him with unbridled delight, and gratitude. "Orielle, I…" He let the sentence drift away.

"It's the least I could do! You saved me afterall," she cut in, her hand falling from his arm.

Colton caught her hand and held it. "Thank you. This means the world to me." He brought her hand to his lips and kissed it gently, then released it.

Orielle's eyes widened in surprise, then she giggled. "It's not a problem. I'm just happy I was able to help."

"Woof!" Imbrose came panting up to them with Ember in tow. "Those kids of yours are making me feel old."

Orielle held Colton's eyes for a second longer before she turned to look at Imbrose. "They seem to have taken a liking to you!" Looking up, Orielle found the sun in the reddened sky. "We really should pick up the pace, we might already be late."

With that, she turned and started jogging away from the others. "Did my eyes deceive me or did you kiss her hand?" Imbrose asked.

"It was a thank you, nothing more," Colton defended sharply.

"Uh huh...Well she's quick, so we'd better get moving," Imbrose said, pointing at her shrinking figure.

The three of them hurried to catch up as they rounded a group of houses to see a large open circular space with long spiral patterns of various rocks extended out from the center. Along the sides of the clearing, multiple tables had been set up, and Colton made for the table that already had people sitting around it.

The people around the table were mostly familiar to him with the exception of three new individuals. There was a grizzled old soldier-type man who stood immediately as they approached the table. Another more roguish male glanced over his shoulder and nodded while raising his mug. On the far side of the table, a beautiful blonde woman in an elegant green gown stood and bowed slightly.

"I'd like to introduce you to our three new members to our delegation. This is Cartwright, Toku, and June." The Keeper gestured to the soldier, cloaked man, and woman in turn. "This is Colton, Imbrose, and Ember. They have agreed to help us get there and back safely."

"A genuine pleasure, sir," Cartwright said, shaking each of their hands with a firm grip.

"Welcome aboard," Toku greeted, not bothering to rise.

"Thank you for your courage! I feel safer knowing you all will be there!" June said brightly with a curtsy.

"We're happy to help," Colton replied, nodding to everyone at the table and taking a seat.

The Keeper nodded as the party exchanged introductions. "Let's not waste time then, we–"

Footsteps approaching from behind caused the Keeper to cut himself off. Colton turned to see Friend walking up to the table with a massive warhammer draped across his shoulders. "I hope I'm not late," he commented.

"Friend! You came!" Orielle exclaimed.

"I always come when asked!" Friend affirmed proudly.

Imbrose stifled a snicker and Ember glared at him.

"You are most welcome! We would love to have your flames with us for this adventure," Colton said.

"Thank you!" Friend said as he moved to take the last seat available.

"Wonderful! Now that we're all here, I'd like to go over what our plans are for this excursion," the Keeper began. "Ultimately, it's time we see these poachers out of our forest, and if possible I would like to avoid bloodshed."

"And if they protest?" Toku asked quietly.

"That, my friend, is why we are bringing all of you with us," George allowed.

That caught Colton's attention. "We? Are you planning on joining us, Keeper?"

George turned and looked at Colton, a grave expression on his face. "I wouldn't be much of a leader if I refused to face the troubles that face my people, now would I?"

"I meant no offense," Colton corrected quickly. "I simply worry for your safety."

"Well, I happen to have a very strong opinion of you all. So, I suspect I will be just as safe out there as I am right now," the Keeper answered with a smile. "Though, I won't be the only one in need of your protection. Miss June will also be joining us as our healer just in case something does happen."

June nodded happily. "I'm honored to be of service, Keeper."

George nodded to her, then turned to look around the table. "We've received word that their current stronghold is three days to the east. If we move quickly and camp in the low hanging branches of the bigger trees, I think we can make it in that timeframe." George paused, taking a sip from his mug. "My intent is to see what they want, and most importantly, find out if they have anything to do with the rising cult activity in the forest."

"Do you think they are involved, sir?" Cartwright asked.

"I can't say, but they have become more active at the same time. So, if they aren't directly connected, there must be something affecting both parties," George said. "Besides, us leaving now gives the tribe time to plan our Welcome Festival."

"Welcome Festival?" Colton asked.

"Yes, when we have new guests or permanent residents join us, we like to welcome them with a festival to show our happiness at their arrival. Six days should be plenty of time for the setup."

"Sir, you do not need to throw a party for us," Ember argued gently.

"But of course we do! It's tradition! It's also a lot of fun, and I think our people could use a bit of fun," George disagreed.

"I'm always excited for a party!" Imbrose said, smiling.

"That's the spirit," George said, raising his glass for Imbrose to toast against.

"Here we are!" Colton watched as Lena, seemingly coming out of nowhere, placed a large bowl with a crispy crust in front of him. "I hope you enjoy it." The aroma of gravy and meat mixed with veggies wafted into his nose and warmed his soul. He smiled happily and closed his eyes excited for the meal to come.

"Thank you, Mrs. Dawson," Colton said as he picked up a fork and broke through the outer crust.

"My pleasure, dear!" she dismissed as she passed out bowls to the others around the table.

A thought struck Colton. "Oh, I forgot to mention that the other prisoner in the cells up by the gate believes he has information that could help us with this mission."

"Oh? What did he say?" George asked.

"He wouldn't say, just that he wanted me to pass that along to you," Colton replied, popping a forkful of gravy-soaked meat into his mouth.

George pursed his lips. "Well, I suppose I should hear him out. He was attacked by the poachers in the forest." Colton caught some movement from the corner of his eye and turned to see Lucas marching toward their table. "Very well, tomorrow morning we will meet at the gate and begin our journey east. Any objections?"

The table went silent aside from a few grunts of assent.

"Orielle." Lucas' voice seemed normal now, maybe it was just Colton's imagination afterall. "Can I speak with you privately?"

Colton turned to look at Orielle without acknowledging Lucas. She was looking into her food with a downcast face. Lena silently walked up and placed a hand on her shoulder. Orielle's face relaxed and she looked up at her mother and nodded. Face growing sterner, she stood and walked around to where Lucas was standing and the two of them walked off some distance.

Colton couldn't help but watch them as they finally stopped and began conversing in hushed tones. He didn't need to be involved in the conversation to know Lucas wasn't happy with the direction it was taking.

"Isn't that right, Colton?" Joel's voice pulled him from his observations.

"I'm sorry, what was that?" Colton asked.

"I said that you're really starting to get a handle on your powers, and I suspect you're starting to have less side effects."

"Oh, yes. I have found it easier to swap between myself and my illusion. Especially when we were fighting the creature in Orielle's head."

"Thank you for helping her, Colton. She can be impulsive at times," George sighed.

"Think nothing of it, sir," Colton dismissed. "I'm just glad I was able to be there when she—"

A loud slap echoed through the air from the direction that Lucas and Orielle were standing. Everyone's head turned to see Orielle cradling the left side of her face and Lucas' hand raised. At once, Colton stood along with Imbrose, Joel, Friend, Ember, and George.

Colton took two steps, then teleported directly to Orielle's side, catching Lucas' hand as he swung for a second time.

"Don't hurt him." Orielle's proud voice echoed from underneath her palm. Straightening herself, she looked Lucas in the eyes, her face already turning a bright shade of scarlet, and a small line of blood dripped down from a split in her lip. "What happened to you, Lucas?"

Lucas' lip twitched and he tried to rip his hand away from Colton, who held firm, staring at him intensely. "Let me go," he snarled.

Colton didn't respond, his own rage barely contained at the sight of Orielle's face. "Let him go, Colton. He's not himself."

Colton slowly relaxed his grip on Lucas' wrist and took a step closer. "Do that again and I'll take your hand, excuses or not," he swore, his voice even.

Lucas narrowed his eyes and stepped into Colton's space, neither backing down. The silence dragged on until Lucas' eyes broke from Colton's and looked behind him. Friend's towering figure shadowed them as the heat from the fire crackling in his hand encroached on the confrontation.

"Lucas, you should leave," Orielle suggested quietly.

At the sound of her voice, Lucas looked at her, his eyes softening ever so slightly. Colton watched as the firm demeanor of Lucas cracked and a small tear formed at the corner of his eye. "I'm sorry." Then he turned and ran off into the settling dusk.

June and Lena rushed to Orielle's side and began fussing over her lip and cheek as Colton's fury slowly calmed. "I can't believe Lucas did that!" Lena stammered, stunned.

"That wasn't Lucas," Orielle stated with finality, her words causing a heavy lump to form in Colton's chest.

Chapter Eighteen: The Sorceress of New Eradin

A silence fell over the small crowd around Orielle as the words left her lips. June was already channeling some kind of energy from her palm into Orielle's swollen face as Ember moved to Orielle, holding out a napkin for her split lip.

With a nod, Orielle took the napkin and pressed it to her face. "Thank you, but I'll be fine."

"Why would he hit you?" Ember asked in concern.

Orielle sighed and looked at her mother. "I told him we weren't going to work out." The admission seemed to take a large weight from her chest as she took another deep breath.

To Colton, it almost seemed like someone who had been submerged in water for too long and finally got their first breath of fresh air. He could still feel the rage at what he just witnessed roiling below the surface. Love made people crazy, that was true, but there were no excuses to strike those you love. His thoughts turned once again to the distorted voice he heard from Lucas back in the prison. The longer he considered it, the more sure he became that it wasn't his imagination. Has Lucas been infected by this Va'Rul?

"What did you mean when you said that wasn't Lucas?" Colton asked quietly.

"He was always so kind until he asked for my hand in marriage. After that, he became different." Orielle waved June away from her with a grateful nod as she rubbed her cheek that was much less swollen than seconds ago. "It feels much better, thank you, June."

June's face twitched up into a small smile. "I'm glad I could help."

"I'll give him some time to calm down then see if he wants to talk. Something else must be on his mind," Orielle defended, as she surveyed the group gathered around her. "Honestly, I'm okay. Please, go finish your food."

Hesitantly, everyone began to make their way back to the table, but as Colton turned to follow suit, he felt a hand close around his wrist. Looking back, he could see Orielle smiling brightly at him.

"Thank you for not hurting him, and thank you for stopping him," she thanked shyly as the group filtered away from them.

Colton felt the rage he had been holding onto melt away as he looked into her eyes. "Of course, I couldn't just stand by."

Orielle blushed. "I'm learning that about you, Colton."

Colton chuckled, then leaned closer to inspect her lip. "Looks pretty minor, but does it hurt much?"

Orielle shook her head, making no effort to increase the distance between them. "Just stings a bit." She pursed her lips. "After dinner, why don't you come with me to Arcadia's house? I think she might need some information if we're going to get your family over here."

Colton smiled, realizing just how close he had leaned in and pulled back slightly. "I look forward to it. Are you sure you're okay?"

Orielle nodded, but Colton could see a small wince as she squinted her eyes. She then let go of his wrist and moved back over to the table, taking the seat to his left this time.

The energy around the table picked back up as they discussed the activities that would occur at the festival. It seemed the delay was an abnormal circumstance, as normally it would have already been prepared by the time new visitors arrived. Everyone laughed and joked, including

181

Orielle, who seemed more alive than she had been since Colton had met her. The only exception was June, who kept glancing in the way Lucas had stormed off with a worried look in her eyes.

As the final bowls were cleared of the delicious meal Lena had prepared, people began to excuse themselves to prepare for the trip the following morning with June being the first to leave. George stood up and gave everyone one last round of thanks before seeing himself and Lena off, no doubt to spend one more evening together prior to leaving. Eventually only Imbrose, Ember, Orielle, and Colton remained at the table.

"Shall we head off to see Arcadia before it gets too much later?" Colton asked Orielle.

She nodded and stood from the table. "She's not too far from here!"

Colton turned to Imbrose and Ember. "You two should come too. After all, it's your mothers who may be able to help us."

Imbrose shuddered visibly. "Wait, you want me to ask *her* for help?"

Ember rolled her eyes. "Oh, come on Imbrose, your mom is lovely. I could actually use some advice on how to handle you."

A devious smile spread across Imbrose's lips. "He said *mothers*, as in yours too."

Ember's eyes widened for a moment but she covered it up quickly. "I heard him! I can't wait to see my mother again." Her voice wavered just enough to betray her nervousness.

"I'm sure…" Imbrose said, the smile never faltering on his face.

Colton shook his head at the two of them and got up to follow Orielle as the two of them kept exchanging jabs about each other's mothers.

"Are they really that bad?" Orielle asked tentatively.

Colton chuckled. "Not in the slightest. Their parents are heroes where we come from, so the two of them feel intense pressure to fill those shoes. Honestly, Aunt Imryth, who's Imbrose's mom, is one of the

182

sweetest women I've ever met. And Meredith is just a very intimidating woman."

"Intimidating, huh? How so?"

"Well, she's easily the most powerful enchanter the world has ever seen." Colton pursed his lips. "Come to think of it, I'm not sure about that anymore. The Archipelago is pretty small, and really only has one major city per continent."

"I'd love to hear about where you're from."

Colton smiled, Imbrose and Ember's bickering still constant in the background. "There are four continents, but they're more like oversized islands. In the north lies the Kingdom of Thebalar which is where Imbrose is originally from. His mother is a princess and should have been the queen, but she turned it down to marry Imbrose's dad."

"Sounds like a romantic story."

"To be honest, I don't know the whole of it. Just that Imbrose's dad, Lucius, was found shipwrecked after his pirate crew abandoned him. Aunt Imryth took him aboard and he never stopped following her. Eventually, she let him marry her."

Orielle laughed out loud. "Let him? You make it sound like she was settling."

Colton smirked. "Not at all! Lucius was a heck of a catch; Aunt Imryth was just a bit fixated on magic. Still is, but now she likes spending most of her time as a mother and wife. From what I understand, that still includes a lot of travel and adventures, but Lucius is quite the far traveler himself."

Orielle looked around nervously. "I've never seen anyone who looks like Imbrose before."

Colton nodded. "He's a bit of a marvel where we come from too. As far as I know, it has something to do with a deal his father made with certain powers to survive after his shipwreck."

"So, his parents don't look like him?" Orielle asked.

"I mean, you can definitely see the resemblance, but neither of them are blue or have horns. Imbrose is unique in that way."

"Interesting... Does the deal affect Imbrose at all, or is it just his appearance?" Orielle asked.

"Just appearance, from what I've seen. Though, there was this one time he..." Colton trailed off.

"He what?" Orielle asked, her curiosity piqued.

Colton pursed his lips, wondering if he should share. Deciding it was probably just nonsense anyway, continued on. "He said that red dagger he has sometimes talks to him, but you know how he is. Besides, he was crazy drunk when he told me that, so it's probably nothing."

Orielle narrowed her eyes. "Hmm, did you ever ask him about it again?"

Colton looked up into the dimming sky. "I don't think so...Come to think of it, I mostly forgot about that until I just told you." Colton shrugged. "That was years ago though, and he hasn't mentioned anything since."

"I see... Sounds like he has a very interesting story. Maybe I'll ask him about it one of these next few days."

"Good luck! You have to catch him in the right mood for that kind of conversation. I still think he keeps certain things from me, but who am I to pry? He's like my brother, and I'd trust him with my life, but if he needs to keep a secret, I just have to trust him."

"True..." Orielle went silent considering. "Alright, here we are!"

Before them was a similar house to all of the others around the village, but with a few distinct differences. The first that caught Colton's attention was the many hanging herbs all around the outside of the building. Additionally, there were distinct glyphs carved in the walls that seemed to give off a faint undulating glow. As the party stepped up to the door, it swung open without Orielle needing to knock. A faint fog drifted out of the opening as the four of them arched their necks to see inside while the door continued to crack open. The whole experience left a sense of the old horror stories Colton used to pry out of his grandmother.

"Come in then," an elegant voice said from within.

Without so much as a second of hesitation, Orielle stepped within the darkened interior. Sighing in resignation, Colton followed in behind to see the darkness of the space dissipate to a fully lit room. For some reason, the inside must not be visible from the outside. As his eyes adjusted to the now extremely bright space, Colton tried to take in his surroundings. All along the walls were the same sigils as outside, but there were far more of them. Some pulsed a dull purple while some were red and others shown in a bluish tint. Blinking a few more times, Colton's eyes finally settled on the home's owner. She was a thin, dark-skinned woman with a long black robe and a pointy, wide-brimmed hat. She was every bit the witch her creepy home suggested she was. Adding to the fairytale Colton was walking into, she also gave off a sense of agelessness, like she was much older than she looked. Her piercing lime green eyes scanned the group quickly before directing her attention at Orielle, a smile splitting her face to reveal perfect teeth.

"Orielle, my dear. Is this the man you spoke about earlier?" The woman's voice was like honey, causing Colton to instinctively smile. The feeling unnerved him deeply, and he took a small step back.

"Oh, Arcadia…Must you keep the runes lit for this meeting?" Orielle chastised lightly.

Arcadia stuck her bottom lip out pouting. "Can't a girl have a little fun?" With a snap, the runes all fell dark, and Colton felt an overwhelming weight fade away. "There!"

Colton shook his head trying to shake off the strange feeling. "H-hello Miss Arcadia. Thank you for helping me with bringing my family over."

Arcadia waved a hand at him and walked to a nearby door. "Just Arcadia is fine, handsome, and think nothing of it. I'm just excited to meet your mage friends from where you come from." The room fell silent as Arcadia whispered a few words and the door in front of her began to swing open. "Now, what I need from you is something that belongs to the mage you think can assist in the teleportation."

Colton looked over his shoulder at Imbrose who sighed and pulled off the cloak he always wore. "It won't be damaged, will it?" Imbrose asked as he held the cloak close.

"No, no, of course not. It is just a way to initiate contact with them. And what is their name?" Arcadia asked as she held out a hand for the cloak.

"Her name's Imryth, and she's my mum," Imbrose hedged, handing the cloak over hesitantly.

"Very well! Follow me." The four trailed after Arcadia as she walked into the next room.

In the center of the room was a large pit of black sand, and the whole space smelled of a mixture of burned incense. Colton watched as Arcadia walked to the edge of the sand pit and smelled the cloak deeply.

"Woah, that's weird," Imbrose mumbled. "I haven't washed that thing in weeks."

Arcadia's eyes shot open as she stared at the cloak in disbelief. "My, my. Your mother is quite the powerful sorceress. The spell that is placed on this cloak is one I couldn't begin to understand. This will do nicely." With reverence, she placed the cloak on the ground next to the edge of the pit and began muttering words in a different language, while simultaneously contorting her fingers in irregular paterns.

The sand began to swirl as it built into a mound then grew into a pile ten feet tall. The entire time, the sand swirled in a circle, making everyone raise their hands to protect from the granular projectiles. Arcadia's chanting reached a crescendo as she brought her hands together in a clap and shouted Imryth's name. All at once, the sand froze in the air and hovered there as if suspended by some invisible force. Suddenly, the sand pulled into the center of the pit, forming a condensed pillar of black. With jerking movements, the pillar began to shape itself into the silhouette of a tall, proud woman. Her long coat stretched to the back of her knees as the leather armor underneath flashed into visibility and the figure made of sand turned to look around the room.

"You had better have a good reason for having my son's cloak, conjurer." The woman's voice was crisp and laced with a threatening tone. However, Colton could still hear the calming voice of Imryth beneath the inherent danger there.

"Sorceress Imryth," Arcadia began, bowing deeply to the sandy figure of Imbrose's mother. "Your son is safe and so are his friends. It is for them that I contact you now."

Imryth's sandy eyes glanced around the interior, seemingly searching for something. "Why should I trust you? Your wards are preventing my vision from seeing you or your surroundings."

Arcadia's eyes looked back up at Imryth in concern. "Apologies, mistress. I simply have these shields in place to protect myself from those who would see me harmed."

Imryth's hand raised as she gestured in quick succession. "I will give you one more chance to prove you are actually helping my son, or I will decimate your wards."

Arcadia quickly beckoned for Imbrose to join her, who walked slowly to the woman's outstretched hand. As soon as Imbrose's hand touched Arcadia's, Imryth dropped her hand and a smile broke her face. "Imbrose, sweetie! How are you? Are you hurt?"

The vast difference in the tone of her voice caused a smile to drift over Colton's face. "Hi, Mum. I'm fine, and no, I'm not hurt. Arcadia is trying to help us get Colton's family over here."

"Oh! Colton's there?" Imryth's form shifted as she leaned forward as if trying to look for something a long ways away. "Does that mean you found what you were looking for?"

Imbrose nodded. "Yes, Mum, and we need your help."

"Of course, dear! What can I do to help?"

"Are you able to help Arcadia open a portal long enough for Colton's family to pass through?" Imbrose asked.

"I'm certain it's possible. I would need her to remove her wards and it may take some time to perfect the connection. Not to mention I would need to get all of the Cobbs in one place, and they like to travel."

187

"Well, we are leaving tomorrow for upwards of a week anyway," Imbrose informed.

"I think I can work with that." The sand sculpture of Imryth raised a hand to her face and rubbed her chin as if thinking. "Arcadia, dear, are you still there?"

"I'm here, mistress," Arcadia intoned.

"I'll need to know the incantation you spoke when you created your teleportation circle."

Imbrose sighed deeply. "It sounds like you have a lot to talk about then!" He started to pull his hand away from Arcadia's.

"Just a moment, mister." Imryth's motherly tone caught everyone's attention, and Imbrose stopped pulling his hand away. "When I get there, you had better tell me everything."

"You plan to come here?" Imbrose asked, his voice rising an octave.

"But of course! There's no way I will miss out on an opportunity to see you, Ember, and Colton. Things have been rather boring since you left."

Imbrose closed his eyes tightly in frustration. "Mother, we have things handled here."

Imryth's form pulled back as if offended. "I would expect nothing less! Don't worry, sweetie, we will only stay as long as we need to make sure everyone makes it over safely."

"We?" Ember asked, a little too loudly.

"Yes, *we*. Is that you, Ember?" Imryth squinted once more, trying to make out where the voice came from. "Your mother is the best enchantress I have ever met. If there is anyone who can make the spell stick, it's your mom."

Arcadia coughed slightly, pulling everyone's focus. She was sweating heavily as the spell to keep talking to Imryth was draining her quickly.

"Right, well, Mum, we look forward to seeing you, but we really should be going now." Imbrose nodded at Arcadia's unspoken request to hurry things along.

"Oh, alright. Be safe out there kids. I love you all!"

"We love you too, Mum."

With a sigh of relief, Arcadia dropped the spell and the sand dropped into a heap back into the pit.

"Sorry about that," Imbrose grimaced as he let go of her hand. "We haven't spoken with her in almost a year."

Arcadia huffed, trying to catch her breath as she waved a hand at him. "It's no problem, but now I need to work." She straightened and looked toward Orielle. "You lot need to shoo! I can't have her thinking I'm some two-bit magician."

Colton started shuffling toward the door as Arcadia began to herd them out of her house. "Thank you again for your help, Arcadia."

"Yes, yes. Off you go!" she nagged, finally pushing them through the front threshold. "Be safe," she managed before slamming the door in their faces.

The four of them stood there in silence, staring at the wooden door before Orielle spoke. "I don't know what you're complaining about! Your mother is great."

Imbrose rolled his eyes and began walking away from the house. "I'm sure you will be great friends."

"You think so?" Orielle asked, her excitement plain to hear.

Imbrose shook his head, a small chuckle escaping him.

The four of them walked back to their respective homes to bed down for the evening, with Orielle trying to pry out more information about Ember and Imbrose's mothers the entire way.

Chapter Nineteen: Moonlit Conversation

T he following morning, the group met at the entrance to the thicket. Colton looked around to see Imbrose, Ember, Orielle, Friend, Cartwright, Toku, Joel, and June all looking down the hill slightly to where the Keeper could be seen saying goodbye to his wife Lena. The two embraced and shared a kiss, the love they shared evident to any onlooker. Colton's eyes drifted to his right, spotting Orielle watching her parents. She had a small smile on her face as they broke apart and George moved to meet with the rest of the group. The Keeper carried a scabbarded shortsword and a pack just like the rest of them. It seemed he wouldn't be asking anyone to carry his stuff for him. Behind him, Lena gave the group a big wave and blew a kiss in Orielle's direction.

Lucas still hadn't been seen since he slapped Orielle the day before, and if Colton was being honest, it left him feeling unsettled not knowing where he was. Though even after such a terrible altercation, Orielle seemed better for it and had a general air of happiness about her. All morning she had been joyfully discussing the trek that was ahead of them as if they were leaving to go on a vacation. However, Colton could tell she wasn't entirely happy leaving the thicket with Jasper still in his current state. He vowed he would find something to help Jasper when they got back home.

Home...the word filled itself in so easily now, and he still couldn't believe his eyes as he surveyed the valley below him. This place was just a fantasy only a month ago. After only a short time, it was home, and by the time he got back, he would be able to show his grandfather just how real it was. The thought brought a smile to his face as a small lump formed in his throat. Swallowing, Colton cleared the emotion away as George drew up to the group.

"Thank you all again for joining me on this expedition," George said, looking around the party. "Let's watch each other's back, and by the grace of Tyrrek we will all return safely."

Everyone nodded their assent and they all moved through the tunnel leading out. Traveling with such a large party would have given Colton pause in the past with how attracted the beasts seemed to be to bigger numbers. However, within the first two hours of leaving, they stumbled upon a large, three-taloned track in the mud, and Toku made it clear why he had been included on this adventure.

"Looks like the albino one," he said simply, as he knelt next to the massive footprint. "She's headed the same way as us. We'll need to be careful if we don't want to attract her attention."

Joel stepped up next to him. Both of them could have comfortably laid down in the impression. "How old is it, do you think?"

Toku clicked his tongue, thinking. "Day or two. It's hard to tell, but judging by her stride, she was moving quickly."

"Not to interrupt, but who or what is the albino one?" Ember asked nervously, scanning the surrounding forest.

"Yeah," added Imbrose, an obvious look of discomfort on his face. "And how do you know its color based on its footprint?"

Orielle turned to address the two of them. "She's the queen of the southern forests, and anyone who survives an encounter can never forget her ghostly white hide. Biggest beastie we have this side of the Andromedus, and the smartest too," Orielle explained, smirking.

"So…why are you smiling? Isn't that a reason to be afraid?" Imbrose questioned, his eyes widening at Orielle's smile.

"Grex'xi is perfectly pleasant to get along with as long as you don't threaten her domain or her young."

191

"You named her? Like a pet?" Imbrose asked incredulously.

"Actually, she told us herself," George corrected quietly as he pushed past the group to look into the distance. "We help her keep the peace in the forest and in turn she lets us pass through without her ire."

"Something must have riled her up to bring her so close to the thicket," Cartwright deduced.

"Maybe..." Toku intoned. "Either way, we need to head this way or lose a day of travel. Joel, maybe you should scout ahead a bit." Joel nodded and began summoning a portal in front of him. A moment later he stepped through and was gone. "Let's keep moving, but be on your toes."

The group picked up the pace from there, wanting to make up as much distance as possible before they lost the light. Joel remained far ahead of them for the rest of the day and only returned when Orielle called to tell him they were bedding down for the evening. Gigantic trees surrounded them on all sides, making it easy to find one that had limbs strong enough to support all of their weight.

With around an hour of daylight remaining, they took the opportunity to make a fire and throw together a small dinner. Toku said that as long as they put the fire out before the sun went down in earnest, they could avoid attracting attention. He also showed Colton and a few others how to mark the surrounding area with a thick jelly he called "monster repellent," but in all actuality, it was a mixture of various glands from predators that were mashed together. However, thinking of it as monster repellent made it easier for Colton to stomach the slimy texture as he spread it on nearby trees.

With everyone fed, they set up a watch schedule which included three separate groups who would watch in four hour intervals. The first watch included Cartwright and Joel, the second Toku and Friend, and the last would be Ember and Imbrose. Colton initially protested, but Toku informed him that he and Orielle would be on watch the following evening. However, before the group could disperse, George called a meeting to discuss something.

"I spoke with our friend in the prison before we left, and he told me that this Skarvald character likely has access to some kind of weapon he might use on us if it comes to open conflict."

Cartwright cleared his throat. "What kind of weapon? Should we double back and get more help before we push forward?"

George shook his head. "We can't trust this information. Since we don't know this Sero fellow, we don't know what his intentions are, and he doesn't strike me as a poacher. For that reason, I can't imagine how he acquired his information." George paused. "As for the nature of the weapon, I couldn't say. He was very vague, which is another reason to question his validity."

"What if he's right?" June asked, her voice betraying her nervousness.

"Then it is as we expected. We know he has weapons, and if he attacks us outright, we will have to respond as we would have anyway." George looked around the gathering. "I just wanted to tell all of you on the slightest chance that he could be telling the truth."

Cartwright nodded. "I appreciate the information. Let's just hope we can talk with him diplomatically and avoid this weapon all together."

"Let's hope," George affirmed, glancing at Orielle. "Anyway, we should get some sleep."

The group nodded and finished preparing for the climb up a nearby trunk.

As everyone found their way up the tree to a ten-foot wide tree branch that was to be their sleeping spot, Colton closed his eyes, trying to get the most of his allotted sleep time. Unfortunately, his mind would not be hushed so easily and his thoughts quickly launched into a smattering of the recent day's events. The vision of the coral-encrusted monstrosity, who he now knew as Va'Rul, haunted him as he tried to get comfortable. Something about the horrible, tooth-filled smile had him grimacing as he tried to clear it from his mind. Eventually, he gave up on sleep and grunted, sitting straight up.

The darkness of the forest made him feel like he hadn't opened his eyes at all and had it not been for the dull light given off by the nearby lichen that clung to the tree, he would be completely blind. He could just barely make out the sitting figure of Joel near the trunk of the tree. Standing, he walked carefully over to him and sat down to his left.

"Can't sleep, huh?" Joel asked, glancing at him before looking ahead again.

"Not a wink. That monster we told you about shows up every time I close my eyes," Colton huffed as he took a swig from his waterskin.

"Based on what you told me, I can't really blame you. It sounds like it was quite the ordeal."

"I'm still not sure what would have happened if we had died in there," Colton admitted, glancing at where Orielle was lying some fifteen feet down the branch. "She came close though."

Joel followed his eyeline. "I wouldn't be so sure. She's as tough as they come."

Colton nodded and turned his attention back to the spanning forest ahead of him. "It's hard to believe that just a month ago I was just a guy trying to track down a fairytale."

Joel scoffed. "I take offense to that. I'm very real."

Colton smiled. "To be honest, I wasn't sure you guys were when we first met. I half expected to wake from a vivid dream still on the ship, lost at sea."

"Sorry to disappoint but it's not a dream, just reality."

"Sometimes reality is preferable to a dream." Colton steepled his hands. "In this case, I'm very happy it is real."

"You are one of us now, Cobb, and while I wasn't keen on picking up any strays when we first met, I have found you and your companions very enjoyable to be around."

Hearing Joel say that made Colton feel a sense of relief. Even though he never thought Joel disliked him, it was nice to hear he was glad they had rescued them. "I appreciate that Joel." Colton held up a finger, a thought coming to him. "Oh, and thank you for helping me with my powers. I'm not sure I'd be talking to you now had you not shown me that night."

Joel waved a hand. "You were a natural. Sometimes it takes years for a person to develop their core as you did."

"Regardless, I appreciate it, and if I can ever help you with something, I hope you won't hesitate to ask."

"Don't worry! I always like being owed favors!" Joel teased.

"I'm sure you do," Colton said, chuckling.

They lapse into silence for a few minutes, enjoying the cool air blowing through the treetops. Small animals could be heard chittering or squeaking as they foraged in the evening shadows for some unseen meal. The whole experience left Colton remembering how it felt to sit on the porch at his grandparents' house. The house was placed just outside of town, so that it felt more secluded than it actually was. In his mindseye, he could see the distant city lights as the two moons of Zerua, Eternius, and Phaseia sat low in the sky.

Phaseia, a brilliant orange, slowly moved across the sky as it had since the beginning of time. Eternius, in contrast, was a swirling mass of purple and green appearing to be constantly in conflict. The edge of Eternius could just barely be seen through the thick forest canopy from where he and Joel sat now. The ever-changing moon had always intrigued Colton as it had only arisen into the night sky after the conclusion of the war. In fact, its arrival only preceded Colton's birth by a few years.

"You should get some sleep. We're going to be pushing pretty hard tomorrow," Joel encouraged, pulling him from his musings.

Colton nodded and pushed himself to his feet. "Yeah, have a good watch, Joel."

Joel waved as Colton retreated to his bedroll. Lying down, Colton found himself staring out at Eternius once more, as the green swirling surface sent a wave of peace over him. Slowly, he felt his eyes close, and instead of seeing Va'Rul, he found himself wrapped in a warm and dreamless sleep.

—

The next day, the group set off just before dawn, most of them still yawning from the difficult sleeping arrangements. Toku pressed the group into a constant and fast pace. Even George and June were forced to keep up with them as they tried to make up as much ground as possible. As they settled down for a midday meal, they all began to relax a bit, talking about the plan heading into the poacher's camp the next day. The idea was for George to offer them safe passage out of the Primal Forest, but if that failed, he suggested they may need to persuade them further. When questioned, he just sighed and placed a hand on his bag, but didn't elaborate.

The conversation was welcome and it helped unveil the mysterious individual, Toku. Apparently, he was from the Thicket of Beasts originally, and had met a woman from the Thicket of Memories before moving there immediately. His wife had since passed, but not before giving him two boys. They, in turn, moved to other thickets, following their own hearts. While Toku told his story, Colton could see Ember and Imbrose move close to one another protectively.

The remainder of the day went without incident as Toku eventually raised his hand for everyone to stop. "We rest here. I don't trust getting any closer to the camp itself."

As everyone began unpacking for the day, Joel walked up to Toku. "I still can't find her, but she definitely came this way. Maybe she finally decided to take out the poachers once and for all."

Toku shrugged. "Perhaps, but whatever upset her took her on a chase."

Colton stepped forward to the duo. "Are you talking about Grex'xi?"

Toku nodded. "I don't like not being able to find her. She's awfully big for being so easy to misplace."

"I'd have to agree with you," Colton said. "I think we saw her when we first landed on Zerua. She was pretty big, even from the distance we saw her at."

"Be grateful she wasn't closer. Something tells me she wouldn't have responded well to your little troop," Toku chuckled, setting his pack against a thick tree. "Let's get camp set up and some dinner going."

Joel and Colton nodded as they set about trying to help get everyone settled in for the evening. To his left, he could see Orielle and June talking quietly and could only make out a few words as he passed by.

"...I still can't believe he struck you. He was always so kind when we were growing up," June whispered, her face screwed up in sadness.

"He hasn't been himself for some time now..." Orielle shared as Colton walked away.

The sun set quickly as Toku judged it too dangerous to build a fire so close to their query, and while Colton didn't care for cold jerky as a meal, he much preferred not becoming something else's dinner. Soon, everyone found their way up a tree to the lowest hanging limb and Colton began his watch alongside Orielle.

The first hour went by without incident, but shortly into the second hour, Colton heard Orielle approach from his right. "Mind if we talk a little bit?" Orielle asked. "I was starting to nod off over there."

Colton nodded and patted the spot next to where he was sitting. "I could use the company."

As Orielle sat down, she adjusted her holsters, trying to get comfortable. "So, tell me about your family." Colton turned to look at her, his eyebrow raising slightly. "What? After meeting Imryth, I'm curious what your parents might be like."

Colton chuckled lightly. "I'm afraid my mother is nothing like Aunt Imryth. She left when I was very young." Colton paused, trying to sift through his memories for a glimpse of his mother's face. "I can't even recall what she looked like, and my father never understood me. So honestly, my grandparents became my parents."

Orielle lowered her head. "I'm sorry. I didn't mean to dredge up bad memories for you."

197

Colton looked at her and placed a gentle hand on her knee. "You didn't! Trust me, my grandmother and grandfather were the best parents a person could ask for." She looked up with a small smile on her face. Colton pulled his hand back and looked into the night. "Now those two, they are heroes. Without my grandmother, I could very easily be blind just like my grandpa. She saved us both, and in turn my grandpa saved all of his future generations."

"They sound like incredible people."

"They absolutely are. Can't imagine what kind of man I'd be if I hadn't been raised by them." Colton blinked rapidly, fighting back the tears forming in his eyes. "You'll love them."

"I'm sure I will…" Orielle replied quietly. "Do you have any siblings?"

"I have a little sister. Her name is Phoebe, and she's quite the talker." Colton smiled thinking of how difficult it was to get a word in while speaking to her. "I swear, she could talk for hours with no one else ever saying a word."

"Jasper was like that," Orielle remembered sadly. "He was definitely the more outgoing of the two of us."

"Is," Colton amended quickly.

"What?" Orielle asked, turning to look at him.

"He *is* the more outgoing of the two of you." Colton paused and met her gaze. "We will get him back, Ori."

Tears welled in her eyes as she sniffed and looked away. "Yes, we will. Thank you, Colton."

Silence fell over them, but Colton felt no discomfort in it. In fact, he just liked being next to her. A strong gust of wind blew through the treetops, causing Orielle's hair to blow wildly to one side. The scent of lavender and marigolds brushed past Colton as she fought to pull her hair back under control. Looking at her once more, Colton felt a pang echo through his chest. From the moment he met this woman, he had felt a connection to her. At first he had assumed it was because she was part of

198

the tribe he had been looking for. But after spending more time with her, he could tell it was more than that.

Colton chastised himself as he remembered that just two days ago this woman had been betrothed and had received a slap as she broke it off. It wasn't the time to pursue the feelings stirring within him. She needed a friend, and he was determined to be there for her.

"I should get back to my post," she said quietly.

Colton nodded, not trusting the words that might leave his mouth.

"Thank you for talking with me." Orielle got to her feet and started to walk away before turning around. "Let's do it again sometime." Then she walked to the other side of the wide tree branch.

Colton smiled as he leaned back on one hand. He nodded to himself, resolving once more to be the friend she needed. Besides, there was plenty else to focus on and he still needed to survive this trip and help Jasper.

The rest of his watch went by quickly as he considered what the next day may hold. After waking Imbrose and Ember, Colton bedded down and found himself drifting off to sleep quickly as the smell of lavender and marigolds blew across the space between him and a nearby bedroll.

Chapter Twenty: Skarvald, King of The Poachers

T oku made sure to wake them early once more. Imbrose complained loudly at the "injustice of it all" as the troop set off, but Colton found himself refreshed and ready for the day. Looking to his right, he could see Orielle talking to June once again, and could tell the young woman was upset about something. Orielle, in turn, rubbed her back and whispered something that had June nodding.

The warmth of the sun increased gradually until everyone was sweating heavily, making each and every person pant as Toku didn't let up on the pace. Eventually, George himself needed to force a break so that they could all catch their breath. That gave Joel the opportunity to scout ahead of them once more. After about an hour break, Joel reappeared with news of the poacher outpost.

"I found it about three miles east," Joel reported, his hands on his knees. "The doors are just open."

"Any sign of guards?" Cartwright asked.

"None," Joel wheezed, still catching his breath.

"That makes me uneasy," Cartwright growled, stepping forward to look down the path Joel had come from. "What about Grex'xi?"

Joel sat down on a fallen log. "No, but I could see tracks leading into the stronghold." Cartwright turned to Joel in alarm as he spoke the last word. "Yes, stronghold. It looks like it was some castle from a very long time ago."

"That complicates things." Cartwright turned to look at George. "Sir, I am not sure I can guarantee your safety if we go into this fortress."

George stepped forward and placed a hand on Cartwright's shoulder. "You don't give yourself enough credit. We have come too far to turn back anyway. We must continue."

Cartwright nodded, offering no argument. "Very well, let's move out. Toku, take up the rear and call out if you see anyone."

The burly ranger nodded and backed up as the rest of the group started to move out with June and George placed in the center. The remainder of the walk to the castle Joel had seen went by slowly as everyone stayed silent. A tense air hung over the party as they tried to consider what might be in store for them. Colton himself tried to pass the time by checking to make sure the hunting knife he purchased before leaving was still sheathed at his side by repeatedly pulling it out and replacing it in its small scabbard. He wished they had left a few days later so he could have made a new whip before this trek. However, he had become more comfortable than he expected using the large sword on his back, which seemed to warm slightly as he thought of it.

He still didn't know much about the sword aside from the fact that it apparently once belonged to Tyrrek himself. Usually though, swords like those tended to have names, but Colton didn't have much hope of learning the name of the sword on his back. Maybe when he got back to the thicket he would ask Terry if there were any records of one.

Ahead of him, Cartwright came to a stop before pushing some thick brambles aside and exiting into a large open space. Being one of the last to pass through, Colton could see the dilapidated front gates of what once must have been a grand hall, wide open as if letting in a glorious host of guests for some feast. However, the vines and ivy that ran up and down the exterior ramparts betrayed the true nature of this abandoned fortress. A long cobblestone pathway ran from the entrance of the fort, into an open courtyard. Massive balconies lined either side of the interior courtyard, as what must have been a once lavish dwelling. From where they were at, the party could easily see the effort that went into clearing out the surrounding trees to give any guards a clear line of sight from the ramparts.

"Still no sign of any guards," Cartwright scanned the ruined towers and open courtyard with practiced eyes."Still, it looks like they could easily hide up in those balconies, and we wouldn't be able to see them until they already shot us dead. There is no way we can protect you from every angle when we walk through." Cartwright warned, as he looked at the Keeper.

"Is it abandoned?" Colton asked, trying to spot any movement from his vantage.

"It appears not…" Ember said, pointing to the open gates.

A scrawny man stepped out from behind cover and raised both hands in the air, clearly disarmed.

"Ho, there!" the man yelled. "My name's Lev, and the boss has been expecting you."

The party shifted uncomfortably as the man continued walking in their direction. "Give the word, and I'll drop him," Imbrose hissed quietly.

"Where there's one, there's more," Toku pacified, making his way to the front of the group. "What do you want to do, George?"

George squinted his eyes then answered confidently. "We came to talk, didn't we? Let's go have a conversation."

Cartwright was visibly uncomfortable with the plan, but nonetheless nodded and strode out into the clearing. Everyone else followed suit, scanning the nearby ramparts for any more movement, but Lev remained the only visible poacher.

"Ah! Now I can see you," Lev croaked, lowering his arms. "If you would follow me, Skarvald would like to have a word with you."

"Just a moment," Cartwright said, and there was no mistaking the menace in his voice. "How do we know you won't just kill us the moment we walk through those gates?"

Lev smiled. "You don't, but I can assure you that you would already be dead if that's all we wanted." With a wave of Lev's hand, thirty crossbowmen stepped out from perfectly camouflaged cover and trained the crossbows on their now seemingly small party.

Everyone in the group drew their weapons and trained them on a nearby poacher, forming a semicircle around June and George. The standoff lasted a moment longer before Lev gestured for the poachers to stand down.

"No need for that just yet," he soothed in a calm tone. "Come, follow me, and let's speak like civilized folk."

Cartwright only lowered his sword when George pushed through the group and nodded toward Lev. "Very well, let's meet this Skarvald you speak of."

Lev smiled once more and gestured for everyone to follow him as he walked through the open gates. George started forward, but Cartwright once again stepped in front of him and started escorting the Keeper as everyone else followed close behind.

Colton blinked and watched the poacher he was targeting melt back into the nearby bush, completely concealing themselves again. If Colton hadn't seen it, he would have no idea that there was a person there, and even now he questioned whether or not the man had simply disappeared into thin air. The display left him holding his knife in his free hand as they approached the entrance to the fort.

Walking through the massive doors, Colton could see they had in fact been broken open by some great force. Whatever left these doors in such a state of disrepair was something Colton wanted to steer clear of. But judging by the trajectory of the gigantic claw prints that led across the courtyard from where he now stood, he would most likely run into it before the end of this walk.

As they followed Lev, the party scanned the crumbling keep all around them. Where there was once a wall blocking the view into the inner corridors high above them, there was only rubble scattered across the cobbled floor. In the empty corridors, there now stood countless crossbowmen, all of their weapons at ease but still loaded. Colton forced himself to look ahead at the upcoming second set of doors Lev was leading them towards. These too had taken recent damage, as one of them hung precariously off one hinge.

"Seems you ran into the Albino Queen," Toku remarked to Lev.

"No, she ran into us, as you can see," Lev explained as he passed beneath the leaning door.

One by one, the group passed under the same door and into the room beyond. What they saw was akin to an ancient throne room, but the ceiling had given out and collapsed on itself centuries ago, leaving the sky visible. Essentially, making the once grand room a glorified courtyard with broken walls and a cracked tile floor.

On the far side of the space, a large steel cage held the prone form of a titanic white beast. Colton recognized it immediately as the one he had seen while scouting on his first days on Zerua. That meant it was Grex'xi, the indomitable apex predator of the Primal Forest. As Colton watched, the behemoth's great chest rose and fell in a balanced rhythm, suggesting she was sleeping. Hundreds of crossbow bolts protruded from the albino hide of Grex'xi, and Colton could tell the poachers deliberately missed anything vital in hopes of capturing her.

Scanning the rest of the room, he could see a long bench that sat right next to the large cage and a massive, charcoal-skinned man sat upon it, smiling broadly. The man wore no shirt and only a hide skirt of sorts. He leaned casually on the long handle of a double bladed greataxe. As the party walked to meet him, he held out a gloved hand to stop them and Lev bowed before scurrying off to one side. Getting a better look at him, Colton could see the man must share the same race as Friend, for he hadn't seen anyone else with a skin such as this. A long black beard covered the man's face on an otherwise hairless head.

With a grunt, the man jumped to his feet and hefted the large ax over one shoulder. "I was beginning to wonder if you got lost in the woods."

The man's voice was deep and guttural as if his voice itself caused the roof to fall from this hall. His accent left Colton wondering as he hadn't heard anything like it since he had arrived in Zerua.

"You must be Skarvald. Might I ask how you knew we were coming?" George asked, stepping forward.

Skarvald chuckled. "Well, Keeper, we have spies all over the forest, so I knew the moment you left your thicket." Skarvald paused walking to one side of the group, causing Cartwright to tense up. "I must say, I never expected to meet one of your leaders. I half anticipated you would send a kill squad when you tired of us. It's what I would have done."

Colton looked over his shoulder at where Friend was standing stock still, his faceplate down, and George continued. "Well, we were hoping to avoid any unneeded conflict. We have enough of that as it is."

Skarvald nodded, his heavy beard bobbing. "Ah, yes, Va'Rul. He's been quite the little thorn in the proverbial bramble, as it were."

Colton watched Orielle tense slightly, her hands moving closer to her pistols. "You know about him?" George asked, unable to hide the surprise in his voice.

"Know him? We've been working for him."

Orielle pulled her pistol faster than Colton could blink and trained it on Skarvald's face. "Explain yourself, poacher," Orielle demanded, her voice curt.

Skarvald smirked and raised his free hand in mock surrender. "Not all talk, I see. This is good. It will make for a more interesting conversation." Skarvald lowered his hand and walked toward a small chest sitting at the base of a broken pillar. "You see, Va'Rul took something of mine and forced me into his service. I wasn't a willing participant if that makes any difference."

Orielle's lip twitched, her pistol lowering an inch.

"I thrive on the hunt, Miss, and this Va'Rul thrives on domination. That taints the purity of the game. There is nothing more thrilling than facing your death at the hands of a creature greater than you." Skarvald

205

reached down and threw open the small chest, producing a small black orb with swirling red light within. "This was how he created his slaves."

"What's that?" Cartwright asked as he pulled his sword halfway out of its scabbard.

Skarvald looked at the melon-sized orb and raised his eyebrows. "Oh, this? From what I was told, it helps to separate the Tyrkin people from their spirit, making it easier to control your mind."

Orielle lowered her pistol to her side, stepping forward. "There's no mind to control if there's no spirit. You're just dead."

"For any other race of people, you would be right, young lady, but the Tyrkin are special. Removing your soul simply makes you an empty meat sack, ripe for Va'Rul's mind games," Skarvald detailed, tossing the orb into the air and catching it again.

The entire party took an unconscious step back at the powerful artifact before them. An object like this was meant to be seized and thrown in a deep hole where no one could use it in the Archipelago. The fact that this man was casually tossing it into the air created a sense of unease around the space.

"Is that what you plan to do with us then?" George asked, eyeing the orb cautiously.

"It's what *he* wants," Skarvald said, pursing his lips. "But he's not here." Skarvald tossed the orb onto the tiled floor between him and the Keeper with a solid thud, betraying its hefty weight and showing no sign of damage. The unassuming globe rolled slowly to a stop, before the red flash of light swirled around its interior then went dark. "I'm no one's slave, and I refuse to act like his any longer." Colton watched the orb intently, as Skarvald began pacing back toward his makeshift throne. "By all means, take it and destroy it if you can find a way. That might help those who have already been consumed to find themselves once more."

Orielle moved to grab the orb when the large metal hand of Friend stopped her from taking another step. "Let me, I am not Tyrkin and it cannot affect me in the same way it does you."

Orielle nodded, her wits returning to her. As Friend put the orb into a satchel, George turned back to Skarvald. "So, does that mean you will help us destroy him?"

Skarvald tilted his head back and forth. "I could, but how can I know that we would succeed? Besides, I heard that you want me and mine to leave the forest for good."

George took another step forward. "That was before we knew about your connection to Va'Rul. Now I believe we can defeat him if we band together."

Skarvald laughed. "You have no idea what you are dealing with. That creepy snake would possess your mind the second you got within one hundred feet of him. It's like the Gods deliberately made him to destroy your people."

"I don't believe that. I think they made him so that we could be tested as a people," George responded quickly.

"Your faith is moving, but my point stands. You can't hope to fight him if you are unable to fight against his mental assault."

"That is where you come in," George proposed. "If you can distract him long enough for us all to get close, we can overwhelm him before he can attack us."

"And if he possesses you all and sends you against us in turn?" Skarvald questioned.

George bit his lip trying to come up with a response. "You're right," Orielle interjected. "We have no way of fighting him now, but if you help us, we may be able to find a solution." Orielle paused, walking up next to her father. "One thing is for certain. When he finds out you are disobeying him, he will come for you, and you wouldn't be talking to us if you thought you could kill him on your own."

Skarvald's face rose into a broad smile again. "I like you. You have guts, and if I'm being honest, I thought the lot of you were a bunch of scared prey. I'm happy to see I was wrong." Skarvald nodded, seeming to come to a decision. "Tell you what, if one of you can beat me one on one, I'll tell you everything I know about Va'Rul and help you kill the slimy bastard."

Before George could interject, Orielle continued. "What are the rules of the duel?"

Skarvald's smile widened further. "If I yield, you win, but if I kill you, I win."

Orielle turned to face the group. "Let me fight him." Her face was stern and unyielding.

"Absolutely not," George refused quickly, his voice offering no room for argument.

"I can do it, Pa! He's slow and I'm quick. I'll have him down before he gets within twenty feet of me."

"And if he hits you with that big ax even once…" George shook his head vehemently. "No, I won't allow it."

"I'll do it," Colton offered, stepping forward. "I think I have a good handle on my power and the sword."

"Sorry, lad. Swords are notoriously bad against axes, and that's one mighty ax," Cartwright winced, pointing at the weapon in Skarvald's hand.

Colton bristled, uncomfortable with the idea of someone else trying to take on that giant.

"It has to be me." Everyone turned to see Friend slowly removing his helm, revealing his charcoal skin. "He is a son of fire, therefore his defeat must come at the hands of another son of fire. I will face him."

Chapter Twenty-One: Dance of Fire

"**Y**ou can't," Orielle argued, her voice rising. "This fight is for my people, not yours."

Friend placed his bag on the floor next to his doffed helm, and looked down at Orielle. "I have come to see you all as my people, but while I was working at the forge, I remembered where I once came from." Friend paused, locking eyes with Skarvald. "We come from a place called the Everglow Plateau, where combats like this are a right of passage."

Skarvald narrowed his eyes as he stepped forward. "You are not familiar to me, brother."

"I left some time ago, it appears," Friend stated simply. "Do you accept my challenge, Skarvald?"

Skarvald bowed his head. "I do, son of fire. May our battle bring glory to your clan and my own."

With that, Friend stepped forward, but Orielle blocked his passage. "I can't let you do this."

Friend looked down once more and placed a hand on her shoulder. "I must do it. He is of my blood, and only I can defeat him in honorable combat." Orielle wrinkled her face, not budging from her place. Seeing her hesitancy, Friend leaned down smiling slightly. "Do you trust me?"

Orielle squinted, her eyes clearly at odds with herself, before nodding. "Yes, I trust you, Friend."

"Then you must let me do this," Friend replied, leaning back once more.

Hesitating only a second longer, Orielle moved away from in front of Friend, allowing him to walk past. "Don't die," she commanded as he stepped away from the group.

"I won't," Friend reassured her before hefting his heavy war hammer with both hands.

Skarvald nodded, his previous mirth wiped away as he too heaved his weapon. The rest of the party moved back to give them room.

With a roar, Skarvald closed the distance between him and Friend, the frightening speed unfit for a man of his size. Friend was ready as he brought his hammer up to intercept the arcing ax. The two weapons clashed in a clang of metal as Friend parried the ax off to one side, unable to bear the weight of the blow. With his gauntleted left hand, Friend released the handle of his hammer and punched Skarvald in the side of the face, forcing the big man back two steps.

As Skarvald stumbled backward, Friend swung his hammer upward toward Skarvald's exposed left side. The weapon met open air as Skarvald gained his footing and took two quick steps back. Undeterred, Friend pressed the advantage, bringing the hammer back down toward his opponent's unprotected head. Skarvald stepped into the blow, bringing his ax head up, catching the haft of the hammer between the blades. Flipping his weapon in his grasp, Skarvald jammed the top of his ax into the ground, pinning Friend's hammer in the dirt. With a grunt of effort, Skarvald planted his shoulder into Friend's chest and shoved him backward, forcing him to release the hammer.

Orielle stiffened next to Colton as she quickly grabbed his hand, gasping as Friend was disarmed. Colton had no time to consider this, however, as Friend stumbled backward, clearly on the back foot.

Sensing victory, Skarvald pressed his advantage, taking two long steps as he brought his ax down in a massive arcing blow. Friend pushed closer to Skarvald in an effort to reduce the impact, as the weapon descended too fast to avoid. With both hands, Friend grabbed the handle of the ax as it slammed into his left pauldron with a *crash*, forcing him to his knees. A terrible screech filled the arena as Skarvald tilted the blade, aiming for Friend's exposed neck.

With a yell of defiance, Friend forced himself to his feet as the ax blade finally bit into the flesh on his shoulder. A massive heat wave rippled away from the clash as Friend's boot caught fire. Skarvald's eyes glanced down at the display just in time to see Friend bring his leg up and kick him in the center of his chest. The force of the kick made every spectator shield their eyes and take a step back.

As the dust cleared, Friend was holding Skarvald's ax in one hand at his side, crimson blood still dripping from one of the blades. Ten feet away, Skarvald was lying on his back, his chest scorched, pain obvious on his face. Pushing himself to his feet, the burly man stared Friend down. In turn, Friend tossed the ax to one side and conjured a small bead of fire in his right hand, bringing it to his wounded shoulder. The sizzle of flesh that followed as Friend cauterized his wound caused even Cartwright to grimace in sympathetic pain.

Friend merely grunted, watching Skarvald carefully. "The old way then," Skarvald smirked, his hands balling into fists.

What followed was a mad exchange of heavy blows from both men, Friend's fists covered in raging flames as Skarvald used his superior strength to compensate for the magical attacks. The two of them refused to take a hit without dishing one in return, Friend connecting with Skarvald's ribs just as a fist forced Friend's head to one side.

Finally, Friend connected with a right hook that forced Skarvald to one knee as another shockwave of heat blasted out from the impact. Stepping forward, Friend brought his own knee into Skarvald's temple with such momentum that Skarvald flopped onto his back once more. Skarvald, blood dripping from his mouth and a cut on his head, swung his legs around, swiping Friend's out from under him. Hitting the ground hard in full plate armor, Friend couldn't adjust in time to prevent Skarvald from straddling him and raining blow after blow down onto his head.

With blood flying as each fist connected, Skarvald let out a guttural yell as he linked his fingers and brought both fists up over his head, intending a crippling blow. Friend seized his moment and leaned forward to wrap his hand behind Skarvald's neck, pulling him down into a gruesome headbutt. Blood spurted from Skarvald's now broken nose as he rolled off of Friend and scrambled to his feet, putting distance between them.

Friend spit a wad of blood mixed with spit onto the cracked tiles to his right and pushed himself to his feet, his eyes catching on a small chunk of stone rubble to his right. Stumbling to the rock, Friend reached down and picked it up in time to see Skarvald regain his bearings.

Skarvald smiled a bloody grin, his nose still bleeding freely. "You're tough, but I nearly had you there. Do you truly believe you can win this?"

Friend returned his smile, panting slightly. "I already have." The rock in his hand began to glow and Friend channeled his fire into it.

Skarvald's eyes widened as he realized what Friend intended to do and he charged toward him as fast as he could. It was too late. Friend pulled the now-flaming, red-hot rock back and heaved the fist-sized projectile directly at Skarvald. The proceeding thunderous explosion of the impact dwarfed any from before, sending broken tiles and dust blasting out in every direction leaving the entire throne room obscured.

Colton's ears rang loudly as he felt around blindly, trying to find Orielle who he had lost as the explosion went off. Eventually, the dust began to settle and Colton could see the seated form of Orielle as she rubbed her own ears. Colton stumbled over the rubble that coated the floor, haphazardly rushing to her side. She coughed slightly as he got close and turned to look at him, her face caked in dust.

Glancing about, Colton spotted June, who was already generating some purple energy around her own ears, no doubt healing herself. With a grimace, Colton raised a hand at Orielle and stood to move toward June, who turned as her ears healed and she could hear his approach. Quickly,

June placed a hand on either side of Colton's head as he reached her, his hearing beginning to return almost immediately.

"Thank you…" Colton said, coughing as he spoke. "Orielle is over there, she needs your help." June nodded and moved to help Orielle who was getting to her feet slowly.

Colton turned in a circle trying to locate anyone else from their party and finding no one. The entire space was slowly becoming less obscured as Colton tried to find his way back to where he had last seen Friend. What he found was the metal clad man lying on his back, his chest slowly rising and falling. Colton shook the armored man, trying to rouse him from unconsciousness as the dust settled enough that the others became visible.

After a minute of shaking Friend, his eyes fluttered open and he tried to sit up, only to fall back down again.

"Rest, Friend. I'll get June to help," Colton said as he looked around to locate the healer once more.

A metallic hand clasped around Colton's wrist. "I cannot be healed until he has yielded," Friend managed, his voice hoarse.

Colton looked down in shock. "There's no way he survived that, and you need help."

"I'm afraid you're wrong," A gravelly voice rasped from behind Colton.

Turning quickly, Colton saw Skarvald in a seated position, holding his mangled left arm close to his chest. "How are you still alive?" Colton asked incredulously.

Skarvald chuckled softly which devolved into hacking coughs. "Luck, it seems."

Friend, finding some deep well of strength, forced himself upright and to his feet. "Do you yield?" Friend's voice betrayed no sense of exhaustion.

Skarvald grimaced as he squeezed his useless left arm. "Aye, I yield."

Friend slumped in relief, falling to one knee as June finally arrived, already conjuring more light at her fingers.

"Mind giving me some of that healing touch once you're done with him?" Skarvald asked weakly, a smile creasing the dried blood and soot that covered his face. "You know, since we're friends now."

Chapter Twenty-Two: To Kill A Nightmare

S hortly after Skarvald and Friend were healed, a long, half-burned throw rug was placed in the center of the damaged throne room, which now sported a ten foot wide crater where Friend had detonated his rock. Everyone was invited to sit and soon a few platters of different meats were brought out and placed on the rug. As a result, they all sat in an awkward silence as Skarvald and a few of his companions—including Lev—all gorged themselves on the meal. As Colton took tentative bites of the extremely bland meat, he watched the others exchanging nervous glances with one another until Orielle could stand the silence no longer.

"Where is he?" she asked abruptly.

Skarvald stopped mid-bite and lowered the greasy leg of meat he had been feasting on. "Where's who?" His voice perfectly imitated an innocent child.

Orielle rolled her eyes. "Va'Rul, where is he?"

Skarvald's face brightened in recognition and Colton wasn't sure if he was faking it. "Oh, yes, him!" Skarvald paused as if to finish the bite Orielle's question had interrupted, then proceeded to answer with his mouth full. "Can't we just enjoy this bounty, and discuss such unpleasantness afterwards?"

"I think you've enjoyed quite a lot of it already!" Orielle scoffed, gesturing to his plate.

The giant man glanced down at the pile of bones he had accumulated, and looked back up in mock hurt. "Making fun of a man for his eating habits, are you?"

Colton watched as Orielle's face darkened even further, not finding this man humorous in the slightest. "She meant nothing by it," George spoke up quickly. "I think we would all just like to discuss our plan moving forward. An informant of mine said that you had a weapon you would likely use if we attacked you outright. Could it be used against Va'Rul?"

Skarvald's mirth vanished and his eyes narrowed at George's words. He wiped his mouth with a sleeve, dropping the leg of meat onto the rug. "As I said, our mutual enemy wanted me to use that orb on you. Though now I'm curious, if you knew about the orb, why did you all come out here in the first place? Seems like quite the gamble."

"We had no idea what the weapon was, and I wasn't sure if I could trust the information," George said.

"I see, well, I'd be very wary of this informant of yours. The only people who know of the orb are myself, Va'Rul, and whichever of his cultists he chose to tell." Skarvald gestured to Lev. "I didn't even tell this joker."

That caused Colton's heart to skip a beat as he imagined them leaving some fanatical cultist back at the thicket without any of their warriors there to protect them. "He didn't seem like one of Va'Rul's," George hummed, his voice taking on a haunted tone. "We've run into quite a few."

Skarvald nodded understandingly. "They are a very distinct lot, with the face of a crab and all that." The space took on a somber tone as everyone lost themselves in thought for a moment. "Anyway, as far as I know, the orb can't be used against Va'Rul. So, unless someone among you has more knowledge on that thing than him, I think he may just turn it against you if we tried to use it on him."

"Where is he?" Orielle asked again, her tone calmer.

"No clue where he actually calls home. He always met me along the coast a day east of here." Skarvald shrugged.

"So, how can you be of assistance to us then?" Toku asked bluntly.

Skarvald turned to look at the grizzled man, the corner of his mouth turning up amusedly. "By all means, face him yourself."

George raised a hand, drawing the poachers' attention back to him. "I think what Toku might mean is that you told us you would share everything you knew about Va'Rul."

Skarvald scratched his beard. "I did say that, didn't I? Well, I suppose a deal is a deal." Lev smirked as he sucked the meat off of a bone. "The first thing you need to know is that he's a forty foot snake with four sets of arms that end in three razor sharp claws." The image of the creature from Orielle's mind flashed uninvited through Colton's head. "If that's not enough to scare you off, then consider the fact that he has hundreds of cultists that do his bidding."

"How could you possibly know that?" Cartwright asked.

"Because I let them stay here when they ranged further south, and I never once saw the same one pass through twice," Skarvald explained, as he reached for his mug full of ale.

"You let them stay here?" Joel asked, his voice sharp.

"Aye, I did tell you he had something of mine, right? Couldn't rightly refuse while he still had it, could I?"

"What does he have?" Friend asked, speaking for the first time since the fight.

Skarvald regarded Friend for a moment before answering. "He took my son."

"As in, he…" Colton let the question hang and Skarvald looked at him tensely.

"Yes, he captured his mind and now controls him like a little puppet." The big man's beard twitched, clearly pushing down his building rage.

217

George swallowed hard. "He took mine too." The admission seemed to leave the Keeper a shadow of himself, and for the first time, Colton could see the effect of Jasper's affliction on the great leader's face.

"I'm sorry," Skarvald sympathized, reaching over and patting George's shoulder. "No parent should have to suffer such a thing."

"Agreed," George assented, rallying. "If he has your son, why rebel now?"

Skarvald scrunched up his face. "Because, if my son were here, he would want me to bury my ax so deeply into Va'Rul's skull that it wasn't possible to remove it. Even if it meant his death."

"I can't imagine..." June sympathized, her voice quiet.

"Neither could I!" Skarvald boomed, his voice becoming more lively again. "That's why I served the slimy serpent for so long. But it wasn't until recently when he came to me saying that I had to wipe you out, that I started to think he could be beaten."

"Why would that–" Joel started.

"I've only ever seen the snake when he was angry, but that day, he was scared," Skarvald recalled, pointing at Joel. "I knew you lot had done something to hurt him, and he felt threatened."

Colton's thoughts raced, a question coming to him. "When did you last speak to him?"

"About four days ago, I'd say."

Colton looked over at Orielle, who was already staring back at him, and nodded. "We forced him out of Orielle's head four days ago."

Skarvald's eyes darted between the two of them. "Forced him out? How?"

Colton cocked his head to one side. "Well, we killed whatever he sent into her head to take her over."

"We? How could anyone do something like that?" Skarvald was visibly intrigued as he leaned across the half-eaten boar in front of him.

"One of the cultists linked its mind with her and opened the door for Va'Rul to come in, I suppose. Then she fell over and started convulsing. I didn't know what else to do, so I connected my mind to hers and it pulled me into her inner battle," Colton shared.

Skarvald went silent for a moment as he looked down, his eyes moving back and forth as if considering something. "That might be the key…" he mused.

"What might be?" Colton asked.

Skarvald nodded, becoming confident in his line of thought. "Va'Rul's power comes from his ability to conquer the minds of others, right? Well, what if we conquered his mind?" Nobody spoke, the idea sounding ludicrous. "Think about it… If you can keep him busy in his head, we can kill him while he's distracted."

Colton shook his head slightly. "He nearly killed us both when it was some remnant of him over what must have been hundreds of miles. I'm willing to wager that the real thing would be far more powerful."

"Probably, but if we can take his most powerful weapon from him, then we can even the playing field."

George held up a finger. "You brought up a good point earlier though. What if he turns us all against you?"

Skarvald shrugged. "Then we're dead anyway."

Joel slowly nodded his head, warming to the idea. "It may be the only way. After all, we have been training with our minds since we were younger than Jasper. If enough of us bombard him at once, we may be able to overwhelm him."

"It's a risk, but we may have no choice," George said, his voice growing somber. "There's no telling what he plans for the children he has already captured."

"There may be someone we aren't considering, Pa," Orielle suggested, looking at him meaningfully.

George pursed his lips before answering. "Do you think he can help?"

"If anyone can, it's him." Orielle hesitated considering something else. "He might also know where Va'Rul is held up."

Colton watched the exchange in confusion. "Who is he?"

Orielle's eyes met his own as a look of uncertainty crossed over her face. "He," she began, placing emphasis on the word, "is someone you will need to meet on your own."

A sinister growl echoed across the room, originating from the large cage in the corner. Everyone turned to see Grex'xi watching them all intently. Colton had almost forgotten about the house-sized creature in the cage, but now that he could see her clearly, he was very glad she was in it. Grex'xi was a fearsome creature with snow-covered scales enveloping her entire body. She bared her multiple rows of sword-length teeth with one extremely large tooth protruding from where the lower left canine should be. A prominent gap sat on the opposite side of her mouth where the other such tooth must have fallen out. From the outside looking in, she could have been considered silly looking with such a lopsided looking smile, but Colton couldn't stop his heart from pounding as the monster forced herself onto her two densely-muscled hind legs. As she placed one foot and then the other, the entire space shook from the impact, causing June to let out a small cry.

"Good morning, beautiful!" Skarvald crooned jovially.

In response, Grex'xi roared so loud everyone had to place their hands over their ears. Then she reached forward with her stunted front legs and tried to pry at the metal bars.

"Is that any way to thank someone for giving you a new house?" Skarvald bemoaned, his lip poking out in a pouting expression.

George stood and walked closer to the albino titan. "May I mindlink with you, Queen Grex'xi?"

Grex'xi stopped biting and tearing at the bars and snorted, seemingly giving George permission. A moment later, George squinted in pain and dropped to one knee cradling his head.

"Pa!" Orielle said, rushing to her father's side.

George waved her away and stood up with some effort. "I'm okay. She's just a little bit angry." George squinted again and grunted as Grex'xi stomped a foot. "Sorry, she's very angry and wants to eat everyone here."

"I would be too if someone threw me in a cage," Ember agreed, looking over at Skarvald.

The big man raised his hands, affronted. "Woah, now! I had every intention of letting her go! We just wanted to give her this lovely castle so that when the cult came by, they would find a large surprise waiting for them."

Grex'xi snorted. "She said to tell us how you lured her here," George relayed.

"That hardly seems important–" Grex'xi slammed her shoulder into the cage, causing it to rock precariously.

"She referred to you as a very edible morsel," George said, his eyebrow twitching in discomfort.

"Touchy, touchy," Skarvald complained before taking a deep breath and rolling his eyes. "I may have relocated her egg here a few days ago."

"You stole her baby?" Imbrose asked, non-believing. "Even I wouldn't do that, mate."

"Stole is a strong word," Skarvald began as Grex'xi began to stomp her feet. "Hey! I planned on giving you a new home where you could protect your egg better! You should be thanking me!"

Grex'xi's eyes narrowed as she moved her foot slightly to reveal an albino egg behind her. "She said that in thanks, she will only eat your firstborn instead of your whole family."

"Wait! What if we promised to remove the cult from the forest?" June asked.

Grex'xi turned her gaze on June and she melted under the pressure. "She doesn't believe we actually can," George shared.

"But what if we did?" June pressed.

Grex'xi growled. "She said that if we did, she would forgive this insult, as long as we never come back to this place."

"Easy enough," Imbrose said. "Kill one terrifying monster in hopes of appeasing another."

Grex'xi growled one more time. "She also says we have one hour to clear out of here or she'll eat us all."

Skarvald stood up and brushed himself off. "Sounds like dinner's over then." He tossed a key at George. "She seems to like you, why don't you let her out after we leave?"

George looked down at the key. "How will we find you when we know where Va'Rul is?"

Skarvald sniffed. "We will set up camp a day north of you, there's an old town there." George nodded, and Skarvald turned to Friend. "Are you certain you won't join me, brother?"

Friend shook his head. "I cannot. Though I look forward to sharing the field of battle with you."

Skarvald nodded in understanding. "And I with you. You always have a place with us." Then all of the poachers followed him out of the dilapidated throne room.

Soon, the only sound in the room was the slow intake and exhale of Grex'xi as she watched the remaining group with hungry eyes.

Imbrose walked up next to Colton. "Do we all have to be here when he lets her out?"

Colton felt a smirk cross his lips as Orielle's voice called out from the other side of the room. "Did you guys see that?"

Everyone turned to see her heavily inspecting an empty bird cage of some kind. "Did we see what?" Ember asked, moving to stand next to Orielle.

"There was a little cat inside this cage a moment ago," she said as she tilted her head to look at it from another angle.

Ember looked at Orielle like she was losing her mind. "There's nothing in there, Ori."

Orielle leaned forward and unlatched the cage and began to open it. "I swear there was a–" The cage burst open as an invisible creature jumped forth and began scurrying across the ground leaving tiny paw prints in its wake.

Everyone stood there for a moment shocked by the speed of the creature until Imbrose piped up. "That'll teach you lot to have doubts about my friend Orielle!" He jogged over and draped an arm across her shoulders. "Didn't think you were losing your mind for a second!"

Orielle scoffed and brushed him off, still staring at the paw prints leading out through the broken doors. "He was really cute. Wish you guys had seen him."

"How do you know it was a he?" Colton asked.

"Just a feeling." Orielle smiled sweetly. "Anyway, I don't know about you, but I don't plan on being in here when he lets her out. Let's get some distance."

Chapter Twenty-Three: The First Shade

Releasing Grex'xi proved to be more anticlimactic than the party anticipated. At first, she seemed just relieved to be out of the cage and even thanked them for their help in getting rid of Skarvald and his poachers. However, she then insisted on the group staying for the evening as well. This took everyone aback as she had essentially promised to devour them if they were around for longer than an hour. Ultimately, it became clear that the massive creature was simply lonely, and she had grown fond of George. Eventually though, the sun rose, and the next day began, signaling it was time to make their way home. While Grex'xi tried to appear nonchalant at the news, she refused to let them leave until they came to an agreement for future meetings.

The three days that it took to return home passed in a blur, as not a single beast larger than a squirrel was seen during the trek. Throughout the days, Colton spent most of his time considering the events ahead of them. What would seeing his family again be like after so long, and what could be done about Va'Rul? Two very different issues, and yet they both left him having sleepless nights.

When questioned about some of the things that came to light about his past, Friend made the attempt to avoid giving any definitive answers. His silence on the matter eventually led to Orielle developing a deep sense of worry for the big man. Fortunately, Friend broke his silence on the final day.

"It's all still coming back to me, but I remember that I was a smith for my village," Friend revealed, as Orielle pressed him for answers once again.

"Do you know how you learned to control flames?" Orielle asked coyly.

"As far as I can tell, I have always known how to control fire. It's not all that uncommon where I come from."

"How long has it been since you were home?" Orielle asked.

Friend hesitated, the pain obvious on his face. "I don't know, but I suspect it has been a very long time."

Orielle flinched, realizing she may have pushed too far. "I'm sorry, I didn't mean to–."

"You didn't do anything," Friend reassured, waving his hand. "It's just, I don't know how long it has been. I just have the feeling that I have been sleeping for longer than I initially thought. I think I will know more as my memories continue to return."

Sensing he was done with the conversation, Orielle just smiled. "Well, if you ever need someone to talk to, don't hesitate."

"Thank you, Orielle." Then Friend lapsed into silence once more.

Finally reaching the entrance to the thicket sent a wave of relief over the group, as everyone seemed more than ready for a full night's sleep in a normal bed.

Upon entering, Cartwright, Toku, George, Joel, and June all left to attend to other matters. However, Orielle insisted the rest join her as she intended to introduce everyone to the elusive "him" mentioned back at what was now Grex'xi's home.

Tired, but eager, the group walked down the main path until they turned off to the left, headed directly for the shining lake in the distance. What caught Colton's interest though was that Orielle seemed to be leading them directly to the stilted cabin that always stood out to him as he walked by. As they approached, Colton couldn't see any light coming from the obviously open windows. Confidently, Orielle walked up the steps and rapped on the door a few times while peaking through the window next to the door.

Colton looked to his right to see Imbrose shifting uneasily as he leaned to see into the shadowed cabin. Slowly, the door cracked open and Orielle started to step through, but Colton caught her arm.

"I'm beginning to think you like taking us to creepy houses," Colton frowned, looking into what he could now see was a mildly lit room via candles.

Orielle chuckled. "The Shade is a perfectly harmless person."

"Ah, yes, because you get a name like 'the Shade' because you are known for saving small animals and raising orphans," Imbrose quipped.

Orielle rolled her eyes but the smile was wide on her face. "You're not afraid of some candles are you?"

"I'm afraid—reasonably so I might add—of the person or thing that lit them. It's clear your scary friend wants to instill such feelings before meeting him," Imbrose theorized, taking a small step back.

Suddenly, the candles in the room brightened significantly to illuminate the entire space, revealing a robed individual sitting in a large armchair at the far end of the cabin.

"Is this better, Imbrose?" The voice of the man sitting in the chair was a deep but silky smooth baritone. His voice alone exuded a sense of strength and power that was directly contrasted by his simple attire.

"The whole 'knowing my name before I introduce myself' thing isn't helping your case, pal," Imbrose pointed out, still standing outside the door.

The man chuckled heartily and stood from his chair. "Please come in and introduce yourself then." He then gestured to five identical arm chairs placed in a semicircle around the cabin.

Colton could see the amusement on Orielle's face as the exchange occurred. Finally, Imbrose huffed and walked into the cabin with the rest of them following in behind him. The entire space was only big enough for a single individual to live comfortably in, with only a small stove and a singular door which likely led to a sleeping quarters. The Shade tracked their movements with a smile barely visible from beneath his darkened hood.

Once inside, Orielle closed the door as the other four sat down. "Let me introduce you to 'him,' also known as the First Shade," Orielle said as she too sat down.

Colton looked at the man once again, noticing his vibrant purple eyes that reflected the color of the Grove Tree. The Shade turned to meet his gaze and smiled genuinely. The whole experience made Colton feel as though he should be very nervous right now, but the presence of this man filled him with peace.

"Mister Cobb, I must say, I am very grateful to finally make your acquaintance," the First Shade welcomed. "And you, Imbrose, Ember, and...Friend."

The hesitation when referring to Friend made him tense slightly as he squinted his eyes at the small man in the chair.

Orielle picked up the conversation while everyone else tried to get a read on this man. "Sir, we've brought you a weapon that was taken from the poacher leader. We know very little about its uses but it seems to be specifically designed to hurt our people." Orielle gestured for Friend to hand over the orb, and he pulled the small sphere from his bag and passed it to the Shade.

"This orb has been corrupted." The Shade's voice seemed far away as he analyzed the glassy surface. "This object once served as a lock to protect the world, but now..." His voice trailed off.

"Now what?" Colton asked, his mind addled.

The Shade looked up, breaking from his trance. "I can say no more, but you must find the others like this. No doubt those who have corrupted them intend to use it for vile purposes."

"What do you mean you can't say anymore?" Imbrose said, frustration clear in his voice. "If you know some way to stop something horrible from happening, isn't it your duty to say it?"

The Shade smiled ruefully. "If it were only that simple. The source that gives me the power I use to protect is held in check by certain…guidelines."

Imbrose opened his mouth to speak again, clearly unimpressed by his explanation, but Orielle spoke first. "What *can* you tell us?"

The Shade sighed and set the orb on the small table between them all and leaned back in his chair. "Not much I'm afraid." Imbrose scoffed but remained otherwise silent. "What I can say is that Va'Rul is but a small cog in a machine. He has some dangerous motivations, but ultimately he's a pawn. Killing him would free the Primal Forest for the time being, but you won't be able to succeed in stopping what is to come by staying here."

Orielle screwed up her face in confusion and leaned forward. "Can you tell us where he is, and would killing him save my brother?"

The Shade smiled sadly. "Your brother can be saved, and killing Va'Rul will help. However, your brother will never be the same, and his path is his own to choose." He shifted slightly in his seat, a sense of discomfort obvious. "As to his location, I cannot say, but if you stay your current path you will find out."

Orielle nodded, her eyes darting back and forth in thought. "What should we do with that?" Colton asked, pointing at the orb.

The Shade glanced down again at the red energy swirling within the orb. "If you will allow it, I can keep it and try to put it back the way it once was. But what comes next would be up to you."

Imbrose sighed and licked his lips. "Then what should we do?" he asked, his emotions calming.

"Well, you have a festival to attend tomorrow, do you not?" the Shade asked, his face serious.

"What does tha–" Imbrose was cut off abruptly by Orielle who stood and snapped her fingers.

"Something is going to happen at the festival isn't it?" Orielle questioned.

The Shade stared at her, his eyes never wavering.

With that, she gestured for everyone to stand, and began moving toward the door. Sparing a final glance at the ominous visage of the Shade, Colton stood and moved to follow Orielle.

"And Colton," the Shade called as he reached the door. "Please try to save him, if you can."

"Save who?" Colton asked as the Shade waved his hand and the candles began to dim the interior.

"You will know when the time is right." The voice of the Shade drifted across the space, and try as he might, Colton could no longer make out the shape of the man in the chair.

Colton started to step back into the cabin but was pulled from it by Orielle. "We have to go."

"What's going on, Ori?" Ember asked as everyone moved down steps while Orielle closed the door behind them.

"He told us exactly what we needed to do," Orielle insisted as she walked down the stairs rapidly.

"Were you having a different conversation in there? He hardly told us anything." Imbrose grumbled, pointing over his shoulder.

"No, you just weren't listening. I've been having this feeling that if Va'Rul was planning anything, then the Festival seems like a good time to do it. The Shade's reaction made that a certainty." she iterated, half jogging down the trail back towards the main thoroughfare. "Besides, Joel just told me that Arcadia is going through the final preparations to bring your families through!"

Imbrose looked over at Colton, Ember, and Friend. "Anyone else less than excited for this party now?"

Ember shrugged. "At least we may know more about our enemy."

But Colton couldn't hear them, as he was just thinking about the last thing the Shade had said to him. "Save him if you can." Save who, and how was he supposed to save someone if he didn't know who they were?

Chapter Twenty-Four: Family

T rying to keep pace with a very excited Orielle tested everyone's stamina, as she navigated the crowds with the ease of a cat. Multiple times, Colton and the others lost track of her only for her to pop up from behind a house or nearby passing crowd of people. Before they knew it, Arcadia's house appeared before them, and a pit of anxiety landed right in the center of Colton's stomach. The idea that he was about to show his family the thicket filled him with both excitement and nervousness. His emotions swelled even more, as he considered his grandfather being able to walk beneath the trees of his ancestors. The thought had occurred to him that his family might pack up their entire lives to move here, and he hoped they wouldn't be disappointed by what he found. Ultimately, he just wasn't sure what he was going to say to them.

The time for thoughts came to an end though as the front door opened to reveal a haggard Arcadia frantically waving for them to enter. Without pause, the group followed her inside and into the back room where the pit of sand was the last time they were there. Upon entering the room, Colton gawked at what he saw. Erected in the center of the sand pit was a massive sandstone archway, and within it was a swirling energy reminiscent of Joel's portals.

The swirling energies sputtered slightly and Arcadia cursed as she ran to a table and threw a handful of some pink powder into the vortex. The maelstrom of magic regulated and Arcadia sighed.

"This has proven to be the biggest pain in butt I have ever attempted." Arcadia trudged back to her desk and plopped down into a chair. "First, I had to tear down my wards and then I had to destroy my teleportation circle." She let out an exasperated sigh and looked at the group. "However, it has also been the greatest feat of magic I have ever been involved in, so thank you for that, I suppose."

Colton pursed his lips and made eye contact with Joel who was seated across the room, apparently interested in the magic being performed here. The other man had a broad smile on his face as he looked back at Colton and nodded enthusiastically.

"I'm glad we could bring you a challenge, Arcadia," Ember replied wryly, surveying the disheveled space. "Any idea how long it will be until they come through?"

Arcadia leaned forward as she blinked a few times. "If what your mother said is accurate, it will be around five more minutes until the enchantment solidifies on their end."

"Oh, if she said it, it's accurate." Ember whispered, as they all settled in for the short wait.

Colton gulped as he watched the magic begin to slow as if gravity no longer affected the space around it. Suddenly, a delicate hand reached through the archway, followed by an arm. A couple seconds later, an elegant woman with a long, graying braid of brunette hair and piercing green eyes walked through the portal wearing a green cloak and stylish leather armor. Colton recognized her immediately as Imryth, and smiled as she crossed the space quickly to embrace a bashful Imbrose.

As soon as she finished crossing the threshold, another figure appeared. This one was a tall aristocratic woman with finely-styled dark red hair and hazel eyes. She held herself upright proudly and glanced around the room with a critical eye. Her distinguished red and white dress matched that of her daughter as she finally located Ember next to Imbrose. Colton immediately recognized Meredith by her stonelike demeanor, though it broke immediately as she smiled at her daughter and the two of them moved to meet one another in a big hug.

Colton felt his gut clench as he watched yet another person pass through the portal. However, he could tell immediately who it was even before they came all the way through. The aging man that stood there wore a simple set of clothes and a blindfold around his eyes. His shoulder length white hair, and wrinkled face did nothing to take away from the impressive physique the man still maintained. Colton felt himself smile as he moved to embrace his grandfather for the first time in months. Despite the man's blindness, he navigated the pit easily and pulled Colton into his arms the moment he was within reach.

"I'm so proud of you, my boy. You actually found them." His grandfather's comforting voice pulled tears to Colton's eyes as he hadn't realized just how much he missed him.

"I did it for you, Grandpa," Colton managed as he tried to swallow his emotion.

Still hugging, Colton felt another set of arms wrap around the two of them as he recognized the faint smell of lavender his grandmother always wore. "We've missed you so much, sweetie." Colton pulled his head back enough to see into his grandma's bright blue eyes, and smiled. There had been nothing to worry about, they were just happy to see him. A loud screech of excitement filled the room as Colton broke away from his grandparents to see his little sister Phoebe charging up and out of the sand to nearly tackle him to the ground in a massive hug.

"You're alive! I honestly didn't know if you had made it. After the first few months, I was beginning to think I would have to console our whole family! What have you seen? Are you still single? What's the tribe like?"

Colton pried Phoebe off of him as the questions began to overlap with one another, and he just placed a hand over her mouth. "It's good to see you too, sis."

With that, one final figure walked through the portal, much to Colton's surprise. Standing there awkwardly was Colton's father Xavier, taking in the surroundings as if preparing for an attack. With a big breath, Colton walked to the edge of the pit and held out a hand for his father to take. Xavier looked up at him with his icy blue eyes and grasped it, allowing himself to be pulled from the pit.

The two men stood there clasping hands. "Well done, son." His father's voice betrayed a sense of embarrassment, as he was the only person in the family who had disapproved of his adventure. "It's good to see you."

"And you, father." Sensing that everyone was watching them, he cleared his throat and released his father's hand. Turning to see the others, he saw that he was in fact right. "I'm so glad you guys could all make it. I really didn't know when I was going to be able to see you all again and I honestly didn't think it would be this soon." Colton surveyed the group of his family and friends all together as a thought struck him. "Oh, everyone, please meet Orielle, Joel, Friend, and Arcadia. They have been some of our greatest allies since we found this place."

"I'm flattered," Arcadia huffed sarcastically. "I hadn't realized you placed so much value in our longtime friendship."

Colton smirked, but continued. "Honestly, this is probably the best time for you guys to be here because there's supposed to be a festival."

Imryth's face brightened as she turned to Imbrose who had yet to escape her embrace. "You didn't tell me there was going to be a party! Your father will be so jealous!" The mage let out a hearty laugh and looked over to Meredith, who looked less than enthused at the idea.

"Yes, well, we still don't really know what's going to happen, but from what we've been told, it should be very fun," Colton enthused.

"Aside from the ominous warning from the Shade earlier." Imbrose mumbled under his breath.

Colton ignored his friend and glanced at Orielle who looked very awkward in the corner of the room. Reaching out, he beckoned her to join him as he indicated her to the group. "Though we never would've made it here had it not been for Orielle."

Orielle blushed heavily as she looked around the room nervously.

"She and Joel over there have saved all three of us so many times now that I doubt I could ever return the favor," Colton gushed.

Orielle lowered her head, embarrassed. "I'm glad we could help."

"Help?" Imbrose scoffed. "You saved my life the first time I met you." Imbrose paused, considering. "In fact, I don't know that I ever thanked you for that, so thank you."

Imryth glanced at her son in worry, and as he nodded, Imryth turned her attention to Orielle. "From the bottom of my heart, thank you for saving my boy."

With that, Joel moved to join Orielle and she seemed to gain a bit of confidence. "You're welcome, ma'am. It turned out to be the smartest thing I could do, as he, Colton, and Ember have helped save me multiple times now too."

Imryth smiled as she looked at the three of them, pride obvious on her face.

"Then there's Friend," Colton added, indicating the big metal man standing in the back of the crowd. "He has been a trusted companion throughout it all."

Their families regarded Friend and he simply nodded at all of them as the attention turned back on Colton.

"So, when are you going to show us around?" his grandfather Xander questioned.

Colton smiled and nodded. "Of course, let's give you the tour."

Orielle and Joel took the lead as they traveled around the thicket. Everyone was thoroughly enchanted by the sights they took in, with Xander asking for visual descriptions on every detail and Colton being all too happy to provide them. The whole time, Colton could only smile as he saw how much this mattered to his family. Even his father loosened up as they approached the great purple tree in the center of the thicket.

"I must admit, it's rather beautiful," Xavier marveled, as Orielle finished explaining the significance of the purple flowers all around the base of the tree.

234

"Maybe you and I can go inside sometime?" Colton asked tentatively.

Xavier turned to look at him, the two of them exchanging a meaningful glance. "I'd like that." The group was led away from the Grove, but Xavier gripped Colton's forearm. "I'm sorry I doubted you, son. You were right to seek out our people."

Colton swallowed hard, his father's apology catching him off guard. "You had your reasons, and I can't fault you for your skepticism."

Xavier chuckled lightly. "I'm a stubborn man, Colton. However, I can admit when I'm wrong." The older man paused, as he placed a hand on Colton's shoulder. "Your mother would be proud of the man you've become, just as I am."

Squeezing his shoulder, Xavier pulled him into a hug before walking with him to catch up to the others.

Eventually, the sun dropped behind the tall walls of the bramble that surrounded them and Orielle suggested they show them to their sleeping quarters. Upon arriving at the cabins, Orielle gracefully excused herself, stating she would come to meet them in the morning. Colton found himself watching her as she left, wishing she had stayed just a little longer.

"She's pretty," Xander commented casually as he walked up next to him.

Colton raised an eyebrow and glanced over at his grandfather. "How do you know? You're blind."

A smirk twitched at the corner of Xander's mouth. "With how much you've been staring at her, she must be. Never noticed you look at someone like that before."

Colton opened his mouth to speak, then closed it as Orielle turned a corner and left his view. With a sigh, he turned and escorted his family into the small cabin that had been set aside for them.

"You're right," Colton confirmed as he stepped through the door just behind Xander. "She is very pretty."

"Come on, let's have a drink," Xander insisted as the family moved into the humble establishment.

Once everyone was seated comfortably inside, Colton surveyed the group. To see them all in one spot after such a long time was a welcome relief from the stresses of the previous months. A smile danced across his face as he watched Imbrose, and Ember who also relished in the comfort of their parents, laughter echoing through the small abode.

"So, tell us about your adventures, Grandson," Xander finally coaxed.

And Colton did. He told them about their landing and how Curtis had betrayed them. He went on to speak about their time trying to survive in the forest and his nearly suicidal attempt to save everyone else. He even told them about his new powers and offered to help them find their own. His father perked up at this, asking a few questions about how it worked.

The evening carried on with Colton regaling his family with tales of heroics and adventures, while conveniently downplaying the danger of it all. The family was content to listen to him and only interjected a few times for clarification.

As Colton spoke, a sense of accomplishment washed over him. His eyes drifted over to his grandfather who smiled broadly, and his heart swelled. Everything he had been through to bring them to Zerua, had been worth it.

Chapter Twenty-Five: Smithing At Its Finest

T he revelries ended much sooner than Colton expected, as his family appeared to be drained from the long-distance travel. Saying their goodnights, Colton, Imbrose, and Ember all returned to their own house and quickly found themselves in bed.

Sleep came quickly to Colton as he found himself far more at ease than he had been in a very long time. However, as soon as he closed his eyes, he found himself transported to a starlit abyss. As he glanced around, he could tell he was dreaming immediately, which came as a shock because he had never had a lucid dream before. The space rippled as if he were looking into a pool of water recently disturbed by a thrown rock. The effect left Colton a bit woozy before the scene shifted, leaving him in a darkened cave. The transition caused the ground to fall out from under him briefly as he dropped two feet to the soft dirt floor of the cave.

Immediately, he reached behind him for the hilt of his blade, only to find it wasn't there. Cursing, he looked around for some sign of where he was and was shocked to recognize the space around him as the caves beneath the Grove Tree. As soon as he came to that realization, the purple flowers began to flair with dim fluorescent light. Looking both ways, he put together that he was in a corridor, leaving only two ways to go. Since neither path gave him any indication as to what he may encounter, he just decided to start walking the way he was originally facing.

Nothing happened for a long time with the exception of the flowers activating as he passed them. The further he walked, the more certain he became that he was traveling the right direction. The tunnel seemed to go on forever until finally, he reached a fork in the cave and he paused, unsure of which way to go.

"Colton…" a barely audible whisper of a female voice echoed from the darkness on his right. Instantly, the voice reminded him of Orielle and he instinctively took a step in its direction.

Turning his back on the other passage, he leaned closer to impenetrable darkness from where the voice came from. "Orielle? Where are you?" His voice echoed loudly down the hall but there was no response.

Taking another step forward, Colton heard a slithering sound behind him and immediately knew there was something there. His skin prickled as he slowly turned his head to look at the other passage, dreading what he may find. Breathing deeply, he turned the rest of the way quickly to reveal…nothing. Colton let the breath out as he tried to calm his racing heart.

In a blink, the massive form of Va'Rul filled the passage less than a foot in front of him with his mouth wide, rows of teeth already closing around Colton's frozen form. Colton winced and closed his eyes as the snake's mouth closed around him, but he felt no pain. Instead, when he opened his eyes he saw himself standing in one of the groves like the one he visited with Terry. All around him, he could see Dream Blooms giving off their vibrant purple glow.

The biggest difference between what he saw the last time he was here and now was that Lucas was standing in the center of the grove, his head bowed. Colton took a tentative step toward the man, shaking his head slightly at the insanity of this dream.

"Lucas, you alright?" His voice came out a hoarse whisper.

Stepping closer, Colton could see a curved dagger loosely grasped in his right hand. Suddenly, Lucas threw his head back and screamed, as hundreds of black tendrils flooded out of his mouth and dove for the various flowers covering the ground. One by one, Colton watched the flowers begin to wilt and die as Lucas continued to scream. The sheer volume and pain in his voice stalled Colton, but upon seeing the flowers succumb to whatever he was doing, he sprinted toward Lucas as fast as he could go.

"Lucas!" Colton yelled the word as he closed the distance. "You need to stop! You're killing them!"

When Colton stepped within ten feet of Lucas, his mouth snapped shut and he lowered his gaze to meet Colton's. "No, I'm consuming them." A terrible smile spread across his face as he brought the dagger to his neck.

"No!" But it didn't matter as Lucas slit his own throat and blood spewed forth. Colton watched in horror as the man's eyes suddenly filled with terror before he collapsed into the dried and dead petals of the once vibrant Dream Blooms.

Sliding to his knees next to the blood-soaked body, Colton raised Lucas' head into his lap and pressed his hands on the gaping wound in his neck in vain.

"You've failed," Lucas coughed as blood filled his mouth. "You couldn't save me." Then Lucas went still as the pulsing stopped beneath Colton's hands.

Colton lifted his hands and stared at his crimson soaked palms, a feeling of complete failure passing over him as Lucas' corpse disintegrated into ash right before his eyes. A loud crash came to his left, and he could vaguely see the large mass of Va'Rul once again bearing down on him. However, he couldn't stop staring at his hands as he blinked in disbelief. The maw closed around him, and his world fell into darkness.

Colton sat bolt upright as his nightmare finally ended. Sweat drenched his skin and clothes as he took heaving breaths. With a shaking hand, he wiped his brow, it coming away soaked with perspiration.

"Are you okay?" Orielle's voice shook him from his post-sleep haze.

He turned to see her standing in the doorway to his room with a look of genuine worry on her face. "Yes, I'm fine. Just a bad dream is all."

Orielle nodded. "Sorry for barging in. We just heard you yelling in the other room and got nervous." Colton shook his head to clear it and swung his legs off the bed. "I was hoping to catch you before you went to see your family again."

"Sure, just let me wash my face off, and I'll meet you in the common room."

Orielle turned to leave, but paused. "Are you sure you're okay?"

Reaching the washbasin in his room, Colton splashed water onto his face and looked over at Orielle still standing in the doorway. "Yeah Ori, I'm alright," he insisted weakly, managing a smile.

"O-okay, I'll just wait for you out here then," she muttered as she closed the door behind her.

Alone, Colton closed his eyes and let out a deep sigh, water dripping off his face. The dream still ran through his mind on repeat, and he found himself getting more anxious the longer he thought about it. Grunting, he dunked his entire head into the chilly water, trying to clear his thoughts of the horrible images. However, the soundlessness of being completely submerged only helped to intensify the visual of Lucas slicing his own throat open in front of him. With a jerk, he yanked his head from the barrel and stumbled back from it as he braced himself on the edge of the bed. *Was that who he meant I needed to save?* The possibility that something like that would actually come to pass and he was expected to prevent it made his head hurt. Why was he having these dreams? He never had such vivid nightmares before coming here.

His thoughts were interrupted as he got a whiff of himself, and cringed. It turned out that a night of sweating through your clothing didn't help with one's odor control. Pulling his linen shirt off, he approached the basin once more and set about the task of cleansing himself before what promised to be a very interesting day. The day the festival was meant to take place had finally arrived. A smile played at the corner of his lips as he considered the merriment to come later that evening.

Drying himself with a linen cloth, Colton looked down to see the wound he received from the porcupine quill had completely healed by now, leaving a grisly scar in its place. He rubbed the physical memento, expecting it to be sensitive, but found it just a bit rough to the touch. This place had changed him in more ways than one, and he knew it would only continue to do so the longer he stayed. The thought made him consider what type of person he would have become if he had just stayed back in the Archipelago. Could he have ever found out how to access the sword? One thing's for certain, he would definitely have less scars and feel a whole lot safer.

Colton shook his head in defiance. It had all been worth it just to see his grandfather's face when he arrived. Then there was…her. Remembering he was being waited on, he quickly tossed the rough, makeshift towel onto the floor and put on another wrinkled shirt he pulled out of his travel pack, and made for the door.

Stepping into the main room he saw Orielle and Ember sitting at a small table sipping some kind of tea. As the door closed behind him, both women turned to look at him. Orielle no longer wore the worried expression she had before she left his room, and instead jumped to her feet with a big smile on her face.

"Are you ready to go?" she exclaimed.

Colton couldn't help but grin back at her, the excitement infectious. "Ready to go? Go where?"

Her face took on a mischievous look as she spoke. "You'll have to wait and find out!"

Colton nodded slowly, glancing down at Ember. "Do you know anything about this?"

Ember drew her finger across her lips. "My lips are sealed." Then she returned to sipping her tea.

Shaking his head in mock frustration, Colton gestured to Orielle. "Well, let's go then! Lead the way."

The young woman pumped her fist in triumph, and opened the front door pointing for Colton to go first. Letting out a sigh, he walked to the door and out into the morning sunlight.

Within moments, Colton knew they were headed to her house since he had traveled the path himself frequently enough. As they approached the house, Orielle exclaimed and reached into her pocket, seeming to remember something.

"I almost forgot! We received word from Genevieve while we were gone." She handed over a folded parchment with the wax seal unbroken. "Here!"

Colton took the letter with a nod, unfolding it and began reading Genevieve's elegant script.

Colton,

We arrived at the Thicket of Rivers to a very friendly group of people! By the end of the first day, they were trying to get us to stay permanently. However, it only took two days for us to realize our hunt for Curtis was likely in vain. From the accounts we received here, his ship did try to cut through the Andromedus but was heavily damaged from some unknown attack. From the looks of it, he and the remaining crew beached the ship and continued north on foot.

I tried to tell Delphine that he's likely dead and eaten by some big beastie, but she wouldn't have any of it and left in the night to chase him. She's too elusive for even the folks here to track down, but if anyone can survive out there alone, it's her.

Since we don't have any other way of locating him, or her, we are going to continue with the original mission to establish communications with the folks of this continent. We'll start with the Glacerian Court to the north, as by all accounts they are the more reasonable of the two powerhouses here. With any luck, we'll run into Delphine and Curtis on the way and we can deal with two birds with one stone.

I hope all is well down there, and if you do send a reply, have it sent up to the Thicket of Frost. Oh, and Quinn finally worked up the courage to make a move so I'm off the market now. Sorry, you missed your shot!

    Be safe,

    Genevieve

Finishing the letter, he handed the unfolded parchment back to Orielle, gesturing for her to read it too. The news that Genevieve and Quinn were finding happiness in this new world helped to dull the frustration of Delphine running off into the woods by herself. Still, somewhere in his gut, he had known she would do something reckless from the moment he let her go after Curtis.

Orielle folded up the letter and held it out for Colton. "Wow, I honestly didn't think Delphine had it in her."

Colton bit his lip. "She's hurting…" He let the words hang in the air, the connection to what Orielle said about Lucas clear.

With a nod, Orielle left the topic alone and led him the rest of the distance to her house. However, unlike every other time he had been here, they didn't walk up to the front door. Instead, Orielle walked around the side of the house to the shed that sat just to the left of the main building. Colton recognized the small dwelling from the day he heard screaming and yelling coming from within, but thought better of mentioning it.

Heaving, Orielle pulled the sliding door open to reveal an interior that could only be described as organized chaos. There were at least six individual work benches with various unfinished works on them. As Colton stepped through the threshold and kicked a small screw across the floor, Orielle closed the door behind them and then crossed to where the screw had scattered to.

"I've been looking for this little guy," she commented, placing it among a large pile of more screws.

"Quite the shop you have here," Colton observed as he walked around the space. To one side he noticed a small workbench that was much closer to the ground than the others and he approached it. "Was this your first one?" he asked, picking up a small hammer from the table.

"No, that was Jasper's before..." Her voice had saddened so dramatically that Colton quickly turned to face her. Orielle had her back to him, and Colton gently laid the small tool back on the worn wooden bench before taking a hesitant step closer.

"I'm sorry, I–" Colton began.

"It's okay." She wiped her face and turned to look at him. "He was the only one who liked being out here with me. So, I made him a bench he could work on while I worked on mine. He spent most of his time over there though, just watching me," she recalled, pointing at a tall stool right next to one of the wooden tables.

Colton looked over at where she was pointing and saw that on the stool now sat a potted Dream Bloom, slowly undulating with purple light. "Is that a Dream Bloom from the Grove?" Colton asked as he approached the flower slowly.

"It's my Dream Bloom," Orielle stated.

Colton froze in place. "Oh, well, it's beautiful."

He heard her scoff and he turned to see her smiling at him. "They all look the same, goof."

"I suppose they do, but yours is beautiful," Colton insisted, his eyes never wavering from hers.

After a moment, Orielle reddened and turned away from him, going to a nearby metal chest nestled in the corner and threw it open. "I find it easier to work in its presence, but I have to take it back every now and then or it'll start to feel lonely."

"Feel lonely?" Colton repeated.

Orielle giggled slightly as she pulled a small bundle from the chest and laid it on the table between her and Colton. "The flower is a part of me, but it belongs with the others. I find that its glow gets dimmer the longer it stays in here. I just assume that it gets lonely."

"Hmm, what do you usually make here?"

Orielle tilted her head, looking down at the bundle on the table. "Lots of things, since I'm a Spirit Smith."

"That's right! Joel told me about that. What does that mean?"

"Well, the short version is that I can make items that take in our spirit power more readily. Take my pistols for example." She pulled an ornate pistol from her thigh holster and laid it on the table. "I channel my power into it, and it creates a blast of energy that shoots out of the barrel here." Colton leaned toward the device, marking this moment as the closest he had ever been to it. "I won't bore you with the details, but there's a lot of rune work that goes into making something like this. Then it takes even more work to get used to shooting your power away from you. Took me months to not pass out every time I shot it."

"It's incredible. I've never seen weapons like these in person, only heard of them."

Orielle's brow furrowed. "There are others like this one?"

"Oh no, nothing like this. It's just that before I was born, there was a war where the creatures who attacked the Archipelago had weapons that shot projectiles. Luckily, Imbrose and Ember's mothers were part of a very powerful group of people who were able to put an end to it."

"Sounds scary... but these pistols are one of a kind around here. Many have tried to get me to make them for their uses, but I always refused. These were the first things I ever made with Jasper, so I like keeping it just between him and I." Colton smiled at the sentiment. "Anyway, I wanted to give you this. Since you lost your other one trying to save us all." She pushed the bundle she had retrieved earlier closer to him.

Gingerly, Colton reached out and unraveled the thick cloth to reveal a dark green, leather-braided handle. He smirked as he quickly pulled away the rest of the fabric to display a ten foot coiled whip with a large blue crystal weaved into the tip. As he admired the craftsmanship, he realized there was a purplish glint being given off as he rotated it in the light.

"I figured I should thank you for helping me at the prison. I felt horrible about how I left without saying anything to you, so I decided I would make you your own unique weapon. Do you like it?" she asked timidly.

245

Colton ran a hand along the tightly wound leather. "Like it? I love it! This has got to be the most amazing thing anyone has ever done for me," he exclaimed, not trying to hide his excitement. "What's this for?" he asked, indicating the gem at the top.

"Oh, that!" she enthused, her voice filled with obvious pleasure at his reaction. "If you channel your power into it, you can create a form of your choosing. I noticed you had a knife on the end of your last one. Well, with this one, you could have anything you want in the end."

"This is glorious, Ori. I can't thank you enough. I've gotten a lot better with the sword, but I must admit I missed the feeling of a whip in my hands."

"I'm glad you like it! That's why I left early last night. I wanted to finish this for you as a gift before the festival this evening."

Colton reached out and took her hand in his, and squeezed it. "I love it, thank you."

After a moment's hesitation, she squeezed back and looked up at him. The two of them gazed at one another for a heart-pounding second before Colton reluctantly released her hand and gathered up the whip to latch it to his belt.

"How do I look?" Colton asked, as he finished attaching his new weapon.

Orielle smirked. "Dashing. It suits you."

"What did you do to get the purple accents?" Colton asked, cocking his head at the phenomenon.

"I weaved in some plant fibers from my flower. It helps to prevent the whole passing out thing I told you about earlier."

Colton looked up in shock. "What? Doesn't that contain your memories?"

Orielle giggled. "The memories are contained in the essence of the flower. Besides, it grows back quickly."

"You promise it didn't damage it at all?" Colton implored worriedly.

Orielle raised her hands, warding off his concern. "I promise! It's standard practice for us Spirit Smiths. It's kind of like an artist's signature, if you will." Colton relaxed, admiring the whip once more. "Speaking of my Dream Bloom, I really should take it back to the grove now. Would you like to come with me?"

"Of course." Orielle walked over and grabbed the flower from the stool as Colton held the door open for her.

The two of them made their way to the Grove Tree in companionable silence, both seemingly happy just to be in the other's presence. The trip felt too quick to Colton as Terry waved at them from the entrance. After exchanging pleasantries, the two of them proceeded into the tree, Colton letting Orielle lead the way. After a few turns down various tunnels, Colton felt himself get turned around and he couldn't help but remember the dream from the previous evening. Just as he felt his mind begin to panic, they turned into a brightly lit grove with purple light illuminating the entire space. Orielle moved to an already pre-dug spot near the center and began planting her flower.

Colton watched the process with interest and an idea came to him. "Could I make my own flower?"

Orielle glanced over her shoulder as she patted the soil around the base of her Dream Bloom. "Certainly. Most kids around the age of six have already cultivated theirs. I bet it would actually be quite easy for you."

"Would you mind showing me how to do it sometime?"

Orielle patted the soft soil next to her. "Why not now?" Accepting the invitation, Colton walked over next to her and kneeled as she shifted slightly to the left facing an empty spot in the grove.

"So, how does this work?" Colton could feel the warmth of her body as she leaned forward and cleared away a small amount of dirt.

"You need to create the seed within yourself, and then plant it here," Orielle instructed, pointing at her chest. "To do that, you have to imagine taking a small piece of your spirit and compressing it into a focused bead of energy."

Colton closed his eyes and focused on his center, locating that same core from before. Taking slow breaths, he reached in and plucked the smallest piece he could and held it in his metaphysical hands.

"Good, now you need to nurture it and pour your memories into it."

Colton listened to her calming voice, and focused on his childhood and how he made his first hat from scratch. He focused on the first time he held a whip and how organic it felt. A memory of a young girl with golden hair popped into his mind as he remembered Cassie, his first crush. His memories flowed into the small piece of himself, and he watched his life play out before him as if the energy—no, the *seed*—was absorbing all of his experiences at once. The first time he visited the great city of New Eradin and every time after that. The day his grandfather told him the story of their tribe, and the subsequent annoyance his father felt when Colton told him. It all ran into the seed like water until it finally reached his present self. The torrent of memories slowed as he watched himself walk into this very grove and then kneel in the dirt, finally catching up to the present.

With a gasp, Colton opened his eyes to see a glowing marble of blue light resting in his hands. "Wow, that was easier than I thought it would be." Orielle's voice caused Colton to look over at her. "Well, go on," she urged. "Plant it!"

Not needing further prompting, Colton placed the seed in the dirt and covered it. Immediately, the dirt began to shift as a stem of vibrant green protruded from the dirt and grew to a foot above the soil. As it reached its apex, a small bulb appeared at the top and a beautiful blue flower unfurled for the first time.

"Is it supposed to be blue?" Colton asked, nervously.

Orielle hesitated. "I've never seen one before, but its energy feels so pure."

Colton focused on the little flower. "Is it okay?"

She leaned forward a bit and observed the flower closer. Then, she pulled back with a broad smile on her face. "Oh, yes. It's very healthy and will continue to grow the more memories you put into it."

Colton smiled, proud of his feat. A memory came to the surface then. Reactively, he reached out and plucked two small petals from the flower as Orielle gasped.

"What are you doing?" she asked.

Colton held out his hand for her. Tentatively, she placed her hand in his, palm up. Gently, Colton placed one of the blue petals in her hand and closed her fist around it. "Joel once said that you can communicate long distances since you both have a petal from your flower."

Orielle glanced down at her hand and swallowed. "That's true, but you shouldn't have plucked them from your flower so soon…" Her voice trailed off as she looked at the flower in disbelief. The petals had already been replaced and the flower had already grown another inch.

"It's like you said. It doesn't hurt the flower any," Colton echoed, looking at her.

Orielle bit her lower lip, then pulled her hand to her chest. "I'll treasure it."

Colton was at war with himself. He felt every instinct in his body wanting to be close to her and lean in. However, something stopped him. He could still tell that she was healing from her recent break up with Lucas, and he didn't want to push her before she was ready. Instead, he stood and held out his hand to help her up. She took it and stood up next to him.

"I should really get going. My grandparents are early risers, and I suspect they're already wondering where I'm at," Colton sighed, his heart still pounding.

Orielle nodded, as her eyes met his. "And I have to prepare for the festival."

Colton chuckled nervously. "Would you mind showing me how to get out of here? I just know I'd get lost if I tried to figure it out on my own."

"Of course." Orielle blushed and walked past him, gently brushing his shoulder. Colton sighed and glanced down one last time at his flower right next to hers before turning to follow her out.

Chapter Twenty-Six: Jailbreak

After parting ways with Orielle, Colton made his way to the house his grandparents were staying in. When he arrived, he was surprised to see that no one was there. Panicking slightly, he rushed back to his house to find Imbrose casually eating a sandwich as Imryth, Ember, and Meredith all talked around a table.

"Oh, there you are, Colton, dear," Imryth greeted as she waved to him. "I'm afraid you just missed your family. They were scooped up by some scrumptious older fellow by the name of George. He said he wanted to show them around."

"Ew, did you actually just call him scrumptious, Mum?" Imbrose intoned from across the room. "I don't even know if I can finish my sandwich with that kind of talk being thrown around."

Imryth just waved her hand at him. "Quit being so dramatic. I'm married, not dead. Besides, I think your father would agree with me if he were here."

"Nope, I'm done," Imbrose declared, tossing his half-eaten sandwich back onto the plate in front of him.

"Guess they couldn't wait for me," Colton said with a chuckle.

"I told them you were…preoccupied," Ember said with a playful smile and a wink.

Colton looked up at the ceiling and sighed as Imbrose approached him from the right. "Come on, let's get out of here and do guy stuff before we start calling old men 'scrumptious.'"

All three women chuckled with glee, and waved at them as they left.

"Hungry?" Imbrose asked, as he closed the door behind them.

Colton looked at his friend incredulously. "Didn't you just throw away half of a sandwich in disgust?"

Imbrose shrugged. "That was then, *now* I'm craving whatever kabobs that guy in the market was selling earlier."

Shaking his head, Colton oriented himself toward the market and started walking. "Alright, I've been meaning to try it anyway." Something popped into Colton's head. "Oh, but I need to make a small side detour while we're there."

"Sure, sure," Imbrose dismissed easily, giving him a thumbs up.

Walking side by side for the first time in what felt like forever was a nice change of pace for both of them. Colton realized there was quite a lot he hadn't filled Imbrose in on, and set about remedying that. He began with how he started to discover his power, and even practiced mindlinking by talking to Imbrose telepathically sometimes. Before now, it had always been a severe struggle to connect with anyone, even with him. Now though, it was as easy as a thought. Colton even decided it was time to tell him about his budding feelings for Orielle and received an unimpressed raised eyebrow in response.

"What?" Colton asked.

"Am I supposed to be shocked?" Imbrose questioned, his hand moving to his mouth to simulate shock. "Oh, really? I never would've guessed! You're so good at hiding how you feel!"

Colton shoved the scrawny blue man none too gently. "Shut up! You're one to talk Mister 'I've been pining after the same woman since I was an infant.'"

Imbrose chuckled and returned to his friend's side. "Ah, well, the days of secret yearning are finally behind us, thank Tyrrek."

252

Colton turned. "Started using Tyrkin sayings, huh?"

"Huh, I suppose so. There are definitely worse Gods to call on when asking for thanks."

He had to agree. Crastia, the Goddess of violence and revenge, being the first that came to mind for him. "That's true enough."

The duo casually walked along a small path, approaching the main road. "Still, I'm happy for you," Imbrose commented as they stepped into the late morning foot traffic. "You deserve happiness, and she might just be enough woman to wrangle in the all desirable Colton Cobb." He finished the last bit with a flourish of his arm, as if he was presenting him.

Colton laughed, and slapped his hand away. "I just don't know if it's proper to push anything so soon after, you know…"

Imbrose smacked his lips. "Yeah, that's a tough one… Just follow your gut, mate. I'm sure she's feeling the same way." The two of them finally spotted the kabob merchant and advanced toward him.

The aroma coming from the little stall was no doubt the cause of the small crowd that prevented their view of the merchants' wares. Pushing their way through the group of people caused at least a couple grumbles, as they finally reached the counter where the man was taking and fulfilling orders as fast as he could.

The man, who must have been in his mid fifties, turned to Imbrose with a weary, but genuine smile. "What can I get for you, lad?"

Imbrose looked past the man and pointed at two foot-long skewers of meat and veggies. "Whatever those are!"

The man reached back and quickly scooped the two kabobs up and held out his free hand. "That'll be ten silver."

Imbrose rustled inside his cloak until he produced empty hands and looked to Colton. Rolling his eyes, Colton tossed a bag of a few gold onto the counter top.

Skeptical, the merchant opened the bag and peaked inside and then smiled brightly. "Oh, thank you sir! Here you are!" With the food extended, Imbrose wasted no time in scooping the two sticks up and passed one to Colton.

His mouth already salivating at the savory scent of the meat, Colton wasted no time in biting off a piece. "So, how much did you pay him?" Imbrose asked, already devouring his second mouthful.

"I'm not sure, found that bag of coins while we were leaving Grex'xi's. Not even certain I ever looked inside."

Imbrose stopped walking. "You mean to say that could have been a small fortune in that bag?"

Colton shrugged. "Could've been, but probably not. Sounded more like five to ten gold if you ask me." Noticing Imbrose wasn't keeping up, he turned around to see him with his mouth full still staring at him.

"I'm never lending you money," he fumed, passing Colton as he squinted his eyes.

"Imbrose! I'm kidding! There were only a few emeralds and a gold coin."

"What!" Imbrose screamed, his food flying out of his mouth at the exasperation. "You gave that man emeralds for a stick of meat?"

"There are veggies on it too..." Colton said defensively.

"Unbelievable." Imbrose threw up his arms, almost losing his meal in the process. Colton smirked and followed behind his friend, who was now actively trying to gain distance from him.

After a while, Imbrose relaxed and returned to Colton's side as they continued joking with one another. That is, until Colton noticed an intricate metal worker's shop off to one side of the path. Casually drifting that direction, he found exactly what he was looking for: a small pendant that had an openable lock.

"How much for this one here?" Colton asked, pointing at the silver locket.

A woman of slight physique walked up to the counter. "Ah, this one," the woman purred as she reached out and flipped the locket over. "As you can see, it has a one of a kind etching on the back in the shape of a phoenix rising from the ashes." The woman paused, seeming to consider something. "I could part with it for...thirty-five gold?"

Colton had to admit, the design on the back was beautiful, but he didn't exactly have thirty-five gold on him. However, he did have something else. "Would you take two emeralds for it?"

Imbrose choked to his left.

The woman eyed him curiously. "They would need to be nearly flawless emeralds."

Colton reached into his pocket and pulled out a small silk pouch. Reaching in, he pinched two of the multitude of stones that were inside between his thumb and index finger, and pulled them out. The emeralds were a brilliant shade of green as the light caught them at just the right angle.

He passed the gems over to her and continued looking around the shop. The woman mumbled something and nodded happily as she appraised the gems. "Yes, these will do nicely."

She quickly plucked the locket from the plush pillow it was lying on and set it into Colton's outstretched hand. "I'd also like that one over there," he asserted, pointing to a plain-looking iron locket.

The woman glanced over at the worn locket, and shrugged. With a swift flick of her wrist she grabbed and tossed the necklace to Colton. "You can have it for free! Consider it a thank you for your patronage."

Bowing his head slightly, Colton turned to leave and bumped directly into Imbrose. "I'm going to steal that bag of gems from you tonight," the hellborn said quietly in a sing-songy voice.

Colton smirked and patted him on the cheek. "You're welcome to try, my little blue friend." Then he walked past him and pulled a little blue petal out of his pocket and placed it in the iron locket, closing it tightly. Realizing the chain was plenty big enough to fit over his head, he simply donned the locket and inspected it happily.

The locket was indeed plain, but Colton could see a small garnet placed into the center of the front face. It also had a small inscription carved into the back in a type of elegant cursive saying: *All My Love*. Colton leaned back in surprise as he considered who this locket may have belonged to in its previous life. The thought that such love went into making it initially filled him with happiness as he let the small necklace drop to his chest.

Next, he opened the phoenix locket to see the inside of the lid was encased in small rubies. They were flawed to be certain, but they held an elegant beauty as the fractals of light danced along the silver metal. He decided it was fit for what he had in mind and pocketed it.

After they left the main market square, they started walking up toward the training grounds, as Imbrose had mentioned he wanted to beat some sense into him. Along the way, a familiar figure waved at the both of them and ran to catch them.

"I'm glad I ran into you two!" Joel exclaimed as he approached.

"Hey Joel, what's up? Colton said, shaking his hand.

Joel pulled a small ring of keys out of his pocket and flipped it around in his hand. "Wanna help me out with this Sero guy?"

Colton narrowed his eyes. "Help how?"

"Well, I've been given the task of deciding whether or not he's trustworthy enough to be let out. So, I was hoping to have a little back up while I question him to find out what his true intentions are."

Colton looked to Imbrose who shrugged. "Sure, we're in."

The trio walked back through the market and past the lake where the First Shade lived. Once they reached the switchbacks, Colton realized it wasn't nearly as tiring as it had been when he was fairly new around the thicket. What was more, as he walked up he was greeted by some of the people he had seen around. This place really was becoming a home to him, and he liked the way that felt. Cresting the final hill, the three men approached the prison's gatehouse. Standing guard as usual was Jerric, who simply nodded at the three of them and opened the door for them to enter.

Colton expected that going back into the prison would prove to be nerve wracking for him, but it didn't really bother him at all. Something about the finality of the encounter he had here with the monster they fought made him feel a sense of hope. Like perhaps defeating this creature that had caused so much misery in its wake really was possible.

Afterall, they had beaten him here. Just him and Orielle. Surely if they had Skarvald and his people as well as their own, they could destroy Va'Rul easily. Yet, there was a deep sense of foreboding nagging at the back of Colton's mind. The nightmares had done their work, and he couldn't help but worry about the alternative. Reaching the end of the hallway, the group turned to see Sero lying on his cot, tossing a small ball into the air and catching it.

As soon as his eyes registered the keys in Joel's hand, he jumped to his feet and came to the bars. "Finally! I was beginning to think you guys forgot about me." Sero laughed nervously, clearly not lying.

Joel casually walked up to the gate then, seeming to think better of it, backed away, and sat down on the bench against the stone wall. "No, Sero, we've been thinking about you quite a lot, actually."

Noticing the intimidating tone Joel was adopting, Colton decided to mirror him and simply stare at the unassuming teen.

"Uh, is that a good thing?" Sero asked, his voice rising.

Joel leaned back and crossed his legs. "That remains to be seen." Joel paused, making Sero's eyes dart around nervously. "Your information proved to be true–"

"You see! I told you I was trustworthy," Sero interjected.

"But…" Joel let the word hang. "We are more curious as to how you know this information."

Sero hesitated, obviously having some internal battle with himself. "Speak up, kid," Colton said gruffly.

Sero backed away from the bars and sat down on the bed. "Look, I didn't just stumble upon your thicket. I was told to come here."

Joel leaned forward, his curiosity piqued. "Told by whom?"

Sero opened his mouth to speak, but closed it again and licked his lips nervously. After a few minutes of silence, Imbrose approached the bars and tapped on them with his red dagger. "Hey, you awake in there? He asked you a question."

Sero glared up at the horned man who didn't back down. "I know, I'm just trying to decide if I trust you with my life, is all," he said through clenched teeth.

Joel looked up at Colton and mindlinked with him. *The kid is scared of something. Let's cool it on the tough-guy approach.*

Colton nodded almost imperceptibly, and stepped forward placing a hand on Imbrose's shoulder. "This place is safe, and the only way we can trust you is if you tell us what you know."

Sero sighed. "His name is Scorpion. At least that's what he makes everyone call him." Joel stood and joined the other two at the bars. "He's been hunting for your thicket. Claims to have been a guest here once, but after the leader at the time figured out why he was really here, they kicked him out."

"Do you know his real name, and where he is?" Joel asked.

"Not a clue what his actual name is, could be Scorpion for all I know. However, he comes from the Barren Steppe. I could tell by his accent. Now, though, he's living in Tri-Spire." Sero's voice was low and shaking. He was obviously afraid of this individual.

"Why did he tell you to come here?" Joel questioned.

"He said I was supposed to look for a flower and bring it to him. A purple one. Said I would know it when I saw it," Sero admitted, his head hung low.

Joel's voice once again sounded off in Colton's head. *I think he's telling the truth, but what do you guys think?*

Looking over at Imbrose, he could tell Joel had projected his thoughts to him as well. After a long moment, Imbrose nodded and stepped away from the bars.

Colton just had one more question. "Why betray him? You're obviously scared of him."

Sero grimaced and looked back up at the two of them. "I wasn't sent alone. There were two of us, and I thought we were friends, but I learned I was wrong." The young man stood up and walked to the corner of the cage. "I saw a group of your scouts making their way through the forest when we first came in. I told him, because he was my direct superior and because like I said, I thought we were friends. When he told me to go kill them, I was shocked. I had never been told to kill innocents before." His voice broke as he recounted what happened to him. "I told him I wouldn't do it, and he said 'Scorpion said I needed to dispose of you anyway' and then he attacked me."

Joel pursed his lips. "I'm sorry, is that why you were injured when we found you?"

Sero nodded. "I somehow managed to land a hit on an artery in his leg and he panicked before bleeding out in front of me. I...I didn't mean to kill him!" Sero brought a hand up to his face with his back still to them. "I just, I didn't have any choice."

Joel cleared his throat. "Look at me, Sero." The boy turned around and looked Joel in the eyes. "What happened to you was horrible, and I want to believe you, but our home is only safe if we are certain about who we let in." Joel walked around the cage until he was face to face with Sero. "Look me in my eyes and tell me you aren't a threat to the people here."

Sero straightened and held Joel's gaze. "I'm not a threat to anyone here, but when I see Scorpion again, I'll kill him."

Joel winced a bit at the venom in the young man's voice, but reached down and unlocked the cage door slowly. "You can stay as long as you need, and you may even find this to be a suitable place to call home in time. Stay true to your promise though, or I'll kill you myself."

Colton turned to look at Joel, surprised at the calmness in his voice. The look on Joel's face held no doubt that he would do what he claimed, and while a few weeks ago he may have been shocked at the coldness of it, now he understood completely. This was his home, and the people here, his family. Anyone or anything that threatened them would face his wrath as well.

Chapter Twenty-Seven: The Festival

After seeing to Sero's needs, Joel, Colton, and Imbrose all made their way to the training grounds so that they could kill some time before the festival started in earnest. Already they could see lanterns being set up and small games for the kids to play. To Colton, it felt like all of these things had appeared out of nowhere, but upon further thought he realized he really hadn't ventured very much around the thicket since returning.

As minutes turned to hours, all three men found themselves sweaty and panting by the time the sky turned orange with early dusk. Deciding it would probably be best to bathe before the party, they all went their separate ways with the intention of meeting up at the tribal center. Colton didn't go straight home though. Instead, he decided to swing by Orielle's workshop and give her the locket he purchased earlier.

As expected, she was hammering away at something as he approached the large sliding doors. "Orielle! I have something for you," he yelled so as to be heard over the hammering.

The pounding stopped and soon after, the slightly dirty face of Orielle peaked out from behind the door. "Oh, Colton! What did you say?"

Colton glanced inside the crack of the door and she shied even further away, concealing herself entirely besides her face. "Uh, I said I have something for you!"

Orielle's face brightened. "You do? You didn't need to get me anything, the whip was me paying you back!"

"I know! This isn't about that." Colton awkwardly fumbled with his pouch trying to pull the necklace free. After a minute of muttered curses, he managed to get ahold of it and present it to her. "I figured this would be a good thing to keep the petal I gave you in."

Orielle glanced down at the locket and her face broke into a smile. "It's very beautiful!" Careful to not reveal any part of her that was unnecessary, she gingerly reached out and plucked the item from his outstretched hands. "One moment!" Then she disappeared behind the door completely and reemerged with the locket in her hand and the blue petal resting inside. "A perfect fit! I love it, thank you!" With a click, she closed the locket and pulled her hand back inside.

"Of course!" Colton narrowed his eyes on her. "Are you okay?"

"Me? Oh yes! Just working out some nerves before the big festival."

"If you say so." Colton couldn't help but wonder what she might be hiding, but it didn't seem to be about him so he let it go. "Well, I should get back and get this grime off me. I'll see you out there?"

"Mhm!" Orielle mumbled as she started to close the door. "See you out there!"

As the door closed, Colton stood there for a moment until the hammering began again. With a shrug, he decided it was time to clean himself up and made for his small house. Walking back, Colton could see there were already people making their way to the tribal center and smiled to see the children running and chasing one another. However, as many children were there playing, there were double that amount just walking quietly next to their parents. Colton vowed that after this they would find Va'Rul and put him down permanently. These children had been under his influence for too long and they deserved to be set free. Shaking the morbid thoughts from his head as he walked up to the front door of his cabin, and made the choice to set aside the horrors of the last few weeks and genuinely enjoy himself tonight.

After cleansing himself, Colton walked out to find a finely sewn outfit waiting for him. Rubbing the fabric between his fingers, he could tell immediately that it was silk and he wondered who would've had this made for him. Coming to the conclusion he was just wasting time, he grabbed the black and purple shirt and a small slip of paper fell onto the floor. Opening the letter, he was surprised at the author.

Colton,
I just want you to look your best. Go get her!
With love,
Aunt Imryth

A smile crept onto his lips. Imryth had always been a forward woman, and he appreciated that about her. Otherwise, he knew Imbrose would have turned out far more insufferable than he already was. With one foot out the door, Colton glanced at his whip as it hung on the nail beside the door. *I won't need this will I?* Remembering the Shade's cryptic warning, he stared at it for a moment before snatching it up and fastening it to his belt. Looking outside, Colton noticed the sun was firmly set at this point and he began to worry he had missed something and rushed to put on the rest of the comfortable clothing.

As soon as he stepped out, he sighed in relief. His family was still trying to get out the door as Phoebe insisted her hair was not "to perfection." Laughing, Colton ran to them and placed a hand on his sister's shoulder.

"You look beautiful, little sister!" And she did, with her elegant blue dress that matched her eyes, and an inconceivably difficult braid running down the side of her head.

She pushed him playfully. "You have to say that! I'd hurt you if you didn't."

"Be that as it may, we should get going," Colton stated as he adjusted his lapel.

Finally galvanized to action, the troop began their walk to the tribal center. It wasn't long before they heard powerful drums playing in the distance and Colton's fears returned as he tried to rush the family along. As they turned the final corner, they could see what must have been the entire village slowly gathering in a place that had been utterly transformed since the last time Colton had been there.

Where there was once only a few tables, there were hundreds and they were all completely filled with people. As Colton looked around, he began to worry that perhaps they were too late and they would need to stand. However, his worries were all for naught as Joel ran up to them yelling Colton's name.

"Colton! About time! We were beginning to worry that we'd have to start without you!" Colton was taken aback by the man's attire as he tried to hear what he was saying. Joel wore no shirt and instead had only a purple cloth skirt and some sort of plant-fiber-like bracelets on his arms and legs. He also wore a strand of purple flowers around his neck and a crown of flowers on his head.

"That's quite the get up you have going on there!" Colton remarked as he tried to avoid looking at Joel's exposed toned torso.

"You like it? Anyway, let's get you to your tables. Imbrose and Ember already showed up with their moms." With that, Joel led the Cobbs through the packed gathering.

All around, there were the same purple glowing lanterns he had seen walking around town, and purple flowers were all around the clearing in full bloom. Colton suddenly had a massive pit form in his stomach as he realized this was being done in his and his family's honor. He had never been treated this way, and the idea of being the center of attention did not appeal to him very much.

Another thing that added to the anxiety was his inability to find Orielle anywhere amongst the crowd. He could easily see Lena who was wearing a beautifully made dress of pearlescent purple, and standing just next to her was George, who was also finely dressed in a dark green jerkin and pants. Even Jasper was visible, his expressionless face contradicting the finery he wore.

"Where's Orielle?" Colton yelled to Joel as they crossed the center of the space.

"She's around!" Joel yelled back as they approached a long empty table save for three people all smiling at them. "Here we are! I've got to go, but get comfortable, things are about to get started!" With a smile, Joel turned and ran off into the crowd as the family started to sit down.

Colton looked down at the end of the table to see Imbrose, Ember, and Meredith all sitting there sipping on some orangish liquid. "Where's your mom?" Aileah asked Imbrose as she took her seat.

Imbrose, who looked more than a little annoyed, simply pointed back into the crowd they had just passed through. There, through the tightly packed group of people, he could see Imryth dancing happily with a group of women to the beat of the drums. Noticing she was being watched, she turned and waved to the group and began to make her way over to them.

"She's insufferable," Imbrose muttered.

"The pot calling the kettle black?" Ember asked quietly.

Imbrose rolled his eyes as his mother finally arrived at the table, her breath coming in gasps. "Wow! These people really know how to throw a party!" She turned to look at Colton. "Don't you look sharp! Dang, I have good taste!" Colton could only smile at her and she moved to sit down next to her son once more.

"Mind if we have a seat?" Friend's familiar voice echoed over the rising music with Sero following close behind.

The boy looked at Imbrose nervously before glancing down. "Sure thing!" the blue man exclaimed happily.

Suddenly, the drums began to beat in a heavy and rhythmic fashion. People began to quickly move to one side and find their seats, as the beat began to pick up in pace. With the center nearly cleared, the drums built to a crescendo and abruptly stopped.

"Welcome everyone!" A vibrant young man Colton had never met and in the same attire as Joel stepped forward to the applause of the surrounding crowd. "We are grateful to celebrate this very special occasion as people from across the great ocean have found their way home!" More applause followed as Colton felt the heat rising to his cheeks once more at the attention. "We invite you to please relax and enjoy the festivities as we welcome you to our great home. To begin, we will start with our dance of greeting led by our First Scion!"

The man ran to one side and jumped in line next to twenty other men dressed exactly like him. Colton could pick out Joel in the group, waving slightly as they stood there at attention.

"What's a First Scion?" Imbrose asked.

"I think it means first born?" Colton stated, unsure.

They watched as the men began to form a semicircle as the drum beat began again. With a strong thump the drums ceased once more, and at the same time the men all turned and let out a deep grunt. Immediately, the drums picked up again as the men continued their guttural chant coupled with rhythmic stomping that matched the drums.

Finally, the men parted down the center to reveal twenty sensually-dressed women who all moved through the men with practiced elegance. Immediately, Colton noticed Orielle at the front of the group, her arms waving fluidly and in complete unison with the other women around her. She wore what was the most revealing outfit Colton had ever seen her in. A lacy black bandeau wrapped around her chest and a long, meshwork black skirt with purple floral design and slits rising nearly to the top of both of her thighs. She and the other women also wore strands of flowers around their necks that swayed gently with their flowing movements and a crown of colorful flowers on top of their heads.

All at once the rhythm changed, and the dancers all began to stomp to the beat of the drums as they clapped their hands. Eventually the crowd also picked up the clap as the women began to dance in a way that could only be described as a story through their movements. The entire time Colton could only watch Orielle, as she flitted around the clearing with everyone else doing elaborate dance moves all the while.

Slowly, the music began to die down as Orielle and the other dancers all began to make their way around the tables. Colton froze as she locked eyes with him and smiled. Then with purposeful poise, she and the other dancers all moved toward someone. His heart pounded in his chest as she approached him, and continued to do so as she bowed slightly before him and removed the flowers from around her neck, placing it over his head.

"Welcome to our thicket," she whispered in his ear as she drew back from him and rejoined the group for one final energetic display.

With the dancers striking a pose, the drums reached a definitive end and the crowd erupted into cheers, the sound deafening. Seeming to not be in any rush, the dancers all stood and waved broad smiles on all of their faces. At last, as the clapping died down, the same young man from before stepped forward through the others.

"Thank you, and now a word from our Keeper!" The man gestured with a flourish to George, who was already moving to the center of the clearing, Lena on his arm.

"On behalf of our thicket, my family and I would like to extend the traditional greeting to each of our lost tribe members!" The crowd cheered once more as George raised his hands to quiet them. "Would the members of the Cobb family as well as their compatriots Ember, Imbrose, and Friend please step forward?"

Hesitant as first, Colton and his whole family stood and began to walk toward the Keeper. As they approached, Orielle, Lena, and Jasper all moved to either side of George. Ultimately, as they all came to a stop George began talking once more.

"Thank you for gracing our village with your presence, and for reuniting our long fractured tribe. We are whole because of you!" Orielle and Lena both stepped forward, looking at one another. "As you are now part of our family, we would like to welcome you with a hug and kiss." Colton flushed slightly at the idea of Orielle kissing not only him, but his father, sister, and grandfather. "On the cheek," George finished, and Lena stepped forward to the person on the far right.

Colton watched as once Lena hugged and kissed someone on either cheek she moved gracefully to the next person and Orielle stepped in behind her to do the same. When the startlingly beautiful wife of the Keeper finally arrived before Colton, she leaned forward and hugged him tightly then kissed him lightly on either cheek. Before moving on, she stopped and placed a hand on his cheek with a warm smile.

He couldn't help but watch as she moved on, and as he turned back he came face to face with Orielle. She smiled and leaned in to hug him. The embrace lasted longer than Colton expected and when she leaned back he felt himself swallow. A smirk plain on her face, Orielle leaned forward and gently kissed one cheek and then the other. When it was over, she straightened and looked at him for a long moment before stepping to the next person in line.

With a loud clap that startled Colton, the Keeper spoke once more. "Be welcome! Now, let's feast shall we?" The crowd, who had been silent throughout the entire exchange, roared loudly, and massive platters began to make their way around the tables.

As everyone made their way back to their table, Colton noticed Orielle split from her family and made her way toward their group. "Do you mind if I sit with you all?"

"Of course not, dear!" Imryth replied quickly. "Here! Have a seat." She then proceeded to quickly shift over from Colton, revealing a spot next to him.

"Thank you!" Orielle exclaimed as she sat down. At this angle, Colton could clearly see she was wearing the locket he gave her earlier, and he surmised it must have been covered by the flowers before.

"That was quite the dance you did out there," Ember praised, breaking the silence.

"Oh! Thank you. I've been doing welcoming dances like this since I was sixteen. We usually do it after each gathering, but this was a significant enough occasion that Pa decided to do it early this year,"

Orielle explained as the platters of food finally made it around to them, and she served herself a healthy portion of meat, vegetables, fruit, and bread.

"It looked pretty tiring!" Aileah noted as she placed a hand on top of Xander's.

"When I first started, it definitely was! Though you get used to it over the years," Orielle shrugged, taking a bite.

"What did you think, Colton?" Imbrose probed.

Colton, realizing the food was now in front of him, began serving himself before answering. "It was beautiful," he blurted. "I've never seen a dance like that before. It was pretty stunning to watch."

Orielle smiled shyly as she looked over at him. "Thank you!"

As the feast continued, the atmosphere began to relax as the wine continued to flow. With the food reaching an end, the drums began playing again as some of the couples began to get up and make their way into the center to dance once more. Even Aileah pulled Xander by the arm to the dance floor. Colton glanced over and caught Imryth's eye, who shifted her eyes in Orielle's direction, the message clear.

Taking a deep breath, Colton drained the last of his cup and stood from his seat. As the liquid courage took effect, he held his hand out for Orielle to take. "Will you dance with me?"

Blushing, Orielle took his hand and together the two of them began walking out into the dancing mass of people.

A hand landed on Colton's shoulder as he turned to look Imryth in the eye. "You won't be needing that will you?" She asked, as she gestured to the still coiled whip hanging from his belt.

Hesitating for only a moment, Colton quickly pulled it from his belt and tossed it on the table before he was whisked away by Orielle, a smile plain on everyone's face at the table.

"I have to apologize, I'm not as good as you are at dancing," Colton admitted as they came to a stop.

Orielle smiled and began tapping her feet to the beat of the drums and held out her hands. "Just follow me!"

Colton took her hands and let her lead him on a dance that had them entangling and pulling apart in equal measure. He couldn't tell if he looked silly or not, but it didn't matter as he watched her beautiful green eyes reflect the lantern light around them. At that moment, he couldn't see anyone else as she moved closer to him. The dance was coming to an end and he felt her pull him into herself as she drew up against him. The motion forced him to drop her into a deep dip, much to the excitement of the crowd around them. As the applause echoed around them, he found himself pulling her up to her full height but she didn't pull away. Instead, her eyes locked on his and then slowly drifted to his lips as she leaned even closer. Colton smiled as his eyes slowly closed and he moved to meet her lips.

Suddenly, he felt Orielle pull from him abruptly and he opened his eyes to see her looking away. Glancing down, he saw Jasper holding her skirt with a broad smile on his face.

She kneeled down to his eye level with a look of concern in her eyes. "Are you okay, Jasper?"

The boy continued to stare at her, his eyes unblinking. "He's coming."

"Who's coming?" Orielle asked, her voice growing increasingly urgent.

"He's coming." It was as if Orielle hadn't spoken. "He's coming. He's coming." Jasper's smile grew wider and wider, a manic light entering his eyes. Startled by the display, Orielle stepped away from her brother. "HE'S COMING," he whispered once more before his eyes rolled back into his head and his mouth hung open as he pointed towards the outskirts of the tribal center.

There, only barely illuminated in the dim light of the purple lanterns stood Lucas, his eyes fixed on Colton and Orielle. With inhuman speed, Lucas turned and sprinted toward the Grove Tree that still shown like a torch in the evening. Colton could barely comprehend what was happening as he watched countless children all repeating the same phrase as Jasper, their voices getting louder and louder. With fear in her eyes,

Orielle turned to look at Colton, as Jasper's and all of the other children's voices became garbled.

As the volume reached a crescendo, Jasper's small body began to rise, lifted off the ground by an unseen force. Orielle gasped as her hands hovered around her brother, as if afraid touching him would make things worse. His legs dangled limply as he lifted up and up until he was a good two feet off the ground. Colton whirled as screams sounded behind him, and found that nearly every child in attendance was levitating

As the situation devolved into utter chaos, Colton's mind cleared as he started to put together a plan. He could tell the events of his dream had begun to play out in reality, and he knew he needed to follow Lucas to prevent its ending.

"I have to go after him," Colton declared as he turned Orielle toward him.

Her eyes were confused and afraid as she tried to make sense of what was happening. "Wh-what about Jasper?" she asked meekly.

"We have to stop Lucas. I think we can help Jasper if we do."

With that, Orielle's eyes cleared and she glanced back at the tree in the distance. "I can't leave him."

"Go," a stern, womanly voice said over the growing din. "I've got him."

The two of them turned to see Lena standing there, pulling Jasper to her chest as he still floated off the ground. "Alright, let's go," Orielle declared as she started running into the night. Colton risked a look over his shoulder, but at this angle, he couldn't see the table where his family was. Realizing time was not on their side, he ran after Orielle, praying his nightmare would not come to pass.

Chapter Twenty-Eight: The Marionette

A s the sounds of the festival behind them grew dimmer, Colton and
Orielle quickly found themselves surrounded by complete
darkness. Before long, a loud scream echoed throughout the night,
coming from directly in front of them. Sharing a glance, the two of them
redoubled their pace and rapidly came across the cause of the commotion.
Lying on the ground and cradling a bloody arm, June was already
beginning to heal a deep cut running along her forearm as tears freely ran
down her face.

"June!" Orielle exclaimed. "Are you okay? Did you see Lucas?"

Through wracking sobs, June managed a jerking nod. "He's not
himself! Don't hurt him!"

Orielle dropped to her knees and pulled June into a hug while
looking over her shoulder at Colton. "Go! Once I know she's okay, I'll
follow you."

Biting his lip, Colton ran off into the shadows once again, his
focus on the looming purple tree in the distance. He knew where Lucas
was going, and his heart began to thump in his chest as he imagined what
he would find when he got there.

With all haste, he found himself running up the small slope to the
entrance of the Grove Tree. Noticing a figure crouched next to the door,
Colton paused and reached over his shoulder, only to find his weapon was
not there. Cursing, Colton closed his eyes, trying to think through what he

should do next. Lucas was obviously armed, and if that was him waiting, Colton knew he would be at a disadvantage in a fight.

A memory flitted through his head as he recalled the fight he had with Va'Rul inside Orielle's mind. A specific moment kept replaying in his head: he had just been thrown from the creature's back and the blade was still lodged in place. A crazy idea formed in his mind as he closed his eyes and reached over his shoulder once more, willing the weapon to be there. He pictured where he knew it was at that moment: leaning against the wall just next to the front door of his cabin.

With an exertion of power, Colton reached out with his spirit across the Reach. The tiny intangible tendrils of himself shot out at an impossible speed, navigating the thicket with ease and eventually arrived at the front of his house. In his mindseye, he could see the house clearly as he slowly pushed his consciousness closer to the door. Pushing through the solid object proved to be the greatest strain so far, and Colton felt his body tremble at the effort. The image of the house began to blur slightly as he felt sweat dripping down his face. The feeling of physically being about a mile from where his spirit was caused his eyes to almost flutter open. The overwhelming desire to see his physical surroundings threatened to collapse his concentration.

Shoving the distractions aside, Colton threw himself into the task at hand. Slowly, his power forced its way through the solid wood, and he found himself in the darkened interior. With a breath of relief, he turned to find the greatsword still leaning against the siding where he had left it. The large sapphire in the pommel began to glow as he inched closer, as his connection to the weapon seemed to call out to him. Exerting himself a final time, he reached for the sword's handle as the gem grew brighter. The moment his spirit touched the leather grip, he felt his tendrils of power snap taut and begin drawing back toward him in a blink of an eye.

Gasping, Colton opened his eyes to see himself still crouching near the entrance to the Grove Tree, the figure before him still unmoving. He suddenly became aware of the heavy object now grasped in his right hand behind his shoulder. Gingerly, he drew the item in front of his face and stared with disbelieving eyes. In his hand was his greatsword, and while the scabbard had not come through with it, he knew he likely wouldn't need it for the night to come. Drawing on his courage, Colton wiped his forehead and hefted his sword.

Approaching the form cautiously, Colton rapidly realized the person he was looking at was already dead. His sword falling limply by his side, he recognized the corpse immediately as Tender Sully, the old man he had seen with Jasper when he first came to the grove. The man's throat was slashed open with the whole front of his robes soaked in crimson. Colton wrinkled his face in sadness. This man seemed very kind and those who mentioned him always spoke of him in a good light.

"Colton!" Orielle's voice sounded from behind him as he continued to look upon the fallen Tender. "Did you find–" Her words cut off abruptly as she drew up next to him.

"Just found him like this, but I suspect Lucas is inside." Turning to look at her he saw tears well in her eyes.

"He was my teacher…" Her voice cracked under the strain of emotion.

"I'm sorry," Colton urged, resting his hand on hers, "but we need to get inside. I have a feeling Lucas isn't finished yet."

With a sharp exhale, Orielle leaned down and grasped the leather straps around her thigh and twisted it revealing her holstered pistol. "You're right, we need to stop him." Then she pulled her pistol and looked at him.

Colton grasped his sword in both hands and after glancing at Tender Sully once more, entered the dimly lit Grove Tree. The space was completely empty as everyone was at the festival, and they walked quickly through the twenty-foot-wide main entryway. However, the two of them stopped abruptly as they reached the first fork in the path.

"Which way?" Orielle asked, her pistol at the ready.

Glancing back and forth, Colton couldn't see much to suggest one way or the other aside from one way being the obviously more traveled of the two. "Maybe he went that way?" he asked, pointing down the wider of the two passages.

"I don't kn–Wait, did you see that?" The surprised tone of her voice caused Colton to look down the much smaller path to their left. "I swear I just saw a…"

"A what?"

"It doesn't make any sense…I saw the cat from the cage back at the poachers' camp," she whispered in disbelief.

"What?" Colton took a few steps down the path and focused ahead. Suddenly, a little green flash contrasted with the purple flowers surrounding the tunnel. Locking his eyes on the source, he saw a diminutive brown, black, and white cat sitting twenty feet down the passage.

"There! I see it again!" Orielle blurted.

"I see him too." The little cat's head tilted to one side as it seemed to be confused, then trotted off down the hallway. "I think it wants us to follow it."

"You want to follow a cat?" Orielle asked incredulously.

"It looks like it knows where it's going," Colton tried with a shrug. "Besides, it's guess is as good as ours."

Shaking her head, Orielle adjusted her skirt and entered the small corridor. "Let's hope it's right. We can't search this whole Grove."

Though as Colton stepped into the passage, he knew immediately that their guide was absolutely right. His gut twisted as he realized this was the path to where the Shield was kept. It made sense to him that Lucas, or Va'Rul who was controlling Lucas, would attack that grove first.

The cat led them through winding hallways of roots and purple flowers, descending deeper into the earth with every step. As they walked, Colton became more and more certain that he knew exactly where this path was going to end. The words of the Shade flashed through his mind then: *save him if you can.* Glancing at the woman just ahead of him, he could see her grasping her weapon with a white-knuckled grip.

Would he have the chance to try and save this man? And even if he could, should he? After all, he had murdered a defenseless old man. Was he worth saving?

As they turned the final corner and walked into the open space of the grove Colton and Terry had come to a week ago, the little feline vanished one final time leaving them alone in the open space. And there, standing in the center of the field of flowers, was Lucas, wielding a blood-stained dagger in his hand.

Lucas watched them both carefully as they entered the room. "It's about time the two of you arrived." His voice was no longer his, as the mocking sound of Va'Rul leaked from him. "I was beginning to worry that my two favorite pawns would fail to play their final roles."

"And what's that?" Orielle asked, her voice laced with poison as she trained her weapon on him.

"To kill him of course!" the sinister voice that came from Lucas said as it pointed the bloody dagger at himself. "He killed one of your tenders and he's going to corrupt your entire Grove Tree!" The creature cackled as black veins began to run up Lucas' neck.

Colton took in his surroundings, the entire space all too familiar. Lucas would open his mouth and it would infect the grove, then he'd die. It played out so clearly as he circled around the raving man in the center. How was he supposed to stop this from happening?

Reacting, Orielle fired her pistol at the man, but it was too late. Lucas opened his mouth and the black oily tendrils sprang forth and dove for the surrounding flowers. The blast from her weapon crashed into the writhing shadows and dissipated as Colton stood frozen, watching the nightmare play out before him once again.

Suddenly, a flash of blue light pulled Colton's attention away from the horror before him to see Tyrrek's shield embedded in the far wall. The sapphire pulsed once more as the room filled with light, and the blade in his hand began to feel warm.

Free him.

The voice was low, but it ran loudly in Colton's head as the events of the room slowed to a crawl and the shield pulsed once more. He felt a presence enter the sword in his grasp as it directed his attention at the wall to his left.

Free him.

Colton blinked as the light blasted once more, and watched the shadows of everything projected on the walls. His eyes focused on Lucas' shadow that looked just like him with one notable exception: there were thick strands of energy connected to his back that stretched to another serpentine creature.

All at once Colton knew what he needed to do as he imagined himself standing just behind Lucas. In a flicker of energy, he appeared right where he anticipated, already bringing his sword down on the invisible strings connected to Lucas. For the briefest moment Colton worried he had got it wrong, as his blade met nothing but empty air. Then, a series of loud, wet, snapping sounds echoed throughout the entire room as the greatsword cut effortlessly through the tension-like strings puppeting Lucas. The black tendrils coming from his mouth cut off abruptly as Lucas began screaming. The ear-piercing wail made Orielle and Colton instinctively pull their hands to their ears, dropping their weapons. Across the wall, Colton watched as the tendons that connected the shadow of Lucas and Va'Rul stretched and snapped, causing the snake-like visage to writhe and wither away.

Finally, the screaming stopped and Lucas fell to his knees, breathing heavily. Letting his hands drop, Colton looked over at Orielle who was staring at him in shock. Movement caught his attention as Lucas brought the dagger in his hand up to his own throat.

"I'm sorry, Ori." Then he started to drag the blade across his exposed neck.

Colton grasped the man's wrist that was wielding the dagger. Fighting him as he tried to pull it deeper into his flesh. "Stop...Lucas," he groaned with effort, trying to prevent the blade from ending his life.

"Let…me…die." Lucas was pulling with all of his might, slowly gaining ground despite the better angle Colton had on his wrist.

Orielle covered the distance between them in a blink as she dropped to her knees in front of Lucas and cradled his face. "Stop, Lucas. I know it wasn't you!"

Lucas' grip loosened and Colton yanked the blade away from him falling onto his backside. "But I killed Sully, and I hurt June!" Lucas' voice was back to his own but it was weary and broken as he sobbed freely.

"Shh, it wasn't you! June is okay, she doesn't blame you," Orielle cooed.

"It was me," Lucas choked out. "I led your brother to him. I led all of the children to him."

Orielle flinched, her heart visibly breaking as she continued to cradle the man's head. "It wasn't you," she repeated, as much for herself as for him.

"I just wanted to be with you, and I thought you would want me if I were more…just more." Lucas gasped for air as he slumped even further. "He promised me that I could be with you if I did what he asked."

Colton watched as Orielle leaned back and forced Lucas to look up at her. "Oh Lucas, you were always an amazing man. It's just, I wasn't meant to be with you."

"Lucas!" June's frantic voice echoed through the chamber as she ran over and pulled Lucas into a tight hug. "Are *you* okay?"

"June, I am so sorry! I never meant to hurt you! Are you okay?" Lucas asked as Orielle stepped away from them.

"I'll be fine, let's get your neck healed up," the young woman fussed as she pressed her hands to Lucas' neck and a brilliant purple light began to shine through her enclosed fingers.

Colton got to his feet, the adrenaline of the situation beginning to settle as he watched Imbrose and Ember run into the room. They all locked eyes with one another as many others began to fill the hallway and Orielle crossed to him.

"Let's get him out of here," she suggested flatly, her voice cold.

Colton reached out for her hand, and she accepted, her eyes glistening. "Are you okay?" Colton asked, as he felt her hand tremble in his.

"No," she said simply before releasing his hand and stooping to grab her weapon. Then she walked toward her father as he made his way into the room.

Colton watched her walk away and then headed for his sword, June and Lucas still holding each other on the damp soil. Bending to pick up the still pulsing weapon, Colton straightened to see the Shade standing before him.

Grasping his chest in fright, Colton settled his breathing and looked back at the Shade. "You did well, Colton. Thank you for saving him."

Colton smacked his lips and glanced over at Orielle who was still talking to her father. "Did I? Do well, I mean."

The Shade placed a hand on his shoulder. "She will recover, and what you did today will be a major reason for said recovery."

Colton turned to look into the man's shadowy cowl. "Why didn't you just tell me what to do?"

"I wish it were that simple," the Shade said with exasperation. "If I want to remain here to help you at all, my intervention must be limited."

"You are a very strange man," Colton remarked as Cartwright and Joel walked into the room and escorted Lucas out of the grove.

The Shade chuckled. "You have no idea."

Chapter Twenty-Nine: Aftermath

"**S**o, what do we do?" Joel's voice echoed in the small dining room. "He killed someone, and he led countless children to be mentally devoured by a horrible monster."

Colton drummed his fingers on the worn wooden table as he looked around the now familiar makeshift council table in the Dawson residence. The tension was high as many of the villagers began to demand some form of punishment for Lucas. However, George had suggested temperance in administering a hasty verdict. No one really knew what was going on with Lucas, and his mother Leilani had begged openly for mercy. With the crowd quickly devolving into a mob, George called a meeting in the house and had Cartwright escort the boy to a prison cell.

The situation was only further exacerbated by the children not regaining their former selves. While they had stopped floating and none of them were harmed, they all returned to their catatonic and emotionless state after Lucas had been confronted. This confirmed that if there was some way to save the children of the thicket, it laid with Va'Rul. Having no way of finding the creature, the meeting held a definitive hopelessness to it.

"The boy had no control over what he was doing," Arcadia, who had been summoned to check Lucas' state of mind, commented. "When I delved into his mind, all I found was constant conflict between him and this monster."

"So, what? We should just free him?" Joel asked, his face reddening.

"Yes, we should." Orielle's frigid voice pulled everyone's attention onto her. "The justice that needs to be dispensed is meant for Va'Rul, not him."

"But, Ori! He led Jasper into his clutches to begin with," Joel argued back.

"I know…and I'm not sure if I can ever truly forgive that, but he was being controlled."

Colton watched as the muscles in Orielle's jaw twitched, her emotions hidden just beneath the veneer she was maintaining on her face. Motion caught his attention as George leaned back in his chair, obviously exhausted.

"Orielle is right. We need to talk with Lucas and find out if he knows where his previous master is," the Keeper reasoned, already beginning to stand. "However, with the festival firmly over, we all need to get some sleep."

Seeing the majority of the table nod in agreement, Colton locked eyes with Joel, the only one who seemed unsatisfied. "I'll question him tonight," Joel declared resolutely.

"You won't," George refuted, his voice taking on a sense of authority that Colton had yet to experience. Joel opened his mouth to speak again but was cut off with a sharp wave from the Keeper. "You are not in a positive state of mind, Joel. I forbid it until you are rested, and only if you take Orielle with you when you speak with him." George deflated slightly, the events of the evening landing on him heavily. "If we go at him like he's an enemy, he may treat us like one. Let's remember that he's still one of us."

"As you say, Keeper." The use of formal titles confirmed that Joel was still not happy with the situation.

George sighed. "I know you were close to Tender Sully. He was my teacher as well, after all. He wouldn't want you storming in there as you are."

Colton could see Joel relax slightly, but nonetheless stood from the table. "Will there be anything else?"

Shaking his head ruefully, George watched as Joel walked out of the home and into the night.

Turning to Orielle, he leaned down and kissed her head. "Watch after him tomorrow."

"Of course, Pa," Orielle said as George reached out for Lena's hand and together, the two of them walked into their room and closed the door.

Arcadia stood from the table, leaving only Colton and Orielle still seated. "I shall take my leave then. If you require my assistance with Lucas, you know where to find me." With that, the witch-like woman exited the home, her long black dress trailing behind her.

"Not the festival we had in mind, was it?" Colton asked, his crude attempt at humor causing a small smile to cross Orielle's face.

"No, it wasn't." She turned to look at him, her face sad. "Why am I so angry with him?"

Colton thought for a moment, his own thoughts on the matter murky at best. "I don't know, but I can only assume you feel a sense of betrayal. Though knowing you, it's more likely that you aren't that mad at him to begin with."

Orielle's eyes narrowed slightly in confusion. "What do you mean?"

"Well, he said that he did all of it to be with you." Colton watched Orielle's eyes drop to the table instantly. "My guess is that you feel responsible for what happened to Lucas, and in turn what happened to Jasper and Sully."

Orielle bit her bottom lip as she continued looking at the table.

Colton leaned forward and took her hand in his. "It's not your fault, Ori. You may blame yourself, but everyone is responsible for their own actions. Lucas chose to accept Va'Rul, and in doing so, is in some ways the most guilty party." Colton swallowed as Orielle grasped his hand tightly. "With that being said, you are right."

"Right about what?" she asked softly.

"Va'Rul is our true enemy and he needs to be put down."

Orielle grimaced. "I shot him. I tried to kill him."

Colton squeezed her hand. "You shot at the thing that was controlling him, and I know Lucas would've wanted you to stop him if you could've."

"I know. I guess I'm just shocked at myself for reacting in that way so quickly. I didn't even think about it before I shot. I just knew he needed to be stopped," Orielle whispered, her voice uncertain.

"You made the right choice. I almost resorted to the same thing before I saw those tendrils connected to him."

"I just wish stopping Lucas had at least helped Jasper, but instead he's just gone back to what he was before."

Colton moved even closer, putting his other hand on her cheek as he gently turned her to look at him, her green eyes glistening in the fading candlelight. "I promised that we would bring Jasper back, and I meant it." Orielle nodded, a small smile breaking the glum expression on her face. "You looked beautiful at the festival this evening. I don't think I'm coordinated enough to dance like that, and I'm definitely not brave enough to wear what Joel was wearing."

Orielle giggled. "I'm sure you would look…amazing in it."

Colton nodded his head to one side, seeming to consider her words. "If it was for only one night perhaps I could be persuaded…" Orielle snorted out a laugh. "I love hearing you laugh," Colton confessed, his eyes locked on hers.

The two of them stared at each other for a long moment, the distance between them shrinking ever so slightly. Orielle's hand tightened on his arm as they both leaned in, and their lips finally met. The feeling sent shockwaves through his body as he felt his heart quicken in pace as she kissed him back. The two of them drew closer together as they put all of the emotion of the evening into a kiss both of them had longed for. The world outside of that moment disappeared as Colton relished the feeling of her warmth against him.

Finally, the two of them broke apart, but continued resting their foreheads against one another. "I promise you Ori, we will bring Jasper back."

"I believe you." Her voice was soft, but she didn't release him. "Will you come with Joel and I tomorrow?"

Colton looked into her eyes once more. Being as close as he was, he could see small gold flakes in her irises. "Of course I will."

A small, but genuine smile crossed her lips as she leaned in and gently kissed him once more. "Thank you, Colton." Pulling back, she continued holding his hands as she looked toward the door. "Imbrose and Ember are probably wondering what's going on."

Colton nodded, his heart still pounding from their newfound intimacy. "They'll probably barge in here soon if I don't get out there," he agreed, reluctantly pulling his hands from hers as he stood. "You should get some sleep."

Getting to her feet, Orielle walked Colton to the door. With her hand on the latch she paused and looked back at him. "I hope that when all of this is over, we can spend some more time together."

Smiling broadly, he took her hand once more. "I'd love nothing more."

As the door swung open to reveal Imbrose and Ember standing there, Colton released her hand, but not before his two friends caught a glimpse of the motion and the look they shared. Orielle smiled, her eyes locked on him as she slowly closed the door.

"Well, it seems like that meeting went very well," Imbrose remarked, his voice low.

Colton glanced at his friend who was looking at him conspiratorially. With a chuckle, he shoved Imbrose and started walking back toward his house as the two of them followed, already berating him with questions.

—

Behind the door, Orielle slumped to the floor and smiled, her own heart thumping rapidly. While the evening had been more than a little

283

stressful, she couldn't help but feel happy at the ending. She knew that the morning would bring more tension, but it felt like it would all be manageable if she had him by her side. And she believed—no, she was certain—that together they would find a way to save Jasper and all of the other children.

With her resolve emboldened, Orielle got to her feet and walked to her room. The dawn would bring another defining day in their search for Va'Rul.

Chapter Thirty: Guilt and Forgiveness

W alking up the switchbacks to the guard house once again, Colton
found himself concerned with just how many times he had
walked up this hill with the intent of interrogating a prisoner. Each time,
he had noticed a definitive difference in how the people acted towards
him, and so far it had always been getting better with each trip up.
However, today it was different. The people who lined the path all the
way to the top seemed far more upset than usual. Some openly wept, their
blank-faced children cradled in their grasp. Others still smiled, but their
faces seemed distant and sunken. What came as the greatest shock though
were the people who were yelling. Colton could hear open requests for
Lucas' head, and for him to be given "justice for the crimes he
committed," It seemed that news of what happened in the grove had
spread rather quickly.

"What is happening?" Colton asked as he struggled to keep up
with the fast pace Joel had set.

"They want answers, and unfortunately, we don't have them,"
Joel seethed through gritted teeth. "The crowd has only grown throughout
the night. Some have even been here since the festival ended."

Colton himself found it difficult to sleep the night before as his
mind continuously played through the events of the evening. Whether it
was remembering the fight with Lucas or the subsequent conversation

with Orielle later, he couldn't say. But the entire endeavor had him questioning what their next move would be.

"We'll do our best to get those answers then," Orielle replied firmly as she walked just to Colton's right. "Who's been keeping the peace?"

The trio crested the hill to see a thick gathering of people leading all the way to the prison door where low shouting could be heard. Picking their way through the crowd, they finally laid eyes on the commotion. Standing in front of the door was a bleary-eyed Leilani, who had obviously not slept a wink last night, and a stoic Cartwright with his hand out to ward off any one that got too close.

"Now, now," Cartwright shouted. "We will get to the bottom of this soon. Please be patient and– ah, Joel! You can't imagine how happy I am to see you!"

Joel raised a hand in welcome before turning to the crowd. "Everyone please calm down." The group all turned to look at Joel as the discontent began to subside. "We are going to get to the bottom of this, but we all know it's not as clear as it seems. The best thing you can do is go home and get some rest."

"What will you do with him?" an angry male voice shouted from the crowd.

"And what about our children?" another female voice screamed.

The mob began to build in volume once more as Joel raised his hands to hush them once more. "Listen! I want nothing more than to answer all of your questions." Joel glanced at Leilani who had once again begun crying at the mention of punishment for her son. "I myself was angry when I found out what happened, but imagine you were Leilani!" Joel gestured to the grieving mother. "She had to find out that something horrible had invaded her son's mind, and now she has stood guard all night as her neighbors called for his punishment."

The crowd stirred awkwardly, as Orielle supported Leilani through her sobs. Slowly, a few citizens approached her and began to surround her protectively. Joel looked over and nodded approvingly.

"This monster wants to sow division among us, but we are better than that!" Joel paused as some of the surrounding group lowered their heads. "We won't give him what he wants, and when the time comes, we will stand united against him."

By now the group had started to disperse, but a few apologies could be heard as people walked away from the prison. Leilani, collecting herself, moved to stand next to Joel.

"Promise you will help him if you can," she pleaded.

Joel looked at her directly, all sense of the rash decision making from last night, gone. "I promise. We will help him if we can."

With a nod, Leilani allowed herself to be directed away from the prison as the crowd broke apart and departed. Colton watched, impressed by Joel's ability to calm such a large group. He had seen riots before in the city of New Eradin, but the entire guard was required to bring peace. Here, it was obvious just how much the people felt connected to one another. Even so, Cartwright being able to keep the energy low enough as just a single defender caused him to smile at the camaraderie of his people.

"Well, now that's settled," Joel began. "Why don't you go get some sleep, Cartwright, and send Jerric to guard the front."

Stifling a yawn, the sentry nodded back. "Jerric is already inside, we were told to have someone watching him at all times."

Joel's eyes narrowed slightly but he didn't say anything else as he moved to the prison door. Following behind, Colton could see Orielle set her shoulders as she took a deep breath. He wondered what it must feel like for her to be seeing Lucas like this, a man she had been set to marry a little over a week ago.

As the door opened, Colton felt a distinctly heavy energy escape the darkened hallway. Torches that lined the wall all flickered as the three of them stepped in and closed the door behind them. Instinctively, Colton reached forward and placed his hand on the wall, attempting to let his eyes adjust to the new lighting. Settling in, the group let out a collective steadying sigh and moved down the corridor.

Eeking closer to the main cell block, the slight rattle of chains could be heard echoing down to them. Before long, the trio turned the corner to see the source of the noise. In front of them they saw Lucas chained by all four limbs to the back wall of the cell. His chin was lowered to his chest and even the blood that had dried from the cut on his neck could still be seen staining his shirt. Brown hair draped over his face and sweat beaded on his skin. Orielle visibly flinched at the state he was in, and scanned the room to find Jerric sitting on the bench looking at the three of them as they entered. The other two cells were left open, and empty.

"Why is he chained up?" Orielle demanded.

Jerric's eyes widened in surprise at her sharp tone, but answered in a leveled voice. "It was your father's orders, Miss."

The corner of Orielle's mouth twitched in frustration and Colton laid a hand on hers. "Thank you for standing guard, Jerric. Has he been talking at all?" Colton asked, noticing Lucas hadn't stirred as they walked in.

The guard turned his attention back to the prisoner. "He only talks when June comes to see him. She was here earlier this morning." Jerric cupped a hand over one side of his mouth as if trying to tell them a secret. "Between you and me, he seems a little ill. I know some daylight would do him good."

"Yes, well, let's see if he feels like talking to us first. Would you mind watching the door, Jerric?" Joel asked as he walked up to the bars.

Picking up on the cue, Jerric promptly stood and walked back down the hallway. Joel waited until the sound of the door shutting echoed back before he leaned on the bars and looked at the man chained to the wall up and down.

"Are you in there, Lucas?" Joel questioned gently. When no response came he tried a different approach. "Your mom has been outside all night. She's worried about you."

Lucas' hand twitched slightly at the mention of his mother, but he still didn't speak.

288

Frustration overcoming her, Orielle stepped forward. "Lucas! You need to talk to us. We want to help you!"

"Why?" The voice that came from him was hoarse, but it was his own.

"Why?" Orielle repeated, confused. "Because I know you, and what I saw last night wasn't you!"

Lucas' head lifted as he met her eyes. "I'm not the same as before. He broke me, and then redesigned me. I don't even know which parts are me and which are him anymore." His head lulled as he winced before locking onto her eyes once more, clearer now. "He likes you two, though. You and your…newcomer."

Orielle stepped back at the sudden change in demeanor. "What do you mean?" Colton asked, raising his voice.

Lucas blinked hard before opening his eyes and looked at Colton. "He craves you. You've defied him multiple times, and now…well, now he wants you to suffer."

"Where is he, Lucas?" Joel asked as Colton tried to make sense of what he just heard.

The prisoner shook his head. "It doesn't matter. We can't stop him. He's targeted us for a reason. Our minds are susceptible to his influence. If I told you where he was, you would just die too."

Orielle regained her wits at the mention of lost lives. "Who else is going to die, Lucas?"

"You may have slowed him down here, but his real plan is already in motion."

"So then tell us!" Orielle pleaded. "Let us try to save the others who are in danger."

"I can't, Ori." Lucas' voice cracked with emotion as he slumped into his chains. "If I tell you, then you will go, and I can't be the reason you die."

Orielle banged on the bars. "For Tyrrek's sake, Lucas! If you know where he's going to attack, you need to tell us!"

Lucas went silent as he just shook his head back and forth. Having an idea, Colton stepped forward. "You said he wants us because we defied him. Is that right?"

Lucas stopped shaking and glanced up at Colton, his eyes peeking through his clumped brown hair. "You're all he would talk about."

"Isn't that proof that we can beat him?" Lucas' eyes narrowed, but he didn't say anything so Colton continued. "If there is anything left of you in there, I know you want to help your people."

"He wants me to tell you, you know that, right?" Lucas asked, tilting his head.

"So, he's still talking to you in your head?" Joel questioned quickly.

"No, he's gone, but the last thing he said before I tried to slit my own throat was 'Tell them everything.'" Lucas shifted his gaze over to Joel. "He's waiting for you."

Orielle sucked in a breath and retrieved the keys hung on the hook near where Jerric had been sitting. Seeing what she had planned, Joel quickly moved to stand between her and the cage but Colton held up a hand. The entire time Orielle unlocked the cage and stepped in, Lucas watched her curiously until she walked right up to him. Gently, she brushed some of the hair from his face as she leaned down to meet his eyes.

"He still has Jasper, and if you don't tell me where I can find him, he will *keep* Jasper." Reaching up, she unshackled one hand, then the other, and helped him to the floor. "If you ever loved me Lucas, you will tell me where he is so that I can save my brother."

With his hands free, Lucas caressed her face. "I'm sorry. I never meant for any of this to happen." His eyes grew desperate as he leaned closer to her. "I just wanted to be more like the man you wanted, I never imagined that going into the woods myself would…"

"You left the Thicket by yourself?" Joel blurted.

Lucas looked over her shoulder, meeting Joel's gaze. "I wanted to show that I could survive on the outside, but then the next thing I knew I was trapped in a horrible nightmare. A puppet in my own body."

"You must have been attacked by one of his cultists like we were," Colton surmised.

Orielle pulled his hand down onto her lap and held it. "I'm sorry you went through that, Lucas. He has attacked us all in one way or another, and I can't imagine what it would have been like to go through that alone. But now I need you to set this right. Help me, Lucas, and maybe we can both learn to forgive ourselves."

A tear streaked down Lucas' grim-covered face. "Can you forgive me?" His voice filled with regret.

Orielle let out a deep breath before answering. "I can try, but I need to stop him." Lucas slumped, pulling his hand back, and sat silently for a few minutes. Just as Colton was about to say something, Lucas looked back up at her with his eyes crystal clear.

"He's going to attack the Gathering," Lucas whispered.

Orielle drew back at the news, her face turning pale. "W-what?"

"He's going to subsume everyone who is there, and send them back to their thickets with instructions to infect everyone else," Lucas revealed, his voice growing more confident.

"The same way that creature attacked you," Joel surmised, his voice low.

"Yes, and when he has us all, he'll consume our memories, taking away our heritage." Lucas paused as Orielle got to her feet. "Then, we will simply be drones in his army as he tries to build his empire."

"But…the Gathering is in five days," Orielle said, her voice disbelieving. "We need to leave now!" Orielle ran to the gate and turned to look at Lucas one more time. "Thank you, Lucas. And for the record, you were always the perfect version of yourself, just the way you are." Then she tossed the keys to Joel as she ran out of the prison.

Chapter Thirty-One: Rushed Execution

C olton rushed out the door behind Orielle as Joel locked the cell once more. Outside, Orielle was standing stock still as she had nearly run into the First Shade who was smiling down at her. The woman apologized as she relayed everything Lucas had just told them, and explained that she needed to leave immediately. To Colton's surprise, the Shade simply nodded in agreement and looked toward him.

"I'm glad you saved him, Colton," he stated, his voice pleasant. "I was concerned you might end him before you noticed the shadows."

Colton tilted his head and narrowed his eyes at the mysterious figure. "You say it as if you were there..."

Pursing his lips, the Shade shrugged. "I suppose in a way, I was." Orielle and Colton exchanged confused glances as the Shade continued, "Alas, you should be going. You will need to leave quickly if you mean to stop what is to come."

"I assume you can't tell us what that is?" Orielle asked, her voice hopeful.

"I'm afraid not," the man stated, his face taking on an apologetic smile. "However, I can tell you to trust yourself. It seems like a simple thing, but when in doubt, ask yourself what you would do, and if what you would do is what you are doing."

"What?" Colton and Orielle asked in unison.

The Shade laughed for the first time since Colton had known him. Placing a hand on both of their shoulders he grew serious. "Question everything." Still unsure what the cryptic message meant, the two of them stood there in silence. "Anyway, I need to get in there and talk with Lucas. He's in need of a friend. You two be safe."

The Shade squeezed their shoulders and moved to the door, waiting a moment before it swung open to show Joel walking briskly out. The hooded figure smiled down at Joel but moved past him and closed the door before he could conjure a response.

"What is he doing here?" Joel asked, confused.

"Who knows…" Orielle dismissed before jogging toward the switchbacks leading into the thicket.

Colton simply shrugged and followed behind her, trying to keep up since he had no idea where she planned to go. It turned out that her plan consisted of rallying their small party, including Friend, Ember, and Imbrose before running to her house. All the while she spouted the plan she had hatched in the small time since their conversation in the prison. Upon reaching her house, she barged in to find her father already speaking with Cartwright, Toku, and the boy from the prison, Sero.

"You're welcome to st–" George cut himself off as the group of six ran into the dining room gasping. "What in Tyrrek's name is going on here? Did you speak with Lucas?"

Orielle gulped air as she settled herself before diving into their interrogation with Lucas. More than once she needed to stop to catch her breath, but eventually she managed to conclude the story.

"…and that's why we need to leave right now!" she finished.

George sat in silence for a moment, trying to make sense of the news he had just received. "We cannot rush into this half-baked. We just survived an attack ourselves! Who's to say the creature won't try to attack us again?"

Imbrose stepped forward. "Both my and Ember's mothers will stay behind and ensure nothing happens while we take the fight to him. Plus, Colton's family aren't slouches at fighting themselves."

George screwed up his face, obviously not liking the direction this conversation was going. "Ori, we don't know what this thing is capable of. It could kill you and any small force you take with you."

Orielle's face flashed in certainty as she crossed the room to her father. "We won't be alone. Friend and Joel are going to head out now and lead Skarvald to the Thicket of Gatherings."

George remained unconvinced. "But you are going to get there before them if you take the cloudstone rails."

"Yes, but we need to know what situation we are headed into," Orielle explained patiently. "It's possible our own people may be under the control of Va'Rul."

"And if they are, what then?" George questioned. "You will have just walked into his trap."

"That's why I'll go too," Sero chimed in.

George turned on the boy. "Why would that make any difference?"

"Because I've been sneaking around the streets of Tri-Spire since I was a child," Sero answered confidently. "If those platinum soldiers couldn't find me, I think I can avoid the eyes of a few unsuspecting villagers. And, if they are hostile, I can slip away just as easily."

"I don't like it," George snapped, his argument dissolving.

Orielle moved to speak again but stopped when her mother held up a hand. "My love, we know where the thing that infected our son is going to be, and when it's going to be there. If we don't act now, we may lose it for good, and Jasper in the process. If you're worried about Orielle's safety, then send Toku and Cartwright with her, but you should know by now that she can handle herself. It's time we put an end to this."

The Keeper furrowed his brow, and remained silent for a long time before looking up at Orielle, his face betraying the fear he still harbored. "Go, take Cartwright and Toku, and this young man if you believe in his abilities. One way or another, this needs to end."

"Thank you, Pa!" Orielle exclaimed as she embraced her father tightly.

George forced a smile to his face, and patted his daughter's back. "Just come back safe."

"I will," Orielle whispered, then she turned to the rest of the group still standing in the small house. "Colton, Ember and Imbrose; you three go situate things with your families. Friend and Joel, you two should prepare for a long trek through the forest, and make it quick! Every minute you delay with Skarvald is another chance for Va'Rul to reveal its presence."

"What about me?" Sero asked, standing from the table.

Orielle glanced at the young man, her eyes assessing him. "Do you think you can do this?" He nodded his head enthusiastically. "Then, get yourself ready." Orielle redirected her eyes to the rest of the group. "We will meet at the entrance in two hours." Everyone sprung into motion as Orielle walked quickly toward Jasper's room.

Colton watched her leave, and turned to go before a hand landed on his shoulder. Glancing back, he noticed Lena looking at him imploringly, a grave look on her face.

"I can sense the way you feel about one another." Colton stood, frozen by her words. "Young love can be beautiful, and it can weather many storms. However, if you truly wish to make things work between the two of you, then you will need to find ways to work around each other's…sharper edges."

"I understand…" Colton managed.

Lena smiled gently. "Not yet you don't, but that's okay. The reason I tell you this now is because she won't stop until that creature is dead or she is." Lena took a deep breath. "I want you to promise me that if she goes too far, you will bring her home. I'd rather have one child alive and well than have both of my children lost to me."

Colton hesitated, unsure of how honest he should be. "I'm not sure she would listen to me."

"She probably won't at first, but you'll need to make her," Lena stated. "Promise me, Colton."

Smacking his lips, he responded. "I'll do my best, Mrs. Dawson. You have my word."

Lena placed a hand on his cheek. "You're a good man, and I'm happy my little Ori found you. Protect her." She turned to leave but looked over her shoulder. "Oh, and call me Lena. Mrs. Dawson sounds so old!"

Colton chuckled slightly as he nodded back at her before rotating to address his friends. The door was just swinging shut as he could see Cartwright, Toku, Friend, and Joel all leave to prepare themselves. Sero, on the other hand, stood right next to Ember as if waiting for directions from Colton. The scarlet-haired woman simply looked at him with confusion.

"Sero?" Colton asked.

"Yeah?" Sero responded quickly.

"Didn't you hear Orielle? You have two hours to get ready," Colton reiterated, walking toward the door.

"Oh, yeah! I heard her, I just don't need to get ready. Everything I own is on me right now," Sero proudly pronounced. "So, I figured I would stay with you, since I know she wouldn't leave you behind."

"And what makes you say that?" Imbrose prompted unabashedly.

Sero squinted, surprised as they exited the house. "You mean, you don't see it? They totally have the hots for each other! One second she's glancing longingly at him, and the next he's doing the same!" Sero rolled his eyes clearly shocked he was the only one who had noticed. "Personally, I'm shocked they haven't wandered off alone and–"

"Thank you," Colton interrupted sharply as Imbrose snickered. "You can stay with us, but keep the chatter to a minimum."

"Yes, sir!" Sero said, his tone mocking.

Colton shook his head, muttering under his breath. "I liked him more when he was locked in prison."

The next two hours consisted of rushed instructions and goodbyes. While Meredith first balked at the idea of them running off to face a potential race-ending threat without their help, Imryth calmed her by reminding her of their own risky endeavors. However, Colton spent most of his time talking to his family, whom he hadn't had much of a chance to speak with since they arrived. Unfortunately, with such a hurried timeline, the conversation ended before it could really get started. Xander, Colton's grandfather, made Colton promise that when he returned he would come and have a nice long talk with him before going on any more adventures.

Before long, Colton found himself standing near the entrance to the cloudstone railway outside the thicket, exchanging goodbyes with Friend and Joel as they made their way north toward where Skarvald was camped. Afterwards, the remaining members descended into the tunnels to find Ulric already walking across the tracks to meet them.

"Hi there! Where are we off to?" Ulric asked enthusiastically.

"We need to get to the Thicket of Gatherings as fast as possible!" Orielle said, walking quickly toward the idle train some distance away.

"Certainly, but your father told me no one from the Thicket of Memories would be attending this year due to problems at home," Ulric stammered as he rushed to catch her.

"There has been a change of plans. Something horrible is going to happen and we need to stop it," Orielle stated as she reached the locomotive.

"Oh no!" The engineer exclaimed. "What's going on?"

Orielle shook her head slightly as she moved aside for everyone to get on. "I wish we had time to tell you, but suffice to say it's really bad." Orielle paused as the last of them went on board. "I also need you to stop any other trains coming from the south."

"O-of course," Ulric stuttered. "Be safe now." The man's voice laced with nervousness as he walked to the controls.

"Thank you, Ulric. We'll see you when we get back," Orielle yelled as she stepped into the train car and sat on a nearby bench.

Colton glanced around the cabin, trying to piece together what the next leg of this journey would look like. As the train lurched into motion, he felt a sudden swell of hope build up inside him, as they were finally taking the fight to the monster that had tried to take everything from the Tyrkin. However, Lucas' words rang through his mind once more. *He wants me to tell you, you know that, right?* An involuntary shudder ran down his spine as he worried for a moment that this was all an elaborate trap. Suddenly, a hand dropped onto his, and he turned to look into Orielle's brilliant green eyes. Releasing the breath he didn't know he was holding, Colton steeled himself once more. As long as he kept faith, they could manage. After all, they had beat the beast before, they could do it again.

—

The depths shifted around Va'Rul's long scaled form, as he lay coiled on the bottom of the great Andromedus River. Long had he waited for the chance to strike at the surface world once more, and these Tyrkin would serve his purposes nicely. For this gathering was to be a defining moment in the rise of his new empire. No Gods could stop him now as they had foolishly locked themselves away, and the broken one was no threat. A sinister snarl split his scaled lips as he remembered the shield revealing his tethers to his pawn. Perhaps he would need to find and devour him after all.

Va'Rul quelled his rising anger, as *his* time would come soon enough. He closed his orange serpentine eyes as he settled into a comfortable position, preparing for his grand re-entrance in only a few days. Va'Rul shuddered with pleasure as he sent a wave of excitement through all of his drones above. Soon, the world would be his once more.

Chapter Thirty-Two: A Time For Action

Whatever Colton thought the two day trip to the Thicket of Gatherings was going to be like, he hadn't imagined it would go the way it did. At first it started as a general planning session to try and find out just what they should do when they got there. This included Orielle trying to lay out just how far ahead of Skarvald and the majority of their forces they would be. Ultimately, Orielle believed they would have a two day head start and the group wanted to use it wisely.

From there they set multiple plans in motion with a majority of them including some form of reconnaissance on Sero and Imbrose's part, while the rest of the team tried to prepare as best as they could outside of the main thicket. Cartwright was the overwhelming favorite for leading the initial endeavor as he had the most experience, and even Orielle preferred to pass the leadership role to someone else. Eventually, they settled on a definitive plan and were left with nothing better to do than try to find a way to pass the time.

"So," Toku began. "You're from Tri-Spire, eh?"

Sero turned to look at the grizzled ranger. "Not originally, but I have lived there most of my life."

Toku nodded slowly. "I see, so what did you do while you were there?"

Sero's eyes darted from person to person seemingly hoping for some kind of bailout. "Uh…well, I worked for someone who…" The young man paused once again, looking around uncomfortably only to see genuine interest on everyone's faces. "Who…acquired things that he didn't have before."

"Riveting," Imbrose intoned.

"What kind of things?" Colton asked, ignoring his friend.

"Things that…other people had and he wanted," Sero finished quickly.

"Ah, so a thief then?" Ember questioned, leaning forward onto her knees. "Did you help him with his business?"

Sero shrunk in on himself as he stammered for an answer. "I-I, uh…"

"Oh, relax, kid!" Imbrose finally blurted, and gestured to the surrounding party. "Everyone here has stolen a thing or two in their time." With that, everyone went silent as Imbrose looked around the room for nods of encouragement, only to get confused looks. "No? None of you have ever… Well fine, at least *one* of us has stolen a thing or two. So, you are in good company."

Colton massaged his forehead, a small grin on his face.

"It's okay, Sero," Orielle said calmly. "We're all friends here! We're just curious about who you are, that's all!"

Sero gulped slightly but smiled tentatively. "When I was a child, I was just an orphan on the streets…"

The young man proceeded to regale the crowd with all of the exploits of his young life, including serving a man known as simply the Scorpion. He explained that at first it was just simple jobs, stealing an odd bag of coins there, a fancy weapon here. Though it quickly escalated to infiltrating noble's homes and digging up dirt on them. Eventually, Scorpion ordered him to eavesdrop on a meeting between two people, and while it seemed like any other task, he was quickly sent on the mission to the Primal Forest after reporting on it.

Cartwright scratched the side of his face as it contorted in thought. "Didn't you say that he wanted your companion to kill you after completing your mission here?"

Sero didn't answer and instead simply nodded in a jerking motion. The memory obviously still caused him pain.

"What was the conversation about?" Colton asked, his curiosity getting the better of him.

"I think they were planning some sort of excursion in the next few days. Seemed pretty harmless, but I think they needed some kind of help," Sero answered, his mood visibly falling.

Sensing the change in the energy around the room, everyone fell into a relatively awkward silence, until Imbrose clapped his hands and stood up.

"You know, only one person in the world is able to find me when I'm trying to stay hidden." The attention of the whole room shifted to the standing blue man. "I wonder if you would fare any better, Sero?" Sero looked up, his eyes brightening at the change in subject. "What do you say, think you can find me?"

The challenge issued, the young man sat up straighter. "Without a doubt."

A fiendish smile crossed Imbrose's face as he looked down at the boy. "I like your confidence."

What followed was a mad scramble as Imbrose hid somewhere in the train and Sero set about trying to locate him. A few times he got close, only to pull back a tablecloth to reveal an empty space underneath as Imbrose had just used his dagger to appear somewhere else. Eventually he allowed himself to be found, only for the group to split into teams and set about a makeshift game of hide and seek. The day went quickly from there, and when the group finally tired themselves out, they ate some of the fresher rations they brought from home.

The following day was much the same, with only a small time in the morning set aside for Cartwright to lay out the plan for the following morning one last time. At the end of his mini lecture, Cartwright could already see the restlessness setting in and ordered everyone to run laps up and down the train until that too devolved into a game. Races between two at a time resulted in a crestfallen Imbrose losing a foot race to his significant other. Colton lost handily to the spry Sero, who made it to the end of the last car before he had even passed the halfway point.

With the day consisting of multiple competitions, one could be forgiven for forgetting about the task before them, but Colton always found his mind drifting to the following morning whenever he sat down. The distraction proved to be welcome as even Toku, who was usually very mild mannered, began to show a more competitive side as Sero continued to run laps around the older among them. At the end of the day, Colton felt a definitive camaraderie among their small group that hadn't been there when they first set out. That only served to strengthen the growing sense of hope that permeated the train as it traveled to their fateful destination.

When the party awoke on the third day to the constant motion below them slowly beginning to stop, they all met in the main cabin to go over the plan one last time.

"We don't know who we can trust right now," Cartwright began. "So, when we get off, Vera will be waiting for us. She is the director of this thicket's cloudstone station. It is important that we don't arouse suspicion, so let me and Toku do most of the talking. If she asks why we have come, just tell her it is for the Gathering."

Everyone nodded around the semicircle, their faces serious.

"Imbrose, Toku, and Sero," Cartwright said, pointing to the three men. "You should make your way into the thicket as soon as we make it out of the tunnel. You have until sundown tonight to scout out the situation inside, then you need to make your way back out to us." Cartwright adjusted his sword belt as he spoke. "If we don't see you by nightfall, we will have to assume you have been captured and we are walking into a hostile environment."

"How will we know where you camped?" Sero asked.

Toku smirked. "Stick with me kid, I've been tracking people down since before your mother ever considered having you."

"If you get captured, we can't risk you revealing our location," Cartwright answered, then he took a breath as the train slowed dramatically. "Listen, we are likely walking into a very dangerous situation, and we could find ourselves in over our heads quickly. If that happens, you need to save as many citizens as you can and leave. We are no use to the other thickets if we can't tell them what happened here should we fail."

The gravity of his instructions sat upon the group as they stood there in silence before nodding one after another, with Orielle being the last. Satisfied everyone was on the right track, Cartwright moved to stand in front of the doors as the train finally came to a stop and they swung open. Outside, a friendly female voice asked them where they were coming from and Cartwright promptly answered her as he exited.

The rest of the group cautiously walked down the stairs and stepped on solid ground, as the two older men busied the woman, who must have been Vera. After a quick discourse the party walked up and out of the tunnels, feeling the first kiss of sunlight in days. Directly to the left, a large wall of brambles and trees made it impossible to see any further in that direction. Seeing an entrance into what had to be the thicket some distance ahead, Cartwright quickly reminded the scouts that they only had until sundown and dismissed them to carry out their duties. Without further prompting, the expedition broke into two groups, with Imbrose giving Ember a parting kiss before jogging after the other two men.

When they were out of sight, Cartwright, Ember, Orielle, and Colton all made their way around to the right, trying to find a way onto the cliff they had just walked out of. The entire hike took just under an hour, as they found themselves looking out into the massive forest all around them. If it hadn't been for the nervousness hovering around their camp, it would have been a breathtaking view.

Cartwright busied them with setting up a defensible perimeter in the form of pit traps and the slime Toku had used to keep predators away from them when traveling to Skarvald. Unfortunately, they quickly ran out of things to keep their mind occupied and the day dragged by slowly. This resulted in Ember showing Orielle a few basic hand to hand combat moves, as she had begun to pace so much that Ember lost her patience.

Colton, on the other hand, stayed near the cliff edge, trying to spot anyone who might be coming from below.

The thicket loomed large to his left as it blotted out the sky, and while it obviously had some similarities to the only one he had seen so far, it had a vastly different shape. Where the Thicket of Memories was very large and oval in shape, this one was nearly a perfectly shaped dome. Additionally, it didn't seem to have any opening at the top, which led Colton to wonder what it must look like in there throughout the day.

His musing only distracted him for so long before the worry began to set in. Since the sun was setting just over his right shoulder, he found himself casually checking its progress more than thirty times per hour.

Desperate to find something to keep his sanity, he drew Tyrrek's greatsword and laid it across his lap. This blade had served him far more than he ever anticipated since he had come to this strange land. Truthfully, he never expected to use it, but now it had become a major part of his fighting style. He remembered his grandfather telling him what it was like to wield the blade back when he was a young man. He always mentioned how the weapon seemed to fill in the gaps of the person holding it. For him, it had given him a certain sense of sight, which only proved to increase his grandfather's swordplay. However, for Colton it almost felt like it was slowly showing him a different version of himself. It was as if the weapon was forging him into someone new, someone stronger.

For as long as he could remember, Colton was barely any good at using a sword. Now though, he felt like the blade was an extension of his very being. Like a piece of him had been returned after being separated for so long. Colton stared at the runed weapon, it's cold steel a comfort in the blazing heat of the forest. There had been times when the sword seemed to be trying to…communicate with him, and he could sense an intention behind it. He had always brushed it off in the moment as he was usually fighting for his life, but the feeling always stayed with him long after the battle ended.

"Brooding alone, are we?" Orielle's playful voice shook him from his musings as she sat down next to him.

"Just slowly going crazy is all. How long until sunset do you think?" Colton queried.

Orielle glanced over her shoulder the same way he had a hundred times over. "I'd say less than an hour now." Colton sighed, his gut twisting at the uselessness he felt. "Don't worry, they'll be back."

"I know, I just feel powerless out here. What if they walked directly into a trap and the entire time we have been sitting here they are in danger?" Colton responded.

"Then we will go in there in about an hour and make them pay," Orielle bantered back, her voice playful.

Colton snickered, her hand grabbing his. "I'd hate to be on your bad side."

"Remember that, so you don't get into any trouble," she teased, bumping his shoulder.

The two of them laughed as Colton set his sword down next to him. They sat there for a while just enjoying the view and the comfort of each other's presence. Suddenly, the peaceful silence was shattered as Cartwright called out to them.

"We got someone approaching," he whispered harshly. "Prepare yourselves for the worst."

Exchanging a glance, the two of them stood up and looked down the slope into the forest. Ember ran up next to them, her naginata gleaming in the fading light of the day. The bushes at the treeline rustled a bit before Toku pulled himself free of the thick underbrush, clearly tired.

Colton took a step toward him but Cartwright held out a hand. "Toku, you sure cut it close."

The winded man took a few steps then stopped. "Apologies, we ran into a bit of trouble."

"We can get into that, but I need to make sure you are still with us, old friend," Cartwright shot back.

Toku nodded, his beard bouncing with the motion. "Go on, then."

Cartwright grimaced. "Your wife," he began. "What was her name?"

Colton could see Toku flinch at the question, but he answered all the same. "Clara."

"And, how did she die?" Cartwright pressed, watching Toku closely.

"Poison, after returning from a hunt," Toku responded blandly. "Now, are you going to let me sit down, or do you want my entire life story?"

Cartwright smirked sadly as he walked up and guided Toku around the traps they had set. "Where are the others?"

"Left them just inside. Figured it would be easier to track you down on my own," Toku said, as he sat down and pulled out a waterskin.

"Tell me what we are dealing with," Cartwright probed.

Wiping his face, Toku nodded. "It has already begun. The entire populace there is acting strangely."

"Strange how?" Orielle cut in.

"Too friendly, and too quiet. Everyone walked around with blank eyes but a wide smile. It reminded me of the kids during the festival," Toku recalled.

"Do you think they found you out?" Colton asked quietly.

"Probably, the beast is cunning. I'll give it that. Even as I was about to leave, the entire population began walking toward the center Gathering Pool as if on cue." Toku paused, taking another swig of water. "I'm not sure we have until the end of tomorrow."

Cartwright cursed. "We aren't prepared for this. We need more time."

"We don't have more time, and those people need us!" Orielle protested.

Cartwright screwed up his face in thought before looking toward Toku once more. "Did you see any of his cultists around?"

Toku shook his head. "Not one. In fact, there wasn't a single armed person that we could see."

Coming to a decision, Cartwright stood up. "The time for planning is over. Now it is a time for action. Let's get down there."

Chapter Thirty-Three: Into The Deep

They hurried down the path they had taken earlier that day, all sense of boredom gone from the group as they closed in on the Thicket of Gatherings. Toku led the way despite his tiredness and eventually they caught sight of their destination. The unguarded doorway made the group pause as they approached.

"Were there always no guards?" Ember asked quietly.

"There were two of them last time I was here," Toku answered grimly as he glanced into the tunnel. In place of the ever-present Dream Bloom, multiple torch sconces were lined along the walls stretching into the darkness.

"No turning back now," Cartwright concluded. "It knows we are here, but remember what I said on the train. If things get too rough, save who you can and leave." Exchanging a nod with Toku, the two of them led the party of five through the illuminated tunnels. The walk through was far shorter than at the Thicket of Memories, and eventually they stepped out and beheld the Thicket of Gatherings.

Colton lowered his sword slightly as he took in the impressive space. The entire area was perfectly circular with the ground descending into a large pool of water placed in the center. As he scanned his surroundings, he noticed the earth was segmented into what seemed like large stairs hundreds of feet across, leading down to the center. Crops were laid out along the stair-like sections as a solid stream of water flowed up the stairs from the pool, defying gravity. He blinked as he registered the canopy above allowing in rays of dying sunlight, which created a beautiful design of shadows all around the thicket.

However, his eyes stopped moving as he locked onto all of the kneeling figures around the pool. Thousands of people all gathered around the water in a prostrating pose, as if praying.

"They haven't moved for over an hour." Imbrose's voice shattered the silence as he and Sero approached the group.

Colton turned to see his friend had grown serious and a haunted look lingered behind his gaze. "Has it been silent this whole time?"

"Yes, not even a chirping bird. It's the loudest silence I've ever had to endure," Imbrose muttered.

"Let's get down there, but keep your eyes open," Cartwright ordered as he started down the normal stairs that led down the layers to the center.

Tentatively, the group followed him as he slowly descended to the pool below, a sense of unease washing over them. It wasn't long before they came up level with the first of the kneeling townsfolk. Jumping clear of the last few stairs, Ember moved to check on a young woman who appeared to be nearing the end of a pregnancy. When the woman didn't respond, Ember backed away and looked back at the group shrugging.

A strong gust of wind blew through the thicket, the kind reserved for abandoned cities. Chills climbed up Colton's spine as he shifted his eyes to the glimmering pool in the center.

"Did you see that?" Orielle asked, before running down the stairs toward the water.

"Orielle!" Colton called out, but she didn't respond. Reacting, he took off after her as the others tried to rouse the other citizens.

Colton huffed as he tried to catch Orielle, but when she reached the edge of the water, she simply started wading into the surf, looking into the depths for something. He stopped at the edge, staring at her in disbelief as she rummaged in the increasingly deep water.

"What are you doing?" he asked, catching his breath.

"I swear I saw something in the water," Orielle's voice called back.

Colton watched as she waded in to above her waist. "How deep does that go?" His voice betrayed the nervousness he felt as she continued further in. "Should you really be going that far?"

"Oh, please, I've been swimming since I was a little girl! There is nothing to–. Wait, I think something just touched me."

Colton's heart pounded at her words. "Get out of the water!"

Orielle seemed to register just how far she had gone and began to frantically swim toward the shore once more. "Colton!"

Without a second thought, he dove into the water, swimming toward her. "Hang on! I'm coming!"

"It's getting closer! Help m–." Just as she was about to reach him, her voice cut off as she abruptly disappeared beneath the surface.

Blinking in shock, he quickly took a breath and dove beneath the surface, looking for any sign of her. The murky water proved to be too difficult to see through, and he emerged before taking another breath and diving under once more. Despair flowed through him freely as he desperately searched in vain for any sign of Orielle. About to go up for a second time he noticed a small glint of something metallic being tussled about in the sandy floor.

Not wanting to risk losing it, he pushed himself down into the depths reaching for the glimmering object. His lungs burned with the effort, begging him to take a breath. Just as he felt the air slipping from between his lips, his hand closed around a metallic object and he quickly rotated and pushed himself to the surface once more.

Bursting through the water, he gasped for air as he tread water. Glancing around, he saw just how far he had swam away from the shore. Now it seemed like miles away as he glanced down at the item in his hand. His heart nearly stopped as he looked at the small locket he had given Orielle.

"No..." His voice came out as barely a whisper.

Steeling himself, he pushed the locket into his pocket and took a deep breath of air and dove once more. This time he didn't stop as he swam deeper and deeper. The light of the waning sun disappeared completely, but Colton didn't care as he pushed himself further. His lungs began to burn once more, but it didn't matter because he had to save her. The darkness seemed to extend forever as he strained his eyes to see through the murk, willing his mind out to find her. If he could just connect with her, maybe he could figure out where she was. His arms ached as he paddled, and he felt himself losing consciousness as the air in his lungs began to escape.

Just as his vision narrowed to a bead, a glimmer of orange light appeared in blackness below. His body went limp as the orange light fast approached, and he felt something grab him under his arms and drag him upwards before his awareness escaped him.

His eyes fluttered open as he saw the canopy of the Thicket of Gatherings high above him. Lurching, he rolled to one side and spat out a stream of water as he coughed.

"Colton! What happened?" Imbrose asked, his voice uncharacteristically accusing.

"She's gone..." he managed between coughing fits. "Something pulled her under."

"So, you let her die, then?" Ember's cold voice startled Colton into looking up at them.

"What? No! I tried to get to her," he pleaded.

"But you didn't, and now she's dead. The Keeper was a fool to trust that you would protect her." Cartwright's venomous tone pulled his attention to his left where the warrior stood with his sword already brandished.

Colton got to his feet and stared at his companions confusedly. They all sounded the same, and looked the same but...no wait, their eyes. All of their eyes were identical orange snake eyes boring into him.

"This isn't real..." Colton stammered as he tried to focus on the world around him.

The space shimmered and he turned to look out at the lake. What was once a pool of water that spanned less than a few hundred feet now stretched into the horizon. Distantly, Colton could make out spires of coral protruding from the water's surface.

"Quicker than I expected," a familiar, sinister voice said behind him.

Colton turned around slowly, coming face to face with the multicolored serpent Va'Rul. Just like when he fought him in Orielle's head, he seemed to be made entirely out of different colored coral. His thirty foot snake-like body coiled beneath him as multiple sets of spindly arms ending in three razor-like fingers braced the creature's bulk on the beach.

A deep sense of loathing washed over Colton as he beheld the monstrosity. "We've come to kill you."

"You've come to try..." Va'Rul taunted. "Unfortunately, you have already failed, and now you are my pet."

"You have tried this once before, and we beat you," Colton fired back.

"True..." Va'Rul's bulk shifted slightly as he lowered his head down to Colton's eye level. "But that was just a small part of my power, and now you have walked directly into my embrace. There is no escape now..." Colton reached behind his shoulder and grasped for the blade, but it wasn't there. "I must say," Va'Rul continued, "taking you was a personal favorite of mine. I want you to know that I plan to have you personally kill your friends and family. Imagine the look on their faces when you stab that fancy sword of yours through their chests." Va'Rul cackled maniacally.

Colton closed his eyes, an overpowering anger building in him as he listened to the fiend threaten his family. He remembered the feeling of complete helplessness as he searched in vain for Orielle, then the admission to himself that he had failed her.

Question everything.

The Shade's words echoed through his mind as he tried to center his thoughts. These feelings weren't his own, because this wasn't real. Va'Rul was trying to drown him in negative emotions so that he couldn't think. A fresh wave of anger crashed over him as he saw the snake smirk with pleasure at his apparent struggle. Ignoring it, Colton delved into the deepest parts of himself. Immediately, he located the soft pulsing of his core within his soul. He could feel the power being suppressed by a heavy fog.

Forcing his way through, Colton could see a version of himself as a child coated in a dull blue light. Dark tendrils coiled around the struggling form of his spirit that solidified into Va'Rul himself. It was obvious that Va'Rul was trying to choke the life out of his very soul. A battle was being waged within himself, but Colton could only smile. He felt the hold the beast had on him was weak, and as he watched, the metaphysical version of himself fought with all of his might to free one hand. A glimmer of energy pulsed as his runed greatsword appeared within reach of the grasping hand in his mindseye.

"Face the truth of it, Colton Cobb. You are weak, and your only purpose was to come here and serve me. Using you, I will rebuild my–."

"No," Colton snarled, opening his eyes as he reached out and seized the blade, prepared to strike at the tendrils that bound him. "You are weak, and you hide behind illusions. You have no power over me." Va'Rul bared his fangs as Colton slashed down at the tendrils holding his power hostage.

The great viper recoiled in pain as the shadowy limbs parted beneath the slashing blade. Colton's very soul pulsed brightly, expelling the influence of Va'Rul from his mind and body. Suddenly, the true blade appeared in his hand as the vista he stood in shattered to reveal a mindspace like Orielle's. All around, he could see his own memories playing out as if he were living them over again.

Before him, Va'Rul screeched as its lithe body writhed in pain. "Tell me, have you ever experienced what you do to others?" Colton asked, walking toward the creature. "Let me show you." With that Colton pointed the blade at Va'Rul and pushed his mind into the monster's.

The ground fell out from under Colton as he fell into open air. He felt his stomach lift into his throat as he fell through the clouds and down towards the fast approaching ground. Only, it wasn't ground, but water as he plummeted toward the crashing waves. Just as he was about to hit, Colton flinched expecting pain but instead he just passed through the water as if it wasn't even there.

His fall came to an abrupt stop as he found himself surrounded in an endless visual of deep blue water. Immediately he could tell he didn't need to breathe as he looked around, trying to take stock of his surroundings. It was obvious that he had pushed himself into some memory of Va'Rul's but he couldn't see anything.

Suddenly, a form became visible in the distance swimming toward him at an incredible speed. It didn't take long for Colton to recognize Va'Rul as it rushed up to and past him, never pausing. The fear in the serpent's eyes were plain to see as Colton directed his eyes back to the way it had come. Passing him in droves, even more coral encrusted monstrosities identical to Va'Rul swam away from some unseen threat.

A small bead of bright light like the sun appeared in the distance, visible from even a vast distance underwater. In an instant the light grew so bright that even Colton had to shield his eyes even though it wasn't real. A loud screech echoed as hundreds of the fleeing creatures were scorched by the approaching light, and Colton watched them dissipate into ash.

Eventually, the light became so bright and hot that Colton felt himself beginning to panic from the sheer force of the memory. Just as quickly as it came, the light and pressure pulled back to just a small bead as Colton risked a glance in the direction of the light to see the figure of a man floating mere feet from him. The figure gave off a presence so powerful that it left Colton breathless, as all of the man's features were shrouded in the same light as before. Instinctively, Colton knew this was a God. A creature of such supreme power that he couldn't even conceive what its face looked like. The God turned and seemed to notice Colton in this mindscape. Even though Colton couldn't see its features, he could tell that it smiled at him before rushing off into the ocean once more in pursuit of Va'Rul and his kin.

The memory shifted and Colton found himself floating just on the outskirts of a massive coral city that seemed to stretch into the horizon. The God was there too, as it proceeded to blast the spires with beams of light that sent shockwaves echoing out in every direction. Colton was witnessing the death of a race. A small piece of him felt sorrow as he watched the coral snakes be decimated one after another, but then he remembered what kind of creature Va'Rul was. He knew what just one of them was capable of, what could an entire race of these creatures do? Besides, Colton knew the God was not evil, but trying to protect his creations. Colton shook his head, confused at how he had come to understand that fact.

Finally, the city lay in ruins and not a single creature remained in the destroyed landscape. The God once more surveyed the space and then with a bright flash of light vanished from the space. The once colorful and beautiful city was now nothing more than a smattering of rubble along the ocean floor. A small movement caught Colton's eye. There in the water floating listlessly was a wounded coral serpent, barely alive.

Focusing on the creature, he could tell immediately that this was Va'Rul, and he had somehow survived the God's decimation. Colton squinted. The memory was accurate and that was Va'Rul then, but it was also him all these years later as Colton knew him. Va'Rul had lived in this memory at this moment to build his hate and desire for revenge. Colton shook his head in sadness. Even after what must have been thousands of years, Va'Rul harbored such hate, and Colton could only pity the creature who must have been the last of his kind.

A pressure swept out from the motionless form, and Colton watched as a wall of inky black water formed on the horizon.

"Insolent insect!" Va'Rul's voice echoed through the space. "I will crush your very soul!" The water around him became colder as the wall of dark water began to rush toward him.

Letting his instincts guide him, he knew that hurting Va'Rul here would hurt him in the waking world. With this realization, he propelled himself toward the injured creature in the water. A roar sounded out as Colton closed in, but the water sped up too. Pushing himself harder, Colton felt himself surge forward, but it wasn't going to be fast enough as the water loomed ever closer. In a spark of inspiration, he reached into himself and used his power to appear next to the creature as he slashed down with all of his strength as blackness surrounded him. He felt the blade bite into something just as an incredible force shoved him away.

Colton gasped as he felt his consciousness return to him in reality. He was kneeling on the ground only a few feet from the water's edge with Orielle kneeling just beside him, still in some kind of trance. With the others not immediately visible, Colton focused his vision on the pool in front of him. The water erupted as a massive form broke the surface. Before him, the true Va'Rul screeched so loud that Colton had to cover his ears. All illusions gone, the viper focused in on Colton and stabbed out with one of its three fingered claws.

Struggling to draw the sword on his back, he knew he wouldn't make it in time and flinched as the attack approached. A clatter to his right revealed Toku diving in front of the blow, having somehow broken free of his own illusion. Colton watched in horror as the three razor sharp claws pierced through Toku, stopping inches from his own body. The ranger's blood splattered onto Colton's face as Toku weakly looked over his shoulder at him.

"Get...her...out..." Toku managed as blood spilled from his mouth before Va'Rul flicked the mortally wounded man to the side.

Reacting quickly, Colton reached out and grabbed Orielle's hand and willed himself to appear with her some two hundred feet away. His powers strained, but obliged him and they disappeared just before another set of claws decimated the space he was kneeling in moments ago.

Upon landing, Orielle jerked to consciousness and pulled a pistol pointing it at him. "Ori! It's me!" Colton cried, already hearing Va'Rul screaming in anger.

Her eyes cleared as she registered the blood on him. "Are you hurt?" she asked, concerned.

Colton shook his head slowly. "Toku sacrificed himself to save us." Fury built in her eyes as she turned to look at the approaching monstrosity, recklessly crushing the kneeling masses with its bulk. "If we are going to leave, we need to go now," Colton warned.

Orielle glanced at him, and he knew they weren't leaving. "Let's end this."

One way or another, it will end today, Colton thought as he nodded and drew his sword, turning to meet the massive Va'Rul, the viper's eyes locked on them.

Chapter Thirty-Four: Va'Rul

O rielle broke off to the left, her pistols already firing as Va'Rul slithered toward Colton, ignoring the barrage leaving scorch marks along his colorful scales. Seeing the snake abandon all pretenses and simply attack him drew a smile to Colton's face. He preferred if no one else was in harm's way, but having Va'Rul focus on him was acceptable as well.

Realizing this fight would only hurt many of the kneeling citizens if it stayed here, he reached out and connected his mind to Orielle.

We need to pull him further away from the pool. There are too many innocents down here. The connection formed easier than ever before.

Orielle sent him a mental affirmation. *I see Cartwright and the others down below. They're still kneeling. Keep him busy, I'm going to try and wake them up. We could use their help.*

Glancing to a clearing further up the side of the area where there was a small bundle of abandoned houses, Colton teleported five hundred feet away, appearing three levels above the highest citizens. Va'Rul redirected immediately and began to use his arms to propel him toward Colton even faster, with no regard for the safety of the prostrated civilians.

With only a few moments before their clash, Colton embedded his sword into the ground and uncoiled the whip at his hip. In a quick motion, he slung the weapon around his body, lashing it in place across his torso for easier access. With that, he drew the blade once more and leveled it on the charging monstrosity.

Leaping the final fifty feet, Va'Rul lunged forward with a razor sharp claw swinging. Not hesitating, Colton rushed to meet him, his sword low for an upward slice. When the claw was within a few feet of him, Colton glanced to the right and warped right next to Va'Rul's exposed flank, his sword already in motion. The rune sword dug in deep as a crash sounded from where Colton had been standing a fraction of a second ago. Rust-red blood oozed from the wound as he ripped the blade free. In turn, the serpent used his large body to slam into Colton, sending him sprawling tens of feet away.

The force of the blow knocked the air out his lungs as he thumped hard onto his back. Struggling to his feet, Colton flinched as Va'Rul had already closed the distance and another set of claws descended. Vanishing once more, Colton appeared on the roof of one of the small houses nearby, stumbling on the wooden planks as he landed.

Colton coughed as a dribble of blood splashed onto the roof below him. *Must've broken a rib,* Colton thought. The gravity of the situation settled in as Va'Rul once more twisted to look at him, murder in his serpentine eyes. If he made a single mistake, it would be the end of him, and everyone below would be next.

In an instant, the titanic monster was upon him again as he plowed through the house beneath Colton. Feeling the roof begin to buckle, he ran toward the end of the building and threw himself off, free falling to the ground below. Reluctantly, Colton let go of his sword and tumbled through the air. Just barely having the time to tuck into a roll as he reached the ground. Unfortunately, he gauged the landing wrong, and instead landed badly on one leg, twisting his ankle.

Hissing in pain, Colton hobbled to his feet to see Va'Rul emerging from the ruined house, already shaking large pieces of the building all over the ground.

"You mortals are such fragile creatures," Va'Rul taunted as he slithered toward Colton slowly. "It almost makes killing you too easy."

Glancing around, Colton saw his blade buried in the ground only a few feet away and started gingerly moving in its direction, hoping the creature would take its time.

"You know what it reminds me of?" Colton managed with a grunt of pain. The colossal creature stalled for a moment, its head cocked to one side as Colton reached his sword once again. "Kinda reminds me of how easily your whole race was decimated as you watched," Colton sneered, a cold smile creeping across his face. Va'Rul's eyes widened in fury as he roared and abandoned all sense of caution, bearing down on Colton for the kill.

The fight was too lopsided; how could one man hope to fight such a thing alone? Then a thought struck him as he realized the full extent of his power. Did he have to be just one man? With a thought, Colton spread out his consciousness, allowing not just one, but two, then three, then four, and more versions of himself appear around the surprised Va'Rul enclosing the beast in a circle.

Freezing in place, Va'Rul glanced around the circle of identical Coltons all holding the rune blade high. Then as one, they all rushed in as if to strike in unison. Va'Rul frantically swiped at one and then another as his claws passed through the illusions harmlessly. Capturing the moment, Colton deftly swapped from one clone to another, landing solid hits on the scaled hide only to swap to another before the creature could react. This hit and run tactic lasted for a number of minutes until Va'Rul roared and coiled into a tight circle before expanding his body out abruptly, hitting all of the illusions and the real Colton all at once.

Once more, he tumbled backwards head over heels as all of his clones dispelled. Slamming into one of the sheer steps that separated one level from another, Colton felt his body creak and crack from the impact.

Cultists are flooding into the valley! Orielle's voice rang out in his head, causing his eyes to snap open and glance at the entrance.

Pouring down the stairs, Colton could see dozens of cultists rushing toward the helpless citizens below. Frustration came over him as he tried to reach for the hilt of the blade only inches from his fingertips. Pain wracked his body as his arms failed to respond properly.

Blinking his bleary eyes, Colton could see Va'Rul turn his head toward him once more and he let his head fall back as he looked at the bright sunlight shining through the holes in the canopy above. His eyes focused as he realized how much time had passed. When they arrived, it was dusk, and now it was late afternoon the following day.

A roar unlike those of Va'Rul echoed throughout the valley as the gigantic albino form of Grex'xi blew open the entrance to the Thicket of Gatherings, already scooping a cultist into her jaws and clamping down. As she continued stampeding, Colton watched as a horde of poachers stormed in behind her, firing their crossbows with abandon, their king leading the charge. Skarvald and his poachers clashed with the cultists as claws and steel met in a cacophony of brutality.

Hope surged within him as Colton weakly reached for his blade once more, determined to rejoin the fight. A shadow covered him as he looked up to see the looming figure of Va'Rul slowly approaching him.

"You have put up more of a fight than I expected, but this ends now." Va'Rul's voice seemed to carry a sense of pride as he opened his mouth wide to devour Colton.

I've got you, a familiar male voice echoed in his mind as a portal appeared in front of him and a metal man stepped through to expel a torrent of flames into the mouth of the creature, forcing Va'Rul back from the sheer force of it. Before Colton could react, Joel reached out and pulled him through the portal.

Landing on soft grass, Colton looked up to see the man already pouring a liquid into his mouth. The bitter taste caused him to sputter before swallowing the viscous substance. Va'Rul was now on the opposite side of the thicket from him as flames enveloped the creature's head.

"Just couldn't wait for us, could you?" Joel admonished as Friend stepped back through the portal, shaking his hands to extinguish the fire in his palms.

Immediately, a warm energy passed through Colton's body as whatever he had just drank began to heal his most grievous wounds. "Sorry," he managed as a rib snapped back into place.

Joel snapped his fingers and the portal vanished as a frustrated roar echoed in the distance. Grex'xi, sensing another apex predator, whipped her head in that direction and returned an ear shattering roar of her own and charged.

"How'd you manage that?" Colton asked as he felt a small amount of his strength returning to him.

Joel shrugged. "I figured we could use the help, so I went and asked her nicely. Turns out, she doesn't like the idea of another beastie attacking her forest."

"Right, but how did you get her here so fast?" Colton groaned as he sat up, the pain in his body quickly abating.

Joel raised an eyebrow. "What? Are you the only one who's capable of improving your skills?" Snapping his fingers once more, a portal appeared over his shoulder and Orielle rushed through with Imbrose, Ember, and Sero shortly behind.

"Colton!" she cried, rushing to his side. "I shouldn't have left you!"

Colton waved her concern away. "You had to save the others." He stood up, taking stock of his surroundings. "This isn't over."

They stood up near where they had originally entered the thicket, but with Grex'xi's entrance decimating the tunnel, the jungle was now visible behind them. The poachers were fighting hard, but it could go either way at any moment. Quickly realizing that Va'Rul was the key to the fight, he redirected his attention toward the serpent just as Grex'xi collided with him in the distance, the sound echoing to where they stood.

"She's going to need help," Colton said, already seeing wounds appear on her white hide.

"What are you going to fight with?" Orielle asked, noticing the sword was missing.

Colton simply reached out a hand, and the blade materialized in his right hand.

"Neat trick," Joel whistled as he threw up another portal. "Ready?"

Everyone nodded as they rushed through the portal together, running out right in the midst of Va'Rul and Grex'xi's grappling. The white Queen of Beasts roared as she was gouged by one slash and then another until she was tossed to one side, stumbling off the edge of the steep, layered terrain and onto the level below.

Va'Rul fell back with the effort, a large chunk torn from his body where an arm used to be. Wasting no time, the group pushed up and attacked Va'Rul, with Friend throwing two large balls of fire at him. Imbrose, Ember, and Sero rushed off to the right as the blue man threw his red dagger, embedding it into Va'Rul's side. Orielle stayed back with Friend, firing blast after blast at the writhing snake. Joel followed alongside Colton as he drew two gleaming shortswords.

As they attacked Va'Rul from every angle, Colton noticed a glowing wound on the serpent's underbelly and immediately knew it had come from the strike he had made while in Va'Rul's mind.

"Aim for the glowing wound on his stomach," Colton shouted as he reached out to the blade in his right hand.

The power it had given him during his suicidal fight in the forest had only happened that one time, but could he call on it at will? Pushing his energy into the blade, the runes began to glow and the familiar feeling of power began to swell within him. The weapon grew light in his grasp as if he had wielded it for a lifetime of battles. One by one, the runes along the center of the sword began to ignite as the whole fight slowed to a crawl for him. He felt himself still running as the sword filled him with power, his lingering wounds forgotten, but all around him his friends had frozen in place as a disembodied voice echoed all around him.

"Yes, I do believe you will suffice." The voice reminded him of his grandfather in a way, but he could tell it wasn't him. "*Penance* accepts you, Champion."

All at once the world returned to motion as Colton had no time to consider what had just happened to him. The sword, no, Penance hummed in his grip as he charged Va'Rul, a mighty battle cry sounding forth as he and his friends clashed with the beast.

Blades met flesh as they laid into the squirming creature. Ember, Sero, and Imbrose pulled Va'Rul's attention to one side as he tried to cover the wound on his stomach. Using the distraction, Joel brought both of his blades down on Va'Rul's hide, causing the massive snake to thrash, catching Sero and Joel off balance, making them both topple to the ground. Va'Rul brought his tail up, attempting to crush Joel into the ground, but Colton threw himself on top of him and teleported them both a few feet away and out of harm's way.

Nodding in appreciation, Joel rolled to his feet as Imbrose continued to irritate the monster by stabbing him in the face and teleporting around elusively. Sero, to his credit, quickly got to his feet and ran to rejoin Ember as they landed blow after blow on Va'Rul's tough scales.

Colton locked in on the wound in the snake's stomach and took a step to attack again up close, but a sudden moment of inspiration struck him. Shaking his head at the absurdity of it, he tossed Penance into the air and unwound his whip in the same motion. With a flick of his wrist he coiled the whip around the handle of Penance and twirled his arm in a large circle. To his surprise the blade didn't weigh down the whip as if it understood his intention as it swung overhead.

Saying a silent prayer to Tyrrek, Colton launched the blade forth, aiming for the glowing cut. Va'Rul's eyes widened as he tried to react and shifted to cover the wound. A massive blast of energy struck the serpent's face as Orielle's weapon barked behind Colton, causing Va'Rul's head to jerk back due to the force. The motion revealed Colton's target once more and the blade sank home, burying itself entirely to the hilt. A shuddering cry pierced the air as Colton was forced to drop the whip. He and all of his allies brought their hands to their ears at the sudden sound.

Screeching, Va'rul writhed in pain as Colton watched all of the cultists in the distance flop to the ground as if they had been puppets and their strings were cut. Finally, the ear splitting sound ended as Va'Rul toppled slightly. With his spindly arms supporting his massive bulk, Va'Rul struggled to hold himself up, Penance still protruding from his abdomen. Still dangerous, Va'Rul lashed out at anyone who got too close, but was trying to gradually move towards the pool in the center of the thicket.

Colton, his ears ringing, watched as Ember frantically pulled Imbrose to one side as he had fallen from Va'Rul. A small pop sounded, his hearing returning to him. He could barely hear Joel who was yelling something right next to him.

"He's trying to escape!" Joel exclaimed, already stumbling toward the slowly slithering Va'Rul.

Colton forced himself to take a step forward, his equilibrium still recovering. Vaguely, he could see his whip handle sliding further from him as the snake increased the distance, and he realized in horror that he was going to get away.

A low rumble of thunder shook the entire space, making everyone look up into the canopy. As they watched, thick black fog pushed its way through and began flowing down toward the ground. Va'Rul, finding some internal strength, forced himself to flee faster, leaving a trail of blood in his wake. Just as he was about to make a jump for the center, a large albino claw slammed down onto his tail, stopping his retreat.

Va'Rul looked back at Grex'xi, who snarled back at him. Even from this distance, Colton could see the fear in the snake's eyes as it glanced up at the descending fog. Desperately, Va'Rul struck out at the Albino Queen, aiming for her throat. However, the fog rapidly increased in speed as it seemed to solidify into black chains and wrap around Va'Rul's body, restraining him.

A pillar of fog landed next to the now prone creature as Lucas stepped out into view. He raised a hand and closed it into a fist as the chains around Va'Rul tightened further. Shocked into action, Colton rushed to the scene as Lucas turned to look at him.

"End it," he said simply, his eyes a swirling black like the fog he seemed to command.

Needing no further encouragement, Colton approached the still embedded blade of Penance and withdrew it with a spray of blood. Va'Rul squirmed as his many arms dug into the earth, but the chains held taut. Approaching the head of the giant snake, Colton met his orange serpentine eyes.

Relaxing in defeat, Va'Rul reached out with his mind. Colton, realizing the creature simply wanted to speak, allowed the connection to form.

I've been alive and in hiding for thousands of years, biding my time to return my race to its former glory, Va'Rul lamented. *In the end, it was another God that shattered that dream.* Colton flinched as he heard Va'Rul's words. *Though I suppose it matters not, you mortals were so focused on killing the monster, that you failed to notice it was mortals who truly sought your demise.*

You wanted to enslave us, Colton shot back.

But you would have lived, now you will all die. A chuckle rumbled in Va'Rul's throat. *I shall find solace in the fact that the precious children of the Gods facilitated their own demise.* A deep sigh echoed through Va'Rul's nose. *My fight is over.* The great serpent closed its eyes as it broke the connection to Colton, submitting to its fate.

Screwing up his face, Colton hefted Penance and brought it down with a mighty blow onto Va'Rul's neck, using all of his strength and gifted power from the blade. The sword cut clean through the once formidable foe's neck, severing his head entirely and digging into the ground underneath.

Colton stood there for a moment, his mind reeling from the fight they had just won, but also the cryptic last words of their enemy. Slowly, his friends gathered around him and Colton eventually turned his gaze away from the corpse of Va'Rul. With a heavy heart, he surveyed the battlefield that had claimed so many innocents. A man could be seen on the shore of the pool with another bearded man lying next to him.

Realizing it was Toku and Cartwright, Colton ran to their side as fast as he could. When he arrived, he saw Toku pale and still with Cartwright kneeling by his side.

"He's with Clara now," Cartwright whispered, his voice raw with emotion.

Without saying a word, Colton laid a hand on the older man's shoulder, and hoped Toku was at peace.

Colton's eyes were drawn to the far off figure of Lucas, who simply stared at him. *What has he become, and what will become of us all?* The harrowing thought lingered in his mind as Colton watched the surviving villagers begin to come to their senses. At least for the time being, they had won. He took in the carnage from Va'Rul's initial charge at him and the countless broken bodies in his path. *But at what cost?*

Chapter Thirty-Five: Turning The Page

T he people who woke from Va'Rul's influence seemed, at first, to be
entirely normal. However, as more and more of them began to stir,
it became increasingly obvious that was not the case. Many seemed to
have no idea how they had ever gotten to the Thicket of Gatherings, and
others had completely forgotten who they were. Luckily, a few were fully
conscious having, from their estimation, been among the last to arrive.
This led to a few families finding their wandering family members and
beginning the process of helping them reclaim lost memories. A process
that would no doubt require many to visit the Thicket of Memories, as
most of their histories would have been stored in a Dream Bloom.

Colton couldn't help but look over at Orielle as she tried
desperately to reunite families and wondered what Jasper was going
through at that exact moment. He had an inkling that she would want to
make her way home as soon as possible to answer that very question. A
request she never made, as she and the others focused on trying to help as
many as they could.

After the initial panic, the party was able to tend to their wounds
as they had finally moved everyone away from the carnage left from
Va'Rul. This led to a rough count of over one hundred and thirty people
dead, with one of them being the Keeper and another being his wife.
Fortunately, their nineteen-year-old daughter, Misha, had survived, and
she valiantly set about restoring structure to the fractured people.

Afternoon turned to evening, and soon Skarvald approached with what remained of his people and a young, but burly man to his left.

"This is my son Dirk, and I thank you for your help in getting him back," Skarvald began gruffly, gesturing to the charcoal-skinned man to his right who just stood there. "Unfortunately, it seems Va'Rul's influence has left him a bit scattered, and I can think of no better place than home to help him recover. So, it's time we made our exit," the large man said simply as he walked up to Orielle, Colton, and Friend.

"Are you certain?" Orielle questioned, looking up into the canopy where the beginnings of twinkling stars could be seen. "The Forest becomes far more active at night."

Skarvald smiled wryly. "Our entire time in your forest has been spent outside. We are more accustomed to the creatures that roam out there than you might think," he bragged, winking at her. "Besides, we made a deal, and I intend to honor that bargain."

"But..." Orielle began. "You've helped save the forest that's been your home for almost a decade. I'm sure my father–"

"But it isn't home, is it?" Skarvald interrupted, looking toward Friend. "Our home is made of fire and soot. We belong there, and we have a nasty little snake of our own to deal with. Will you join us, brother?"

Friend appeared to consider for a moment before glancing over at Sero, who was ferrying food to a nearby gathering of people. "I wish that I could, but I'm afraid I no longer belong there either." Friend stopped, looking down at his armor. "The moment I put this on, I became part of something bigger. And in my time away, someone has made a mockery of what this armor was supposed to represent."

Colton glanced at Friend, curiosity written all over his face. Skarvald, on the other hand, simply nodded and stepped forward. "Should you ever find yourself once more, Everglow calls to you, Brother Friend."

"Call me Murkane, Murkane Forgekeeper." Friend, or rather, Murkane, replied. "Know that when this is over, I will return to Everglow to hear of your victory."

Skarvald clasped Murkane's forearm, then turned away and marched with his son and poachers out of the Thicket of Gatherings, never looking back.

"Murkane?" Orielle asked, beating Colton to the same question.

Murkane smiled. "Aye, it was my name before I put on this armor. I have been dreaming a lot lately, and with Terry's help back at the Grove, I have begun to remember who I was."

"Oh? Well, I'm happy for you!" she exclaimed, her voice a little extra excited to cover the many other questions she still had.

Murkane chuckled. "Not to worry, Ori, we will have plenty of time to talk about me. For now, let's focus on getting these people settled before we leave."

It was the first time anyone had said anything about leaving, and Colton could see Orielle's face brighten at the mere mention. He determined that they would do what they could for the evening, but in the morning he would push the party to head back home. Misha already seemed to be taking charge, despite her young age, and it was obvious that their presence wasn't really needed any longer. That fact became even more obvious when the young Keeper approached the group as they had just finished bundling up Toku for his final journey home.

"I thank you for your help in saving this thicket." Her voice was extremely youthful, yet commanding. "I must ask another favor of you though."

"Of course! Anything we can do, we shall try," Orielle affirmed.

"Please take those who lost their memories with you. They could be from any of the northern thickets and the sooner we help them recover what they can, the sooner they can return to their families," Misha requested. "Oh, and please take...*her* as well, if you don't mind," she added, pointing at the sleeping Grex'xi in the field. "We can't begin repairs on the entrance until after she has left."

Joel bit his lip nervously. "Yeah, sorry about that, I just figured we would need the help."

Misha waved away the concern. "We are grateful for her help as well, but I think she may be making some of the children feel nervous." Ignoring the fact that she herself was barely an adult, Joel just nodded understandingly.

Following a hasty dinner, Joel managed to finally muster up the courage to approach Grex'xi. After a short two or three minute talk, the large reptile stood and made for the Grex'xi-shaped hole she had made earlier that day.

"How are you doing?" Colton asked Orielle as they sat next to each other.

"I'm…okay, I think," she answered softly, her face lifting into a small smile. "I guess I'm just anxious about getting home to Jasper. And I also can't help but worry about Lucas, he hasn't walked away from Va'Rul even once today."

Colton looked over at the massive corpse, and sure enough, standing about five feet away, was Lucas. "Ignoring the obvious, something else has changed within him. He's…" Colton let the sentence hang, unsure of what to say. Quickly adjusting himself to be face to face with her, he took her hand. "We will be home soon, and Jasper is going to be okay now. You saved him!"

Orielle smiled, and looked down. "I can feel it in my bones, he's lost right now." A small tear ran down her cheek. "I doubt he even remembers his own name, let alone me."

Colton brushed the tear from her face and pulled her gaze up to meet his own. "Then you'll have to make him remember you. Take it as an opportunity to build new memories with your brother. What matters is that he will be back, and he will be safe."

Orielle nodded, wiping her eyes. "You're right. I suppose I'm just worried that I've forgotten what it was like to be an older sister." A small chuckle escaped her.

"You've never stopped being his big sister." Colton pointed at his chest. "I've personally watched you fight monsters people tell horror stories about for the sake of your brother. If that's not being an older sister, I don't know what is."

Orielle leaned forward and kissed Colton gently. "Thank you for always standing by my side, even when I was being foolish."

"That's what being in a relationship means, right?" Colton asked sheepishly.

"Is that what we are?" Orielle pressed, her hand tightening in his. "In a relationship?"

"I'd love nothing more," Colton admitted, squeezing her hand back.

Orielle kissed him again, his heart soaring.

"Well, that's a new look," Joel called, returning to the group with a smile plain to see. The two of them broke apart blushing as they turned to look at him. "How long has this been going on?"

"A while," Orielle stated simply.

"Ah, well, the Queen says she will await us outside to demand her payment. Refused to tell me what it was though." The nervousness in Joel's voice made it clear how he felt about it.

"Did she seem angry?" Orielle asked.

"Not in the slightest." Joel sat down next to them, a cheeky grin splitting his face. "But I want to hear more about you two!"

Colton stood up, looking at the motionless Lucas in the distance. "Seems like you have a lot to talk about."

Orielle scoffed, her face playful. "Brave man you are!" Then, noticing where he was looking, she grew more serious. "Fine, but don't be gone long. It looks like the rest of the group is getting antsy."

Colton nodded as he saw Imbrose, Ember, Friend, and Sero all running around with children on their shoulders as they giggled furiously. "Looks like they're having a terrible time," he said jokingly before excusing himself and making his way to Lucas.

"I was wondering when you would finally come over here," Lucas commented flatly, not looking up. "I imagine you have some questions after what you have seen."

Colton stopped a few paces back, his instincts encouraging him to keep a small distance. "Wouldn't you?"

Lucas smirked, and finally pulled his gaze from the large corpse next to him. "I suppose I would." The young man gestured to a nearby boulder and Colton obliged. "You know, there was a time when I thought I would simply live out my life in Ma's apple orchard."

"It's a beautiful place to live," Colton acknowledged, his posture relaxing.

"It is, isn't it?" Lucas tilted his head back and looked at the night sky through the twisting branches. "Now, I don't know what the world has in store for me. The Shade told me things, things I can't even tell you if I wanted to, and they have changed me."

Colton studied the other man. "Lucas, are you okay?"

Lucas' eyes dropped to the ground in front of him. "Truthfully, I'm better now than I've ever been. I thought I knew what I wanted and what I was meant to do, but the world was small back then. Ori was right, we were never meant for each other, but I'm glad I was able to help put an end to the horrors I brought on our people in my pursuit of that fiction." The younger man looked at Colton genuinely. "I'm happy for the two of you. It's what you both deserve."

Colton nodded. "Thank you, Lucas." They lapsed into silence for a few minutes before Colton spoke again. "Will you come with us tomorrow?"

"No, I need to stay here and help this thicket recover, but if I could ask you a favor...?"

Leaning forward, Colton nodded once more. "Of course."

"Tell my mom I'm sorry, and I'll be home soon."

"I will," Colton affirmed.

Lucas nodded in appreciation as the two of them lapsed into a comfortable silence.

The evening ended rather quickly, as most of the villagers wanted to put the toils of today behind them. The group found a small house that was purposely left empty for when the Gathering occurred each year and promptly fell asleep.

That night, they all slept better than they had since arriving in Zerua, and when the morning dawn came, they awoke ready to begin the next chapter of their journey.

Refreshed and revitalized, the party made their departure as organized as possible. Upwards of seventy-five people were set to come with them back home in search of their memories, with another three hundred staying behind due to lack of room on the train. Misha assured them that once word got out about what had happened, the other thickets would send more transportation to help expedite the process.

True to her word, Grex'xi waited outside with her request for payment already thought out. The fearsome Queen of Monsters had decided that in return for assisting with Va'Rul, she would like someone from the Thicket of Memories to visit at least once a month. She additionally required that when her baby hatched, it would be the thicket's responsibility to guard the baby while she hunted for meat. With those terms agreed upon, the albino mother-to-be ran back to her den.

It took a little over an hour to load everyone into the train, as Vera had been under the influence of Va'Rul as well and seemed very confused when a massive group of people arrived. Luckily, Colton was becoming a bit of an expert with this mode of transportation and helped lead the boarding process. Helping to carry all of the fallen proved to be the most difficult part. Though, with the Thicket of Memories being the cemetery for all Tyrkin, they did what was necessary. Cartwright never left Toku's side as the train finally departed.

With their quest complete, they returned home.

Chapter Thirty-Six: Long Overdue

With the train being far more cramped than the last time, the trip was significantly more somber. Many people stared listlessly out windows, their minds still muddled from what they had gone through. The hardest for Colton and the others to see were the countless children who wandered up and down the train, seemingly lost at all times. Others still cried endlessly, but no one had the heart to stop them and instead settled on just holding them tightly. Ultimately, the group spent most of their time trying to help the dozens of people on the train.

Though even with all of the people struggling to find themselves, Colton and the others felt a profound sense of accomplishment. They had saved the forest, and these people would have another chance because of it. This was only heightened when a woman who had previously just been playing with a small piece of fabric between her fingers looked up to see a little girl standing before her. The two of them stared at one another, before a look of recognition flashed onto the woman's face and she pulled the little girl into a tight hug after referring to her as "my sweet daughter." More of these reunions occurred before finally reaching the Thicket of Memories, but most still seemed to require a trip to their flower in the Grove. Colton sensed that Terry would have his hands full for the foreseeable future.

After arriving at the thicket, Colton and the others rushed in to tell everyone of their arrival. Countless citizens offered to help those in need, and even offered lodging while they recovered their memories. This freed up the group to pursue their own agendas, and while Colton desperately wanted to follow Imbrose and Ember to go speak with their families, he also wanted to see how Jasper was doing. Confident his grandfather would understand, Colton followed Orielle to her house for her reunion with her brother.

From the moment the train had come to a stop, Colton could see deep emotions playing across the young woman's face. She was nervous, but also excited. It was as if she were trying to temper her expectations so as to not be disappointed in the result. She had not said a word to them as they closed in on her home, but he could understand the roiling feelings she was likely going through. So, when she reached the door and it flew open to reveal a very lively young boy smiling up at her, Colton wasn't surprised to see her break down in tears of relief.

As it turned out, Jasper had been nearly catatonic, even after Va'Rul's spell was eliminated. However, he had finally recognized his own mother and father for the first time in almost a year. Shortly after that, when the other children started acting closer to normal, it became obvious what they needed to do next. Taking Jasper to his Dream Bloom had been the next step, and almost immediately after, he began asking where Orielle was. The boy was still scarred from his experience, that was clear, but his bubbly personality lit up the room as Colton watched him flit from one adult to another, laughing and smiling all the while.

As the reunion continued, Jasper eventually made his way over to Colton, a gleeful look in his eye.

"Thank you for helping me, and for being there for my sister," Jasper said, bashfully.

Lowering himself to the child's eye level, Colton placed a hand on his shoulder. "Of course Jasper, I can't begin to tell you how happy I am to finally meet you."

The boy smiled once more, and leaned in. "Can you promise me something?"

"Sure, pal."

"Keep protecting her," Jasper pleaded, his eyes drifting over to Orielle who had just walked back into the room with an armful of drinks.

Colton followed his eyeline and locked eyes with her, the relief and unbridled joy written on her face making him smile. "Always."

"Good, because if you don't, I'll have to beat you up!" Jasper exclaimed.

Returning his attention, Colton held out a hand with the pinky extended and nodded. "I promise."

Satisfied, Jasper seized the extended digit with his own before running off to continue his rambunctious antics.

Before long, Colton started to feel a bit out of place as it was clear the family needed some time alone. So, with a gentle kiss on Orielle's cheek, which drew her mother's attention, he excused himself and made his way to his own family.

The lonely walk proved to be just what he needed as he considered the events of the last week. What had Va'Rul meant by his final words? Was there some greater threat at work that he was unaware of? Until now, Va'Rul seemed like the only threat worth considering, but now his mind turned to a foe he had almost forgotten: Curtis Nezva. Of course, that also drew his thoughts toward Delphine, and what had become of her. It had been such a long time since he had received the letter from Genevieve that... Did he ever respond? Colton froze mid stride as he realized he had never replied to the letter he received. Sighing at the fact that he never seemed to get a break, Colton pushed his concerns aside as he approached the door to where his family was staying. Only pausing for a moment to consider whether he should knock or not, he just shrugged and walked through the door, surprising four people inside.

Xander, Aileah, Xavier, and Phoebe all sat around a small table, enjoying some delicious smelling stew. The four of them all turned to see him, aside from his grandfather, who simply patted the bench to his right.

Taking the invitation, Colton removed his hat and leaned his sword against the wall. "I'm sorry it took me so long to sit down with all of you. It has been a crazy week."

"Are you kidding?" Phoebe exclaimed. "This place is amazing! I haven't been bored for a single second! First, there was the whole teleporting thing, then the festival. Which was scary to be honest, but still fun! Then, after you left, we went to that cider house near the pond! Then we–."

"Phoebe, dear," their grandmother graciously interrupted. "Why don't you tell Colton about that Jerric fellow you met."

Phoebe's face turned a dark shade of crimson at the name. "I uh…he probably doesn't want to…" she stammered.

Seizing on his sister's discomfort, Colton leaned onto the table. "Oh, but I do! Jerric has always seemed like a nice young man. Tell me, how long have you two been…drinking cider together?"

Phoebe's blush darkened as she glared at her brother. "Sure, I'll tell you, just as soon as you tell me how long you've been wooing the Keeper's daughter!" she fired back.

The two of them argued about their love interests until the last of the stew was eaten. The familiar banter drew a smile from even their father, who otherwise said nothing during the exchange. After dinner, Phoebe excused herself, claiming she needed some air. However, Colton noted she turned definitively towards the switchbacks leading to the guardhouse where Jerric was no doubt standing guard.

"Gods have mercy on that boy," Aileah sighed, a smile playing at her lips. "He has no idea what he's gotten himself into."

Colton just nodded, a relaxed feeling settling over him as the remaining four of them all moved to more comfortable seating arrangements.

"So, did you succeed?" Xander finally asked.

"I believe we did, but I can't help but worry about what comes next," Colton confided.

"Tell us what happened," Aileah pressed.

338

Taking a deep breath, Colton told them about their trip to the Thicket of Gatherings, and what they found there. He recounted the scene they had arrived to, and the preceding fight with the great serpent.

After explaining the creature's ending, and its cryptic final words Aileah interjected. "Do you know what he could be talking about?"

Colton shook his head.

"Whatever it is, I know you can handle it," Xander assured, his voice calm.

"I hope so," Colton said.

A silence fell over the family, until Aileah decided to turn the conversation to tales about their first visit to the Memory Grove. Apparently, the whole family had created their own flowers, and each Cobb now had a uniquely blue Dream Bloom surrounding Colton's own. Taking the opportunity to let someone else share, Colton simply smiled and enjoyed their experience and company. Eventually, Xavier excused himself and went to his room, and Aileah, sensing Xander wanted to speak with Colton alone, shortly did the same.

When the two men sat alone in the room with the fire crackling gently in the corner, Xander smiled and leaned back comfortably. "It seems you have had more adventure than you bargained for," the old man chortled.

Colton smiled broadly, and leaned back himself. "I suppose I have, but I never would have done it if you hadn't told me about our people."

Xander waved a hand in the air. "Oh, you had a traveler's heart long before I ever filled your head with tales of grandeur."

"That's true enough. I'm just glad I was able to find this place for you."

Xander nodded slowly. "As am I. It started to feel like I would never find my way here, and yet here we are." The old man gestured around the room. "I must admit, when I heard you were leaving, I almost wanted to jump on that ship with you!" The two of them laughed heartily.

"But, your grandmother keeps me in line these days, and this was your journey, not mine."

Colton grunted in agreement. "It would have been fun to go on another trip with you, like we used to."

"There's time for all that yet, my boy. Now that we are here, there is a whole world to discover. I've already talked your father into touring the other thickets with me."

Colton gasped in mock hurt. "Am I not invited?"

A smirk played on the elder's lips. "I wager you will be busy with your own exploits. Besides, being here has been good for Xavier and I. We never did see eye to eye on the whole Tyrkin thing, and now that it's behind us, we have grown much closer." Xander paused and turned in Colton's direction. "I have to thank you for that as well. Before Imryth came to collect us to come here, I hadn't seen your father since the day we said goodbye to you. It has been a welcome change of pace to get to know my son once again."

Colton felt a lump of emotions form in his throat. "It makes me happier than you know to hear you two are doing better."

Xander smiled contentedly. "What about you, Colton? Are you happy with yourself?"

Colton thought about his answer, knowing his grandfather could pull apart any lie he might try to conjure. "For the most part, I would say yes."

"But?" Xander prompted.

"But, I just feel like there are still so many unknowns about this place, and I'm afraid of what I may uncover if I dig into them," Colton admitted.

"Hmm, you know, when I was about your age, I had just heard a rumor about my tribe." A log in the fire crackled loudly as Xander continued. "Until then I had always just believed that we were correct in our beliefs, but then I heard that Tyrrek had never wished for us to maim ourselves. Well, it led me to question everything." Colton took a drink from his glass, intrigued by the story. "Then, I met your grandmother, and my own father wanted me to kill her on the spot. This was difficult for me, because this woman had just saved my life and that of my father, so I was confused as to why she needed to die." Xander sighed heavily. "One stroke of a sword, and I was a fugitive." The old man seemed to age significantly after the admission.

"That must have been unbearable," Colton sympathized.

"Oh, it was, but your grandmother pulled me through it as best she could. Even still, in the matter of a few days my entire life had changed. All because I chose to dig into the unknown," Xander declared, leaning closer to Colton.

"Do you regret it?" Colton asked tentatively.

"Not for a second," Xander answered confidently. "Without that choice, I wouldn't have married your grandmother, or had your father, or lived to see my grandson fulfill such great achievements." He paused, considering. "Living in the light of truth is far better than hiding from the shadow of the unknown."

"So, you think I should pursue it even if it's dangerous?" Colton questioned.

"Especially if it's dangerous! If it were easy, it would already be known!" The old man stood and walked to his grandson. "Follow your heart, Colton. It has brought us all this far, and I for one can't wait to see what you achieve next." Colton hugged his grandfather, the lean man still pulling him into a crushing embrace. "Now, go and get some rest, you've earned it, my boy."

Yawning, Colton felt extremely tired, and could tell his grandfather also longed for his bed. "You too, Gramps. I'll see you in the morning."

With a wave, Colton exited the house and made his way to his own bed, a new sense of certainty rising within him.

Chapter Thirty-Seven: Radio Silence

I n the following weeks, Meredith and Imryth both returned home,
accepting their children's desire to stay in Zerua. Though not before
insisting that the portal remain open to facilitate any visiting the two
women deemed necessary. Arcadia was more than happy to
accommodate this, as Imryth had shown her magic she hadn't yet begun
to imagine. In truth, the young witch was probably the saddest to see the
two sorceresses leave.

With the Grove slowly helping to restore the memories of those
affected by Va'Rul, life around the Thicket of Memories was beginning
to return to normal. This left Colton, Imbrose, and Ember with little to do
except train and mostly be in the way. So, after relaying Lucas' message
to his mother and writing a response to Genevieve, the trio set off to make
good on the deal they had made with Grex'xi. Originally, Orielle planned
on coming with them, but after Jasper had asked her to help him build
something, she had backed out at the last minute. Colton didn't get upset,
but instead found himself grateful for the time he was able to spend with
his oldest friends.

The trip was uneventful, with the exception of another viewing of
the strange cat Orielle had seen. Just as before when leading them to
Lucas' location in the Grove, it had a strange green glow around it. This
time, however, the strange creature allowed them to approach and they
even noticed a small collar and a star-shaped name tag that read "Comet."

The little cat proved to be an adorable companion as it led them through the forest. Of course, Colton was most intrigued by its seemingly sentient nature as it constantly made eye contact with him. Something about the tiny animal made Colton feel like it was constantly trying to tell him a secret.

The evening before arriving at their destination, the trio of friends sat comfortably around a low burning campfire.

"Never thought I'd be sitting in a mile-high tree with a bunch of bloodthirsty beasts just waiting for one of us to fall, and a fire burning in said tree," Imbrose piped up.

"Don't worry, I rubbed the repellent on nearly every surface within a hundred foot radius," Colton informed. "But I agree with you. We've come a long way."

"Definitely the wildest adventure we've been on so far, eh?" Ember asked.

"Without a doubt," Imbrose agreed, leaning back. "Wouldn't trade it for the world."

Colton smiled. "Couldn't have imagined doing this without you two."

Ember placed a hand on Colton's arm and squeezed. "We'll follow you on any ill-advised adventure you find yourself on."

"Don't be too hasty now," Colton chuckled. "I think Va'Rul was just the beginning."

"Good," Imbrose smirked. "Ember and I have been talking, and we like it here."

"So, you'll stay?" Colton asked, the question had been weighing on him.

Imbrose moved over next to Colton and draped an arm across his shoulders. "Where you go, we go, mate."

Ember scooched in closer. "Who else is going to make sure you don't get yourself killed?"

Colton scoffed and wrapped an arm around each of them. "Thank you both."

The three of them fell into companionable silence as the night wore on and eventually Colton found himself dozing off as Imbrose took first watch.

The following morning they reached Grex'xi to find a rather disheveled mother chasing a tiny rambunctious baby around the interior of the nearly completely destroyed courtyard. Sending Imbrose in to distract the little monster with his teleporting dagger allowed the grateful Queen to lie down, her chest heaving.

After Colton mindlinked with her, Grex'xi panted, *I don't expect you little fleshlings to understand what it is like to be the mother of a creature with this much energy, but I appreciate your intervention.*

Colton made meaningful eye contact with Ember, which held all of the memories of shenanigans they had gotten into. Nevermind how much trouble they got in for said shenanigans. However, they wisely chose to simply nod at Grex'xi's assertion.

Tiring out the little beastie proved to be an all-day affair, and after Imbrose nearly lost a finger from allowing the little guy to get too close, he was grateful when the beast collapsed. The albino mother, on the other hand, was just getting started as she was far chattier than Colton remembered. Though he also realized he had never spoken directly to her until that day, and now he finally understood why George had a headache for days after their initial meeting.

In all, the trip helped to allow the friends a much needed getaway, but eventually Colton received a message from Orielle. At first he had flinched in surprise at the sudden echo of her voice in his head, but the feeling subsided as he glanced fondly at the necklace dangling around his neck. She explained that he should return as soon as possible, because her father had requested they go on a diplomatic mission for him. Eager to be of use, Imbrose, Ember, and Colton all bid farewell to Grex'xi and made their way back to the thicket.

Upon arriving back home, the trio was immediately met by Orielle who ran to embrace Colton in a big hug and kiss. "Why don't you hug me like that?" Imbrose muttered to Ember.

"Because you never leave me alone," she replied simply.

Imbrose shrugged. "True enough."

After exchanging greetings, they made their way to the Keeper who was waiting for them with Sero and Murkane in the Tribal Center.

"Ah! I'm glad you guys made it back safely!" the Keeper began. "I must apologize for the lack of things to do around here. After the funeral, everything started to go back to normal. But if you're anything like Ori here, I know you must be itching for something to do."

"It has been quiet, sir," Colton answered honestly.

"Unfortunately, the lack of noise is why I have asked for you. Or to be more precise, the lack of communication," the Keeper said cryptically.

"What do you mean, Pa?" Orielle asked, her voice concerned.

"Keeper Gerald has been silent for a few weeks now," George started. "At first, I thought maybe his people were just recovering from Va'Rul like the rest of us, but now I'm beginning to worry."

"Who's Keeper Gerald?" Imbrose asked.

"He's the leader of the Thicket of Borders, and the only thing standing between us and the Platinum Dominion," Orielle answered.

Sero shuddered. "That can't be good," he said nervously.

George smiled slightly. "It's probably nothing. Gerald has always been a bit of a recluse, so I half expect him to be drinking wine and staring at the sunset when you get there."

"When do you want us to leave?" Colton asked.

"By the end of the day, if possible. It'll take you the better part of a day to get down there, and if something has happened, I'd like to know sooner than later." George pulled out a small metallic case and passed it over to Orielle. "Contact me as soon as you know what's going on."

Orielle nodded and turned to the rest of the group. "Meet up at the gate in two hours?" The party exchanged nods and set off to prepare for their trip south.

An hour and forty-five minutes later, the six of them exited through the glowing cave and descended into the Cloudstone Railway.

Before long, the group had secured transport from Ulric, and they were underway once more.

Colton found himself spending most of the time in the main cabin with all of his friends. They laughed and talked about the time they had shared so far, and even Sero began to fit into their little troop nicely.

Since this trip was only going to be an overnighter, the party stayed up for a large majority of the night. Eventually, Murkane and Sero wandered off after the metal man convinced the kid to bet on a game of "Badger Hole," and not long after, Ember and Imbrose retreated to their room.

Left alone, Orielle gestured for Colton to follow her down the hallway. A few doors down, she walked into a room Colton was very familiar with. He entered to see the large glass window that showed the walls of the tunnel speeding by. He had spent a vast majority of his time when he was injured sitting here and watching the earth race by. However, Colton also loved the flowing streamers of blue light that flickered across the window, no doubt part of the magic that allowed the train to move in the first place.

Colton watched as Orielle walked over and sat on a two-seater couch that looked out the window and gestured for him to join. Smiling, he quickly moved to join her as she snuggled into his shoulder.

"Sometimes, I can imagine the trees of the forest flying by at incredible speeds. Is that silly?" she asked coyly.

"Not at all!" Colton said, wrapping his arm around her tightly. "Where I come from, the fastest thing we have is a horse, so the pretty lights keep my attention well enough."

Orielle giggled. "How are you adjusting to life in the forest?"

"Surprisingly well. It helps that I've found someone to share my time with," Colton smiled. "How's Jasper doing?"

Orielle adjusted slightly, the two of them sinking into the couch. "He's doing good! Almost back to the same kid he was before." She paused, biting her lip. "But I can tell there are some scars there. At first, I wanted to just stay with him until he had completely healed. Though now,

I've figured out that he will need to do that on his own." She looked up at him. "Still, thank you for keeping your promise. You helped bring Jasper back to me."

"I'd do just about anything for you," he whispered.

She blushed and he leaned in to kiss her. When they parted, she snuggled into him once more, and they both watched as the long blue rays of light cascaded over the window in beautiful patterns.

After some time, Orielle sat up and looked back at him. "Well, we should probably get some rest. Tomorrow could be a very interesting day."

Disappointed at the loss of closeness, Colton nodded. "Yeah, you're probably right."

Orielle smirked and got up to leave, when she reached the door she stopped and looked back at Colton. "Are you coming?" her voice a sultry invitation.

Wide eyed, Colton turned to see her beckoning him to follow. Hurriedly, he moved to the door as she walked to her cabin. A sensual smile played on her lips, as she stepped through the door, leaving it open. A sigh escaped him as he realized, *Yes, I really am beginning to love it here.*

Preview for Book II: Invasion

Prologue: In Defiance

T he woman stood at the crest of a small hill. A winter chill kissing the exposed bits of her charcoal skin, as the metal plates of her battle gear scraped together gently. To her right, a man with red skin and two long jet-black horns protruding from his brow stared into the distance.

"Is this what you had in mind?" the man asked.

The woman didn't respond immediately as she glanced over her shoulder, taking in her surroundings. An army of twenty thousand strong stood behind her, ready to charge if she gave the order. However, what gave her pause was the sight in front of her.

A force that rivaled her own stood between her and the city that lay beyond. Her destination.

"It wasn't supposed to be like this," she lamented. "They were meant to see the folly of their charge and join us in claiming what is ours."

The man smiled fiendishly, revealing long pointed canines. "Ah, but not all are blessed with your sight, Kanathi." He swept a hand across the soon to be battlefield. "They are a relic of a bygone age. Let them fall into history where they belong."

Kanathi pursed her lips as she inspected the banners across from her, a six pointed shape on a blue background with a singular star directly in the center. "It's too late anyway, it's them or us." With resolution she turned her back on the distant army and faced her own. "My friends," she began, her voice echoing across the field, "today marks a moment in history when the races of this world took back our own destinies." Kanathi swept her arm behind her. "The Guardians are afraid of what being unshackled by the Gods would mean for us, but that is because they have never tasted true free will. They would rather live under a design they themselves cannot see, than face their future and establish their own path." Kanathi paused as she paced back and forth atop the mound. "It is our duty to usher in a new age, and in this new world there will be no room for those who cower beneath the divine. We are the chosen few, and our children's child will look back on this day and praise us for the courage we had to stand against the bigotry that has loomed so large for too long." Kanathi took a deep breath. "Our families in the north may have shied away from our path, but I know they will see the truth when we prevail today."

Kanathi looked up at her red-skinned compatriot, his face a mask and impossible to read save a small nod.

"Will you fight with me, one last time, to claim your lives as your own?"

The crowd of soldiers yelled their assent.

Kanathi stepped forward, her fist raised high. "Then follow me into the annals of history!"

Letting out a guttural cry, Kanathi pulled her longsword and stormed down the side of the hill, leading the charge across the open plains that separated her from her destiny. The thunderous roar of twenty thousand soldiers shaking the ground beneath her feet as she watched the red man disappear in a cloud of red smoke.

Chapter One: The Platinum Legion

The low humming of the Cloudstone Railway jostled Colton from a peaceful sleep. Yawning, he rolled to one side and looked into the stunning green eyes of Orielle and kissed her gently on the nose. His heart felt happy, and his mood was brighter than it had been in a very long time. He finally felt like his life had a direction, and he was happy Orielle was standing by his side. The mere thought of what things could have been like had she not found them that day, threatened to overthrow his bright demeanor, and so he ignored the useless thought. Instead, he basked in the glow of waking up next to the beautiful woman who made him feel like a better man.

A burst of laughter from the main corridor broke the silence between them, as they nodded with resignation and moved to dress themselves. Unable to ignore her, Colton approached from behind and kissed her neck as she pulled a shirt over her head.

Orielle snickered as she gently placed a hand on the side of his head. "If we take any more time getting out there, it's going to be even more awkward."

Sighing in mock exasperation, Colton pulled away from her and reached for his own shirt. "Ah, you're right, but I hate that you are."

Still smiling, she turned to look at him. "Not to worry, I suspect we will have more alone time in the very near future."

"I'll hold you to that," Colton whispered as they kissed. "Now, you need to quit distracting me or I won't be able to control myself."

Orielle giggled and playfully shoved him away and tossed his hat at him. "Keep your clothes on Mr. Cobb."

They both laughed and finished getting ready. When the two of them finally exited their shared room, it caused quite the disturbance as the other four all turned in unison, watching them. For a painful moment, they all stared at each other until Murkane broke the silence.

"Bacon?" he asked cheerfully.

"Yes please!" Colton announced, happily seizing the lifeline.

The conversation picked back up as they moved past the awkwardness of the situation, but Imbrose couldn't resist winking at Colton when he caught his attention. The gesture drew a chuckle from Colton as his eyes latched onto a blur of movement to Imbrose's left. With lightning speed, Ember slapped Imbrose on the leg, his blue skin darkening in shade at the strike. Ignoring his protests, her amber gaze softened as she apologetically smiled at Colton. Returning the smile, Colton suddenly felt a shadow loom over him as Murkane held out a plate of food in his direction. The tall charcoal-skinned man wore his ever-present plate armor, but seemed to have left his helm elsewhere. Thanking him, Colton accepted the plate and began eating as he immersed himself in the comradery around him.

"I've put some thought into it," Murkane began, "I think I would like you all to call me by the name you first knew me by."

Orielle wiped her mouth with a cloth, her eyebrows scrunched together. "Is everything okay?"

Murkane nodded. "Yes, I just feel like the name Murkane no longer suits me. But instead, it feels like a reminder of a past that I left behind."

"I can understand that," Colton said as he smiled at the big man. "We'll call you Friend, if that's what you would like."

"Thank you," Murkane, now Friend once more, appreciated. "I've grown rather fond of the name."

"It suits you!" Ember encouraged, as she tossed her newly braided long red hair over her shoulder.

"Well," Imbrose started, his voice carrying a mischievous tone, "if we are changing our names, can I be called the Lord of Zer–."

"No." Colton stated plainly as everyone laughed.

"That seems unfair…" Imbrose lamented. No one paid him any mind as they joked heartily at his expense.

After breakfast, everyone busied themselves with getting prepared for the day ahead by filling their rations and packing their bags. With the nature of their quest seeming so mundane, the group tried their best to not get caught up in complacency. The entire group had been through too much on Zerua to not assume something was amiss. And this time, even Orielle had no idea what to expect when they got there. So, when the bright blue streamers that encompassed the locomotive began to visibly slow, the party all gathered in the main common room and waited until they arrived.

Stepping off, Colton immediately noticed the vast difference in how the air around him felt from where they had come. He had grown accustomed to the stifling heat mixed with heavy moisture. Though where he now found himself seemed to be a much drier climate. The unexpected change left Colton wondering what the landscape beyond the forest would look like, as he stepped toward a small man who jogged to meet them.

The station engineer proved to be a nice man by the name of Nicholas, and not for the first time, Colton wondered if being nice was a requirement for the job. However, unlike Ulric, Nicholas was brief and understood the importance of getting somewhere on time. So, after stating their business, Nicholas directed them to exactly where the Keeper held most of his meetings. Unfortunately, he didn't have any information on why the Thicket of Borders had gone silent, aside from the lack of traffic coming through.

Once again, Colton was dumbstruck at how different the various parts of the forest could be. Here, the trees were much shorter but denser, it was almost like they were trying to hide what was within from anybody looking inside the forest. Additionally, the path leading out of the underground railway was simply a ramp that ascended up and out of a large oak trunk similar to the outpost they had spent some time in when they first arrived. The true vista that took everyone's breath away was what they saw when they turned around and looked at the Thicket of Borders.

It took Colton a moment to realize where it was, but once he looked down, he froze in place. This thicket was not covered and instead sat in a low valley with high walls leading up hundreds of feet. What caught him by surprise was that they were standing at the top of the valley walls looking down on the thicket below. A large path cut through the village from east to west, and Colton could make out the vast fields of green that stretched into the distance beyond the Primal Forest. He found himself staring in wonder as up until now he had only been surrounded by dense forest or jungle and hadn't seen an open field of this size since before, he left the Archipelago. Smiling, he turned to see his friends' reactions were much the same. Even Orielle gawked in amazement.

"Are you coming or what?" a gruff voice called out to them from near the edge of the canyon wall.

Standing there was a man on a rickety wooden platform about fifteen feet across. He held a rope levered to a pulley system looped throughout the trees above them and seemed to be waiting.

"Sorry! None of us have ever been here before," Orielle answered honestly.

"Mhm," the man grunted in reply.

With nothing left to say, the group boarded the platform, and the man began the slow task of lowering them to the canyon floor. The view going down was just as stunning as above. The sunlight landed perfectly down the main thoroughfare and people bustled from one place to the next. Colton could see a wide gate that spanned the entirety of the canyon that blocked entrance into the forest. At about the halfway point, a ray of sunlight revealed a slight shimmer in the space that divided The Primal Forest and what Colton could only guess was the Platinum Dominion.

As the platform thudded to the ground, the group hurried to disembark with Orielle thanking the grumpy man before he slowly started to climb once more.

"State your purpose," another rough voice called to them.

A man in full armor stood down a ramp and at another gate which barred the lift from the rest of the thicket.

"Um…we've come to speak with Keeper Gerald. We were sent by the Keeper of the Thicket of Memories," Orielle responded, her voice guarded.

The man looked down and glanced at a small piece of parchment. "We aren't expecting any visitors today."

"Well," Orielle said, her tone shifting to one of annoyance, "if you had been answering us when we tried to speak with you, there would be no visitors today!"

The guard stared blankly at Orielle, clearly measuring her response. "Very well, the Keeper is attending a war council at the moment. You will find him at the Overlook." With that, the guard promptly opened the gate and stood aside.

Orielle, still irritated at the reception they had received, tried to calm herself. "And where can we find the Overlook?"

The guard simply pointed down the road toward the massive gates that blocked all visual of the fields beyond. Taking a deep breath, Orielle led the group through the gate and down into the busy road.

"Did he say war council?" Ember asked.

"I believe he did," Colton winced, as the hope for a simple task began to slip away.

"Who is he going to war with?" Imbrose wondered aloud.

"I don't know, but let's go and find out," Orielle muttered.

As they stepped into traffic, Colton found himself struggling to maintain line of sight on everyone in their party, which proved to be even more difficult when wagons being pulled by horses started forcing their way through the crowds. This caused Colton to pause as even though he had seen horses countless times back in the Archipelago, it was the first time he saw them in the Primal Forest. The sight of them made him feel a bit more comfortable, as until now, all of the creatures had been spawned from nightmares. So, something that remained docile as he passed by it was a welcome development.

A loud horn sounded from the main gates and people began to move more rapidly. Making it increasingly more difficult for the party to stay together and eventually resorted to linking hands. Slowly, the street began to clear until the once bustling roadway was almost completely devoid of life.

"I'm scared to ask, but what does the horn mean?" Sero questioned.

With no one knowing the answer, they simply picked up the pace, rushing for the gates. As they got closer, they could see hundreds of soldiers manning the ramparts over three hundred feet in the air and upwards of a thousand foot soldiers in formation behind said gate.

Colton grabbed a nearby running merchant. "Where is the Overlook?"

The man's eyes darted around frantically before pointing up and to the right of the giant portcullis, clearly what was happening here was not normal. There, a small pathway led up the side of the cliff face and out of sight. Colton released the merchant before breaking into a run, as the group made their way up the narrow walkway. After another ten minutes of precarious footing, they finally turned a corner to reveal a large plateau-like shelf that extended away from the cliffs. As the name might suggest, it overlooked the spanning fields just outside the Primal Forest.

Having no time to take anything in, spears were lowered to block their path moving forward. "Who goes there?" a shout echoed from behind the line of pointed weapons.

"Or-Orielle Dawson! First Scion of the Thicket of Memories," Orielle yelled back, her voice gaining volume as she spoke.

A pause lingered over the crowd as no one spoke, but Colton slowly moved his hand to his whip handle, preparing for the worst.

"What in the blazes are you doing here?" a deep commanding voice called as the spearmen parted to reveal a middle-aged man in a set of full plate armor.

"We've come to check in with Keeper Gerald. We hadn't heard from him in–" Orielle began.

"Well, you've found him, but I don't have the time to talk. I'm running a war here," Keeper Gerald thundered, gesturing for them to follow him.

The party tentatively stepped through the ranks of guards to see multiple tents positioned on the rocky surface. Gerald walked quickly as soldiers saluted him until he reached a raised wooden platform. Trying to keep up, the party all piled onto the command post.

"As you can see," the Keeper began, holding his hand out over the fields below, "I've got my hands full."

Colton looked over the small railing in front of him. Despite the breath-taking view, thousands of soldiers marched toward the large gate that guarded the Primal Forest. An invading army was hours away from assaulting the Thicket of Borders.

Sero gasped behind him. "That's them. The Platinum Legion."

To Be Continued in Book Two: Invasion

ACKNOWLEDGEMENTS

When I first set about writing Heritage I thought: "Man this is going to be so simple, and once I'm done writing all I have to do is publish!" Boy was I wrong! The sheer volume of people who have made this book a reality is too many to count, but I will do my best to thank as many of them as I can! Thank you to my friends and family who, behind the scenes, cheered me on daily! Thank you Sammi and Andrew for your patience and assistance while I navigate this crazy journey. Thank you to my cousins Mckenzie and Colby as well as Papa for taking the time to read the entirety of my novel, and for always being open with your feedback (it really does help). Thank you to my best friend Chris, for without you my friend there would be no cover and there would be no website! Lastly, thank you once more to my beautiful and endlessly supportive wife! I doubt there will ever be another individual who has read my novel cover to cover more than you (including me)! You made this journey a magical one, and I can't wait to share more of Zerua with you!

Dear Grandpa,

Oh, how I wish you could read this novel. Alas, you have likely been reading it over my shoulder this whole time. I would have cherished your critiques as the only person I know who will finish a book, even if you can't stand it. I look forward to hearing what you think when we meet again. Rest easy, and I suppose this makes me a professional writer now, doesn't it?

Thank you for everything,
Brady

ABOUT THE AUTHOR

Brady E. Moxley is a debuting author who prides himself on the ability to create vivid worlds that complement the vast array of characters, which give it life. As a husband, teacher, and RPG gamer, he draws from the inspiration in his personal life, and molds it with a creative imagination to put every ounce of himself into everything he writes. Zerua Unchained is but the first in his quest for literary immortality.

To Learn More About Zerua Unchained Please Visit:

BradyEMoxley.com

And Add Your Dream Bloom To The Grove!